W9-DIS-244

MISERY

ALSO BY STEPHEN KING

NOVELS

Carrie	Firestarter
'Salem's Lot	Cujo
The Shining	The Dark Tower
The Stand	Christine
The Dead Zone	Pet Semetary

The Talisman (with Peter Straub)

It

The Eyes of the Dragon

AS RICHARD BACHMAN

Rage

The Long Walk

Roadwork

The Running Man

Thinner

COLLECTIONS

Night Shift

Different Seasons

Skeleton Crew

NONFICTION

Danse Macabre

SCREENPLAYS

Creepshow

Cat's Eye

Silver Bullet

Maximum Overdrive

STEPHEN KING

MISERY

VIKING

VIKING

Viking Penguin Inc., 40 West 23rd Street, New York, New York 10010, U.S.A.
Penguin Books Ltd, Harmondsworth, Middlesex, England
Penguin Books Australia Ltd, Ringwood, Victoria, Australia
Penguin Books Canada Limited, 2801 John Street, Markham, Ontario, Canada L3R 1B4
Penguin Books (N.Z.) Ltd, 182–190 Wairau Road, Auckland 10, New Zealand

Copyright © Stephen King, Tabitha King, and Arthur B. Greene, Trustee, 1987
All rights reserved

First published in 1987 by Viking Penguin Inc.
Published simultaneously in Canada

Grateful acknowledgment is made for permission to reprint excerpts from
the following copyrighted material:
"King of the Road," by Roger Miller. © 1964 Tree Publishing Co., Inc.
International copyright secured. All rights reserved. Used by permission
of the publisher.
"Fifty Ways to Leave Your Lover," by Paul Simon. Copyright © 1975 by Paul
Simon. Used by permission.
The Collector, by John Fowles. Copyright © 1963 by John Fowles Ltd. By
permission of Little, Brown and Company.
"Those Lazy, Hazy, Crazy Days of Summer," by Hans Carste and Charles Tobias.
© 1962 Edition Primus Budde KG Berlin, Germany. © 1963 Comet Music Corp.
All rights for the U.S.A. and Canada controlled and administered by April
Music Inc. under license from ATV Music (Comet). All rights reserved.
International copyright secured. Used by permission.
"Girls Just Want to Have Fun." © Heroic Music 1979. Permission to use
lyric granted by Heroic Music (ASCAP), for songwriter, Robert Hazard.
"Santa Claus Is Comin' to Town," by Haven Gillespie and J. Fred Coots. © 1934,
renewed 1962 Leo Feist Inc. Rights assigned to SBK Catalogue Partnership.
All rights controlled and administered by SBK Feist Catalog Inc. All rights
reserved. International copyright secured. Used by permission.
"Chug-a-Lug," by Roger Miller. © 1964 Tree Publishing Company, Inc. International
copyright secured. All rights reserved. Used by permission of the publisher.
"Disco Inferno," by Leroy Green and Ron "Have Mercy" Kersey. Copyright © 1977
by Six Strings Music and Golden Fleece Music; assigned to Six Strings Music,
1978. All rights reserved.

LIBRARY OF CONGRESS CATALOGING IN PUBLICATION DATA
King, Stephen, 1947–
Misery.
I. Title.
PS3561.I483M5 1987   813'.54   86-40504
ISBN 0-670-81364-8

Printed in the United States of America by
R. R. Donnelley & Sons, Harrisonburg, Virginia
Set in Garamond No. 3
Designed by Amy Hill

Without limiting the rights under copyright reserved above, no part of this
publication may be reproduced, stored in or introduced into a retrieval system,
or transmitted, in any form or by any means (electronic, mechanical, photo-
copying, recording or otherwise), without the prior written permission of both
the copyright owner and the above publisher of this book.

This is for Stephanie and Jim Leonard, who know why.
Boy, *do* they.

goddess

Africa

I'd like to gratefully acknowledge the help of three medical people who helped me with the factual material in this book. They are:

Russ Dorr, P.A.
Florence Dorr, R.N.
Janet Ordway, M.D. and Doctor of Psychiatry

As always, they helped with the things you don't notice. If you see a glaring error, it's mine.

There is, of course, no such drug as Novril, but there are several codeine-based drugs similar to it, and, unfortunately, hospital pharmacies and medical practice dispensaries are sometimes lax in keeping such drugs under tight lock and close inventory.

The places and characters in this book are fictional.

S.K.

I

ANNIE

When you look into the abyss, the abyss also looks into you.

—Friedrich Nietzsche

1

umber whunnnn
yerrrnnn umber whunnnn
fayunnnn
These sounds: even in the haze.

2

But sometimes the sounds—like the pain—faded, and then there was only the haze. He remembered darkness: solid darkness had come before the haze. Did that mean he was making progress? Let there be light (even of the hazy variety), and the light was good, and so on and so on? Had those sounds existed in the darkness? He didn't know the answers to any of these questions. Did it make sense to ask them? He didn't know the answer to that one, either.

The pain was somewhere below the sounds. The pain was east of the sun and south of his ears. That was all he *did* know.

For some length of time that seemed very long (and so *was*, since the pain and the stormy haze were the only two things which existed) those sounds were the only outer reality. He had no idea who he was or where he was and cared to know neither. He wished he was dead, but through the pain-soaked haze that filled his mind like a summer storm-cloud, he did not know he wished it.

As time passed, he became aware that there were periods of nonpain, and that these had a cyclic quality. And for the first time since emerging from the total blackness which had prologued the haze, he had a thought which existed apart from whatever his current situation was. This thought was of a broken-off piling which had jutted from the sand at Revere Beach. His mother and father had taken him to Revere Beach often when he was a kid, and he had always insisted that they spread their blanket where he could keep an eye on that piling, which looked to him like the single jutting fang of a buried monster. He liked to sit and watch the water come up until it covered the piling. Then, hours later, after the sandwiches and potato salad had been eaten, after the last few drops of Kool-Aid had been coaxed from his father's big Thermos, just before his mother said it was time to pack up and start home, the top of the rotted piling would begin to show again—just a peek and flash between the incoming waves at first, then more and more. By the time their trash was stashed in the big drum with KEEP YOUR BEACH CLEAN stencilled on the side, Paulie's beach-toys picked up

(*that's my name Paulie I'm Paulie and tonight ma'll put Johnson's Baby Oil on my sunburn* he thought inside the thunderhead where he now lived)

and the blanket folded again, the piling had almost wholly reappeared, its blackish, slime-smoothed sides surrounded by sudsy scuds of foam. It was the tide, his father had tried to explain, but he had always known it was the piling. The tide came and went; the piling stayed. It was just that sometimes you couldn't see it. Without the piling, there *was* no tide.

This memory circled and circled, maddening, like a sluggish fly. He groped for whatever it might mean, but for a long time the sounds interrupted.

fayunnnn

red everrrrrythinggg

umberrrrr whunnnn

Sometimes the sounds stopped. Sometimes *he* stopped.

His first really clear memory of this *now*, the *now* outside the storm-haze, was of stopping, of being suddenly aware he just couldn't pull another breath, and that was all right, that was good, that was in fact just peachy-keen; he could take a certain level of pain but enough was enough and he was glad to be getting out of the game.

Then there was a mouth clamped over his, a mouth which was unmistakably a woman's mouth in spite of its hard spitless lips, and the wind from this woman's mouth blew into his own mouth and down his throat, puffing his lungs, and when the lips were pulled back he smelled his warder for the first time, smelled her on the outrush of the breath she had forced into him the way a man might force a part of himself into an unwilling woman, a dreadful mixed stench of vanilla cookies and chocolate ice cream and chicken gravy and peanut-butter fudge.

He heard a voice screaming, "Breathe, goddammit! *Breathe*, Paul!"

The lips clamped down again. The breath blew down his throat again. Blew down it like the dank suck of wind which follows a fast subway train, pulling sheets of newspaper and candy-wrappers after it, and the lips were withdrawn, and he thought *For Christ's sake don't let any of it out through your nose* but he couldn't help it and oh that *stink*, that *stink* that *fucking STINK*.

"*Breathe, goddam you!*" the unseen voice shrieked, and he thought *I will, anything, please just don't do that anymore, don't infect me anymore,* and he *tried,* but before he could really get started her lips were clamped over his again, lips as dry and dead as strips of salted leather, and she raped him full of her air again.

When she took her lips away this time he did not *let* her breath out but *pushed* it and whooped in a gigantic breath of his own. Shoved it out. Waited for his unseen chest to go up again on its own, as it had been doing his whole life without any help from him. When it didn't, he gave another giant whooping gasp, and then he was breathing again on his own, and doing it as fast as he could to flush the smell and taste of her out of him.

Normal air had never tasted so fine.

He began to fade back into the haze again, but before the dimming world was gone entirely, he heard the woman's voice mutter: "Whew! That was a close one!"

Not close enough, he thought, and fell asleep.

He dreamed of the piling, so real he felt he could almost reach out and slide his palm over its green-black fissured curve.

When he came back to his former state of semiconsciousness, he was able to make the connection between the piling and his current situation—it seemed to float into his hand. The pain wasn't tidal. That was the lesson of the dream which was really a memory. The pain only *appeared* to come and go. The pain was like the piling, sometimes covered and sometimes visible, but always there. When the pain wasn't harrying him through the deep stone grayness of his cloud, he was dumbly grateful, but he was no longer fooled— it was still there, waiting to return. And there was not just *one* piling but *two*; the pain was the pilings, and part of him knew for a long time before most of his mind had knowledge of knowing that the shattered pilings were his own shattered legs.

But it was still a long time before he was finally able to break the dried scum of saliva that had glued his lips together and croak out "Where am I?" to the woman who sat by his bed with a book in her hands. The name of the man who had written the book was Paul Sheldon. He recognized it as his own with no surprise.

"Sidewinder, Colorado," she said when he was finally able to ask the question. "My name is Annie Wilkes. And I am—"

"I know," he said. "You're my number-one fan."

"Yes," she said, smiling. "That's just what I am."

3

Darkness. Then the pain and the haze. Then the awareness that, although the pain was constant, it was sometimes buried by an uneasy compromise which he supposed was relief. The first real memory: stopping, and being raped back into life by the woman's stinking breath.

Next real memory: her fingers pushing something into his mouth at regular intervals, something like Contac capsules, only since there was no water they only sat in his mouth and when they melted there was an incredibly bitter taste that was a little like the taste of aspirin. It would have been good to spit that bitter taste out, but he knew better than to do it. Because it was that bitter taste which brought the high tide in over the piling

(*PILINGS it's PILINGS there are TWO okay there are two fine now just hush just you know hush shhhhhh*)

and made it seem gone for awhile.

These things all came at widely spaced intervals, but then, as the pain itself began not to recede but to erode (as that Revere Beach piling must itself have eroded, he thought, because nothing is for-ever—although the child he had been would have scoffed at such heresy), outside things began to impinge more rapidly until the objective world, with all its freight of memory, experience, and prejudice, had pretty much re-established itself. He was Paul Shel-don, who wrote novels of two kinds, good ones and best-sellers. He had been married and divorced twice. He smoked too much (or had before all this, whatever "all this" was). Something very bad had happened to him but he was still alive. That dark-gray cloud began to dissipate faster and faster. It would be yet awhile before his number-one fan brought him the old clacking Royal with the

grinning gapped mouth and the Ducky Daddles voice, but Paul
understood long before then that he was in a hell of a jam.

4

That prescient part of his mind saw her before he knew he was
seeing her, and must surely have understood her before he knew
he was understanding her—why else did he associate such dour,
ominous images with her? Whenever she came into the room he
thought of the graven images worshipped by superstitious African
tribes in the novels of H. Rider Haggard, and stones, and doom.

   The image of Annie Wilkes as an African idol out of *She* or *King
Solomon's Mines* was both ludicrous and queerly apt. She was a big
woman who, other than the large but unwelcoming swell of her
bosom under the gray cardigan sweater she always wore, seemed
to have no feminine curves at all—there was no defined roundness
of hip or buttock or even calf below the endless succession of wool
skirts she wore in the house (she retired to her unseen bedroom
to put on jeans before doing her outside chores). Her body was
big but not generous. There was a feeling about her of clots and
roadblocks rather than welcoming orifices or even open spaces,
areas of hiatus.

   Most of all she gave him a disturbing sense of *solidity*, as if she
might not have any blood vessels or even internal organs; as if she
might be only solid Annie Wilkes from side to side and top to
bottom. He felt more and more convinced that her eyes, which
appeared to move, were actually just painted on, and they moved
no more than the eyes of portraits which appear to follow you to
wherever you move in the room where they hang. It seemed to
him that if he made the first two fingers of his hand into a V and
attempted to poke them up her nostrils, they might go less than an
eighth of an inch before encountering a solid (if slightly yielding)
obstruction; that even her gray cardigan and frumpy house skirts
and faded outside-work jeans were part of that solid fibrous unchannelled body. So his feeling that she was like an idol in a per-
fervid novel was not really surprising at all. Like an idol, she gave
only one thing: a feeling of unease deepening steadily toward terror.
Like an idol, she took everything else.

No, wait, that wasn't quite fair. She *did* give something else. She gave him the pills that brought the tide in over the pilings.

The pills were the tide; Annie Wilkes was the lunar presence which pulled them into his mouth like jetsam on a wave. She brought him two every six hours, first announcing her presence only as a pair of fingers poking into his mouth (and soon enough he learned to suck eagerly at those poking fingers in spite of the bitter taste), later appearing in her cardigan sweater and one of her half-dozen skirts, usually with a paperback copy of one of his novels tucked under her arm. At night she appeared to him in a fuzzy pink robe, her face shiny with some sort of cream (he could have named the main ingredient easily enough even though he had never seen the bottle from which she tipped it; the sheepy smell of the lanolin was strong and proclamatory), shaking him out of his frowzy, dream-thick sleep with the pills nestled in her hand and the poxy moon nestled in the window over one of her solid shoulders.

After awhile—after his alarm had become too great to be ignored—he was able to find out what she was feeding him. It was a pain-killer with a heavy codeine base called Novril. The reason she had to bring him the bedpan so infrequently was not only because he was on a diet consisting entirely of liquids and gelatines (earlier, when he was in the cloud, she had fed him intravenously), but also because Novril had a tendency to cause constipation in patients taking it. Another side-effect, a rather more serious one, was respiratory depression in sensitive patients. Paul was not particularly sensitive, even though he had been a heavy smoker for nearly eighteen years, but his breathing had *stopped* nonetheless on at least one occasion (there might have been others, in the haze, that he did not remember). That was the time she gave him mouth-to-mouth. It might have just been one of those things which happened, but he later came to suspect she had nearly killed him with an accidental overdose. She didn't know as much about what she was doing as she believed she did. That was only one of the things about Annie that scared him.

He discovered three things almost simultaneously, about ten days after having emerged from the dark cloud. The first was that Annie Wilkes had a great deal of Novril (she had, in fact, a great many drugs of all kinds). The second was that he was hooked on Novril. The third was that Annie Wilkes was dangerously crazy.

5

The darkness had prologued the pain and the storm-cloud; he began to remember what had prologued the darkness as she told him what had happened to him. This was shortly after he had asked the traditional when-the-sleeper-wakes question and she had told him he was in the little town of Sidewinder, Colorado. In addition she told him that she had read each of his eight novels at least twice, and had read her *very* favorites, the *Misery* novels, four, five, maybe six times. She only wished he would write them faster. She said she had hardly been able to believe that her patient was *really that Paul Sheldon* even after checking the ID in his wallet.

"Where *is* my wallet, by the way?" he asked.

"I've kept it safe for you," she said. Her smile suddenly collapsed into a narrow watchfulness he didn't like much—it was like discovering a deep *crevasse* almost obscured by summer flowers in the midst of a smiling, jocund meadow. "Did you think I'd *steal* something out of it?"

"No, of course not. It's just that—" *It's just that the rest of my life is in it,* he thought. *My life outside this room. Outside the pain. Outside the way time seems to stretch out like the long pink string of bubble-gum a kid pulls out of his mouth when he's bored. Because that's how it is in the last hour or so before the pills come.*

"Just *what*, Mister Man?" she persisted, and he saw with alarm that the narrow look was growing blacker and blacker. The *crevasse* was spreading, as if an earthquake was going on behind her brow. He could hear the steady, keen whine of the wind outside, and he had a sudden image of her picking him up and throwing him over her solid shoulder, where he would lie like a burlap sack slung over a stone wall, and taking him outside, and heaving him into a snowdrift. He would freeze to death, but before he did, his legs would throb and scream.

"It's just that my father always told me to keep my eye on my wallet," he said, astonished by how easily this lie came out. His father had made a career out of not noticing Paul any more than he absolutely had to, and had, so far as Paul could remember, offered him only a single piece of advice in his entire life. On Paul's fourteenth birthday his father had given him a Red Devil condom in a foil envelope. "Put that in your wallet," Roger Sheldon said, "and if you ever get excited while you're making out at the drive-in, take a second between excited enough to want to and too excited to care and slip that on. Too many bastards in the world already, and I don't want to see you going in the Army at sixteen."

Now Paul went on: "I guess he told me to keep my eye on my wallet so many times that it's stuck inside for good. If I offended you, I'm truly sorry."

She relaxed. Smiled. The *crevasse* closed. Summer flowers nodded cheerfully once again. He thought of pushing his hand through that smile and encountering nothing but flexible darkness. "No offense taken. It's in a safe place. Wait—I've got something for you."

She left and returned with a steaming bowl of soup. There were vegetables floating in it. He was not able to eat much, but he ate more than he thought at first he could. She seemed pleased. It was while he ate the soup that she told him what had happened, and he remembered it all as she told him, and he supposed it was good to know how you happened to end up with your legs shattered, but the manner by which he was coming to this knowledge was disquieting—it was as if he was a character in a story or a play, a character whose history is not recounted like history but created like fiction.

She had gone into Sidewinder in the four-wheel drive to get feed for the livestock and a few groceries . . . also to check out the paperbacks at Wilson's Drug Center—that had been the Wednesday that was almost two weeks ago now, and the new paperbacks always came in on Tuesday.

"I was actually *thinking* of you," she said, spooning soup into his mouth and then professionally wiping away a dribble from the corner with a napkin. "That's what makes it such a remarkable coincidence, don't you see? I was hoping *Misery's Child* would finally be out in paperback, but no such luck."

A storm had been on the way, she said, but until noon that day the weather forecasters had been confidently claiming it would veer south, toward New Mexico and the Sangre de Cristos.

"Yes," he said, remembering as he said it: "They said it would turn. That's why I went in the first place." He tried to shift his legs. The result was an awful bolt of pain, and he groaned.

"Don't do that," she said. "If you get those legs of yours talking, Paul, they won't shut up . . . and I can't give you any more pills for two hours. I'm giving you too much as it is."

Why aren't I in the hospital? This was clearly the question that wanted asking, but he wasn't sure it was a question either of them wanted asked. Not yet, anyway.

"When I got to the feed store, Tony Roberts told me I better step on it if I was going to get back here before the storm hit, and I said—"

"How far *are* we from this town?" he asked.

"A ways," she said vaguely, looking off toward the window. There was a queer interval of silence, and Paul was frightened by what he saw on her face, because what he saw was nothing; the black nothing of a *crevasse* folded into an alpine meadow, a blackness where no flowers grew and into which the drop might be long. It was the face of a woman who has come momentarily untethered from all of the vital positions and landmarks of her life, a woman who has forgotten not only the memory she was in the process of recounting but memory itself. He had once toured a mental asylum—this was years ago, when he had been researching *Misery*, the first of the four books which had been his main source of income over the last eight years—and he had seen this look . . . or, more precisely, this un-look. The word which defined it was *catatonia*, but what frightened him had no such precise word—it was, rather, a vague comparison: in that moment he thought that her thoughts had become much as he had imagined her physical self: solid, fibrous, unchannelled, with no places of hiatus.

Then, slowly, her face cleared. Thoughts seemed to flow back into it. Then he realized *flowing* was just a tiny bit wrong. She wasn't filling up, like a pond or a tidal pool; she was *warming* up. *Yes . . . she is warming up, like some small electrical gadget. A toaster, or maybe a heating pad.*

"I said to Tony, 'That storm is going south.' " She spoke slowly at first, almost groggily, but then her words began to catch up to normal cadence and to fill with normal conversational brightness. But now he was alerted. *Everything* she said was a little strange, a little offbeat. Listening to Annie was like listening to a song played in the wrong key.

"But he said, 'It changed its mind.'

" 'Oh poop!' I said. 'I better get on my horse and ride.'

" 'I'd stay in town if you can, Miz Wilkes,' he said. 'Now they're saying on the radio that it's going to be a proper jeezer and nobody is prepared.'

"But of course I *had* to get back—there's no one to feed the animals but me. The nearest people are the Roydmans, and they are miles from here. Besides, the Roydmans don't like me."

She cast an eye shrewdly on him as she said this last, and when he didn't reply she tapped the spoon against the rim of the bowl in peremptory fashion.

"Done?"

"Yes, I'm full, thanks. It was very good. Do you have a lot of livestock?"

Because, he was already thinking, *if you do, that means you've got to have some help. A hired man, at least.* "Help" was the operant word. Already that seemed like the operant word, and he had seen she wore no wedding ring.

"Not very much," she said. "Half a dozen laying hens. Two cows. And Misery."

He blinked.

She laughed. "You won't think I'm very nice, naming a sow after the brave and beautiful woman you made up. But that's her name, and I meant no disrespect." After a moment's thought she added: "She's very friendly." The woman wrinkled up her nose and for a moment *became* a sow, even down to the few bristly whiskers that grew on her chin. She made a pig-sound: *"Whoink! Whoink! Whuh-Whuh-WHOINK!"*

Paul looked at her wide-eyed.

She did not notice; she had gone away again, her gaze dim and musing. Her eyes held no reflection but the lamp on the bed-table, twice reflected, dwelling faintly in each.

At last she gave a faint start and said: "I got about five miles and then the snow started. It came fast—once it starts up here, it always does. I came creeping along, with my lights on, and then I saw your car off the road, overturned." She looked at him disapprovingly. "You didn't have *your* lights on."

"It took me by surprise," he said, remembering only at that moment how he had been taken by surprise. He did not yet remember that he had also been quite drunk.

"I stopped," she said. "If it had been on an upgrade, I might not have. Not very Christian, I know, but there were three inches on the road already, and even with a four-wheel drive you can't be sure of getting going again once you lose your forward motion. It's easier just to say to yourself, 'Oh, they probably got out, caught a

ride,' et cetera, et cetera. But it was on top of the third big hill past
the Roydmans', and it's flat there for awhile. So I pulled over, and
as soon as I got out I heard groaning. That was *you*, Paul."

She gave him a strange maternal grin.

For the first time, clearly, the thought surfaced in Paul Sheldon's
mind: *I am in trouble here. This woman is not right.*

6
————————

She sat beside him where he lay in what might have been a spare
bedroom for the next twenty minutes or so and talked. As his body
used the soup, the pain in his legs reawakened. He willed himself
to concentrate on what she was saying, but was not entirely able to
succeed. His mind had bifurcated. On one side he was listening to
her tell how she had dragged him from the wreckage of his '74
Camaro—that was the side where the pain throbbed and ached like
a couple of old splintered pilings beginning to wink and flash between the heaves of the withdrawing tide. On the other he could
see himself at the Boulderado Hotel, finishing his new novel, which
did not—thank God for small favors—feature Misery Chastain.

There were all sorts of reasons for him not to write about Misery,
but one loomed above the rest, ironclad and unshakable. Misery—
thank God for *large* favors—was finally dead. She had died five
pages from the end of *Misery's Child*. Not a dry eye in the house
when *that* had happened, including Paul's own—only the dew falling from *his* oculiaries had been the result of hysterical laughter.

Finishing the new book, a contemporary novel about a car-thief,
he had remembered typing the final sentence of *Misery's Child*: "So
Ian and Geoffrey left the Little Dunthorpe churchyard together,
supporting themselves in their sorrow, determined to find their
lives again." While writing this line he had been giggling so madly
it had been hard to strike the correct keys—he had to go back
several times. Thank God for good old IBM CorrectTape. He had
written THE END below and then had gone capering about the
room—this same room in the Boulderado Hotel—and screaming
*Free at last! Free at last! Great God Almighty, I'm free at last! The
silly bitch finally bought the farm!*

The new novel was called *Fast Cars*, and he hadn't laughed when it was done. He just sat there in front of the typewriter for a moment, thinking *You may have just won next year's American Book Award, my friend.* And then he had picked up—

"—a little bruise on your right temple, but that didn't look like anything. It was your legs. . . . I could see right away, even with the light starting to fade, that your legs weren't—"

—the telephone and called room service for a bottle of Dom Pérignon. He remembered waiting for it to come, walking back and forth in the room where he had finished all of his books since 1974; he remembered tipping the waiter with a fifty-dollar bill and asking him if he had heard a weather forecast; he remembered the pleased, flustered, grinning waiter telling him that the storm currently heading their way was supposed to slide off to the south, toward New Mexico; he remembered the chill feel of the bottle, the discreet sound of the cork as he eased it free; he remembered the dry, acerbic-acidic taste of the first glass and opening his travel bag and looking at his plane ticket to New York; he remembered suddenly, on the spur of the moment, deciding—

"—that I better get you home right away! It was a struggle getting you to the truck, but I'm a big woman—as you may have noticed— and I had a pile of blankets in the back. I got you in and wrapped you up, and even then, with the light fading and all, I thought you looked *familiar!* I thought maybe—"

—he would get the old Camaro out of the parking garage and just drive west instead of getting on the plane. What the hell was there in New York, anyway? The townhouse, empty, bleak, un-welcoming, possibly burgled. *Screw it!* he thought, drinking more champagne. *Go west, young man, go west!* The idea had been crazy enough to make sense. Take nothing but a change of clothes and his—

"—bag I found. I put that in, too, but there wasn't anything else I could see and I was scared you might die on me or something so I fired up Old Bessie and I got your—"

—manuscript of *Fast Cars* and hit the road to Vegas or Reno or maybe even the City of the Angels. He remembered the idea had also seemed a bit silly at first—a trip the kid of twenty-four he had been when he had sold his first novel might have taken, but not one for a man two years past his fortieth birthday. A few more glasses of champagne and the idea no longer seemed silly at all. It seemed, in fact, almost noble. A kind of Grand Odyssey to Somewhere, a way to reacquaint himself with reality after the fictional terrain of the novel. So he had gone—

"—out like a light! I was sure you were going to die. . . . I mean, I was *sure!* So I slipped your wallet out of your back pocket, and I looked at your driver's license and I saw the name, *Paul Sheldon,* and I thought, 'Oh, that must be a coincidence,' but the picture on the license *also* looked like you, and then I got so scared I had to sit down at the kitchen table. I thought at first that I was going to faint. After awhile I started thinking maybe the *picture* was just a coincidence, too—those driver's-license photos really don't look like anybody—but then I found your Writers' Guild card, and one from PEN, and I knew you were—"

—in trouble when the snow started coming down, but long before that he had stopped in the Boulderado bar and tipped George twenty bucks to provide him with a second bottle of Dom, and he had drunk it rolling up I-70 into the Rockies under a sky the color of gunmetal, and somewhere east of the Eisenhower Tunnel he had diverted from the turnpike because the roads were bare and dry, the storm was sliding off to the south, what the hay, and also the goddam tunnel made him nervous. He had been playing an old Bo Diddley tape on the cassette machine under the dash and never turned on the radio until the Camaro started to seriously slip and slide and he began to realize that this wasn't just a passing upcountry flurry but the real thing. The storm was maybe not sliding off to the south after all; the storm was maybe coming right at him and he was maybe in a bucket of trouble

(the way you are in trouble now)

but he had been just drunk enough to think he could drive his way out of it. So instead of stopping in Cana and inquiring about shelter, he had driven on. He could remember the afternoon turning into a dull-gray chromium lens. He could remember the champagne beginning to wear off. He could remember leaning forward to get his cigarettes off the dashboard and that was when the last skid began and he tried to ride it out but it kept getting worse; he could remember a heavy dull thump and then the world's up and down had swapped places. He had—

"—*screamed!* And when I heard you screaming, I knew that you would live. Dying men rarely scream. They haven't the energy. I know. I decided I would *make* you live. So I got some of my pain medication and made you take it. Then you went to sleep. When you woke up and started to scream again, I gave you some more. You ran a fever for awhile, but I knocked that out, too. I gave you Keflex. You had one or two close calls, but that's all over now. I promise." She got up. "And now it's time you rested, Paul. You've got to get your strength back."

"My legs hurt."

"Yes, I'm sure they do. In an hour you can have some medication."

"Now. Please." It shamed him to beg, but he could not help it. The tide had gone out and the splintered pilings stood bare, jaggedly real, things which could neither be avoided nor dealt with.

"In an hour." Firmly. She moved toward the door with the spoon and the soup-bowl in one hand.

"Wait!"

She turned back, looking at him with an expression both stern and loving. He did not like the expression. Didn't like it at *all*.

"Two weeks since you pulled me out?"

She looked vague again, and annoyed. He would come to know that her grasp of time was not good. "Something like that."

"I was unconscious?"

"Almost all the time."

"What did I eat?"

She considered him.

"IV," she said briefly.

"IV?" he said, and she mistook his stunned surprise for ignorance.

"I fed you intravenously," she said. "Through tubes. That's what those marks on your arms are." She looked at him with eyes that were suddenly flat and considering. "You owe me your life, Paul. I hope you'll remember that. I hope you'll keep that in mind."

Then she left.

7

The hour passed. Somehow and finally, the hour passed.

He lay in bed, sweating and shivering at the same time. From the other room came first the sounds of Hawkeye and Hot Lips and then the disc jockeys on WKRP, that wild and crazy Cincinnati radio station. An announcer's voice came on, extolled Ginsu knives,

gave an 800 number, and informed those Colorado watchers who
had simply been panting for a good set of Ginsu knives that Op-
erators Were Standing By.

Paul Sheldon was also Standing By.

She reappeared promptly when the clock in the other room
struck eight, with two capsules and a glass of water.

He hoisted himself eagerly on his elbows as she sat on the bed.

"I *finally* got your new book two days ago," she told him. Ice
tinkled in the glass. It was a maddening sound. "*Misery's Child*. I
love it. . . . It's as good as all the rest. Better! The best!"

"Thank you," he managed. He could feel the sweat standing out
on his forehead. "Please . . . my legs . . . very painful . . ."

"I *knew* she would marry Ian," she said, smiling dreamily, "and
I believe Geoffrey and Ian will become friends again, eventually.
Do they?" But immediately she said: "No, don't tell! I want to find
out for myself. I'm making it last. It always seems so long before
there is another one."

The pain throbbed in his legs and made a deep steel circlet around
his crotch. He had touched himself down there, and he thought his
pelvis was intact, but it felt twisted and weird. Below his knees it
felt as if *nothing* was intact. He didn't want to look. He could see
the twisted, lumpy shapes outlined in the bedclothes, and that was
enough.

"Please? Miss Wilkes? The pain—"

"Call me Annie. All my friends do."

She gave him the glass. It was cool and beaded with moisture.
She kept the capsules. The capsules in her hand were the tide. She
was the moon, and she had brought the tide which would cover the
pilings. She brought them toward his mouth, which he immediately
dropped open . . . and then she withdrew them.

"I took the liberty of looking in your little bag. You don't mind,
do you?"

"No. No, of course not. The medicine—"

The beads of sweat on his forehead felt alternately hot and cold.
Was he going to scream? He thought perhaps he was.

"I see there is a manuscript in there," she said. She held the
capsules in her right hand, which she now slowly tilted. They fell
into her left hand. His eyes followed them. "It's called *Fast Cars*.
Not a *Misery* novel, I know that." She looked at him with faint
disapproval—but, as before, it was mixed with love. It was a *ma-*

ternal look. "No cars in the nineteenth century, fast or otherwise!" She tittered at this small joke. "I also took the liberty of glancing through it. . . . You don't mind, do you?"

"Please," he moaned. "No, but please—"

Her left hand tilted. The capsules rolled, hesitated, and then fell back into her right hand with a minute clicking sound.

"And if I read it? You wouldn't mind if I read it?"

"No—" His bones were shattered, his legs filled with festering shards of broken glass. "No . . ." He made something he hoped was a smile. "No, of course not."

"Because I would never presume to do such a thing without your permission," she said earnestly. "I respect you too much. In fact, Paul, I love you." She crimsoned suddenly and alarmingly. One of the capsules dropped from her hand to the coverlet. Paul snatched at it, but she was quicker. He moaned, but she did not notice; after grabbing the capsule she went vague again, looking toward the window. "Your *mind*," she said. "Your *creativity*. That is all I meant."

In desperation, because it was the only thing he could think of, he said: "I know. You're my number-one fan."

She did not just warm up this time; she *lit* up. "That's it!" she cried. "That's it *exactly*! And you wouldn't mind if I read it in that spirit, would you? That spirit of . . . of fan-love? Even though I don't like your other books as well as the *Misery* stories?"

"No," he said, and closed his eyes. *No, turn the pages of the manuscript into paper hats if you want, just . . . please . . . I'm dying in here. . . .*

"You're *good*," she said gently. "I *knew* you would be. Just reading your books, I knew you would be. A man who could think of Misery Chastain, first think of her and then *breathe life* into her, could be nothing else."

Her fingers were in his mouth suddenly, shockingly intimate, dirtily welcome. He sucked the capsules from between them and swallowed even before he could fumble the spilling glass of water to his mouth.

"Just like a baby," she said, but he couldn't see her because his eyes were still closed and now he felt the sting of tears. "But *good*. There is so much I want to ask you . . . so much I want to know."

The springs creaked as she got up.

"We are going to be very happy here," she said, and although a bolt of horror ripped into his heart, Paul still did not open his eyes.

8

He drifted. The tide came in and he drifted. The TV played in the
other room for awhile and then didn't. Sometimes the clock chimed
and he tried to count the chimes but he kept getting lost between.

IV. Through tubes. That's what those marks on your arms are.

He got up on one elbow and pawed for the lamp and finally got
it turned on. He looked at his arms and in the folds of his elbows
he saw fading, overlapped shades of purple and ocher, a hole filled
with black blood at the center of each bruise.

He lay back, looking at the ceiling, listening to the wind. He was
near the top of the Great Divide in the heart of winter, he was with
a woman who was not right in her head, a woman who had fed him
with IV drips when he was unconscious, a woman who had an
apparently never-ending supply of dope, a woman who had told no
one he was here.

These things were important, but he began to realize that something else was more important: the tide was going out again. He
began to wait for the sound of her alarm clock upstairs. It would
not go off for some long while yet, but it was time for him to start
waiting for it to be time.

She was crazy but he needed her.

Oh I am in so much trouble he thought, and stared blindly up at
the ceiling as the droplets of sweat began to gather on his forehead
again.

9

The next morning she brought him more soup and told him she
had read forty pages of what she called his "manuscript-book." She
told him she didn't think it was as good as his others.

"It's hard to follow. It keeps jumping back and forth in time."

"Technique," he said. He was somewhere between hurting and
not hurting, and so was able to think a little better about what she
was saying. "Technique, that's all it is. The subject . . . the subject
dictates the form." In some vague way he supposed that such tricks
of the trade might interest, even fascinate her. God knew they had

fascinated the attendees of the writers' workshops to whom he had
sometimes lectured when he was younger. "The boy's mind, you
see, is confused, and so—"

"Yes! He's *very* confused, and that makes him less interesting.
Not *un*interesting—I'm sure you couldn't create an *un*interesting
character—but *less* interesting. And the profanity! Every other word
is that effword! It has—" She ruminated, feeding him the soup
automatically, wiping his mouth when he dribbled almost without
looking, the way an experienced typist rarely looks at the keys; so
he came to understand, effortlessly, that she had been a nurse. Not
a doctor, oh no; doctors would not know when the dribbles would
come, or be able to forecast the course of each with such a nice
exactitude.

*If the forecaster in charge of that storm had been half as good at his
job as Annie Wilkes is at hers, I would not be in this fucking jam,* he
thought bitterly.

"It has no *nobility!*" she cried suddenly, jumping and almost
spilling beef-barley soup on his white, upturned face.

"Yes," he said patiently. "I understand what you mean, Annie.
It's true that Tony Bonasaro has no nobility. He's a slum kid trying
to get out of a bad environment, you see, and those words
. . . everybody uses those words in—"

"They do *not!*" she said, giving him a forbidding look. "What do
you think I do when I go to the feed store in town? What do you
think I *say*? 'Now Tony, give me a bag of that effing pigfeed and a
bag of that bitchly cow-corn and some of that Christing ear-mite
medicine'? And what do you think he says to me? 'You're effing
right, Annie, coming right the eff up'?"

She looked at him, her face now like a sky which might spawn
tornadoes at any instant. He lay back, frightened. The soup-bowl
was tilting in her hands. One, then two drops fell on the coverlet.

"And then do I go down the street to the bank and say to Mrs.
Bollinger, 'Here's one big bastard of a check and you better give
me fifty effing dollars just as effing quick as you can'? Do you think
that when they put me up there on the stand in Den—"

A stream of muddy-colored beef soup fell on the coverlet. She
looked at it, then at him, and her face twisted. "There! Look what
you made me do!"

"I'm sorry."

"Sure! You! Are!" she screamed, and threw the bowl into the

corner, where it shattered. Soup splashed up the wall. He gasped.

She turned off then. She just sat there for what might have been thirty seconds. During that time Paul Sheldon's heart did not seem to beat at all.

She roused a little at a time, and suddenly she tittered.

"I have such a *temper*," she said.

"I'm sorry," he said out of a dry throat.

"You *should* be." Her face went slack again and she looked moodily at the wall. He thought she was going to blank out again, but instead she fetched a sigh and lifted her bulk from the bed.

"You don't have any need to use such words in the *Misery* books, because they didn't use such words at all back then. They weren't even invented. Animal times demand animal words, I suppose, but that was a *better* time. You ought to stick to your *Misery* stories, Paul. I say that sincerely. As your number-one fan."

She went to the door and looked back at him. "I'll put that manuscript-book back in your bag and finish *Misery's Child*. I may go back to the other one later, when I'm done."

"Don't do that if it makes you mad," he said. He tried to smile. "I'd rather not have you mad. I sort of depend on you, you know."

She did not return his smile. "Yes," she said. "You do. You do, don't you, Paul?"

She left.

10

The tide went out. The pilings were back. He began to wait for the clock to chime. Two chimes. The chimes came. He lay propped up on the pillows, watching the door. She came in. She was wearing an apron over her cardigan and one of her skirts. In one hand she held a floor-bucket.

"I suppose you want your cockadoodie medication," she said.

"Yes, please." He tried to smile at her ingratiatingly and felt that shame again—he felt grotesque to himself, a stranger.

"I have it," she said, "but first I have to clean up the mess in the corner. The mess *you* made. You'll have to wait until I do that."

He lay in the bed with his legs making shapes like broken branches under the coverlet and cold sweat running down his face in little slow creeks, he lay and watched as she crossed to the corner and set the bucket down and then picked up the pieces of the bowl and took them out and came back and knelt by the bucket and fished in it and brought out a soapy rag and wrung it out and began to wash the dried soup from the wall. He lay and watched and at last he began to shiver and the shivering made the pain worse but he could not help it. Once she turned around and saw him shivering and soaking the bedclothes in sweat, and she favored him with such a sly knowing smile that he could easily have killed her.

"It's dried on," she said, turning her face back into the corner. "I'm afraid this is going to take awhile, Paul."

She scrubbed. The stain slowly disappeared from the plaster but she went on dipping the cloth, wringing it out, scrubbing, and then repeating the whole process. He could not see her face, but the idea—the *certainty*—that she had gone blank and might go on scrubbing the wall for hours tormented him.

At last—just before the clock chimed once, marking two-thirty—she got up and dropped the rag into the water. She took the bucket from the room without a word. He lay in bed, listening to the creaking boards which marked her heavy, stolid passage, listening as she poured the water out of her bucket—and, incredibly, the sound of the faucet as she drew more. He began to cry soundlessly. The tide had never gone out so far; he could see nothing but drying mudflats and those splintered pilings which cast their eternal damaged shadows.

She came back and stood for just a moment inside the doorway, observing his wet face with that same mixture of sternness and maternal love. Then her eyes drifted to the corner, where no sign of the splashed soup remained.

"Now I must rinse," she said, "or else the soap will leave a dull spot. I must do it all; I must make everything right. Living alone as I do is no excuse whatever for scamping the job. My mother had a motto, Paul, and I live by it. 'Once nasty, never neat,' she used to say."

"Please," he groaned. "Please, the pain, I'm dying."

"No. You're not dying."

"I'll scream," he said, beginning to cry harder. It hurt to cry. It hurt his legs and it hurt his heart. "I won't be able to help it."

"Then scream," she said. "But remember that *you* made that mess. Not me. It's nobody's fault but your own."

Somehow he was able to keep from screaming. He watched as
she dipped and wrung and rinsed, dipped and wrung and rinsed.
At last, just as the clock in what he assumed was the parlor began
to strike three, she rose and picked up the bucket.

*She's going to go out now. She's going to go out and I'll hear her
pouring the rinse-water down the sink and maybe she won't come back
for hours because maybe she's not done punishing me yet.*

But instead of leaving, she walked over to the bed and fished in
her apron pocket. She brought out not two capsules but three.

"Here," she said tenderly.

He gobbled them into his mouth, and when he looked up he
saw her lifting the yellow plastic floor-bucket toward him. It filled
his field of vision like a falling moon. Grayish water slopped over
the rim onto the coverlet.

"Wash them down with this," she said. Her voice was still tender.

He stared at her, and his face was all eyes.

"Do it," she said. "I know you can dry-swallow them, but please
believe me when I say I can make them come right back up again.
After all, it's only rinse-water. It won't hurt you."

She leaned over him like a monolith, the bucket slightly tipped.
He could see the rag twisting slowly in its dark depths like a drowned
thing; he could see a thin scrum of soap on top. Part of him groaned
but none of him hesitated. He drank quickly, washing the pills
down, and the taste in his mouth was as it had been on the occasions
when his mother made him brush his teeth with soap.

His belly hitched and he made a thick sound.

"I wouldn't throw them up, Paul. No more until nine tonight."

She looked at him for a moment with a flat empty gaze, and then
her face lit up and she smiled.

"You won't make me mad again, will you?"

"No," he whispered. Anger the moon which brought the tide?
What an idea! What a *bad* idea!

"I love you," she said, and kissed him on the cheek. She left,
not looking back, carrying the floor-bucket the way a sturdy coun-
trywoman might carry a milk-pail, slightly away from her body with
no thought at all, so that none would spill.

He lay back, tasting grit and plaster in his mouth and throat.
Tasting soap.

I won't throw up . . . won't throw up . . . won't throw up.

At last the urgency of this thought began to fade and he realized he was going to sleep. He had held everything down long enough for the medication to begin its work. He had won.

This time.

11

He dreamed he was being eaten by a bird. It was not a good dream. There was a bang and he thought, *Yes, good, all right! Shoot it! Shoot the goddamned thing!*

Then he was awake, knowing it was only Annie Wilkes, pulling the back door shut. She had gone out to do the chores. He heard the dim crunch of her footsteps in the snow. She went past his window, wearing a parka with the hood up. Her breath plumed out, then broke apart on her moving face. She didn't look in at him, intent on her chores in the barn, he supposed. Feeding the animals, cleaning the stalls, maybe casting a few runes—he wouldn't put it past her. The sky was darkening purple—sunset. Five-thirty, maybe six o'clock.

The tide was still in and he could have gone back to sleep—*wanted* to go back to sleep—but he had to think about this bizarre situation while he was still capable of something like rational thought.

The worst thing, he was discovering, was that he didn't want to think of it even while he could, even when he knew he could not bring the situation to an end without thinking about it. His mind kept trying to push it away, like a child pushing away his meal even though he has been told he cannot leave the table until he has eaten it.

He didn't want to think about it because just *living* it was hard enough. He didn't want to think about it because whenever he did unpleasant images intervened—the way she went blank, the way she made him think of idols and stones, and now the way the yellow plastic floor-bucket had sped toward his face like a crashing moon. Thinking of *those* things would not change his situation, was in fact worse than not thinking at all, but once he turned his mind to Annie Wilkes and his position here in her house, they were the thoughts that came, crowding out all others. His heart would start to beat too fast, mostly in fear, but partly in shame, too. He saw himself putting his lips to the rim of the yellow floor-bucket, saw the rinse-

water with its film of soap and the rag floating in it, saw these things
but drank anyway, never hesitating a bit. He would never tell anyone about that, assuming he ever got out of this, and he supposed
he might try to lie about it to himself, but he would never be able
to do it.

Yet, miserable or not (and he was), he still wanted to live.

*Think about it, goddammit! Jesus Christ, are you already so cowed
you can't even* try?

No—but *almost* that cowed.

Then an odd, angry thought occurred to him: *She doesn't like the
new book because she's too stupid to understand what it's up to.*

The thought wasn't just odd; under the circumstances, how she
felt about *Fast Cars* was totally immaterial. But thinking about the
things she had said was at least a new avenue, and feeling angry *at*
her was better than feeling scared *of* her, and so he went down it
with some eagerness.

*Too stupid? No. Too set. Not just unwilling to change, but antag-
onistic to the very* idea *of change.*

Yes. And while she might be crazy, was she so different in her
evaluation of his work from the hundreds of thousands of other
people across the country—ninety percent of them women—who
could barely wait for each new five-hundred-page episode in the
turbulent life of the foundling who had risen to marry a peer of
the realm? No, not at all. They wanted Misery, Misery, Misery.
Each time he had taken a year or two off to write one of the other
novels—what he thought of as his "serious" work with what was at
first certainty and then hope and finally a species of grim desperation—he had received a flood of protesting letters from these
women, many of whom signed themselves "your number-one fan."
The tone of these letters varied from bewilderment (that always
hurt the most, somehow), to reproach, to outright anger, but the
message was always the same: *It wasn't what I expected, it wasn't
what I* wanted. *Please go back to Misery. I want to know what Misery
is doing.* He could write a modern *Under the Volcano, Tess of the
D'Urbervilles, The Sound and the Fury*; it wouldn't matter. They
would still want Misery, Misery, Misery.

It's hard to follow . . . he's not interesting . . . and the profanity!

The anger sparked again. Anger at her obdurate density, anger
that she could actually kidnap him—keep him prisoner here, force
him into a choice between drinking dirty rinse-water from a floor-

bucket or suffering the pain of his shattered legs—and then, on top of all that, find the nerve to *criticize* the best thing he had ever written.

"Bugger you and the effword you rode in on," he said, and he suddenly felt better again, felt *himself* again, even though he knew this rebellion was petty and pitiful and meaningless—she was in the barn where she couldn't hear him, and the tide was safely in over the splintered pilings. Still . . .

He remembered her coming in here, withholding the capsules, coercing permission to read the manuscript of *Fast Cars*. He felt a flush of shame and humiliation warming his face, but now they were mixed with *real* anger: it had bloomed from a spark into a tiny sunken flame. He had *never* shown anyone a manuscript before he had proof-read it and then retyped it. *Never.* Not even Bryce, his agent. *Never.* Why, he didn't even—

For a moment his thoughts broke off cleanly. He could hear the dim sound of a cow mooing.

Why, he didn't even make a *copy* until the second draft was done.

The manuscript copy of *Fast Cars* which was now in Annie Wilkes's possession was, in fact, the only existing copy in the whole world. He had even burned his notes.

Two years of hard work, she didn't like it, and she was crazy.

Misery was what *she* liked; Misery was *who* she liked, not some foul-talking little spic car-thief from Spanish Harlem.

He remembered thinking: *Turn the pages of the manuscript into paper hats if you want, just . . . please . . .*

The anger and humiliation surged again, awakening the first dull answering throb in his legs. Yes. The work, the pride in your work, the worth of the work itself . . . all those things faded away to the magic-lantern shades they really were when the pain got bad enough. That she would do that to him—that she *could*, when he had spent most of his adult life thinking the word *writer* was the most important definition of himself—made her seem utterly monstrous, something he *must* escape. She really *was* an idol, and if she didn't kill him, she might kill what was *in* him.

Now he heard the eager squeal of the pig—she had thought he would mind, but he thought Misery was a wonderful name for a pig. He remembered how she had imitated it, the way her upper lip had wrinkled toward her nose, how her cheeks had seemed to flatten, how she had actually *looked* like a pig for a moment: *Whoink!* *WHOINKK!*

From the barn, her voice: "*Sooo-ey, pig-pig-pig!*"

He lay back, put his arm over his eyes, and tried to hold onto the anger, because the anger made him feel brave. A brave man could think. A coward couldn't.

Here was a woman who had been a nurse—he was sure of that. Was she still a nurse? No, because she did not go to work. Why did she no longer practice her trade? That seemed obvious. Not all her gear was stowed right; lots of it was rolling around in the holds. If it was obvious to him even through the haze of pain he had been living in, it would surely have been obvious to her colleagues.

And he had a little extra information on which to judge just how *much* of her gear wasn't stowed right, didn't he? She had dragged him from the wreck of his car and instead of calling the police or an ambulance she had installed him in her guest-room, put IV drips in his arms and a shitload of dope in his body. Enough so he had gone into what she called respiratory depression at least once. She had told no one he was here, and if she hadn't by now, that meant she didn't mean to.

Would she have behaved in this same fashion if it had been Joe Blow from Kokomo she had hauled out of the wreck? No. No, he didn't think so. She had kept *him* because he was Paul Sheldon, and *she*—

"She's my number-one fan," Paul muttered, and put an arm over his eyes.

An awful memory bloomed there in the dark: his mother had taken him to the Boston Zoo, and he had been looking at a great big bird. It had the most beautiful feathers—red and purple and royal blue—that he had ever seen . . . and the saddest eyes. He had asked his mother where the bird came from and when she said *Africa* he had understood it was doomed to die in the cage where it lived, far away from wherever God had meant it to be, and he cried and his mother bought him an ice-cream cone and for awhile he had stopped crying and then he remembered and started again and so she had taken him home, telling him as they rode the trolley back to Lynn that he was a bawl-baby and a sissy.

Its feathers. Its *eyes*.

The throbbing in his legs began to cycle up.

No. No, no.

He pressed the crook of his elbow more tightly against his eyes. From the barn he could hear spaced thudding noises. Impossible to tell what they were, of course, but in his imagination

(*your* MIND *your* CREATIVITY *that is all I meant*)

he could see her pushing bales of hay out of the loft with the heel of her boot, could see them tumbling to the barn floor.

Africa. That bird came from Africa. From—

Then, cutting cleanly through this like a sharp knife, came her agitated, almost screaming voice: *Do you think that when they put me up there on the stand in Den—*

Up on the stand. When they put me up on the stand in Denver.

Do you swear to tell the truth, the whole truth, and nothing but the truth, so help you God?

(*"I don't know where he gets it."*)

I do.

(*"He's* ALWAYS *writing things like this down."*)

State your name.

(*"Nobody on* MY *side of the family had an imagination like his."*)

Annie Wilkes.

(*"So vivid!"*)

My name is Annie Wilkes.

He willed her to say more; she would not.

"Come on," he muttered, his arm over his eyes—this was the way he thought best, the way he *imagined* best. His mother liked to tell Mrs. Mulvaney on the other side of the fence what a marvellous imagination he had, so vivid, and what wonderful little stories he was always writing down (except, of course, when she was calling him a sissy and a bawl-baby). "Come on, come on, come on."

He could see the courtroom in Denver, could see Annie Wilkes on the stand, not wearing jeans now but a rusty purple-black dress and an awful hat. He could see that the courtroom was crowded with spectators, that the judge was bald and wearing glasses. The judge had a white moustache. There was a birthmark beneath the white moustache. The white moustache covered most of it but not quite all.

Annie Wilkes.

(*"He read at just three! Can you imagine!"*)

That spirit of . . . of fan-love . . .

("He's always writing things down, making things up.")
Now I must rinse.
("Africa. That bird came from")

"Come *on*," he whispered, but could get no further. The bailiff asked her to state her name, and over and over again she said it was Annie Wilkes, but she said no more; she sat there with her fibrous solid ominous body displacing air and said her name over and over again but no more than that.

Still trying to imagine why the ex-nurse who had taken him prisoner might have once been put on the stand in Denver, Paul drifted off to sleep.

12

He was in a hospital ward. Great relief swept through him—so great he felt like crying. Something had happened when he was asleep, someone had come, or perhaps Annie had had a change of heart or mind. It didn't matter. He had gone to sleep in the monster-woman's house and had awakened in the hospital.

But surely they would not have put him in a long ward like this? It was as big as an airplane hangar! Identical rows of men (with identical bottles of nutrient hung from identical IV trays beside their beds) filled the place. He sat up and saw that the men themselves were also identical—they were all *him*. Then, distantly, he heard the clock chime, and understood that it was chiming from beyond the wall of sleep. This was a dream. Sadness replaced the relief.

The door at the far end of the huge ward opened and in came Annie Wilkes—only she was dressed in a long aproned dress and there was a mobcap on her head; she was dressed as Misery Chastain in *Misery's Love*. Over one arm she held a wicker basket. There was a towel over the contents. She folded the towel back as he watched. She reached in and took out a handful of something and flung it into the face of the first sleeping Paul Sheldon. It was sand, he saw—this was Annie Wilkes pretending to be Misery Chastain pretending to be the sandman. Sand*woman*.

Then he saw that the first Paul Sheldon's face had turned a ghastly white as soon as the sand struck it and fear jerked him out of the dream and into the bedroom, where Annie Wilkes was standing over him. She was holding the fat paperback of *Misery's Child* in one hand. Her bookmark suggested she was about three-quarters of the way through.

"You were moaning," she said.

"I had a bad dream."

"What was it about?"

The first thing which was not the truth that popped into his head was what he replied:

"Africa."

13

She came in late the following morning, her face the color of ashes. He had been dozing, but he came awake at once, jerking up on his elbows.

"Miss Wilkes? Annie? Are you all r—"

"No."

Christ, she's had a heart attack, he thought, and there was a moment's alarm which was immediately replaced by joy. *Let* her have one! A *big* one! A fucking chest-buster! He would be more than happy to crawl to the telephone, no matter how much it might hurt. He would crawl to the telephone over broken glass, if that was what it took.

And it *was* a heart attack . . . but not the right kind.

She came toward him, not quite staggering but *rolling,* the way a sailor will when he's just gotten off his ship at the end of a long voyage.

"What—" He tried to shrink away from her, but there was no place to go. There was only the headboard, and behind that, the wall.

"*No!*" She reached the side of the bed, bumped it, wavered, and for a moment seemed on the verge of falling on top of him. Then she just stood there, looking down at him out of her paper-white face, the cords on her neck standing out, one vein pulsing in the center of her forehead. Her hands snapped open, hooked shut into solid rocklike fists, then snapped open again.

"You . . . you . . . you *dirty bird!*"

"What—I don't—" But suddenly he did, and his entire midsection first seemed to turn hollow and then to entirely disappear. He remembered where her bookmark had been last night, three-quarters of the way through. She had finished it. She knew all there was to know. She knew that Misery hadn't been the barren one, after all; it had been *Ian*. Had she sat there in her as-yet-unseen-by-him parlor with her mouth open and her eyes wide as Misery finally realized the truth and made her decision and sneaked off to Geoffrey? Had her eyes filled with tears when she realized that Misery and Geoffrey, far from having a clandestine affair behind the back of the man they both loved, were giving him the greatest gift they could—a child he would believe to be his own? And had her heart risen up when Misery told Ian she was pregnant and Ian had crushed her to him, tears flowing from his eyes, muttering "My dear, oh, my dear!" over and over again? He was sure, in those few seconds, that all of those things had happened. But instead of weeping with exalted grief as she should have done when Misery expired giving birth to the boy whom Ian and Geoffrey would presumably raise together, she was mad as hell.

"*She can't be dead!*" Annie Wilkes shrieked at him. Her hands snapped open and hooked closed in a faster and faster rhythm. "*Misery Chastain CANNOT BE DEAD!*"

"Annie—Annie, please—"

There was a glass water-pitcher on the table. She seized it up and brandished it at him. Cold water splashed his face. An ice-cube landed beside his left ear and slid down the pillow into the hollow of his shoulder. In his mind

(*"So vivid!"*)

he saw her bringing the pitcher down into his face, he saw himself dying of a fractured skull and a massive cerebral hemorrhage in a freezing flood of ice-water while goosepimples formed on his arms.

She wanted to do it; there was no question of that.

At the very last moment she pivoted away from him and flung the water-pitcher at the door instead, where it shattered as the soup-bowl had the other day.

She looked back at him and brushed her hair away from her face—two hard little spots of red had now bloomed in the white—with the backs of her hands.

"Dirty bird!" she panted. "Oh you dirty birdie, how *could* you!"

He spoke rapidly, urgently, eyes flashing, riveted on her face—

he was positive in that moment that his life might depend on what he was able to say in the next twenty seconds.

"Annie, in 1871 women *frequently* died in childbirth. Misery gave her life for her husband and her best friend and her child. The *spirit* of Misery will always—"

"I don't want her *spirit!*" she screamed, hooking her fingers into claws and shaking them at him, as if she would tear his eyes out. "I want *her!* You *killed* her! You *murdered* her!" Her hands snapped shut into fists again and she drove them down like pistons, one on either side of his head. They punched deep into the pillow and he bounced like a ragdoll. His legs flared and he cried out.

"*I didn't kill her!*" he screamed.

She froze, staring at him with that narrow black expression—that look of *crevasse.*

"Of *course* not," she said, bitterly sarcastic. "And if you didn't, Paul Sheldon, who did?"

"No one," he said more quietly. "She just died."

Ultimately he knew this to be the truth. If Misery Chastain had been a real person, he knew he might very well have been called upon "to aid the police in their inquiries," as the euphemism went. After all, he had a motive—he had hated her. Ever since the third book, he had hated her. For April Fools' Day four years ago he'd had a small booklet privately printed and had sent it to a dozen close acquaintances. It had been called *Misery's Hobby.* In it Misery spent a cheerful country weekend boffing Growler, Ian's Irish setter.

He might have murdered her . . . but he hadn't. In the end, in spite of his having grown to despise her, Misery's death had been something of a surprise to him. He had remained true enough to himself for art to imitate life—however feebly—to the very end of Misery's hackneyed adventures. She had died a mostly unexpected death. His cheerful capering had in no way changed the fact.

"You lie," Annie whispered. "I thought you were *good,* but you are *not* good. You are just a lying old dirty birdie."

"She slipped away, that's all. Sometimes that happens. It was like life, when someone just—"

She overturned the table by the bed. The one shallow drawer spilled out. His wristwatch and pocket-change spilled out with it. He hadn't even known they were in there. He cringed back from her.

"You must think I was born *yesterday*," she said. Her lips drew back from her teeth. "In my job I saw dozens of people die—hundreds, now that I think about it. Sometimes they go screaming and sometimes they go in their sleep—they just slip away, the way you said, sure.

"But characters in stories DO NOT just slip away! God takes us when He thinks it's time and a writer is God to the people in a story, he made them up just like God made US up and no one can get hold of God to make him explain, all right, okay, but as far as Misery goes I'll tell you one thing you dirty bird, I'll tell you that God just happens to have a couple of broken legs and God just happens to be in MY house eating MY food . . . and . . ."

She went blank then. She straightened up with her hands hanging limply by her sides, looking at the wall where an old photograph of the Arc de Triomphe was hung. She stood there and Paul lay in his bed with round marks in the pillow beside his ears and looked at her. He could hear the water which had been in the pitcher dripping on the floor, and it came to him that he could commit murder. This was a question which had occurred to him from time to time, strictly academic, of course, only now it wasn't and he had the answer. If she hadn't thrown the pitcher, he would have shattered it on the floor himself and tried to shove one of the broken pieces of glass into her throat while she stood there, as inert as an umbrella-stand.

He looked down into the spillage from the drawer, but there was only the change, a pen, a comb, and his watch. No wallet. More important, no Swiss Army knife.

She came back a little at a time, and the anger, at least, was gone. She looked down at him sadly.

"I think I better go now. I don't think I better be around you for awhile. I don't think it's . . . wise."

"Go? Where?"

"It doesn't matter. A place I know. If I stay here, I'll do something unwise. I need to think. Goodbye, Paul."

She strode across the room.

"Will you be back to give me my medication?" he asked, alarmed.

She grasped the doorknob and pulled the door shut without answering. For the first time he heard the rattle of a key.

He heard her footsteps going off down the hall; he winced as she cried out angrily—words he couldn't understand—and something else fell and shattered. A door slammed. An engine cranked over and then started up. The low, crunching squeal of tires turning on packed snow. Now the motor-sound began to go away. It dwindled to a snore and then to a drone and was finally gone.

He was alone.

Alone in Annie Wilkes's house, locked in this room. Locked in this bed. The distance between here and Denver was like . . . well, like the distance between the Boston Zoo and Africa.

He lay in bed looking at the ceiling, his throat dry and his heart beating fast.

After awhile the parlor clock chimed noon and the tide began to go out.

14

Fifty-one hours.

He knew just how long because of the pen, the Flair Fine-Liner he had been carrying in his pocket at the time of the crash. He had been able to reach down and snag it. Every time the clock chimed he made a mark on his arm—four vertical marks and then a diagonal slash to seal the quintet. When she came back there were ten groups of five and one extra. The little groups, neat at first, grew increasingly jagged as his hands began to tremble. He didn't believe he had missed a single hour. He had dozed, but never really slept. The chiming of the clock woke him each time the hour came around.

After awhile he began to feel hunger and thirst—even through the pain. It became something like a horse race. At first King of Pain was far in the lead and I Got the Hungries was some twelve furlongs back. Pretty Thirsty was nearly lost in the dust. Then, around sunup on the day after she had left, I Got the Hungries actually gave King of Pain a brief run for his money.

He had spent much of the night alternately dozing and waking in a cold sweat, sure he was dying. After awhile he began to *hope* he was dying. Anything to be out of it. He'd never had any idea how bad hurting could get. The pilings grew and grew. He could see the barnacles which encrusted them, could see pale drowned things lying limply in the clefts of the wood. They were the lucky things. For them the hurting was over. Around three he had lapsed into a bout of useless screaming.

By noon of the second day—Hour Twenty-four—he realized that, as bad as the pain in his legs and pelvis was, something else was also making him hurt. It was withdrawal. Call this horse Junkie's Revenge, if you wanted. He needed the capsules in more ways than one.

He thought of trying to get out of bed, but the thought of the thump and the drop and the accompanying escalation of pain constantly deterred him. He could imagine all too well

("*So vivid!*")

how it would feel. He might have tried anyway, but she had locked the door. What could he do besides crawl across to it, snaillike, and lie there?

In desperation he pushed back the blankets with his hands for the first time, hoping against hope that it wasn't as bad as the shapes the blankets made seemed to suggest it was. It wasn't *as* bad; it was worse. He stared with horror at what he had become below the knees. In his mind he heard the voice of Ronald Reagan in *King's Row*, shrieking *"Where's the rest of me?"*

The rest of him was here, and he might get out of this; the prospects for doing so seemed ever more remote, but he supposed it was technically possible . . . but he might well never walk again—and surely not until each of his legs had been rebroken, perhaps in several places, and pinned with steel, and mercilessly overhauled, and subjected to half a hundred shriekingly painful indignities.

She had splinted them—of course he had known that, felt the rigid ungiving shapes, but until now he had not known what she had done it with. The lower parts of both legs were circled with slim steel rods that looked like the hacksawed remains of aluminum crutches. The rods had been strenuously taped, so that from the knees down he looked a bit like Im-Ho-Tep when he had been discovered in his tomb. The legs themselves meandered strangely up to his knees, turning outward here, jagging inward there. His left knee—a throbbing focus of pain—no longer seemed to exist at all. There was a calf, and a thigh, and then a sickening bunch in the middle that looked like a salt-dome. His upper legs were badly swollen and seemed to have bowed slightly outward. His thighs, crotch, even his penis, were all still mottled with fading bruises.

He had thought his lower legs might be shattered. That was not so, as it turned out. They had been *pulverized.*

Moaning, crying, he pulled the blankets back up. No rolling out of bed. Better to lie here, die here, better to accept this level of pain, terrific as it was, until all pain was gone.

Around four o'clock of the second day, Pretty Thirsty made its move. He had been aware of dryness in his mouth and throat for a long time, but now it began to seem more urgent. His tongue felt thick, too large. Swallowing hurt. He began to think of the pitcher of water she had dashed away.

He dozed, woke, dozed.

Day passed away. Night fell.

He had to urinate. He laid the top sheet over his penis, hoping to create a crude filter, and urinated through it into his cupped and shaking hands. He tried to think of it as recycling and drank what he had managed to hold and then licked his wet palms. Here was something else he reckoned he would not tell people about, if he lived long enough to tell them anything.

He began to believe she was dead. She was deeply unstable, and unstable people frequently took their own lives. He saw her

(*"So vivid"*)

pulling over to the side of the road in Old Bessie, taking a .44 from under the seat, putting it in her mouth, and shooting herself. *"With Misery dead I don't want to live. Goodbye, cruel world!" Annie cried through a rain of tears, and pulled the trigger.*

He cackled, then moaned, then screamed. The wind screamed with him . . . but took no other notice.

Or an accident? Was that possible? Oh, yes, sir! He saw her driving grimly, going too fast, and then

(*"He doesn't get it from* MY *side of the family!"*)

going blank and driving right off the side of the road. Down and down and down. Hitting once and bursting into a fireball, dying without even knowing it.

If she was dead he would die in here, a rat in a dry trap.

He kept thinking unconsciousness would come and relieve him, but unconsciousness declined; instead Hour Thirty came, and Hour Forty; now King of Pain and Pretty Thirsty merged into one single horse (I Got the Hungries had been left in the dust long since) and he began to feel like nothing more than a slice of living tissue on

a microscope slide or a worm on a hook—something, anyway, twisting endlessly and waiting only to die.

15

When she came in he thought at first that she must be a dream,
but then reality—or mere brute survival—took over and he began
to moan and beg and plead, all of it broken, all of it coming from
a deepening well of unreality. The one thing he saw clearly was
that she was wearing a dark-blue dress and a sprigged hat—it was
exactly the sort of outfit he had imagined her wearing on the stand
in Denver.

Her color was high and her eyes sparkled with life and vivacity.
She was as close to pretty as Annie Wilkes ever could be, and when
he tried to remember that scene later the only clear images he could
fix upon were her flushed cheeks and the sprigged hat. From some
final stronghold of sanity and evaluative clarity the rational Paul
Sheldon had thought: *She looks like a widow who just got fucked after
a ten-year dry spell.*

In her hand she held a glass of water—a tall glass of water.

"Take this," she said, and put a hand still cool from the out-of-
doors on the back of his neck so he could sit up enough to drink
without choking. He took three fast mouthfuls, the pores on the
arid plain of his tongue widening and clamoring at the shock of the
water, some of it spilling down his chin and onto the tee-shirt he
wore, and then she drew it away from him.

He mewled for it, holding his shaking hands out.

"No," she said. "No, Paul. A little at a time, or you'll vomit."

After a bit she gave it back to him and allowed two more swallows.

"The stuff," he said, coughing. He sucked at his lips and ran his
tongue over them and then sucked his tongue. He could vaguely
remember drinking his own piss, how hot it had been, how salty.
"The capsules—pain—please, Annie, please, for God's sake help
me *the pain is so bad*—"

"I know it is, but you must listen to me," she said, looking at
him with that stern yet maternal expression. "I had to get away and
think. I have thought deeply, and I hope I've thought well. I was
not entirely sure; my thoughts are often muddy, I know that. I

accept that. It's why I couldn't remember where I was all those times they kept asking me about. So I prayed. There *is* a God, you know, and He answers prayers. He always does. So I prayed. I said, 'Dear God, Paul Sheldon may be dead when I get back.' But God said, 'He will not be. I have spared him, so you may shew him the way he must go.'"

She said *shew* as *shoe*, but Paul was barely hearing her anyway; his eyes were fixed on the glass of water. She gave him another three swallows. He slurped like a horse, burped, then cried out as shudder-cramps coursed through him.

During all of this she looked at him benignly.

"I will give you your medication and relieve your pain," she said, "but first you have a job to do. I'll be right back."

She got up and headed for the door.

"*No!*" he screamed.

She took no notice at all. He lay in bed, cocooned in pain, trying not to moan and moaning anyway.

16

At first he thought he had lapsed into delirium. What he was seeing was too bizarre to be sane. When Annie returned, she was pushing a charcoal grill in front of her.

"Annie, I'm in terrible pain." Tears coursed down his cheeks.

"I know, my dear." She kissed his cheek, the touch of her lips as gentle as the fall of a feather. "Soon."

She left and he looked stupidly at the charcoal grill, something meant for an outdoor summer patio which now stood in his room, calling up relentless images of idols and sacrifices.

And sacrifice was what she had in mind, of course—when she came back she was carrying the manuscript of *Fast Cars*, the only existing result of his two years' work, in one hand. In the other she had a box of Diamond Blue Tip wooden matches.

17

"No," he said, crying and shaking. One thought worked at him, burned in him like acid: for less than a hundred bucks he could have had the manuscript photocopied in Boulder. People—Bryce, both of his ex-wives, hell, even his mother—had always told him he was crazy not to make at least one copy of his work and put it aside; after all, the Boulderado could catch on fire, or the New York townhouse; there might be a tornado or a flood or some other natural disaster. He had constantly refused, for no rational reason: it was just that making copies seemed a jinx thing to do.

Well, here was the jinx and the natural disaster all rolled up in one; here was Hurricane Annie. In her innocence it had apparently never even crossed her mind that there might be another copy of *Fast Cars* someplace, and if he had just *listened*, if he had just invested the lousy hundred dollars—

"Yes," she replied, holding out the matches to him. The manuscript, clean white Hammermill Bond with the title page topmost, lay on her lap. Her face was still clear and calm.

"No," he said, turning his burning face away from her.

"Yes. It's filthy. That aside, it's also no good."

"You wouldn't know good if it walked up and bit your nose off!" he yelled, not caring.

She laughed gently. Her temper had apparently gone on vacation. But, Paul thought, knowing Annie Wilkes, it could arrive back unexpectedly at any moment, bags in hand: *Couldn't stand to stay away! How ya doin?*

"First of all," she said, "good would *not* bite my nose off. *Evil* might, but not good. Second of all, I *do* know good when I see it— *you* are good, Paul. All you need is a little help. Now, take the matches."

He shook his head stiffly back and forth. "No."

"Yes."

"No!"

"Yes."

"No goddammit!"

"Use all the profanity you want. I've heard it all before."

"I won't do it." He closed his eyes.

When he opened them she was holding out a cardboard square

with the word NOVRIL printed across the top in bright blue letters.
SAMPLE, the red letters just below the trade name read. NOT TO
BE DISPENSED WITHOUT PHYSICIAN'S PRESCRIPTION. Below the
warning were four capsules in blister-packs. He grabbed. She pulled
the cardboard out of his reach.

"When you burn it," she said. "Then I'll give you the capsules—
all four of these, I think—and the pain will go away. You will begin
to feel serene again, and when you've got hold of yourself, I will
change your bedding—I see you've wet it, and it must be uncom-
fortable—and I'll also change *you*. By then you will be hungry and
I can give you some soup. Perhaps some unbuttered toast. But until
you burn it, Paul, I can do nothing. I'm sorry."

His tongue wanted to say *Yes! Yes, okay!* and so he bit it. He
rolled away from her again—away from the enticing, maddening
cardboard square, the white capsules in their lozenge-shaped trans-
parent blisters. "You're the devil," he said.

Again he expected rage and got the indulgent laugh, with its
undertones of knowing sadness.

"Oh yes! *Yes!* That's what a child thinks when mommy comes
into the kitchen and sees him playing with the cleaning fluid from
under the sink. He doesn't say it *that* way, of course, because he
doesn't have your education. He just says, 'Mommy, you're mean!' "

Her hand brushed his hair away from his hot brow. The fingers
trailed down his cheek, across the side of his neck, and then squeezed
his shoulder briefly, with compassion, before drawing away.

"The mother feels badly when her child says she's mean or if he
cries for what's been taken away, as you are crying now. But she
knows she's right, and so she does her duty. As I am doing mine."

Three quick dull thumps as Annie dropped her knuckles on the
manuscript—190,000 words and five lives that a well and pain-free
Paul Sheldon had cared deeply about, 190,000 words and five lives
that he was finding more dispensable as each moment passed.

The pills. The pills. He had to have the goddam pills. The lives
were shadows, the pills were not. *They* were real.

"Paul?"

"*No!*" he sobbed.

The faint rattle of the capsules in their blisters—silence—then
the woody shuffle of the matches in their box.

"Paul?"

"*No!*"

"I'm waiting, Paul."

Oh why in Christ's name are you doing this asshole Horatio-at-the-bridge act and who in Christ's name are you trying to impress? Do you think this is a movie or a TV show and you are getting graded by some audience on your bravery? You can do what she wants or you can hold out. If you hold out you'll die and then she'll burn the manuscript anyway. So what are you going to do, lie here and suffer for a book that would sell half as many copies as the least successful Misery *book you ever wrote, and which Peter Prescott would shit upon in his finest genteel disparaging manner when he reviewed it for that great literary oracle,* Newsweek? *Come on, come on, wise up! Even Galileo recanted when he saw they really meant to go through with it!*

"Paul? I'm waiting. I can wait all day. Although I rather suspect that you may go into a coma before too long; I believe you are in a near-comatose state now, and I have had a lot of . . ."

Her voice droned away.

Yes! Give me the matches! Give me a blowtorch! Give me a Baby Huey and a load of napalm! I'll drop a tactical nuke on it if that's what you want, you fucking beldame!

So spoke the opportunist, the survivor. Yet another part, failing now, near-comatose itself, went wailing off into the darkness: *A hundred and ninety thousand words! Five lives! Two years' work!* And what was the real bottom line: The *truth! What you knew about* THE FUCKING TRUTH!

There was the creak of bedsprings as she stood up.

"Well! You *are* a very stubborn little boy, I must say, and I can't sit by your bed all night, as much as I might like to! After all, I've been driving for nearly an hour, hurrying to get back here. I'll drop by in a bit and see if you've changed y—"

"*You* burn it, then!" he yelled at her.

She turned and looked at him. "No," she said, "I cannot do that, as much as I would like to and spare you the agony you feel."

"Why not?"

"Because," she said primly, "you must do it of your own free will."

He began to laugh then, and her face darkened for the first time since she had come back, and she left the room with the manuscript under her arm.

18

When she came back an hour later he took the matches.

She laid the title page on the grill. He tried to light one of the Blue Tips and couldn't because it kept missing the rough strip or falling out of his hand.

So Annie took the box and lit the match and put the lit match in his hand and he touched it to the corner of the paper and then let the match fall into the pot and watched, facinated, as the flame tasted, then gulped. She had a barbecue fork with her this time, and when the page began to curl up, she poked it through the gaps in the grill.

"This is going to take forever," he said. "I can't—"

"No, we'll make quick work of it," she said. "But you must burn a few of the single pages, Paul—as a symbol of your understanding."

She now laid the first page of *Fast Cars* on the grill, words he remembered writing some twenty-four months ago, in the New York townhouse: " *'I don't have no wheels,' Tony Bonasaro said, walking up to the girl coming down the steps, 'and I am a slow learner, but I am a fast driver.' "*

Oh it brought that day back like the right Golden Oldie on the radio. He remembered walking around the apartment from room to room, big with book, more than big, *gravid*, and here were the labor pains. He remembered finding one of Joan's bras under a sofa cushion earlier in the day, and she had been gone a full three months, showed you what kind of a job the cleaning service did; he remembered hearing New York traffic, and, faintly, the monotonous tolling of a church bell calling the faithful to mass.

He remembered sitting down.

As always, the blessed relief of starting, a feeling that was like falling into a hole filled with bright light.

As always, the glum knowledge that he would not write as well as he wanted to write.

As always, the terror of not being able to finish, of accelerating into a blank wall.

As always, the marvellous joyful nervy feeling of *journey begun*.

He looked at Annie Wilkes and said, clearly but not loud: "Annie, please don't make me do this."

She held the matches immovably before him and said: "You can do as you choose."

So he burned his book.

19

She made him burn the first page, the last page, and nine pairs of pages from various points in the manuscript—because nine, she said, was a number of power, and nine doubled was lucky. He saw that she had used a magic marker to black out the profanities, at least as far as she had read.

"Now," she said, when the ninth pair was burned. "You've been a good boy and a real sport and I know this hurts you almost as badly as your legs do and I won't draw it out any longer."

She removed the grill and set the rest of the manuscript into the pot, crunching down the crispy black curls of the pages he had already burned. The room stank of matches and burned paper. *Smells like the devil's cloakroom,* he thought deliriously, and if there had been anything in the wrinkled walnut-shell that had once been his stomach, he supposed he would have vomited it up.

She lit another match and put it in his hand. Somehow he was able to lean over and drop the match into the pot. It didn't matter anymore. It didn't matter.

She was nudging him.

Wearily, he opened his eyes.

"It went out." She scratched another match and put it in his hand.

So he somehow managed to lean over again, awakening rusty bandsaws in his legs as he did so, and touched the match to the corner of the pile of manuscript. This time the flame spread instead of shrinking and dying around the stick.

He leaned back, eyes shut, listening to the crackling sound, feeling the full, baking heat.

"Goodness!" she cried, alarmed.

He opened his eyes and saw that charred bits of paper were wafting up from the barbecue on the heated air.

Annie lumbered from the room. He heard water from the tub taps thud into the floorpail. He idly watched a dark piece of manuscript float across the room and land on one of the gauzy curtains.

There was a brief spark—he had time to wonder if perhaps the room was going to catch on fire—that winked once and then went out, leaving a tiny hole like a cigarette burn. Ash sifted down on the bed. Some landed on his arms. He didn't really care, one way or the other.

Annie came back, eyes trying to dart everywhere at once, trying to trace the course of each carbonized page as it rose and seesawed. Flames flipped and flickered over the edge of the pot.

"Goodness!" she said again, holding the bucket of water and looking around, trying to decide where to throw it or if it needed to be thrown at all. Her lips were trembling and wet with spit. As Paul watched, her tongue darted out and slicked them afresh. "Goodness! Goodness!" It seemed to be all she could say.

Even caught in the squeezing vise of his pain, Paul felt an instant of intense pleasure—this was what Annie Wilkes looked like when she was frightened. It was a look he could come to love.

Another page wafted up, this one still running with little tendrils of low blue fire, and that decided her. With another "Goodness!" she carefully poured the bucket of water into the barbecue pot. There was a monstrous hissing and a plume of steam. The smell was wet and awful, charred and yet somehow creamy.

When she left he managed to get up on his elbow one final time. He looked into the barbecue pot and saw something that looked like a charred lump of log floating in a brackish pond.

After awhile, Annie Wilkes came back.

Incredibly, she was humming.

She sat him up and pushed capsules into his mouth.

He swallowed them and lay back, thinking: *I'm going to kill her.*

20

"Eat," she said from far away, and he felt stinging pain. He opened his eyes and saw her sitting beside him—for the first time he was actually on a level with her, facing her. He realized with bleary, distant surprise that for the first time in untold eons he was sitting, too . . . actually sitting up.

Who gives a shit? he thought, and let his eyes slip shut again. The tide was in. The pilings were covered. The tide had finally come in and the next time it went out it might go out forever and so he was going to ride the waves while there were waves left to ride, he could think about sitting up later. . . .

"*Eat!*" she said again, and this was followed by a recurrence of pain. It buzzed against the left side of his head, making him whine and try to pull away.

"Eat, Paul! You've got to come out of it enough to eat or . . ."

Zzzzzing! His earlobe. She was pinching it.

" 'Kay," he muttered. " '*Kay!* Don't yank it off, for God's sake."

He forced his eyes open. Each lid felt as if it had a cement block dangling from it. Immediately the spoon was in his mouth, dumping hot soup down his throat. He swallowed to keep from drowning.

Suddenly, out of nowhere—*the most amazing comeback this announcer has ever seen, ladies and gentlemen!*—I Got the Hungries came bursting into view. It was as if that first spoonful of soup had awakened his gut from a hypnotic trance. He took the rest as fast as she could spoon it into his mouth, seeming to grow more rather than less hungry as he slurped and swallowed.

He had a vague memory of her wheeling out the sinister, smoking barbecue and then wheeling in something which, in his drugged and fading state, he had thought might be a shopping cart. The idea had caused him to feel neither surprise nor wonder; he *was* visiting with Annie Wilkes, after all. Barbecues, shopping carts; maybe tomorrow a parking meter or a nuclear warhead. When you lived in the funhouse, the laff riot just never stopped.

He had drifted off, but now he realized that the shopping cart had been a folded-up wheelchair. He was sitting in it, his splinted legs stuck stiffly out in front of him, his pelvic area feeling uncomfortably swollen and not very happy with the new position.

She put me in it while I was conked out, he thought. *Lifted me. Dead weight. Christ she must be strong.*

"Finished!" she said. "I'm pleased to see how well you took that soup, Paul. I believe you are going to mend. We will not say 'Good as new'—alas, no—but if we don't have any more of these . . . these *contretemps* . . . I believe you'll mend just fine. Now I'm going to change your nasty old bed, and when that's done I'm going to change nasty old *you*, and then, if you're not having too much pain and still feel hungry, I am going to let you have some toast."

"Thank you, Annie," he said humbly, and thought: *Your throat. If I can, I'll give you a chance to lick your lips and say 'Goodness!' But only once, Annie.*

Only once.

21

Four hours later he was back in bed and he would have burned *all* his books for even a single Novril. Sitting hadn't bothered him a bit while he was doing it—not with enough shit in his bloodstream to have put half the Prussian Army to sleep—but now it felt as if a swarm of bees had been loosed in the lower half of his body.

He screamed very loudly—the food must have done *something* for him, because he could not remember being able to scream so loudly since he had emerged from the dark cloud.

He sensed her standing just outside the bedroom door in the hallway for a long time before she actually came in, immobile, turned off, unplugged, gazing blankly at no more than the doorknob or perhaps the pattern of lines on her own hands.

"Here." She gave him his medication—two capsules this time.

He swallowed them, holding her wrist to steady the glass.

"I bought you two presents in town," she said, getting up.

"Did you?" he croaked.

She pointed at the wheelchair which brooded in the corner with its steel leg-rests stuck stiffly out.

"I'll show you the other one tomorrow. Now get some sleep, Paul."

22

But for a long time no sleep came. He floated on the dope and thought about the situation he was in. It seemed a little easier now. It was easier to think about than the book which he had created and then uncreated.

Things . . . isolated things like pieces of cloth which may be pieced together to make a quilt.

They were miles from the neighbors who, Annie said, didn't like her. What was the name? Boynton. No, *Roydman.* That was it. Roydman. And how far from town? Not too far, surely. He was in a circle whose diameter might be as small as fifteen miles, or as large as forty-five. Annie Wilkes's house was in that circle, and the

Roydmans', and downtown Sidewinder, however pitifully small that
might be. . . .

*And my car. My Camaro's somewhere in that circle, too. Did the police
find it?*

He thought not. He was a well-known person; if a car had been
found with tags registered in his name, a little elementary checking
would have shown he had been in Boulder and had then dropped
out of sight. The discovery of his wrecked and empty car would
have prompted a search, stories on the news. . . .

*She never watches the news on TV, never listens to the radio at all—
unless she's got one with an earplug, or phones.*

It was all a little like the dog in the Sherlock Holmes story—the
one that didn't bark. His car hadn't been found because the cops
hadn't come. If it *had* been found, they would have checked everyone in his hypothetical circle, wouldn't they? And just how many
people could there be in such a circle, here close to the top of the
Western Slope? The Roydmans, Annie Wilkes, maybe ten or twelve
others?

And just because it hadn't been found so far didn't mean it
wouldn't be found.

His vivid imagination (which he had not gotten from anyone on
his *mother's* side of the family) now took over. The cop was tall,
handsome in a cold way, his sideburns perhaps a bit longer than
regulation. He was wearing dark sunglasses in which the person
being questioned would see his own face in duplicate. His voice
had a flat Midwestern twang.

*We've found an overturned car halfway down Humbuggy Mountain
which belongs to a famous writer named Paul Sheldon. There's some blood
on the seats and the dashboard, but no sign of him. Must have crawled
out, may even have wandered away in a daze—*

That was a laugh, considering the state of his legs, but of course
they would not know what injuries he might have sustained. They
would only assume that, if he was not here, he must have been
strong enough to get at least a little way. The course of their deductions was not apt to lead to such an unlikely possibility as kid-
napping, at least not at first, and probably never.

*Do you remember seeing anyone on the road the day of the storm? Tall
man, forty-two years old, sandy hair? Probably wearing blue jeans and
a checked flannel shirt and a parka? Might have looked sort of bunged
up? Hell, might not even have known who he was?*

Annie would give the cop coffee in the kitchen; Annie would be mindful that all the doors between there and the spare bedroom should be closed. In case he should groan.

Why, no, officer—I didn't see a soul. In fact, I came back from town just as quick as I could chase when Tony Roberts told me that bad old storm wasn't turning south after all.

The cop, setting down the coffee cup and getting up: *Well, if you should see anyone fitting the description, ma'am, I hope you'll get in touch with us just as fast as you can. He's quite a famous person. Been in* People *magazine. Some other ones, too.*

I certainly will, officer!

And away he would go.

Maybe something like that had *already* happened and he just didn't know about it. Maybe his imaginary cop's actual counterpart or counterparts had visited Annie while he was doped out. God knew he spent enough time doped out. More thought convinced him it was unlikely. He *wasn't* Joe Blow from Kokomo, just some transient blowing through. He had been in *People* (first best-seller) and *Us* (first divorce); there had been a question about him one Sunday in Walter Scott's *Personality Parade*. There would have been re-checks, maybe by phone, probably by the cops themselves. When a celebrity—even a quasi-celebrity like a writer—disappeared, the heat came on.

You're only guessing, man.

Maybe guessing, maybe deducing. Either way it was better than just lying here and doing nothing.

What about guardrails?

He tried to remember and couldn't. He could only remember reaching for his cigarettes, then the amazing way the ground and the sky had switched places, then darkness. But again, deduction (or educated guesswork, if you wanted to be snotty) made it easier to believe there had been none. Smashed guardrails and snapped guywires would have alerted roadcrews.

So what exactly *had* happened?

He had lost control at a place where there wasn't much of a drop, that was what—just enough grade to allow the car to flip over in space. If the drop had been steeper, there would have been guardrails. If the drop had been steeper, Annie Wilkes would have found it difficult or impossible to get to him, let alone drag him back to the road by herself.

So where was his car? Buried in the snow, of course.

Paul put his arm over his eyes and saw a town plow coming up the road where he has crashed only two hours earlier. The plow is a dim orange blob in the driving snow near the end of this day. The man driving is bundled to the eyes; on his head he wears an old-fashioned trainman's cap of blue-and-white pillowtick. To his right, at the bottom of a shallow slope which will, not far from here, deepen into a more typical upcountry gorge, lies Paul Sheldon's Camaro, with the faded blue HART FOR PRESIDENT sticker on the rear bumper just about the brightest thing down there. The guy driving the plow doesn't see the car; bumper sticker is too faded to catch his eye. The wing-plows block most of his side-vision, and besides, it's almost dark and he's beat. He just wants to finish this last run so he can turn the plow over to his relief and get a hot cup of joe.

He sweeps past, the plow spuming cloudy snow into the gully. The Camaro, already drifted to the windows, is now buried to the roof-line. Later, in the deepest part of a stormy twilight when even the things directly in front of you look unreal, the second-shift man drives by, headed in the opposite direction, and entombs it.

Paul opened his eyes and looked at the plaster ceiling. There was a fine series of hairline cracks up there that seemed to make a trio of interlocked W's. He had become very familiar with them over the endless run of days he had lain here since coming out of the cloud, and now he traced them again, idly thinking of w words such as *wicked* and *wretched* and *witchlike* and *wriggling*.

Yes.

Could have been that way. Could have been.

Had she thought of what might happen when his car was found?

She *might* have. She was nuts, but being nuts didn't make her stupid.

Yet it had never crossed her mind that he might have a duplicate of *Fast Cars*.

Yeah. And she was right. The bitch was right. I didn't.

Images of the blackened pages floating up, the flames, the sounds, the smell of the uncreation—he gritted his teeth against the images and tried to shut his mind away from them; *vivid* was not always *good*.

*No, you didn't, but nine out of ten writers would have—at least they would if they were getting paid as much as you have been for even the non-*Misery *books. She never even thought of it.*

She's not a writer.

Neither is she stupid, as I think we have both agreed. I think that she is filled with herself—she does not just have a large ego but one which is positively grandiose. Burning it seemed to her the proper thing to do, and the idea that her concept of the proper thing to do might be short-circuited by something so piddling as a bank Xerox machine and a couple of rolls of quarters . . . that blip just never crossed her screen, my friend.

His other deductions might be like houses built on quicksand, but this view of Annie Wilkes seemed to him as solid as the Rock of Gibraltar. Because of his researches for *Misery*, he had rather more than a layman's understanding of neurosis and psychosis, and he knew that although a borderline psychotic might have alternating periods of deep depression and almost aggressive cheerfulness and hilarity, the puffed and infected ego underlay all, positive that all eyes were upon him or her, positive that he or she was starring in a great drama; the outcome was a thing for which untold millions waited with held breath.

Such an ego simply forbade certain lines of thought. These lines were predictable because they all stretched in the same direction: from the unstable person to objects, situations, or other persons outside of the subject's field of control (or fantasy: to the neurotic there might be some difference but to the psychotic they were one and the same).

Annie Wilkes had wanted *Fast Cars* destroyed, and so, to her, there had been only the one copy.

Maybe I could have saved the damn thing by telling her there were more. She would have seen destroying the manuscript was futile. She—

His breathing, which had been slowing toward sleep, suddenly caught in his throat and his eyes widened.

Yes, she would have seen it was futile. She would have been forced to acknowledge one of those lines leading to a place beyond her control. The ego would be hurt, squealing—

I have such a temper!

If she had been clearly faced with the fact that she *couldn't* destroy his "dirty book," might she not have decided to destroy the *creator* of the dirty book instead? After all, there was no copy of Paul Sheldon.

His heart was beating fast. In the other room the clock began to bong, and overhead he heard her thumping footfalls cross his ceiling. The faint sound of her urinating. The toilet flushing. The heavy pad of her feet as she went back to bed. The creak of the springs.

You won't make me mad again, will you?

His mind suddenly tried to break into a gallop, an overbred trotter trying to break stride. What, if anything, did all this dime-store psychoanalysis mean in terms of his car? About when it was found? What did it mean to *him?*

"Wait a minute," he whispered in the dark. "Wait a minute, wait a minute, just hold the phone. Slow down."

He put his arm across his eyes again and again conjured up the state trooper with the dark sunglasses and the overlong sideburns. *We've found an overturned car halfway down Humbuggy Mountain,* the state trooper was saying, and blah-de-blah-de-blah.

Only *this* time Annie doesn't invite him to stay for coffee. This time she isn't going to feel safe until he's out of her house and far down the road. Even in the kitchen, even with two closed doors between them and the guest-room, even with the guest doped to the ears, the trooper might hear a groan.

If his car was found, Annie Wilkes would know she was in trouble, wouldn't she?

"Yes," Paul whispered. His legs were beginning to hurt again, but in the dawning horror of this recognition he barely noticed.

She would be in trouble not because she had taken him to her house, especially if it was closer than Sidewinder (and so Paul believed it to be); for that they would probably give her a medal and a lifetime membership in the Misery Chastain Fan Club (to Paul's endless chagrin there actually was such a thing). The problem *was,* she had taken him to her house and installed him in the guest-room and told no one. No phone-call to the local ambulance service: "This is Annie up on the Humbuggy Mountain Road and I've got a fellow here, looks a little bit like King Kong used him for a trampoline." The problem *was,* she had filled him full of dope to which she was certainly not supposed to have access—not if he was even half as hooked as he thought he was. The problem *was,* she had followed the dope with a weird sort of treatment, sticking IV needles in his arms, splinting his legs with sawed-off pieces of aluminum crutches. The problem *was,* Annie Wilkes had been on the stand up there in Denver . . . *and not as a supporting witness, either,* Paul thought. *I'd bet the house and lot on that.*

So she watches the cop go down the road in his spandy-clean cruiser (spandy-clean except for the caked chunks of snow and salt nestled in the wheel-wells and under the bumpers, that is), and she feels safe again . . . but not *too* safe, because now she is like an animal with its wind up. Way, *way* up.

The cops will look and look and look, because he is not just good old Joe Blow from Kokomo; he is Paul Sheldon, the literary Zeus from whose brow sprang Misery Chastain, darling of the dump-bins and sweetheart of the supermarkets. Maybe when they don't find him they'll stop looking, or at least look someplace else, but maybe one of the Roydmans saw her going by that night and saw something funny in the back of Old Bessie, something wrapped in a quilt, something vaguely manlike. Even if they hadn't seen a thing, she wouldn't put it past the Roydmans to make up a story to get her in trouble; they didn't like her.

The cops might come back, and next time her house-guest might not be so quiet.

He remembered her eyes darting around aimlessly when the fire in the barbecue pot was on the verge of getting out of control. He could see her tongue slicking her lips. He could see her walking back and forth, hands clenching and unclenching, peeking every now and then into the guest-room where he lay lost in his cloud. Every now and then she would utter "Goodness!" to the empty rooms.

She had stolen a rare bird with beautiful feathers—a rare bird which came from Africa.

And what would they do if they found out?

Why, put her up on the stand again, of course. Put her up on the stand again in Denver. And this time she might not walk free.

He took his arm away from his eyes. He looked at the inter-locking W's swaying drunkenly across the ceiling. He didn't need his elbow over his eyes to see the rest. She might hang on to him for a day or a week. It might take a follow-up phone-call or visit to make her decide to get rid of her *rara avis*. But in the end she would do it, just as wild dogs begin to bury their illicit kills after they have been hunted awhile.

She would give him five pills instead of two, or perhaps smother him with a pillow; perhaps she would simply shoot him. Surely there was a rifle around somewhere—almost everyone living in the high country had one—and that would take care of the problem.

No—not the gun.

Too messy.

Might leave evidence.

None of that had happened yet because no one had found the car. They might be looking for him in New York or in L.A., but no one was looking for him in Sidewinder, Colorado.

But in the spring.

The W's straggled across the ceiling. *Washed. Wiped. Wasted.*

The throbbing in his legs was more insistent; the next time the clock bonged she would come, but he was almost afraid she would read his thoughts on his face, like the bare premise of a story too gruesome to write. His eyes drifted left. There was a calendar on the wall. It showed a boy riding a sled down a hill. It was February according to the calendar, but if his calculations were right it was already early March. Annie Wilkes had just forgotten to turn the page.

How long before the melting snows revealed his Camaro with its New York plates and its registration in the glove compartment proclaiming the owner to be Paul Sheldon? How long before that trooper called on her, or until she read it in the paper? How long until the spring melt?

Six weeks? Five?

That could be the length of my life, Paul thought, and began shuddering. By then his legs were fully awake, and it was not until she had come in and given him another dose of medicine that he was able to fall asleep.

23

The next evening she brought him the Royal. It was an office model from an era when such things as electric typewriters, color TVs, and touch-tone telephones were only science fiction. It was as black and as proper as a pair of high-button shoes. Glass panels were set into the sides, revealing the machine's levers, springs, ratchets, and rods. A steel return lever, dull with disuse, jutted to one side like a hitchhiker's thumb. The roller was dusty, its hard rubber scarred and pitted. The letters ROYAL ran across the front of the machine in a semicircle. Grunting, she set it down on the foot of the bed between his legs after holding it up for his inspection for a moment.

He stared at it.

Was it grinning?

Christ, it *looked* like it was.

Anyway, it already looked like trouble. The ribbon was a faded two-tone, red over black. He had forgotten there *were* such ribbons. The sight of this one called up no pleasant nostalgia.

"Well?" She was smiling eagerly. "What do you think?"

"It's nice!" he said at once. "A real antique."

Her smile clouded. "I didn't buy it for an antique. I bought it for second-hand. *Good* second-hand."

He responded with immediate glibness. "Hey! There ain't no such *thing* as an antique typewriter—not when you come right down to it. A good typewriter lasts damn near forever. These old office babies are *tanks!*"

If he could have reached it he would have patted it. If he could have reached it he would have *kissed* it.

Her smile returned. His heartbeat slowed a little.

"I got it at Used News. Isn't that a silly name for a store? But Nancy Dartmonger, the lady who runs it, is a silly woman." Annie darkened a little, but he saw at once that she was not darkening at *him*—the survival instinct, he was discovering, might *be* only instinct in itself, but it created some really amazing shortcuts to empathy. He found himself becoming more attuned to her moods, her cycles; he listened to her tick as if she were a wounded clock.

"As well as silly, she's *bad*. Dartmonger! Her name ought to be *Whoremonger*. Divorced twice and now she's living with a *bartender*. That's why when you said it was an antique—"

"It looks fine," he said.

She paused a long moment and then said, as if confessing: "It has a missing n."

"Does it?"

"Yes—see?"

She tilted the typewriter up so he could peer at the banked semicircle of keys and see the missing striker like a missing molar in a mouthful of teeth worn but otherwise complete.

"I see."

She set it back down. The bed rocked a little. Paul guessed the typewriter might weigh as much as fifty pounds. It had come from a time when there were no alloys, no plastics . . . also no six-figure book advances, no movie tie-in editions, no *USA Today*, no *Entertainment Tonight*, no celebrities doing ads for credit cards or vodka.

The Royal grinned at him, promising trouble.

"She wanted forty-five dollars but gave me five off. Because of the missing n." She offered him a crafty smile. No fool she, it said.

He smiled back. The tide was in. That made both smiling and lying easy. "*Gave* it to you? You mean you didn't dicker?"

Annie preened a little. "I told her n was an important letter," she allowed.

"Well good for you! *Damn!*" Here was a new discovery. Sycophancy was easy once you got the hang of it.

Her smile grew sly, inviting him to share a delicious secret.

"I told her n was one of the letters in my favorite writer's name."

"It's *two* of the letters in my favorite *nurse's* name."

Her smile became a glow. Incredibly, a blush rose in her solid cheeks. *That's what it would look like,* he thought, *if you built a furnace inside the mouth of one of those idols in the H. Rider Haggard stories. That is what it would look like at night.*

"You *fooler!*" she simpered.

"I'm not!" he said. "Not at all."

"Well!" She looked off for a moment, not blank but just pleased, a little flustered, taking a moment to gather her thoughts. Paul could have taken some pleasure in the way this was going if not for the weight of the typewriter, as solid as the woman and also damaged; it sat there grinning with its missing tooth, promising trouble.

"The wheelchair was much more expensive," she said. "Ostomy supplies have gone right out of *sight* since I—" She broke off, frowned, cleared her throat. Then she looked back at him, smiling. "But it's *time* you began sitting up, and I don't begrudge the cost one tiny bit. And of course you can't type lying down, can you?"

"No . . ."

"I've got a board . . . I cut it to size . . . and paper . . . wait!"

She dashed from the room like a girl, leaving Paul and the typewriter to regard each other. His grin disappeared the moment her back was turned. The Royal's never varied. He supposed later that he had pretty well known what all this was about, just as he supposed he had known what the typewriter would sound like, how it would clack through its grin like that old comic-strip character Ducky Daddles.

She came back with a package of Corrasable Bond in shrink-wrap and a board about three feet wide by four feet long.

"Look!" She put the board on the arms of the wheelchair that stood by his bed like some solemn skeletal visitor. Already he could see the ghost of himself behind that board, pent in like a prisoner.

She put the typewriter on the board, facing the ghost, and put the package of Corrasable Bond—the paper he hated most in all the world because of the way the type blurred when the pages were shuffled together—beside it. She had now created a kind of cripple's study.

"What do you think?"

"It looks good," he said, uttering the biggest lie of his life with perfect ease, and then asked the question to which he already knew the answer. "What will I write there, do you think?"

"Oh, but Paul!" she said, turning to him, her eyes dancing animatedly in her flushed face. "I don't *think*, I *know!* You're going to use this typewriter to write a new novel! Your best novel! *Misery's Return!*"

24

Misery's Return. He felt nothing at all. He supposed a man who had just cut his hand off in a power saw might feel this same species of nothing as he stood regarding his spouting wrist with dull surprise.

"Yes!" Her face shone like a searchlight. Her powerful hands were clasped between her breasts. "It will be a book just for me, Paul! My payment for nursing you back to health! The one and only copy of the newest *Misery* book! I'll have something no one else in the world has, no matter how much they might want it! *Think* of it!"

"Annie, Misery is dead." But already, incredibly, he was thinking, *I could bring her back.* The thought filled him with tired revulsion but no real surprise. After all, a man who could drink from a floorbucket should be capable of a little directed writing.

"No she's not," Annie replied dreamily. "Even when I was . . . when I was so mad at you, I knew she wasn't really dead. I knew you couldn't really kill her. Because you're *good.*"

"Am I?" he said, and looked at the typewriter. It grinned at him. *We're going to find out just how good you are, old buddy,* it whispered.

"Yes!"

"Annie, I don't know if I can sit in that wheelchair. Last time—"

"Last time it hurt, you bet it did. And it will hurt next time, too.

Maybe even a little more. But there will come a day—and it won't be long, either, although it may seem longer to you than it really is—when it hurts a little less. And a little less. And a little less."

"Annie, will you tell me one thing?"

"Of course, dear!"

"If I write this story for you—"

"*Novel!* A nice big one like all the others—maybe even bigger!"

He closed his eyes for a moment, then opened them. "Okay— if I write this *novel* for you, will you let me go when it's done?"

For a moment unease slipped cloudily across her face, and then she was looking at him carefully, studiously. "You speak as though I were keeping you *prisoner*, Paul."

He said nothing, only looked at her.

"I think that by the time you finish, you should be up to the . . . up to the strain of meeting people again," she said. "Is that what you want to hear?"

"That's what I wanted to hear, yes."

"Well, honestly! I knew writers were supposed to have big egos, but I guess I didn't understand that meant ingratitude, too!"

He went on looking at her and after a moment she looked away, impatient and a little flustered.

At last he said: "I'll need all the *Misery* books, if you've got them, because I don't have my concordance."

"Of course I have them!" she said. Then: "What's a concordance?"

"It's a loose-leaf binder where I have all my *Misery* stuff," he said. "Characters and places, mostly, but cross-indexed three or four different ways. Time-lines. Historical stuff . . ."

He saw she was barely listening. This was the second time she'd shown not the slightest interest in a trick of the trade that would have held a class of would-be writers spellbound. The reason, he thought, was simplicity itself. Annie Wilkes was the perfect audience, a woman who loved stories without having the slightest interest in the mechanics of making them. She was the embodiment of that Victorian archetype, Constant Reader. She did not want to hear about his concordance and indices because to her Misery and the characters surrounding her were perfectly real. Indices meant nothing to her. If he had spoken of a village census in Little Dunthorpe, she might have shown some interest.

"I'll make sure you get the books. They're a little dog-eared, but that's a sign a book has been well read and well loved, isn't it?"

"Yes," he said. No need to lie this time. "Yes it is."

"I'm going to study up on book-binding," she said dreamily. "I'm going to bind *Misery's Return* myself. Except for my mother's Bible, it will be the only *real* book I own."

"That's good," he said, just to say something. He was feeling a little sick to his stomach.

"I'll go out now so you can put on your thinking cap," she said. "This is exciting! Don't you think so?"

"Yes, Annie. I sure do."

"I'll be in with some breast of chicken and mashed potatoes and peas for you in half an hour. Even a little Jell-O because you've been such a good boy. And I'll make sure you get your pain medication right on time. You can even have an extra pill in the night if you need it. I want to make sure you get your sleep, because you have to go back to work tomorrow. You'll mend faster when you're working, I'll bet!"

She went to the door, paused there for a moment, and then, grotesquely, blew him a kiss.

The door closed behind her. He did not want to look at the typewriter and for awhile resisted, but at last his eyes rolled helplessly toward it. It sat on the bureau, grinning. Looking at it was a little like looking at an instrument of torture—boot, rack, strappado—which is standing inactive, but only for the moment.

I think that by the time you finish, you should be . . . up to the strain of meeting people again.

Ah, Annie, you were lying to both of us. I knew it, and you did, too. I saw it in your eyes.

The limited vista now opening before him was extremely unpleasant: six weeks of life which he would spend suffering with his broken bones and renewing his acquaintance with Misery Chastain, née Carmichael, followed by a hasty interment in the back yard. Or perhaps she would feed his remains to Misery the pig—*that* would have a certain justice, black and gruesome though it might be.

Then don't do it. Make her mad. She's like a walking bottle of nitroglycerine as it is. Bounce her around a little. Make her explode. Better than lying here suffering.

He tried looking up at the interlocked W's, but all too soon he was looking at the typewriter again. It stood atop the bureau, mute and thick and full of words he did not want to write, grinning with its one missing tooth.

*I don't think you believe that, old buddy. I think you want to stay
alive even if it* does *hurt. If it means bringing Misery back for an encore,
you'll do it. You'll* try, *anyway—but first you are going to have to deal
with me . . . and I don't think I like your face.*

"Makes us even," Paul croaked.

This time he tried looking out the window, where fresh snow
was falling. Soon enough, however, he was looking at the typewriter
again with avid repulsed fascination, not even aware of just when
his gaze had shifted.

25

Getting into the chair didn't hurt as much as he had feared, and
that was good, because previous experience had shown him that he
would hurt *plenty* afterward.

She set the tray of food down on the bureau, then rolled the
wheelchair over to the bed. She helped him to sit up—there was
a dull, thudding flare of pain in his pelvic area but it subsided—
and then she leaned over, the side of her neck pressing against his
shoulder like the neck of a horse. For an instant he could feel the
thump of her pulse, and his face twisted in revulsion. Then her
right arm was firmly around his back, her left under his buttocks.

"Try not to move from the knees down while I do this," she
said, and then simply slid him into the chair. She did it with the
ease of a woman sliding a book into an empty slot in her bookcase.
Yes, she was strong. Even in good shape the outcome of a fight
between him and Annie would have been in doubt. As he was now
it would be like Wally Cox taking on Boom Boom Mancini.

She put the board in front of him. "See how well it fits?" she
said, and went to the bureau to get the food.

"Annie?"

"Yes."

"I wonder if you could turn that typewriter around. So it faces
the wall."

She frowned. "Why in the world would you want me to do that?"

Because I don't want it grinning at me all night.

"Old superstition of mine," he said. "I always turn my typewriter
to the wall before I start writing." He paused and added: "Every
night while I *am* writing, as a matter of fact."

"It's like step on a crack, break your mother's back," she said. "I never step on a crack if I can help it." She turned it around so it grinned at nothing but blank wall. "Better?"

"Much."

"You are such a *silly*," she said, and came over and began to feed him.

26

He dreamed of Annie Wilkes in the court of some fabulous Arabian caliph, conjuring imps and genies from bottles and then flying around the court on a magic carpet. When the carpet banked past him (her hair streamed out behind her; her eyes were as bright and flinty as the eyes of a sea-captain navigating among icebergs), he saw it was woven all in green and white; it made a Colorado license plate.

Once upon a time, Annie was calling. *Once upon a time it came to pass. This happened in the days when my grandfather's grandfather was a boy. This is the story of how a poor boy. I heard this from a man who. Once upon a time. Once upon a time.*

27

When he woke up Annie was shaking him and bright morning sun was slanting in the window—the snow had ended.

"Wake up, sleepyhead!" Annie was almost trilling. "I've got yogurt and a nice boiled egg for you, and then it will be time for you to begin."

He looked at her eager face and felt a strange new emotion—hope. He had dreamed that Annie Wilkes was Scheherazade, her solid body clad in diaphanous robes, her big feet stuffed into pink sequined slippers with curly toes as she rode on her magic carpet and chanted the incantatory phrases which open the doors of the best stories. But of course it wasn't *Annie* that was Scheherazade. *He* was. And if what he wrote was good enough, if she could not bear to kill him until she discovered how it all came out no matter how much or how loudly her animal instincts yelled for her to do it, that she *must* do it . . .

Might he not have a chance?

He looked past her and saw she had turned the typewriter around before waking him; it grinned resplendently at him with its missing tooth, telling him it was all right to hope and noble to strive, but in the end it was doom alone which would count.

28

She rolled him over to the window so the sun fell on him for the first time in weeks, and it seemed to him he could feel his pasty-white skin, dotted here and there with minor bedsores, murmur its pleasure and thanks. The window-panes were edged on the inside with a tracery of frost, and when he held out his hand he could feel a bubble of cold like a dome around the window. The feel of it was both refreshing and somehow nostalgic, like a note from an old friend.

For the first time in weeks—it felt like years—he was able to look at a geography different from that of his room with its un-changing verities—blue wallpaper, picture of the Arc de Triomphe, the long, long month of February symbolized by the boy sliding downhill on his sled (he thought that his mind would turn to that boy's face and stocking cap each time January became February, even if he lived to see that change of months another fifty times). He looked into this new world as eagerly as he had watched his first movie—*Bambi*—as a child.

The horizon was near; it always was in the Rockies, where longer views of the world were inevitably cut off by uptilted plates of bedrock. The sky was a perfect early-morning blue, innocent of clouds. A carpet of green forest climbed the flank of the nearest mountain. There were perhaps seventy acres of open ground be-tween the house and the edge of the forest—the snow-cover over it was a perfect and blazing white. It was impossible to tell if the land beneath was tilled earth or open meadow. The view of this open square was interrupted by only one building: a neat red barn. When she spoke of her livestock or when he saw her trudging grimly past his window, breaking her breath with the impervious

prow of her face, he had imagined a ramshackle outbuilding like
an illustration from a child's book of ghost stories—rooftree bowed
and sagging from years of snow-weight, windows blank and dusty,
some broken and blocked with pieces of cardboard, long double
doors perhaps off their tracks and swaying outward. This neat and
tidy structure with its dark-red paint and neat cream-colored trim
looked like the five-car garage of a well-to-do country squire mas-
querading as a barn. In front of it stood a Jeep Cherokee, maybe
five years old but obviously well cared for. To one side stood a
Fisher plow in a home-made wooden cradle. To attach the plow to
the Jeep, she would only need to drive the Jeep carefully up to the
cradle so that the hooks on the frame matched the catches on the
plow, and throw the locking lever on the dashboard. The perfect
vehicle for a woman who lived alone and had no neighbor she could
call upon for help (except for those dirty-birdie Roydmans, of course,
and Annie probably wouldn't take a plate of pork chops from them
if she was dying of starvation). The driveway was neatly plowed, a
testament to the fact that she did indeed use the blade, but he could
not see the road—the house cut off the view.

"I see you're admiring my barn, Paul."

He looked around, startled. The quick and uncalculated movement awoke his pain from its doze. It snarled dully in what remained
of his shins and in the bunched salt-dome that had replaced his left
knee. It turned over, needling him from where it lay imprisoned
in its cave of bones, and then fell lightly asleep again.

She had food on a tray. Soft food, invalid food . . . but his stomach growled at the sight of it. As she crossed to him he saw that
she was wearing white shoes with crepe soles.

"Yes," he said. "It's very handsome."

She put the board on the arms of the wheelchair and then put
the tray on the board. She pulled a chair over beside him and sat
down, watching him as he began to eat.

"Fiddle-de-foof! Handsome is as handsome does, my mother
always said. I keep it nice because if I didn't, the neighbors would
yap. They are always looking for a way to get at me, or start a rumor
about me. So I keep everything nice. Keeping up appearances is
very, very important. As far as the barn goes, it really isn't much
work, as long as you don't let things pile up. Keeping the snow
from breaking in the roof is the oogiest part."

The oogiest part, he thought. *Save that one for the Annie Wilkes*

*lexicon in your memoirs—if you ever get a chance to write your memoirs,
that is. Along with dirty birdie and fiddle-de-foof and all the others
which I'm sure will come up in time.*

"Two years ago I had Billy Haversham put heat-tapes in the roof.
You throw a switch and they get hot and melt the ice. I won't need
them much longer *this* winter, though—see how it's melting on its
own?"

He had a forkful of egg halfway to his mouth. It stopped in
midair as he looked out at the barn. There was a row of icicles along
the eave. The tips of these icicles were dripping—dripping fast.
Each drop sparkled as it fell onto a narrow canal of ice which lay
at the base of the barn's side.

"It's up to forty-five degrees and it's not even nine o'clock!"
Annie was going on gaily as Paul imagined the rear bumper of his
Camaro surfacing through the rotted snow for the sun to twinkle
on. "Of course it won't last—we've got a hard snap or three ahead
of us yet, and probably another big storm as well—but spring is
coming, Paul, and my mother always used to say that the hope of
spring is like the hope of heaven."

He put his fork back down on the plate with the egg still on it.

"Don't want that last bite? All done?"

"All done," he agreed, and in his mind he saw the Roydmans
driving up from Sidewinder, saw a bright arrow of light strike Mrs.
Roydman's face, making her wince and put a shielding hand up—
*What's down there, Ham? . . . Don't tell me I'm crazy, there's something
down there! Reflection damn near burned m'eye out! Back up, I want
to take another look!*

"Then I'll just take the tray," she said, "and you can get started."
She favored him with a glance that was very warm. "I just can't tell
you how excited I am, Paul."

She went out, leaving him to sit in the wheelchair and look at
the water running from the icicles which clung to the edge of the
barn.

29

"I'd like some different paper, if you could get it," he said when
she came back to put the typewriter and paper on the board.

"Different from this?" she asked, tapping the cellophane-wrapped package of Corrasable Bond. "But this is the most expensive of *all!* I *asked* when I went into the Paper Patch!"

"Didn't your mother ever tell you that the most expensive is not always the best?"

Annie's brow darkened. Her initial defensiveness had been replaced by indignation. Paul guessed her fury would follow.

"No, she did *not*. What she *told* me, Mister Smart Guy, is that when you *buy* cheap, you *get* cheap."

The climate inside her, he had come to discover, was like springtime in the Midwest. She was a woman full of tornadoes waiting to happen, and if he had been a farmer observing a sky which looked the way Annie's face looked right now, he would have at once gone to collect his family and herd them into the storm cellar. Her brow was too white. Her nostrils flared regularly, like the nostrils of an animal scenting fire. Her hands had begun to spring limberly open and then snatch closed again, catching air and squashing it.

His need for her and his vulnerability to her screamed at him to back off, to placate her while there was still time—if indeed there still was—as a tribe in one of those Rider Haggard stories would have placated their goddess when she was angry, by making sacrifice to her effigy.

But there was another part of him, more calculating and less cowed, which reminded him that he could not play the part of Scheherazade if he grew frightened and placatory whenever she stormed. If he did, she would storm all the more. *If you didn't have something she badly wants,* this part of him reasoned, *she would have taken you to the hospital right away or killed you later on to protect herself from the Roydmans—because for Annie the world is full of Roydmans, for Annie they're lurking behind every bush. And if you don't bell this bitch right now, Paulie my boy, you may never be able to.*

She was beginning to breathe more rapidly, almost to hyperventilate; the rhythm of her clenching hands was likewise speeding up, and he knew that in a moment she would be beyond him.

Gathering up the little courage he had left, trying desperately to summon exactly the right note of sharp and yet almost casual irritability, he said: "And you might as well stop that. Getting mad won't change a thing."

She froze as if he had slapped her and looked at him, wounded.

"Annie," he said patiently, "this is no big deal."

"It's a trick," she said. "You don't want to write my book and so you're making up tricks not to start. I knew you would. Oh boy. But it's not going to work. It—"

"That's silly," he said. "Did I say I wasn't going to start?"

"No . . . no, but—"

"That's right. Because I *am*. And if you come here and take a look at something, I'll show you what the problem is. Bring that Webster Pot with you, please."

"The what?"

"Little jar of pens and pencils," he said. "On newspapers, they sometimes call them Webster Pots. After Daniel Webster." This was a lie he had made up on the spur of the moment, but it had the desired effect—she looked more confused than ever, lost in a specialists' world of which she had not the slightest knowledge. The confusion had diffused (and thus defused) her rage even more; he saw she now didn't even know if she had any *right* to be angry.

She brought over the jar of pens and pencils and slammed them down on the board and he thought: *Goddam! I won!* No—that wasn't right. *Misery* had won.

But that isn't right, either. It was Scheherazade. Scheherazade won.

"What," she said grumpily.

"Watch."

He opened the package of Corrasable and took out a sheet. He took a freshly sharpened pencil and drew a line on the paper. Then he took a ballpoint pen and drew another line parallel to the first. Then he slid his thumb across the slightly waffled surface of the paper. Both lines blurred smudgily in the direction his thumb was travelling, the pencil-line slightly more than the one he had drawn with the pen.

"See?"

"So what?"

"Ribbon-ink will blur, too," he said. "It doesn't blur as much as that pencil-line, but it's worse than the ballpoint-ink line."

"Were you going to sit and rub every page with your thumb?"

"Just the shift of the pages against each other will accomplish plenty of blurring over a period of weeks or even days," he said, "and when a manuscript is in work, it gets shifted around a lot. You're always hunting back through to find a name or a date. My God, Annie, one of the first things you find out in this business is that editors hate reading manuscripts typed on Corrasable Bond almost as much as they hate hand-written manuscripts."

"Don't call it that. I hate it when you call it that."

He looked at her, honestly puzzled. "Call what *what?*"

"When you pervert the talent God gave you by calling it a business. I *hate* that."

"I'm sorry."

"You ought to be," she said stonily. "You might as well call yourself a whore."

No, Annie, he thought, suddenly filled with fury. *I'm no whore. Fast Cars was about not being a whore. That's what killing that goddamned bitch Misery was about, now that I think about it. I was driving to the West Coast to celebrate my liberation from a state of whoredom. What you did was to pull me out of the wreck when I crashed my car and stick me back in the crib again. Two dollar straight up, four dollar I take you aroun the worl. And every now and then I see a flicker in your eyes that tells me a part of you way back inside knows it too. A jury might let you off by reason of insanity, but not me, Annie. Not this kid.*

"A good point," he said. "Now, going back to the subject of the paper—"

"I'll get you your cockadoodie paper," she said sullenly. "Just tell me what to get and I'll get it."

"As long as you understand I'm on your side—"

"Don't make me laugh. No one has been on my side since my mother died twenty years ago."

"Believe what you want, then," he said. "If you're so insecure you can't believe I'm grateful to you for saving my life, that's your problem."

He was watching her shrewdly, and again saw a flicker of uncertainty, of wanting to believe, in her eyes. Good. Very good. He looked at her with all the sincerity he could muster, and again in his mind he imagined shoving a chunk of glass into her throat, once and forever letting out the blood that serviced her crazy brain.

"At least you should be able to believe that I am on the *book's* side. You spoke of binding it. I assume that you meant binding the manuscript? The typed pages?"

"Of course that's what I meant."

Yes, you bet. Because if you took the manuscript to a printer, it might raise questions. You may be naive about the world of books and publishing, but not that naive. Paul Sheldon is missing, and your printer might remember receiving a book-length manuscript concerning itself with Paul Sheldon's most famous character right around the time the man

*himself disappeared, mightn't he? And he'd certainly remember the in-
structions—instructions so queer any printer would remember them. One
printed copy of a novel-length manuscript.*

Just one.

*"What did she look like, officer? Well, she was a big woman. Looked
sort of like a stone idol in an H. Rider Haggard story. Just a minute,
I've got her name and address here in the files. . . . Just let me look up
the carbons of the invoices. . . ."*

"Nothing wrong with the idea, either," he said. "A bound manuscript can be damned handsome. Looks like a good folio edition.
But a book should last a long time, Annie, and if I write this one
on Corrasable, you're going to have nothing but a bunch of blank
pages in ten years or so. Unless, of course, you just put it on the
shelf."

But she wouldn't want that, would she? Christ, no. She'd want
to take it down every day, maybe every few hours. Take it down
and gloat over it.

An odd stony look had come onto her face. He did not like this
mulishness, this almost ostentatious look of obduration. It made
him nervous. He could calculate her rage, but there was something
in this new expression which was as opaque as it was childish.

"You don't have to talk anymore," she said. "I already told you
I'll get you your paper. What kind?"

"In this business-supply store you go to—"

"The Paper Patch."

"Yes, the Paper Patch. You tell them you'd like two reams—a
ream is a package of five hundred sheets—"

"I know that. I'm not stupid, Paul."

"I know you're not," he said, becoming more nervous still. The
pain had begun to mutter up and down his legs again, and it was
speaking even more loudly from the area of his pelvis—he had
been sitting up for nearly an hour, and the dislocation down there
was complaining about it.

Keep cool, for God's sake—don't lose everything you've gained!

But have I gained anything? Or is it only wishful thinking?

"Ask for two reams of white long-grain mimeo. Hammermill
Bond is a good brand; so is Triad Modern. Two reams of mimeo
will cost less than this one package of Corrasable, and it should be
enough to do the whole job, write and rewrite."

"I'll go right now," she said, getting up suddenly.

He looked at her, alarmed, understanding that she meant to leave him without his medication again, and sitting up this time, as well. Sitting already hurt; the pain would be monstrous by the time she got back, even if she hurried.

"You don't have to do that," he said, speaking fast. "The Corrasable is good enough to start with—after all, I'll have to rewrite anyway—"

"Only a silly person would try to start a good work with a bad tool." She took the package of Corrasable Bond, then snatched the sheet with the two smudged lines and crumpled it into a ball. She tossed both into the wastebasket and turned back to him. That stony, obdurate look covered her face like a mask. Her eyes glittered like tarnished dimes.

"I'm going to town now," she said. "I know you want to get started as soon as you can, since you're *on my side*"—she spoke these last words with intense, smoking sarcasm (and, Paul believed, more self-hate than she would ever know)—"and so I'm not even going to take time to put you back in your bed."

She smiled, a pulling of the lips that was grotesquely puppet-like, and slipped to his side in her silent white nurse's shoes. Her fingers touched his hair. He flinched. He tried not to but couldn't help it. Her dead-alive smile widened.

"Although I suspect we may have to put off the actual start of *Misery's Return* for a day . . . or two . . . perhaps even three. Yes, it may be as long as three days before you are able to sit up again. Because of the pain. Too bad. I had champagne chilling in the fridge. I'll have to put it back in the shed."

"Annie, really, I can start if you'll just—"

"No, Paul." She moved to the door and then turned, looking at him with that stony face. Only her eyes, those tarnished dimes, were fully alive under the shelf of her brow. "There is one thought I would like to leave you with. You may think you can fool me, or trick me; I know I look slow and stupid. But I am not stupid, Paul, and I am not slow."

Suddenly her face broke apart. The stony obduracy shattered and what shone through was the countenance of an insanely angry child. For a moment Paul thought the extremity of his terror might kill him. Had he thought he had gained the upper hand? Had he? Could one possibly play Scheherazade when one's captor was insane?

She rushed across the room at him, thick legs pumping, knees flexing, elbows chopping back and forth in the stale sickroom air like pistons. Her hair bounced and joggled around her face as it came loose from the bobby-pins that held it up. Now her passage was not silent; it was like the tread of Goliath striding into the Valley of Bones. The picture of the Arc de Triomphe clacked affrightedly on the wall.

"Geeeee-yahhh!" she screamed, and brought her fist down on the bunched salt-dome that had been Paul Sheldon's left knee.

He threw his head back and howled, veins standing out in his neck and on his forehead. Pain burst out from his knee and shrouded him, whitely radiant, in the center of a nova.

She tore the typewriter off the board and slammed it down on the mantel, lifting its weight of dead metal as he might have lifted an empty cardboard box.

"So you just sit there," she said, lips pulled back in that grinning rictus, "and you think about who is in charge here, and all the things I can do to hurt you if you behave badly or try to trick me. You sit there and you scream if you want to, because no one can hear you. No one stops here because they all know Annie Wilkes is crazy, they all know what she did, even if they did find me innocent."

She walked back to the door and turned again, and he screamed again when she did, in anticipation of another bull-like charge, and that made her grin more widely.

"I'll tell you something else," she said softly. "They think I got away with it, and they are right. Think about that, Paul, while I'm in town getting your cockadoodie paper."

She left, slamming the bedroom door enough to shake the house. Then there was the click of the lock.

He leaned back in the chair, shaking all over, trying not to shake because it hurt, not able to help it. Tears streamed down his cheeks. Again and again he saw her flying across the room, again and again he saw her bringing her fist down on the remains of his knee with all the force of an angry drunk hammering on an oak bar, again and again he was swallowed in that terrible blue-white nova of pain.

"Please, God, please," he moaned as the Cherokee started outside with a bang and a roar. "Please, God, please—let me out of this or kill me . . . let me out of this or kill me."

The roar of the engine faded off down the road and God did

neither and he was left with his tears and the pain, which was now fully awake and raving through his body.

30

He thought later that the world, in its unfailing perversity, would probably construe those things which he did next as acts of heroism. And he would probably let them—but in fact what he did was nothing more than a final staggering grab for self-preservation.

Dimly he seemed to hear some madly enthusiastic sports-caster—Howard Cosell or Warner Wolf or perhaps that all-time crazy Johnny Most—describing the scene, as if his effort to get at her drug supply before the pain killed him was some strange sporting event—a trial substitution for *Monday Night Football*, perhaps. What would you call a sport like that, anyway? *Run for the Dope?*

"I just *can*not believe the guts this Sheldon kid is displaying today!" the sportscaster in Paul Sheldon's head was enthusing. "I don't believe anyone in Annie Wilkes Stadium—or in the home viewing audience, for that matter—thought he had the *sly*-test *chance* of getting that wheelchair moving after the blow he took, but I believe . . . yes, it is! It's moving! Let's look at the replay!"

Sweat ran down his forehead and stung his eyes. He licked a mixture of salt and tears off his lips. The shuddering would not stop. The pain was like the end of the world. He thought: *There comes a point when the very discussion of pain becomes redundant. No one knows there is pain the size of this in the world. No one. It is like being possessed by demons.*

It was only the thought of the pills, the Novril that she kept somewhere in the house, which got him moving. The locked bed-room door . . . the possibility the dope might not be in the down-stairs bathroom as he had surmised but hidden somewhere . . . the chance she might come back and catch him . . . these things mat-tered not at all, these things were only shadows behind the pain. He would deal with each problem as it came up or he would die. That was all.

Moving caused the band of fire below his waist and in his legs to sink in deeper, cinching his legs like belts studded with hot, inward-pointing spikes. But the chair *did* move. Very slowly the chair began to move.

He had managed about four feet before realizing he was going to do nothing more useful than roll the wheelchair past the door and into the far corner unless he could turn it.

He grasped the right wheel, shuddering,

(*think of the pills, think of the relief of the pills*)

and bore down on it as hard as he could. Rubber squeaked minutely on the wooden floor, the cries of mice. He bore down, once strong and now flabby muscles quivering like jelly, lips peeling back from his gritted teeth, and the wheelchair slowly pivoted.

He grasped both wheels and got the chair moving again. This time he rolled five feet before stopping to straighten himself out. Once he'd done it, he grayed out.

He swam back to reality five minutes later, hearing the dim, goading voice of that sportscaster in his head: "He's trying to get going again! I just cannot be-*leeve* the guts of this Sheldon kid!"

The front of his mind only knew about the pain; it was the back that directed his eyes. He saw it near the door and rolled over to it. He reached down, but the tips of his fingers stopped a clear three inches short of the floor, where one of the two or three bobby-pins that had fallen from her hair as she charged him lay. He bit his lip, unaware of the sweat running down his face and neck and darkening his pajama shirt.

"I don't think he can get that pin, folks—it's been a fan-*tas*-tic effort, but I'm afraid this is where it all ends."

Well, maybe not.

He let himself slouch to the right in the wheelchair, at first trying to ignore the pain in his right side—pain that felt like an increasing bubble of pressure, something similar to a tooth impaction—and then giving way and screaming. As she said, there was no one to hear him anyway.

The tips of his fingers still hung an inch from the floor, brushing back and forth just above the bobby-pin, and his right hip really felt as if it might simply explode outward in a squirt of some vile white bone-jelly.

Oh God please please help me—

He slumped farther in spite of the pain. His fingers brushed the pin but succeeded only in pushing it a quarter of an inch away. Paul slid down in the chair, still slumped to the right, and screamed again at the pain in his lower legs. His eyes were bulging, his mouth was open, his tongue hung straight down between his teeth like the pull on a windowshade. Little drops of spittle ran from its tip and spatted on the floor.

He pinched the bobby-pin between his fingers . . . tweezed it . . . almost lost it . . . and then it was locked in his fist.

Straightening up brought a fresh slough of pain, and when the act was accomplished he could do no more than sit and pant for awhile, his head tilted as far as the uncompromising back of the wheelchair would allow, the bobby-pin lying on the board across the chair's arms. For awhile he was quite sure he was going to puke, but that passed.

What are you doing? part of his mind scolded wearily after awhile. *Are you waiting for the pain to go away? It won't. She's always quoting her mother, but your own mother had a few sayings, too, didn't she?*

Yes. She had.

Sitting there, head thrown back, face shiny with sweat, hair plastered to his forehead, Paul spoke one of them aloud now, almost as an incantation: "There may be fairies, there may be elves, but God helps those who help themselves."

Yeah. So stop waiting, Paulie—the only elf that's going to show up here is that all-time heavyweight, Annie Wilkes.

He got moving again, rolling the wheelchair slowly across to the door. She had locked it, but he believed he might be able to unlock it. Tony Bonasaro, who was now only so many blackened flakes of ash, had been a car-thief. As part of his preparation for writing *Fast Cars*, Paul had studied the mechanics of car-thievery with a tough old ex-cop named Tom Twyford. Tom had shown him how to hotwire an ignition, how to use the thin and limber strip of metal car-thieves called Slim Jims to yank the lock on a car door, how to short out a car burglar alarm.

Or, Tom had said on a spring day in New York some two and a half years ago, *let's say you don't want to steal a car at all. You got a car, but you're a little low on gas. You got a hose, but the car you pick for the free donation has got a locking gas-cap. Is this a problem? Not if you know what you're doing, because most gas-cap locks are strictly Mickey Mouse. All you really need is a bobby-pin.*

It took Paul five endless minutes of backing and filling to get the wheelchair exactly where he wanted it, with the left wheel almost touching the door.

The keyhole was the old-fashioned sort, reminding Paul of John Tenniel's *Alice in Wonderland* drawings, set in the middle of a tarnished keyplate. He slid down a bit in the wheelchair—giving out a single barking groan—and looked through it. He could see a short hallway leading down to what was clearly the parlor: a dark-red rug on the floor, an old-fashioned divan upholstered in similar material, a lamp with tassels hanging from its shade.

To his left, halfway down the hallway, was a door which stood ajar. Paul's pulsebeat quickened. That was almost surely the downstairs bathroom—he had heard her running enough water in there (including the time she had filled the floor-bucket from which he had enthusiastically drunk), and wasn't it also the place she always came from before giving him his medicine?

He thought it was.

He grasped the bobby-pin. It spilled out of his fingers onto the board and then skittered toward the edge.

"No!" he cried hoarsely, and clapped a hand over it just before it could fall. He clasped it in one fist and then grayed out again.

Although he had no way of telling for sure, he thought he was out longer this second time. The pain—except for the excruciating agony of his left knee—seemed to have abated a tiny bit. The bobby-pin was on the board across the arms of the wheelchair. This time he flexed the fingers of his right hand several times before picking it up.

Now, he thought, unbending it and holding it in his right hand. *You will not shake. Hold that thought.* YOU WILL NOT SHAKE.

He reached across his body with the pin and slipped it into the keyhole, listening as the sportscaster in his mind

(so vivid!)

described the action.

Sweat ran steadily down his face like oil. He listened . . . but even more, he *felt.*

The tumbler in a cheap lock is nothing but a rocker, Tom Twyford had said, seesawing his hand to demonstrate. *You want to turn a rocking chair over? Easiest thing in the world, right? Just grab the rockers and flip the mother right over . . . nothing to it. And that's all you got to do with a lock like this. Slide the tumbler up and then open the gas-cap quick, before it can snap back.*

He had the tumbler twice, but both times the bobby-pin slipped off and the tumbler snapped back before he could do more than begin to move it. The bobby-pin was starting to bend. He thought that it would break after another two or three tries.

"Please God," he said, sliding it in again. "Please God, what do you say? Just a little break for the kid, that's all I'm asking."

("Folks, Sheldon has performed heroically today, but this has got to be his last shot. The crowd has fallen silent. . . .")

He closed his eyes, the sportscaster's voice fading as he listened avidly to the minute rattle of the pin in the lock. Now! Here was resistance! The tumbler! He could see it lying in there like the curved foot of a rocking chair, pressing the tongue of the lock, holding it in place, holding *him* in place.

It's strictly Mickey Mouse, Paul. Just stay cool.

When you hurt this badly, it was hard to stay cool.

He grasped the doorknob with his left hand, reaching under his right arm to do it, and began to apply gentle pressure to the bobby-pin. A little more . . . a little more . . .

In his mind he could see the rocker beginning to move in its dusty little alcove; he could see the lock's tongue begin to retract. No need for it to go all the way, good God, no—no need to overturn the rocking chair, to use Tom Twyford's metaphor. Just the instant it cleared the doorframe—a push—

The pin was simultaneously starting to bend and slip. He felt it happening, and in desperation he pushed upward as hard as he could, turned the knob, and shoved at the door. There was a *snap* as the pin broke in two, the part in the lock falling in, and he had a dull moment to consider his failure before he saw that the door was slowly swinging open with the tongue of the lock sticking out of the plate like a steel finger.

"Jesus," he whispered. "Jesus, thank you."

Let's go to the videotape! Warner Wolf screamed exultantly in his mind as the thousands in Annie Wilkes Stadium—not to mention the untold millions watching at home—broke into thunderous cheers.

"Not now, Warner," he croaked, and began the long, draining job of backing and filling the wheelchair so he could get a straight shot at the door.

31

He had a bad—no, not just bad; terrible, horrible—moment when it seemed the wheelchair was not going to fit. It was no more than two inches too wide, but that was two inches too much. *She brought it in collapsed, that's why you thought it was a shopping cart at first,* his mind informed him drearily.

In the end he was able to squeeze through—barely—by positioning himself squarely in the doorway and then leaning forward enough to grab the jambs of the door in his hands. The axle-caps of the wheels squalled against the wood, but he was able to get through.

After he did, he grayed out again.

32

Her voice called him out of his daze. He opened his eyes and saw she was pointing a shotgun at him. Her eyes glittered furiously. Spit shone on her teeth.

"If you want your freedom so badly, Paul," Annie said, "I'll be happy to grant it to you."

She pulled back both hammers.

33

He jerked, expecting the shotgun blast. But she wasn't there, of course; his mind had already recognized the dream.

Not a dream—a warning. She could come back anytime. Anytime at all.

The quality of the light fanning through the half-open bathroom door had changed, grown brighter. It looked like noonlight. He wished the clock would chime and tell him just how close to right he was, but the clock was obstinately silent.

She stayed away fifty hours before.

So she did. And she might stay away eighty this time. Or you might hear that Cherokee pulling in five seconds from now. In case you didn't know it, friend, the Weather Bureau can post tornado warnings, but when it comes to telling exactly when and where they'll touch down, they don't know fuck-all.

"True enough," he said, and rolled the wheelchair down to the bathroom. Looking in, he saw an austere room floored with hexagonal white tiles. A bathtub with rusty fans spreading below the faucets stood on clawed feet. Beside it was a linen closet. Across from the tub was a sink. Over the sink was a medicine cabinet.

The floor-bucket was in the tub—he could see its plastic top.

The hall was wide enough for him to swing the chair around and face the door, but now his arms were trembling with exhaustion. He had been a puny kid and so he had tried to take reasonably good care of himself as an adult, but his muscles were now the muscles of an invalid and the puny kid was back, as if all that time spent doing laps and jogging and working out on the Nautilus machine had only been a dream.

At least this doorway was wider—not much, but enough to make his passage less hair-raising. Paul bumped over the lintel, and then the chair's hard rubber wheels rolled smoothly over the tiles. He smelled something sour that he automatically associated with hospitals—Lysol, maybe. There was no toilet in here, but he had already suspected that—the only flushing sounds came from upstairs, and now that he thought of it, one of those upstairs flushes always followed his use of the bedpan. Here there was only the tub, the basin, and the linen closet with its door standing open.

He gazed briefly at the neat piles of blue towels and washcloths— he was familiar with both from the sponge-baths she had given him—and then turned his attention to the medicine cabinet over the washstand.

It was out of reach.

No matter how much he strained, it was a good nine inches above the tips of his fingers. He could see this but reached anyway, unable to believe Fate or God or Whoever could be so cruel. He looked like an outfielder reaching desperately for a home-run ball he had absolutely no chance of catching.

Paul made a wounded, baffled noise, lowered his hand, and then leaned back, panting. The gray cloud lowered. He willed it away and looked around for something he could use to open the medicine cabinet's door and saw an O-Cedar mop leaning stiffly in the corner on a long blue pole.

You going to use that? Really? Well, I guess you could. Pry open the medicine cabinet door and then just knock a bunch of stuff out into the basin. But the bottles will break and even if there are no bottles, fat chance, everyone has at least a bottle of Listerine or Scope or something in their medicine cabinet, you have no way of putting back what you knock down. So when she comes back and sees the mess, what then?

"I'll tell her it was Misery," he croaked. "I'll tell her she dropped by looking for a tonic to bring her back from the dead."

Then he burst into tears . . . but even through the tears his eyes were conning the room, looking for something, anything, inspiration, a break, just a fucking br—

He was looking into the linen closet again, and his rapid breath suddenly stopped. His eyes widened.

His first cursory glance had taken in the shelves with their stacks of folded sheets and pillow-cases and washcloths and towels. Now he looked at the *floor* and on the floor were a number of square cardboard cartons. Some were labelled UPJOHN. Some were labelled LILLY. Some were labelled CAM PHARMACEUTICALS.

He turned the wheelchair roughly, hurting himself, not caring.

Please God don't let it be her cache of extra shampoo or her tampons or pictures of her dear old sainted mother or—

He fumbled for one of the boxes, dragged it out, and opened the flaps. No shampoo, no Avon samples. Far from it. There was a wild jumble of drugs in the carton, most of them in small boxes marked SAMPLES. At the bottom a few pills and capsules, different colors, rolled around loose. Some, like Motrim and Lopressor, the hypertension drug his father had taken during the last three years of his life, he knew. Others he had never heard of.

"Novril," he muttered, raking wildly through the box while sweat ran down his face and his legs pounded and throbbed. "Novril, where's the fucking *Novril?*"

No Novril. He pushed the flaps of the carton closed and shoved it back into the linen closet, making only a token effort to replace it in the same place it had been. Should be all right, the place looked like a goddam junk-heap—

Leaning far to his left, he was able to snag a second carton. He opened it and was hardly able to credit what he was seeing.

Darvon. Darvocet. Darvon Compound. Morphose and Mor-

phose Complex. Librium. Valium. And Novril. Dozens and dozens
and dozens of sample boxes. Lovely boxes. Dear boxes. O lovely
dear sainted boxes. He clawed one open and saw the capsules she
gave him every six hours, enclosed in their little blisters.

NOT TO BE DISPENSED WITHOUT PHYSICIAN'S PRESCRIPTION,
the box said.

"Oh dear Jesus, the doctor is *in!*" Paul sobbed. He tore the
cellophane apart with his teeth and chewed up three of the capsules,
barely aware of the bruisingly bitter taste. He halted, stared at the
five that were left encased in their mutilated cellophane sheet, and
gobbled a fourth.

He looked around quickly, chin down on his breastbone, eyes
crafty and frightened. Although he knew it was too soon to be
feeling any relief, he *did* feel it—*having* the pills, it seemed, was
even more important than *taking* the pills. It was as if he had been
given control of the moon and the tides—or had just reached up
and taken it. It was a huge thought, awesome . . . and yet also frightening, with undertones of guilt and blasphemy.

If she comes back now—

"All right—okay. I get the message."

He looked into the carton, trying to calculate how many of the
sample boxes he might be able to take without her realizing a little
mouse named Paul Sheldon had been nibbling away at the supply.

He giggled at this, a shrill, relieved sound, and he realized the
medication wasn't just working on his legs. He had gotten his fix,
if you wanted to be perfectly vulgar about it.

Get moving, idiot. You have no time to enjoy being stoned.

He took five of the boxes—a total of thirty capsules. He had to
restrain himself from taking more. He stirred the remaining boxes
and bottles around, hoping the result would look no more or less
helter-skelter than it had when he first peered into the box. He
refolded the flaps and slipped the box back into the linen closet.

A car was coming.

He straightened up, eyes wide. His hands dropped to the arms
of the wheelchair and gripped them with panicky tightness. If it
was Annie, he was screwed and that was the end of it. He would
never be able to maneuver this balky, oversized thing back to the
bedroom in time. Maybe he could whack her once with the O-
Cedar mop or something before she wrung his neck like a chicken.

He sat in the wheelchair with the sample boxes of Novril in his

lap and his broken legs stuck stiffly out in front of him and waited
for the car to pass or turn in.

The sound swelled endlessly . . . then began to diminish.

Okay. Do you need a more graphic warning, Paul-baby?

As a matter of fact, he did not. He took a final glance at the
cartons. They looked to him about as they had when he had first
seen them—although he had been looking at them through a haze
of pain and could not be completely sure—but he knew that the
piles of boxes might not be as random as they had looked, oh, not
at all. She had the heightened awareness of the deep neurotic, and
might have had the position of each box carefully memorized. She
might take one casual glance in here and immediately realize in
some arcane way what had happened. This knowledge did not bring
fear but a sense of resignation—he had needed the medication, and
he had somehow managed to escape his room and get it. If there
were consequences, punishment, he could face them with at least
the understanding that he could have done nothing but what he
had done. And of all she had done to him, this resignation was
surely a symptom of the worst—she had turned him into a pain-
wracked animal with no moral options at all.

He slowly backed the wheelchair across the bathroom, glancing
behind himself occasionally to make sure he wasn't wandering off-
course. Before, such a movement would have made him scream
with pain, but now the pain was disappearing under a beautiful
glassiness.

He rolled into the hall and then stopped as a terrible thought
struck him: if the bathroom floor had been slightly damp, or even
a bit dirty—

He stared at it, and for a moment the idea that he must have left
tracks on those clean white tiles was so persuasive that he actually
saw them. He shook his head and looked again. No tracks. But the
door was open farther than it had been. He rolled forward, swung
the wheelchair slightly to the right so he could lean over and grab
the knob, and pulled the door half-closed. He eyed it, then pulled
it a bit closer to the jamb. There. That looked right.

He was reaching for the wheels, meaning to pivot the chair so
he could roll back to his room, when he realized he was pointed
more or less toward the living room, and the living room was where
most people kept their telephone and—

Light bursting in his mind like a flare over a foggy meadow.

"Hello, Sidewinder Police Station, Officer Humbuggy speaking."

"Listen to me, Officer Humbuggy. Listen very carefully and don't interrupt, because I don't know how much time I have. My name is Paul Sheldon. I'm calling you from Annie Wilkes's house. I've been her prisoner here for at least two weeks, maybe as long as a month. I—"

"Annie Wilkes!"

"Get out here right away. Send an ambulance. And for Christ's sake get here before she gets back. . . ."

"Before she gets back," Paul moaned. "Oh yeah. Far out."

What makes you think she even has a phone? Who have you ever heard her call? Who would she call? Her good friends the Roydmans?

Just because she doesn't have anyone to chatter with all day doesn't mean she is incapable of understanding that accidents can happen; she could fall downstairs and break an arm or a leg, the barn might catch on fire—

How many times have you heard this supposed telephone ring?

So now there's a requirement? Your phone has to ring at least once a day or Mountain Bell comes and takes it out? Besides, I haven't even been conscious most of the time.

You're pushing your luck. You're pushing your luck and you know it.

Yes. He knew it, but the thought of that telephone, the imagined sensation of the cool black plastic under his fingers, the click of the rotary dial or the single booping sound as he touch-toned 0—these were seductions too great to resist.

He worked the wheelchair around until it was directly facing the parlor, and then he rolled down to it.

The place smelled musty, unaired, obscurely tired. Although the curtains guarding the bow windows were only half-drawn, affording a lovely view of the mountains, the room seemed too dark—because its colors were too dark, he thought. Dark red predominated, as if someone had spilled a great deal of venous blood in here.

Over the mantel was a tinted photograph portrait of a forbidding woman with tiny eyes buried in a fleshy face. The rosebud mouth was pursed. The photograph, enclosed in a rococo frame of gold gilt, was the size of the President's photograph in the lobby of a big-city post office. Paul did not need a notarized statement to tell him that this was Annie's sainted mother.

He rolled farther into the room. The left side of the wheelchair struck a small occasional table covered with ceramic gewgaws. They chattered together and one of them—a ceramic penguin sitting on a ceramic ice-block—fell off the side.

Without thinking, he reached out and grabbed it. The gesture was almost casual . . . and then reaction set in. He held the penguin tightly in his curled fist, trying to will the shakes away. *You caught it, no sweat, besides, there's a rug on the floor, probably wouldn't have broken anyway—*

But if it HAD! his mind screamed back. *If it HAD! Please, you have to go back to your room before you leave something . . . a track. . . .*

No. Not yet. Not yet no matter how frightened he was. Because this had cost him too much. If there was a payoff, he was going to have it.

He looked around the room, which was stuffed with heavy grace-less furniture. It should have been dominated by the bow windows and the gorgeous view of the Rockies beyond them but was instead dominated by the picture of that fleshy woman imprisoned in the ghastly glaring frame with its twists and curlicues and frozen gilded swags.

On a table at the far end of the couch, where she would sit to watch TV, was a plain dialer telephone.

Gently, hardly daring to breathe, he put the ceramic penguin (NOW MY TALE IS TOLD! the legend on the block of ice read) back on the knick-knack table and rolled across the room toward the phone.

There was an occasional table in front of the sofa; he gave it a wide berth. On it was a spray of dried flowers in an ugly green vase, and the whole thing looked topheavy, ready to tip over if he so much as brushed it.

No cars coming outside—only the sound of the wind.

He grasped the handset of the phone in one hand and slowly picked it up.

A queer predestinate sense of failure filled his mind even before he got the handset to his ear and heard the nothing. He replaced the receiver slowly, a line from an old Roger Miller song occurring to him and seeming to make a certain senseless sense: *No phone, no pool, no pets . . . I ain't got no cigarettes. . . .*

He traced the phone cord with his eye, saw the small square module on the baseboard, saw that the jack was plugged into it. Everything looked in perfect working order.

Like the barn, with its heat-tapes.

Keeping up appearances is very, very important.

He closed his eyes and saw Annie removing the jack and squeezing Elmer's Glue into the hole in the module. Saw her replacing the jack in the dead-white glue, where it would harden and freeze forever. The phone company would have no idea that anything was wrong unless someone attempted to call her and reported the line out of service, but no one called Annie, did they? She would receive regular monthly bills on her dead line and she would pay them promptly, but the phone was only stage dressing, part of her never-ending battle to *keep up appearances,* like the neat barn with its fresh red paint and cream trim and heat-tapes to melt the winter ice. Had she castrated the phone in case of just such an expedition as this? Had she foreseen the possibility that he might get out of the room? He doubted it. The phone—the *working* phone—would have gotten on her nerves long before he came. She would have lain awake at night, looking up at the ceiling of her bedroom, listening to the high-country whine of the wind, imagining the people who must be thinking of her with either dislike or outright malevolence—all the world's Roydmans—people who might, any of them, at any time, take a notion to call her on the telephone and scream: *You did it, Annie! They took you all the way to Denver, and we know you did it! They don't take you all the way to Denver if you're innocent!* She would have asked for and gotten an unlisted number, of course— anyone tried for and acquitted of some major crime (and if it had been Denver, it had been major) would have done that—but even an unlisted number would not comfort a deep neurotic like Annie Wilkes for long. *They* were all in league against her, *they* could get the number if *they* wanted, probably the lawyers who had been against her would be glad to pass it out to anyone who asked for it, and people *would* ask, oh yes—for she would see the world as a dark place full of moving human masses like seas, a malevolent universe surrounding a single small stage upon which a single savagely bright pinspot illuminated . . . only her. So best to eradicate the phone, silence it, as she would silence *him* if she knew he had gotten even this far.

Panic burst shrilly up in his mind, telling him that he *had* to get out of here and back into his room, hide the pills somewhere, return to his place by the window so that when she returned she would see *no difference, no difference at all,* and this time he agreed with the voice. He agreed wholeheartedly. He backed carefully

away from the phone, and when he gained the room's one reasonably clear area, he began the laborious job of turning the
wheelchair around, careful not to bump the occasional table as he
did so.

He had nearly finished the turn when he heard an approaching
car and knew, simply *knew* it was her, returning from town.

34

He nearly fainted, in the grip of the greatest terror he had ever
known, a terror that was filled with deep and unmanning guilt. He
suddenly remembered the only incident in his life that came re-
motely close to this one in its desperate emotional quality. He had
been twelve. It was summer vacation, his father working, his mother
gone to spend the day in Boston with Mrs. Kaspbrak from across
the street. He had seen a pack of her cigarettes and had lit one of
them. He smoked it enthusiastically, feeling both sick and fine,
feeling the way he imagined robbers must feel when they stick up
banks. Halfway through the cigarette, the room filled with smoke,
he had heard her opening the front door. *"Paulie? It's me—I've
forgotten my purse!"* He had begun to wave madly at the smoke,
knowing it would do no good, knowing he was caught, knowing he
would be spanked.

It would be more than a spanking this time.

He remembered the dream he'd had during one of his gray-outs:
Annie cocking the shotgun's twin triggers and saying *If you want
your freedom so badly, Paul, I'll be happy to grant it to you.*

The sound of the engine began to drop as the approaching car
slowed down. It *was* her.

Paul settled hands he could barely feel on the wheels and rolled
the chair toward the hallway, sparing one glance at the ceramic
penguin on its block of ice. Was it in the same place it had been?
He couldn't tell. He would have to hope.

He rolled down the hall toward the bedroom door, gaining speed.
He hoped to shoot right through, but his aim was a little off. Only
a little . . . but the fit was so tight that a little was enough. The
wheelchair thumped against the right side of the doorway and bounced
back a little.

Did you chip the paint? his mind screamed at him. *Oh Jesus Christ, did you chip the paint, did you leave a track?*

No chip. There was a small dent but no chip. Thank God. He backed and filled frantically, trying to navigate the fineness of the doorway's tight fit.

The car motor swelled, nearing, still slowing. Now he could hear the crunch of its snow tires.

Easy . . . easy does it . . .

He rolled forward and then the hubs of the wheels stuck solid against the sides of the bedroom door. He pushed harder, knowing it wasn't going to do any good, he was stuck in the doorway like a cork in a wine-bottle, unable to go either way—

He gave one final heave, the muscles in his arms quivering like overturned violin strings, and the wheelchair passed through with that same low squealing noise.

The Cherokee turned into the driveway.

She'll have packages, his mind gibbered, *the typewriter paper, maybe a few other things as well, and she'll be careful coming up the walk because of the ice, you're in here now, the worst is over, there's time, still time. . . .*

He rolled farther into the room, then turned in a clumsy semicircle. As he rolled the wheelchair parallel to the open bedroom door, he heard the Cherokee's engine shut off.

He leaned over, grasped the doorknob, and tried to pull the door shut. The tongue of the lock, still stuck out like a stiff steel finger, bumped the jamb. He pushed it with the ball of his thumb. It began to move . . . then stopped. Stopped dead, refusing to let the door close.

He stared at it stupidly for a moment, thinking of that old Navy maxim: *Whatever CAN go wrong WILL go wrong.*

Please God, no more, wasn't it enough she killed the phone?

He let go of the tongue. It sprang all the way out again. He pushed it in again and encountered the same obstruction. Inside the guts of the lock he heard an odd rattling and understood. It was the part of the bobby-pin which had broken off. It had fallen in some way that was keeping the lock's tongue from retracting completely.

He heard the Cherokee's door open. He even heard her grunt as she got out. He heard the rattle of paper bags as she gathered up her parcels.

"Come *on*," he whispered, and began to chivvy the tongue gently
back and forth. It went in perhaps a sixteenth of an inch each time
and then stopped. He could hear the goddam bobby-pin rattling
inside there. "Come on . . . come on . . . come on. . . ."

He was crying again and unaware of it, sweat and tears mingling
freely on his cheeks; he was vaguely aware that he was still in great
pain despite all the dope he had swallowed, that he was going to
pay a high price for this little piece of work.

Not so high as the one she'll *make you pay if you can't get this goddam
door closed again, Paulie.*

He heard her crunching, cautious footsteps as she made her way
up the path. The rattle of bags . . . and now the rattle of her house-
keys as she took them from her purse.

"Come on . . . come on . . . come on. . . ."

This time when he pushed the tongue there was a flat click from
inside the lock and the jut of metal slid a quarter of an inch into
the door. Not enough to clear the jamb . . . but almost.

"Please . . . come *on*. . . ."

He began to chivvy the tongue faster, diddling it, listening as she
opened the kitchen door. Then, like a hideous flashback to that day
when his mother had caught him smoking, Annie called cheerily:
"Paul? It's me! I've got your paper!"

Caught! I'm caught! Please God, no God, don't let her hurt me God—

His thumb pressed convulsively tight against the tongue of the
lock, and there was a muffled snap as the bobby-pin broke. The
tongue slid all the way into the door. In the kitchen he heard a
zipper-rasp as she opened her parka.

He closed the bedroom door. The click of the latch
(did she hear that? must have must have heard that!)
sounded as loud as a track-starter's gun.

He backed the wheelchair up toward the window. He was still
backing and filling as her footsteps began to come down the hallway.

"I've got your paper, Paul! Are you awake?"

Never . . . never in time . . . She'll hear. . . .

He gave the guide-lever a final wrench and rolled the wheelchair
into place beside the window just as her key rattled in the lock.

It won't work . . . the bobby-pin . . . and she'll be suspicious. . . .

But the piece of alien metal must have fallen all the way to the
bottom of the lock, because her key worked perfectly. He sat in
his chair, eyes half-closed, hoping madly that he had gotten the

chair back where it had been (or at least close enough to it so she wouldn't notice), hoping that she would take his sweat-drenched face and quivering body simply as reactions to missing his medication, hoping most of all that he hadn't left a track—

It was as the door swung open that he looked down and saw that by looking for individual tracks with such agonized concentration, he had ignored a whole buffalo run: the boxes of Novril were still in his lap.

35

She had two packages of paper, and she held one up in each hand, smiling. "Just what you asked for, isn't it? Triad Modern. Two reams here, and I have two more in the kitchen, just in case. So you see—"

She broke off, frowning, looking at him.

"You're *dripping* with sweat . . . and your color is *very* hectic." She paused. "What have you been doing?"

And although that set the panicky little voice of his lesser self to squealing again that he was caught and might as well give it up, might as well confess and hope for her mercy, he managed to meet her suspicious gaze with an ironic weariness.

"I think you know what I've been doing," he said. "I've been suffering."

From the pocket of her skirt she took a Kleenex and wiped his brow. The Kleenex came away wet. She smiled at him with that terrible bogus maternity.

"Has it been very bad?"

"Yes. Yes, it has. Now can I—"

"I *told* you about making me mad. Live and learn, isn't that what they say? Well, if you live, I guess you'll learn."

"Can I have my pills now?"

"In a minute," she said. Her eyes never left his sweaty face, its waxy pallor and red rashlike blotches. "First I want to make sure there's nothing *else* you want. Nothing else stupid old Annie Wilkes forgot because she doesn't know how a Mister Smart Guy goes about writing a book. I want to make sure you don't want me to go back to town and get you a tape recorder, or maybe a special pair of writing slippers, or something like that. Because if you want me to, I'll go. Your wish is my command. I won't even wait to give you your pills. I'll hop right into Old Bessie again and go. So what do you say, Mister Smart Guy? You all set?"

"I'm all set," he said. "Annie, please—"

"And you won't make me mad anymore?"

"No. I won't make you mad anymore."

"Because when I get mad I'm not really myself." Her eyes dropped. She was looking down to where his hands were cupped tightly together over the sample boxes of Novril. She looked for a very long time.

"Paul?" she asked softly. "Paul, why are you holding your hands like that?"

He began to cry. It was guilt he cried from, and he hated that most of all: in addition to everything else that this monstrous woman had done to him, she had made him feel guilty as well. So he cried from guilt . . . but also from simple childish weariness.

He looked up at her, tears flowing down his cheeks, and played the absolute last card in his hand.

"I want my pills," he said, "and I want the urinal. I held it all the time you were gone, Annie, but I can't hold it much longer, and I don't want to wet myself again."

She smiled softly, radiantly, and pushed his tumbled hair off his brow. "You poor dear. Annie has put you through a lot, hasn't she? Too much! Mean old Annie! I'll get it right away."

36

He wouldn't have dared put the pills under the rug even if he thought he had time to do so before she came back—the packages were small, but the bulges would still be all too obvious. As he heard her go into the downstairs bathroom, he took them, reached painfully around his body, and stuffed them into the back of his underpants. Sharp cardboard corners poked into the cleft of his buttocks.

She came back with the urinal, an old-fashioned tin device that looked absurdly like a blow-dryer, in one hand. She had two Novril capsules and a glass of water in the other.

Two more of those on top of the ones you took half an hour ago may drop you into a coma and then kill you, he thought, and a second voice answered at once: *Fine with me.*

He took the pills and swallowed them with water.

She held out the urinal. "Do you need help?"

"I can do it," he said.

She turned considerately away while he fumbled his penis into the cold tube and urinated. He happened to be looking at her when the hollow splashing sounds commenced, and he saw that she was smiling.

"All done?" she asked a few moments later.

"Yes." He actually had needed to urinate quite badly—in all the excitement he hadn't had time to think of such things.

She took the urinal away from him and set it carefully on the floor. "Now let's get you back in bed," she said. "You must be exhausted . . . and your legs must be singing grand opera."

He nodded, although the truth was that he could not feel *any-thing*—this medication on top of what he'd already given himself was rolling him toward unconsciousness at an alarming rate, and he was beginning to see the room through gauzy layers of gray. He held onto one thought—she was going to lift him into bed, and when she did that she would have to be blind as well as numb not to notice that the back of his underwear happened to be stuffed with little boxes.

She got him over to the side of the bed.

"Just a minute longer, Paul, and you can take a snooze."

"Annie, could you wait five minutes?" he managed.

She looked at him, gaze narrowing slightly.

"I thought you were in a lot of pain, buster."

"I am," he said. "It hurts . . . too much. My knee, mostly. Where you . . . uh, where you lost your temper. I'm not ready to be picked up. Could I have five minutes to . . . to . . ."

He knew what he wanted to say but it was drifting away from him. Drifting away and into the gray. He looked at her helplessly, knowing he was going to be caught after all.

"To let the medication work?" she asked, and he nodded gratefully.

"Of course. I'll just put a few things away and come right back."

As soon as she was out of the room he was reaching behind him, bringing out the boxes and stuffing them under the mattress one by one. The layers of gauze kept thickening, moving steadily from gray toward black.

Get them as far under as you can, he thought blindly. *Make sure you do that so if she changes the bed she won't pull them out with the ground sheet. Get them as far under as you . . . you . . .*

He shoved the last under the mattress, then leaned back and looked up at the ceiling, where the W's danced drunkenly across the plaster.

Africa, he thought.

Now I must rinse, he thought.

Oh, I am in so much trouble here, he thought.

Tracks, he thought. *Did I leave tracks? Did I—*

Paul Sheldon fell unconscious. When he woke up, fourteen hours had gone by and outside it was snowing again.

MISERY

Writing does not cause misery, it is born of misery.

—Montaigne

1

MISERY'S RETURN

By Paul Sheldon

For Annie Wilkes

CHAPTER 1

Although Ian Carmichael would not have moved from
Little Dunthorpe for all the jewels in the Queen's treasury,
he had to admit to himself that when it rained in Cornwall,
it rained harder than anywhere else in England.

There was an old strip of towelling hung from a hook
in the entryway, and after hanging up his dripping coat
and removing his boots, he used it to towel his dark-blonde
hair dry.

Distantly, from the parlor, he could hear the rippling
strains of Chopin, and he paused with the strip of towel
still in his left hand, listening.

The moisture running down his cheeks now was not
rainwater but tears.

He remembered Geoffrey saying <u>You must not cry in</u>

<u>front of her, old man--that is the one thing you must
never do!</u>

Geoffrey was right, of course--dear old Geoffrey
was rarely wrong--but sometimes when he was alone, the
nearness of Misery's escape from the Grim Reaper came
forcibly home to him, and it was nearly impossible to
hold the tears back. He loved her so much; without her
he would die. Without Misery, there would simply be no
life left for him, or in him.

Her labor had been long and hard, but no longer and
no harder than that of many other young ladies she had
seen, the midwife declared. It was only after midnight,
an hour after Geoffrey had ridden into the gathering storm.
to try and fetch the doctor, that the midwife had grown
alarmed. That was when the bleeding had started.

"Dear old Geoffrey!" He spoke it aloud this time as
he stepped into the huge and stuporously warm West Country
kitchen.

"Did ye speak, young sair?" Mrs. Ramage, the Car-
michaels' crotchety but lovable old housekeeper, asked him
as she came in from the pantry. As usual, her mobcap was
askew and she smelled of the snuff she still firmly believed, after all these years, to be a secret vice.

"Not on purpose, Mrs. Ramage," Ian said.

"By the sound o' ye coat a-drippin' out there in the
entry, ye nairly drowned between the sheds and the hoose!"

"Aye, so I nearly did," Ian said, and thought: <u>If</u>
<u>Geoffrey had returned with the doctor even ten minutes</u>
<u>later, I believe she would have died</u>. This was a
thought he tried consciously to discourage--it was both
useless and gruesome--but the thought of life without
Misery was so terrible that it sometimes crept up on him
and surprised him.

Now, breaking into these gloomy meditations, there
came the healthy bawl of a child--his son, awake and more
than ready for his afternoon meal. Faintly he could hear
the sound of Annie Wilkes, Thomas's capable nurse, as she
began to soothe him and change his napkin.

"The wee bairn's in good voice today," Mrs. Ramage
observed. Ian had one moment to think again, with sur-
passing wonder, that he was the father of a son, and then
his wife spoke from the doorway:

"Hello, darling."

He looked up, looked at his Misery, his darling. She
stood lightly poised in the doorway, her chestnut hair
with its mysterious deep-red glints like dying embers
flowing over her shoulders in gorgeous profusion. Her
complexion was still too pallid, but in her cheeks Ian
could see the first signs of returning color. Her eyes
were dark and deep, and the glow of the kitchen lamps
sparkled in each, like small and precious diamonds lying
upon darkest jewellers' felt.

"My darling!" he cried, and ran to her, as he had
that day in Liverpool, when it seemed certain that the pir-
ates had taken her away as Mad Jack Wickersham had sworn
they would.

Mrs. Ramage suddenly remembered something she had
left undone in the parlor and left them together--she went,
however, with a smile on her face. Mrs. Ramage, too, had
her moments when she could not help wondering what life
might have been like if Geoffrey and the doctor had arrived
an hour later on that dark and stormy night two months ago,
or if the experimental blood transfusion in which her young
master had so bravely poured his own life's blood into
Misery's depleted veins had not worked.

"Och, girrul," she told herself as she hurried down
the hall. "Some things dinna bear thinkin' a'." Good
advice--advice Ian had given himself. But both had discovered that good advice was sometimes easier to give than
receive.

In the kitchen, Ian hugged Misery tightly to him,
feeling his soul live and die and then live again in the
sweet smell of her warm skin.

He touched the swell of her breast and felt the strong
and steady beat of her heart.

"If you had died, I should have died with you," he
whispered.

She put her arms about his neck, bringing the firm-

ness of her breast more fully into his hand. "Hush, my
darling," Misery whispered, "and don't be silly. I'm
here...right here. Now kiss me! If I die, I fear it will
be with desire for you."

He pressed his mouth against hers and plunged his
hands deeply into the glory of her chestnut hair, and for
a few moments there was nothing at all, except for the
two of them.

2

Annie laid the three pages of typescript on the night-table beside
him and he waited to see what she would say about them. He was
curious but not really nervous—he had been surprised, really, at
how easy it had been to slip back into Misery's world. Her world
was corny and melodramatic, but that did not change the fact that
returning there had been nowhere near as distasteful as he had
expected—it had been, in fact, rather comforting, like putting on
a pair of old slippers. So his mouth dropped open and he was frankly
and honestly flabbergasted when she said:

"It's not right."

"You—you don't like it?" He could hardly believe it. How could
she have liked the other *Misery* novels and not like this? It was so
Misery-esque it was nearly a caricature, what with motherly old Mrs.
Ramage dipping snuff in the pantry, Ian and Misery pawing each
other like a couple of horny kids just home from the Friday-night
high-school dance, and—

Now *she* was the one who looked bewildered.

"*Like* it? Of course I like it. It's *beautiful*. When Ian swept her
into his arms, I cried. I couldn't help it." Her eyes actually were a
bit red. "And you naming baby Thomas's nurse after me . . . that
was very sweet."

He thought: *Smart, too—at least, I hope so. And by the way, toots,
the baby's name started out to be Sean, in case you're interested; I changed
it because I decided that was just too fucking many n's to fill in.*

"Then I'm afraid I don't understand—"

"No, you don't. I didn't say anything about not *liking* it, I said it wasn't *right*. It's a cheat. You'll have to change it."

Had he once thought of her as the perfect audience? Oh boy. *Have to give you credit, Paul—when you make a mistake, you go whole hog.* Constant Reader had just become Merciless Editor.

Without his even being aware that it was happening, Paul's face rearranged itself into the expression of sincere concentration he always wore while listening to editors. He thought of this as his Can I Help You, Lady? expression. That was because most editors were like women who drive into service stations and tell the mechanic to fix whatever it is that's making that knocking sound under the hood or going *wonk-wonk* inside the dashboard, and please have it done an hour ago. A look of sincere concentration was good because it flattered them, and when editors were flattered, they would sometimes give in on some of their mad ideas.

"How is it a cheat?" he asked.

"Well, Geoffrey rode for the doctor," she said. "*That's* all right. That happened in Chapter 38 of *Misery's Child*. But the doctor never came, as you well know, because Geoffrey's horse tripped on the top rail of that rotten Mr. Cranthorpe's toll-gate when Geoffrey tried to jump it—I hope *that* dirty bird gets his comeuppance in *Misery's Return,* Paul, I really do—and Geoffrey broke his shoulder and some of his ribs and lay there most of the night in the rain until the sheep-herder's boy came along and found him. So the doctor never came. You see?"

"Yes." He found himself suddenly unable to take his eyes from her face.

He had thought she was putting on an editor's hat—maybe even trying on a collaborator's chapeau, preparing to tell him what to write and how to write it. But that was not so. Mr. Cranthorpe, for instance. She *hoped* Mr. Cranthorpe would get his comeuppance, but she did not demand it. She saw the story's creative course as something outside of her hands, in spite of her obvious control of *him.* But some things simply could not be done. Creativity or the lack of it had no bearing on these things; to do them was as foolish as issuing a proclamation revoking the law of gravity or trying to play table-tennis with a brick. She really *was* Constant Reader, but Constant Reader did not mean Constant Sap.

She would not allow him to kill Misery . . . but neither would she allow him to cheat Misery back to life.

But Christ, I DID kill her, he thought wearily. *What am I going to do?*

"When I was a girl," she said, "they used to have chapter-plays at the movies. An episode a week. The Masked Avenger, and Flash Gordon, even one about Frank Buck, the man who went to Africa to catch wild animals and who could subdue lions and tigers just by staring at them. Do you remember the chapter-plays?"

"I remember them, but *you* can't be that old, Annie—you must have seen them on TV, or had an older brother or sister who told you about them."

At the corners of her mouth dimples appeared briefly in the solidity of flesh and then disappeared. "Go on with you, you fooler! I *did* have an older brother, though, and we used to go to the movies every Saturday afternoon. This was in Bakersfield, California, where I grew up. And while I always used to enjoy the newsreel and the color cartoons and the feature, what I really looked forward to was the next installment of the chapter-play. I'd find myself thinking about it at odd moments all week long. If a class was boring, or if I had to babysit Mrs. Krenmitz's four brats downstairs. I used to hate those little brats."

Annie lapsed into a moody silence, staring into the corner. She had become unplugged. It was the first time this had happened in some days, and he wondered uneasily if it meant she was slipping into the lower part of her cycle. If so, he had better batten down his hatches.

At last she came out of it, as always with an expression of faint surprise, as if she had not really expected the world to still be here.

"Rocket Man was my favorite. There he would be at the end of Chapter 6, Death in the Sky, unconscious while his plane went into a power dive. Or at the end of Chapter 9, Fiery Doom, he'd be tied to a chair in a burning warehouse. Sometimes it was a car with no brakes, sometimes poison gas, sometimes electricity."

Annie spoke of these things with an affection which was bizarre in its unmistakable genuineness.

"Cliff-hangers, they called them," he ventured.

She frowned at him. "I know that, Mister Smart Guy. Gosh, sometimes I think you must believe I'm awful stupid!"

"I don't, Annie, really."

She waved a hand at him impatiently, and he understood it would be better—today, at least—not to interrupt her. "It was fun to try and think how he would get out of it. Sometimes I could, sometimes

I couldn't. I didn't really care, as long as they played fair. The people who made the story."

She looked at him sharply to make sure he was taking the point. Paul thought he could hardly have missed it.

"Like when he was unconscious in the airplane. He woke up, and there was a parachute under his seat. He put it on and jumped out of the plane and that was fair enough."

Thousands of English-comp teachers would disagree with you, my dear, Paul thought. *What you're talking about is called a* deus ex machina, *the god from the machine, first used in Greek amphitheaters. When the playwright got his hero into an impossible jam, this chair decked with flowers came down from overhead. The hero sat down in it and was drawn up and out of harm's way. Even the stupidest swain could grasp the symbolism—the hero had been saved by God. But the* deus ex mach- ina—*sometimes known in the technical jargon as "the old parachute- under-the-airplane-seat trick," finally went out of vogue around the year 1700. Except, of course, for such arcana as the Rocket Man serials and the Nancy Drew books. I guess you missed the news, Annie.*

For one gruesome, never-to-be-forgotten moment, Paul thought he was going to have a laughing fit. Given her mood this morning, that would almost surely have resulted in some unpleasant and painful punishment. He raised a hand quickly to his mouth, pasting it over the smile trying to be born there, and manufactured a cough- ing fit.

She thumped him on the back hard enough to hurt.

"Better?"

"Yes, thanks."

"Can I go on now, Paul, or were you planning to have a sneezing fit? Should I get the bucket? Do you feel as if you might have to vomit a few times?"

"No, Annie. Please go on. What you're saying is fascinating."

She looked a little mollified—not much, but a little. "When he found that parachute under the seat, it was fair. Maybe not all that *realistic,* but fair."

He thought about this, startled—her occasional sharp insights never failed to startle him—and decided it was true. *Fair* and *re- alistic* might be synonyms in the best of all possible worlds, but if so, this was not that world.

"But you take another episode," she said, "and this is *exactly* what's wrong with what you wrote yesterday, Paul, so listen to me."

"I'm all ears."

She looked at him sharply to see if he was joking. His face, however, was pale and serious—very much the face of a conscientious student. The urge to laugh had dissipated when he realized that Annie might know everything about the *deus ex machina* except the name.

"All right," she said. "This was a no-brakes chapter. The bad guys put Rocket Man—only it was Rocket Man in his secret identity—into a car that didn't have any brakes, and then they welded all the doors shut, and then they started the car rolling down this twisty-turny mountain road. I was on the edge of my seat that day, I can tell you."

She was sitting on the edge of his bed—Paul was sitting across the room in the wheelchair. It had been five days since his expedition into the bathroom and the parlor, and he had recuperated from that experience faster than he would ever have believed. Just not being caught, it seemed, was a marvellous restorative.

She looked vaguely at the calendar, where the smiling boy rode his sled through an endless February.

"So there was poor old Rocket Man, stuck in that car without his rocket pack or even his special helmet with the one-way eyes, trying to steer and stop the car and open the side door, all at the same time. He was busier than a one-armed paperhanger, I can tell you!"

Yes, Paul could suddenly see it—and in an instinctive way he understood exactly how such a scene, absurdly melodramatic as it might be, could be milked for suspense. The scenery, all of it canted at an alarming downhill angle, rushing by. Cut to the brake-pedal, which sinks bonelessly to the mat when the man's foot (he saw the foot clearly, clad in a 1940s-style airtip shoe) stomps on it. Cut to his shoulder, hitting the door. Cut to the outside reverse, showing us an irregular bead of solder where the door has been sealed shut. Stupid, sure—not a bit literary—but you could do things with it. You could speed up pulses with it. No Chivas Regal here; this was the fictional equivalent of backwoods popskull.

"So then you saw that the road just ended at this cliff," she said, "and everyone in the theater knew that if Rocket Man didn't get out of that old Hudson before it got to the cliff, he was a gone goose. Oh boy! And here came the car, with Rocket Man still trying to put on the brakes or bash the door open, and then . . . over it went! It flew out into space, and then it went down. It hit the side of the cliff about halfway down and burst into flames, and then it went into the ocean, and then this ending message came up on the screen that said NEXT WEEK CHAPTER 11, THE DRAGON FLIES."

She sat on the edge of his bed, hands tightly clasped together, her large bosom rising and falling rapidly.

"Well!" she said, not looking at him, only at the wall, "after that I hardly *saw* the movie. I didn't just think about Rocket Man once in awhile that next week; I thought about him *all* the time. How could he have gotten out of it? I couldn't even guess.

"Next Saturday, I was standing in front of the theater at noon, although the box office didn't open until one-fifteen and the movie didn't start until two. But, Paul . . . what happened . . . well, you'll never guess!"

Paul said nothing, but he could guess. He understood how she could like what he had written and still know it was not right— know it and say it not with an editor's sometimes untrustworthy literary sophistication but with Constant Reader's flat and uncontradictable certainty. He understood, and was amazed to find he was ashamed of himself. She was right. He *had* written a cheat.

"The new episode always started with the ending of the *last* one. They showed him going down the hill, they showed the cliff, they showed him banging on the car door, trying to open it. Then, just before the car got to the edge, the door banged open and out he flew onto the road! The car went over the cliff, and all the kids in the theater were cheering because Rocket Man got out, but *I* wasn't cheering, Paul. I was *mad!* I started yelling, 'That isn't what happened last week! That isn't what happened last week!' "

Annie jumped up and began to walk rapidly back and forth in the room, her head down, her hair falling in a frizzy cowl about her face, smacking one fist steadily into her other palm, eyes blazing.

"My brother tried to make me stop and when I wouldn't he tried to put his hand over my mouth to shut me up and I bit it and went on yelling 'That isn't what happened last week! Are you all too stupid to remember? Did you all get amnesia?' And my brother said 'You're crazy, Annie,' but I knew I wasn't. And the manager came and said if I didn't shut up I'd have to leave and I said 'You bet I'm going to leave because that was a dirty *cheat,* that wasn't what happened last week!' "

She looked at him and Paul saw clear murder in her eyes.

"He didn't get out of the cockadoodie car! It went over the edge and he was still inside it! Do you understand that?"

"Yes," Paul said.

"DO YOU UNDERSTAND THAT?"

She suddenly leaped at him with that limber ferocity, and although he felt certain she meant to hurt him as she had before, possibly because she couldn't get at the dirty birdie of a scriptwriter who had cheated Rocket Man out of the Hudson before it went over the cliff, he did not move at all—he could see the seeds of her current instability in the window of past she had just opened for him, but he was also awed by it—the injustice she felt was, in spite of its childishness, completely, inarguably real.

She didn't hit him; she seized the front of the robe he was wearing and dragged him forward until their faces were nearly touching.

"DO YOU?"

"Yes, Annie, yes."

She stared at him, that furious black gaze, and must have seen the truth in his face, because after a moment she slung him contemptuously back in the chair.

He grimaced against the thick, grinding pain, and after awhile it began to subside.

"Then you know what is wrong," she said.

"I suppose I do." *Although I'll be goddamned if I know how I'm going to fix it.*

And that other voice returned at once: *I don't know if you'll be damned by God or saved by Him, Paulie, but one thing I do know: if you don't find a way to bring Misery back to life—a way she can believe— she's going to kill you.*

"Then do it," she said curtly, and left the room.

3

Paul looked at the typewriter. The typewriter was there. N's! He had never realized how many n's there were in an average line of type.

I thought you were supposed to be good, the typewriter said—his mind had invested it with a sneering and yet callow voice: the voice of a teen-age gunslinger in a Hollywood western, a kid intent on making a fast reputation here in Deadwood. *You're not so good. Hell, you can't even please one crazy overweight ex-nurse. Maybe you broke your writing bone in that crash, too . . . only that bone isn't healing.*

He leaned back as far as the wheelchair would allow and closed his eyes. Her rejection of what he had written would be easier to bear if he could blame it on the pain, but the truth was that the pain had finally begun to subside a little.

The stolen pills were safely tucked away between the mattress and the box spring. He had taken none of them—knowing he had them put aside, a form of Annie-insurance, was enough. She would find them if she took it into her head to turn the mattress, he supposed, but that was a chance he was prepared to take.

There had been no trouble between them since the blow-up over the typewriter paper. His medication came regularly, and he took it. He wondered if she knew he was hooked on the stuff.

Hey, come on now, Paul, that's a bit of a dramatization, isn't it?

No, it wasn't. Three nights ago, when he was sure she was upstairs, he had sneaked one of the sample boxes out and had read everything on the label, although he supposed he had read everything he needed when he saw what Novril's principal ingredient was. Maybe you spelled *relief* R-O-L-A-I-D-S, but you spelled Novril C-O-D-E-I-N-E.

The fact is, you're healing up, Paul. Below the knees your legs look like a four-year-old's stick-drawing, but you are healing up. You could get by on aspirin or Empirin now. It's not you that needs the Novril; you're feeding it to the monkey.

He would have to cut down, have to duck some of the caps. Until he could do that, she would have him on a chain as well as in a wheelchair—a chain of Novril capsules.

Okay, I'll duck one of the two capsules she gives me every other time she brings them. I'll put it under my tongue when I swallow the other one, then stick it under my mattress with the other pills when she takes the drinking glass out. Only not today. I don't feel ready to start today. I'll start tomorrow.

Now in his mind he heard the voice of the Red Queen lecturing Alice: *Down here we got our act clean yesterday, and we plan to start getting our act clean tomorrow, but we* never *clean up our act today.*

Ho-ho, Paulie, you're a real riot, the typewriter said in the tough gunsel's voice he had made up for it.

"Us dirty birdies are never all that funny, but we never stop trying—you have to give us that," he muttered.

Well, you better start thinking about all the dope you are taking, Paul. You better start thinking about it very seriously.

He decided suddenly, on the spur of the moment, that he would start dodging some of the medication as soon as he got a first chapter that Annie liked on paper—a chapter which Annie decided wasn't a cheat.

Part of him—the part that listened to even the best, fairest editorial suggestions with ill-grace—protested that the woman was crazy, that there was no way to tell what she might or might not accept; that anything he tried would be only a crapshoot.

But another part—a far more sensible part—disagreed. He would know the real stuff when he found it. The real stuff would make the crap he had given Annie to read last night, the crap it had taken him three days and false starts without number to write, look like a dog turd sitting next to a silver dollar. Hadn't he known it was all wrong? It wasn't like him to labor so painfully, nor to half-fill a wastebasket with random jottings or half-pages which ended with lines like "Misery turned to him, eyes shining, lips murmuring the magic words Oh you numb shithead THIS ISN'T WORKING AT ALL!!!" He had chalked it off to the pain and to being in a situation where he was not just writing for his supper but for his life. Those ideas had been nothing but plausible lies. The fact was, things had gone dry. The work had gone badly because he was cheating and he had known it himself.

Well, she saw through you, shit-for-brains, the typewriter said in its nasty, insolent voice. *Didn't she? So what are you going to do now?*

He didn't know, but he supposed he would have to do something, and in a hurry. He hadn't cared for her mood this morning. He supposed he should count himself lucky that she hadn't re-broken his legs with a baseball bat or given him a battery-acid manicure or something similar to indicate her displeasure with the way he had begun her book—such critical responses were always possible, given Annie's unique view of the world. If he got out of this alive, he thought he might drop Christopher Hale a note. Hale reviewed books for the New York *Times.* The note would say: "Whenever my editor called me up and told you were planning to review one of my books in the daily *Times,* my knees used to knock together—you gave me some good ones, Chris old buddy, but you also torpedoed me more than once, as you well know. Anyway, I just wanted to tell you to go ahead and do your worst—I've discovered a whole new critical mode, my friend. We might call it the

Colorado Barbecue and Floor Bucket school of thought. It makes the stuff you guys do look about as scary as a ride on the Central Park carousel."

This is all very amusing, Paul, writing critics little billets-doux *in one's head is always good for a giggle, but you really ought to find yourself a pot and get it boiling, don't you think?*

Yes. Yes indeed.

The typewriter sat there, smirking at him.

"I hate you," Paul said morosely, and looked out the window.

4

The snow-storm to which Paul had awakened the day after his expedition to the bathroom had gone on for two days—there had been at least eighteen inches of new fall, and heavy drifting. By the time the sun finally peered through the clouds again, Annie's Cherokee was nothing but a vague hump in the driveway.

Now, however, the sun was out again and the sky was brilliant once more. That sun had heat as well as brilliance—he could feel it on his face and hands as he sat here. The icicles along the barn were dripping again. He thought briefly of his car in the snow, and then picked up a piece of paper and rolled it into the Royal. He typed the words MISERY'S RETURN in the upper left-hand corner, the number 1 in the upper right. He banged the carriage-return lever four or five times, centered the carriage, and typed CHAPTER 1. He hit the keys harder than necessary, so she would be sure to hear he was typing *something,* at least.

Now there was all this white space below CHAPTER 1, looking like a snowbank into which he could fall and die, smothered in frost.

Africa.

As long as they played fair.

That bird came from Africa.

There was a parachute under his seat.

Africa.

Now I must rinse.

He was drifting off and knew he shouldn't—if she came in here and caught him cooping instead of writing she would be mad—but he let himself drift anyway. He was not just dozing; he was, in an odd way, thinking. Looking. *Searching.*

Searching for what, Paulie?

But that was obvious. The plane was in a power-dive. He was searching for the parachute under the seat. Okay? Fair enough?

Fair enough. When he found the parachute under the seat, it was fair. Maybe not all that realistic, but fair.

For a couple of summers his mother had sent him to day-camp at the Malden Community Center. And they had played this game . . . they sat in a circle, and the game was like Annie's chapter-plays, and he almost always won. . . . What was that game called?

He could see fifteen or twenty little boys and girls sitting in a circle in one shady corner of a playground, all of them wearing Malden Community Center tee-shirts, all listening intently as the counsellor explained how the game was played. *Can You?, the name of that game was Can You?, and it really* was *just like the Republic cliff-hangers, the game you played then was Can You?, Paulie, and that's the name of the game now, isn't it?*

Yes, he supposed it was.

In Can You? the counsellor would start a story about this guy named Careless Corrigan. Careless was lost in the trackless jungles of South America. Suddenly he looks around and sees there are lions behind him . . . lions on either side of him . . . and by-God lions ahead of him. Careless Corrigan is surrounded by lions . . . and they are starting to move in. It's only five in the afternoon, but that is no problem for these kitties; as far as South American lions are concerned, that dinner-at-eight shit is for goofballs.

The counsellor had had a stopwatch, and Paul Sheldon's dozing mind saw it with brilliant clarity, although he had last held its honest silver weight in his hand more than thirty years ago. He could see the fine copperplate of the numbers, the smaller needle at the bottom which recorded tenths of seconds, he could see the brand name printed in tiny letters: ANNEX.

The counsellor would look around the circle and pick one of the day-campers. "Daniel," he would say. "Can you?" The moment *Can you?* was out of his mouth, the counsellor would click the stopwatch into motion.

Daniel then had exactly ten seconds to go on with the story. If he did not begin to speak during those ten seconds, he had to leave the circle. But if he got Careless away from the lions, the counsellor would look at the circle again and ask the game's other question, one that recalled his current situation clearly to mind again. This question was *Did he?*

The rules for this part of the game were Annie's exactly. Realism was not necessary; fairness was. Daniel could say, for instance: "Luckily, Careless had his Winchester with him, and plenty of ammo. So he shot three of the lions and the rest ran away." In a case like that, Daniel *did.* He got the stopwatch and went on with the story, ending his segment with Careless up to his hips in a pool of quicksand or something, and then he would ask someone else if he or she could, and bang down the button on the stopwatch.

But ten seconds wasn't long, and it was easy to get jammed up . . . easy to cheat. The next kid might well say something like "Just then this great big bird—an Andean vulture, I think—flew down. Careless grabbed its neck and made it pull him out of that quicksand."

When the counsellor asked *Did she?,* you raised your hand if you thought she had, left it down if you thought she had blown it. In the case of the Andean vulture, the kid would almost surely have been invited to leave the circle.

Can you, Paul?

Yeah. That's how I survive. That's how come I'm able to maintain homes in both New York and L.A. and more rolling iron than there is in some used-car lots. Because I can, *and it's not something to apologize for, goddammit. There are lots of guys out there who write a better prose line than I do and who have a better understanding of what people are really like and what humanity is supposed to mean—hell, I know that. But when the counsellor asks* Did he? *about those guys, sometimes only a few people raise their hands. But they raise their hands for me . . . or for Misery . . . and in the end I guess they're both the same. Can I? Yeah. You bet I can. There's a million things in this world I can't do. Couldn't hit a curve ball, even back in high school. Can't fix a leaky faucet. Can't roller-skate or make an F-chord on the guitar that sounds like anything but shit. I have tried twice to be married and couldn't do it either time. But if you want me to take you away, to scare you or involve you or make you cry or grin, yeah. I can. I can bring it to you and keep bringing it until you holler uncle. I am able. I CAN.*

The typewriter's insolent gunslinger-voice whispered into this deepening dream.

What we got here, friends, is a lot of two things—big talk and white space.

Can You?
Yes. Yes!
Did *he?*
No. He cheated. In Misery's Child *the doctor never came. Maybe the rest of you forgot what happened last week, but the stone idol never forgets. Paul has to leave the circle. Pardon me, please. Now I must rinse. Now I must—*

5

"—rinse," he muttered, and slid over to the right. This dragged his left leg slightly askew, and the bolt of pain in his crushed knee was enough to wake him up. Less than five minutes had gone by. He could hear Annie washing dishes in the kitchen. Usually she sang as she did her chores. Today she was not singing; there was only the rattle of plates and the occasional hiss of rinsewater. Another bad sign. *Here's a special weather bulletin for residents of Sheldon County— a tornado watch is in effect until 5:00 P.M. tonight. I repeat, a tornado watch—*

But it was time to stop playing games and get down to business. She wanted Misery back from the dead, but it had to be fair. Not necessarily realistic, just fair. If he could do it this morning, he could just maybe he could derail the depression he sensed coming on before it could get a real start.

Paul looked out the window, his chin on his palm. He was fully awake now, thinking fast and hard, but not really aware of the process. The top two or three layers of his conscious mind, which dealt with such things as when he had last shampooed, or whether or not Annie would be on time with his next dope allotment, seemed to have departed the scene entirely. That part of his head had quietly gone out to get a pastrami on rye, or something. There was sensory input, but he was not doing anything with it—not seeing what he was seeing, not hearing what he was hearing.

Another part of him was furiously trying out ideas, rejecting them, trying to combine them, rejecting the combinations. He sensed this going on but had no direct contact with it and wanted none. It was dirty down there in the sweatshops.

He understood what he was doing now as TRYING TO HAVE AN IDEA. TRYING TO HAVE AN IDEA wasn't the same thing as GETTING

AN IDEA. GETTING AN IDEA was a more humble way of saying *I am inspired,* or *Eureka! My muse has spoken!*

The idea for *Fast Cars* had come to him one day in New York City. He had gone out with no more in mind than buying a VCR for the townhouse on 83rd Street. He had passed a parking lot and had seen an attendant trying to jimmy his way into a car. That was all. He had no idea if what he had seen was licit or illicit, and by the time he had walked another two or three blocks, he no longer cared. The attendant had become Tony Bonasaro. He knew everything about Tony but his name, which he later plucked from a telephone book. Half the story existed, full-blown, in his mind, and the rest was rapidly falling into place. He felt jivey, happy, almost drunk. The muse had arrived, every bit as welcome as an unexpected check in the mail. He had set out to get a video recorder and had gotten something much better instead. He had GOTTEN AN IDEA.

This other process—TRYING TO HAVE AN IDEA—was nowhere near as exalted or exalting, but it was every bit as mysterious . . . and every bit as necessary. Because when you were writing a novel you almost always got roadblocked somewhere, and there was no sense in trying to go on until you'd HAD AN IDEA.

His usual procedure when it was necessary to HAVE AN IDEA was to put on his coat and go for a walk. If he didn't need to HAVE AN IDEA, he took a book when he went for a walk. He recognized walking as good exercise, but it was boring. If you didn't have someone to talk to while you walked, a book was a necessity. But if you needed to HAVE AN IDEA, boredom could be to a roadblocked novel what chemotherapy was to a cancer patient.

Halfway through *Fast Cars,* Tony had killed Lieutenant Gray when the lieutenant tried to slap the cuffs on him in a Times Square movie theater. Paul wanted Tony to get away with the murder—for awhile, anyway—because there could be no third act with Tony sitting in the cooler. Yet Tony could not simply leave Gray sitting in the movie theater with the haft of a knife sticking out of his left armpit, because there were at least three people who knew Gray had gone to meet Tony.

Body disposal was the problem, and Paul didn't know how to solve it. It was a roadblock. It was the game. It was *Careless just killed this guy in a Times Square movie theater and now he's got to get the body back to his car without anyone saying "Hey mister, is that guy as dead as he looks or did he just pitch a fit or something?"* If he gets

Gray's corpse back to the car, he can drive it to Queens and dump it in
this abandoned building project he knows about. Paulie? Can You?

There was no ten-second deadline, of course—he'd had no con-
tract for the book, had written it on spec, and hence there was no
delivery date to think about. Yet there was *always* a deadline, a
time after which you had to leave the circle, and most writers knew
it. If a book remained roadblocked long enough, it began to decay,
to fall apart; all the little tricks and illusions started to show.

He had gone for a walk, thinking of nothing on top of his mind,
the way he was thinking of nothing on top right now. He had walked
three miles before someone sent up a flare from the sweatshops
down below: *Suppose he starts a fire in the theater?*

That looked like it might work. There was no sense of giddiness,
no true feeling of inspiration; he felt like a carpenter looking at a
piece of lumber that might do the job.

He could set a fire in the stuffing of the seat next to him, how's that?
Goddam seats in those theaters are always torn up. And there'd be smoke.
Lots of it. He could hold off leaving as long as possible, then drag Gray
out with him. He can pass Gray off as a smoke-inhalation victim. What
do you think?

He had thought it was okay. Not great, and there were plenty
of details still to be worked out, but it looked okay. He'd HAD AN
IDEA. The work could proceed.

He'd never needed to HAVE AN IDEA to *start* a book, but he
understood instinctively that it could be done.

He sat quietly in the chair, chin on hand, looking out at the barn.
If he'd been able to walk, he would have been out there in the
field. He sat quietly, almost dozing, waiting for something to happen, really aware of nothing at all except that things were happening
down below, that whole edifices of make-believe were being erected,
judged, found wanting, and torn down again in the wink of an eye.
Ten minutes passed. Fifteen. Now she was running the vacuum
cleaner in the parlor (but still not singing). He heard it but did
nothing with the hearing of it; it was unconnected sound which ran
into his head and then out again like water running through a
flume.

Finally the guys down below shot up a flare, as they always eventually did. Poor buggers down there *never* stopped busting their
balls, and he didn't envy them one little bit.

Paul sat quietly, beginning to HAVE AN IDEA. His conscious mind returned—THE DOCTOR IS *IN*—and picked the idea up like a letter pushed through the mail-slot in a door. He began to examine it. He almost rejected it (was that a faint groan from down there in the sweatshops?), reconsidered, decided half of it could be saved.

A second flare, this one brighter than the first.

Paul began to drum his fingers restlessly on the windowsill.

Around eleven o'clock he began to type. This went very slowly at first—individual clacks followed by spaces of silence, some as long as fifteen seconds. It was the aural equivalent of an island archipelago seen from the air—a chain of low humps broken by broad swaths of blue.

Little by little the spaces of silence began to shorten, and now there were occasional bursts of typing—it would have sounded fine on Paul's electric typewriter, but the clacking sound of the Royal was thick, actively unpleasant.

But Paul did not notice the Ducky Daddles voice of the typewriter. He was warming up by the bottom of the first page. By the bottom of the second he was in high gear.

After awhile Annie turned off the vacuum cleaner and stood in the doorway, watching him. Paul had no idea she was there—had no idea, in fact, that *he* was. He had finally escaped. He was in Little Dunthorpe's churchyard, breathing damp night air, smelling moss and earth and mist; he heard the clock in the tower of the Presbyterian church strike two and dumped it into the story without missing a beat. When it was very good, he could see through the paper. He could see through it now.

Annie watched him for a long time, her heavy face unsmiling, moveless, but somehow satisfied. After awhile she went away. Her tread was heavy, but Paul didn't hear that, either.

He worked until three o'clock that afternoon, and at eight that night he asked her to help him back into the wheelchair again. He wrote another three hours, although by ten o'clock the pain had begun to be quite bad. Annie came in at eleven. He asked for another fifteen minutes.

"No, Paul, it's enough. You're white as salt."

She got him into bed and he was asleep in three minutes. He slept the whole night through for the first time since coming out of the gray cloud, and his sleep was for the first time utterly without dreams.

He had been dreaming awake.

6

MISERY'S RETUR*N*

By Paul Sheldo*n*

For An*n*ie Wilkes

CHAPTER 1

For a mome*n*t Geoffrey Alliburto*n* was *n*ot sure who the
old ma*n* at the door was, a*n*d this was *n*ot e*n*tirely because
the bell had awake*n*ed him from a deepe*n*i*n*g doze. The ir-
ritati*n*g thing about village life, he thought, was that
there were*n*'t e*n*ough people for there to be a*n*y perfect
stra*n*gers; i*n*stead there were just e*n*ough to keep o*n*e from
knowi*n*g immediately who ma*n*y of the villagers were. Sometimes all o*n*e really had to go o*n* was a family resembla*n*ce
--and such resembla*n*ces, of course, *n*ever precluded the
u*n*likely but hardly impossible coi*n*cide*n*ce of bastardy.
O*n*e could usually ha*n*dle such mome*n*ts--*n*o matter how much
o*n*e might feel o*n*e was e*n*teri*n*g o*n*e's dotage while tryi*n*g
to maintai*n* an ordi*n*ary co*n*versatio*n* with a perso*n* whose
*n*ame o*n*e should be able to recall but could *n*ot; thi*n*gs
o*n*ly reached the more cosmic realms of embarrassme*n*t whe*n*
two such familiar faces arrived at the same time, a*n*d o*n*e
felt called upo*n* to make i*n*troductio*n*s.

"I hope I'll not be disturbin' ye, sair," this visitor
said. He was twisting a cheap cloth cap restlessly in
his hands, and in the light cast by the lamp Geoffrey held
up, his face looked lined and yellow and terribly
worried--frightened, even. "It's just that I didn't want
to go to Dr. Bookings, nor did I want to disturb His
Lordship. Not, at least, until I'd spoken to you, if
ye take my meaning, sair."

Geoffrey didn't, but quite suddenly he did know one
thing--who this late-coming visitor was. The mention of
Dr. Bookings, the C of E Minister, had done it. Three
days ago Dr. Bookings had performed Misery's few last
rites in the churchyard which lay behind the rectory,
and this fellow had been there--but lurking considerately
in the background, where he was less apt to be noticed.

His name was Colter. He was one of the church sex-
tons. To be brutally frank, the man was a gravedigger.

"Colter," he said. "What can I do for you?"

Colter spoke hesitantly. "It's the noises, sair.
The noises in the churchyard. Her Ladyship rests not
easy, sair, so she doesn't, and I'm afeard. I--"

Geoffrey felt as if someone had punched him in the
midsection. He pulled in a gasp of air and hot pain
needled his side, where his ribs had been tightly taped
by Dr. Shinebone. Shinebone's gloomy assessment had been
that Geoffrey would almost certainly take pneumonia

after lying in that ditch all night in the chilly rain,
but three days had passed and there had been no onset of
fever and coughing. He had known there would not be;
God did not let off the guilty so easily. He believed
that God would let him live to perpetuate his poor lost
darling's memory for a long, long time.

"Are ye all right, sair?" Colter asked. "I heard
ye were turrible bunged up t'other night." He paused.
"The night herself died."

"I'm fine," Geoffrey said slowly. "Colter, these
sounds you say you hear...you know they are just imaginings, don't you?"

Colter looked shocked.

"Imaginings?" he asked. "Sair! Next ye'll be tellin'
me ye have no belief in Jesus and the life everlastin'!
Why, didn't Duncan Fromsley see old man Patterson not
two days after his funeral, glowin' just as white as marsh-
fire (which was just what it probably was, Geoffrey thought,
marsh-fire plus whatever came out of old Fromsley's last
bottle)? And ain't half the bleedin' town seen that old
Papist monk that walks the battlements of Ridgeheath Manor?
They even sent down a coupler ladies from the bleedin'
London Psychic Serciety to look inter that 'un!"

Geoffrey knew the ladies Colter meant; a couple of
hysterical beldames probably suffering from the alternate

calms and monsoons of midlife, both as dotty as a child's
Draw-It-Name-It puzzle.

"Ghosts are just as real as you or me, sair,"
Colter was saying earnestly. "I don't mind the <u>idea</u>
of them--but these noises are fearsome spooky, so they
are, and I hardly even like to go near the churchyard--
and I have to dig a grave for the little Roydman babe
tomorrow, so I do."

Geoffrey said an inward prayer for patience. The
urge to bellow at this poor sexton was almost insurmount-
able. He had been dozing peacefully enough in front of his
own fire with a book in his lap when Colter came, waking
him up...and he was coming more and more awake all the
time, and at every second the dull sorrow settled more deeply over him, the awareness that his darling was gone.
She was three days in her grave, soon to be a week...a
month...a year...ten years. The sorrow, he thought, was
like a rock on the shoreline of the ocean. When one was
sleeping it was as if the tide was in, and there was some
relief. Sleep was like a tide which covered the rock of
grief. When one woke, however, the tide began to go out
and soon the rock was visible again, a barnacle-encrusted
thing of inarguable reality, a thing which would be there
forever, or until God chose to wash it away.

And this fool dared to come here and prate of ghosts!

But the man's face looked so wretched that Geoffrey was
able to control himself.

"Miss Misery--Her Ladyship--was much loved," Geoffrey said quietly.

"Aye, sair, so she was," Colter agreed fervently. He switched custody of his cloth cap to his left hand solely, and with his right produced a giant red handkerchief from his pocket. He honked mightily into it, his eyes watering.

"All of us sorrow at her passing." Geoffrey's hands went to his shirt and rubbed the heavy muslin wrappings beneath it restlessly.

"Aye, so we do, sair, so we do." Colter's words were muffled in the handkerchief, but Geoffrey could see his eyes; the man was really, honestly weeping. The last of his own selfish anger dissolved in pity. "She were a good lady, sair! Aye, she were a _great_ lady, and it's a turrible thing the way His Lordship's took on about it--"

"Aye, she was fine," Geoffrey said gently, and found to his dismay that his own tears were now close, like a cloudburst which threatens on a late summer's afternoon. "And sometimes, Colter, when someone especially fine passes away--someone especially dear to us all--we find it hard to let that someone go. So we may imagine that they have _not_ gone. Do you follow me?"

"Aye, sair!" Colter said eagerly. "But these sounds... sair, if ye heard them!"

Patiently, Geoffrey said: "What sort of sounds do you mean?"

He thought Colter would then speak of sounds which might

be no more than the wind in the trees, sounds amplified by his

own imagination, of course--or perhaps a badger bumbling its way

down to Little Dunthorpe Stream, which lay behind the church-

yard. And so he was hardly prepared when Colter whispered in

an affrighted voice: "Scratchin' sounds, sair! It sounds as

if she were still alive down there and tryin' to work her way

back up to the land o' the livin', so it does!"

CHAPTER 2

    Fifteen minutes later, alone again, Geoffrey approached

the dining-room sideboard. He was reeling from side to side

like a man negotiating the foredeck of a ship in a gale. He

felt like a man in a gale. He might have believed that the

fever Dr. Shinebone had almost gleefully predicted had come

on him at last, and with a vengeance, but it wasn't fever

which had simultaneously brought wild red roses to his cheeks

and turned his forehead to the color of candlewax, not fever

which made his hands shake so badly that he almost dropped

the decanter of brandy as he brought it out of the sideboard.

    If there was a chance--the slightest chance--that the

monstrous idea Colter had planted in his mind was true, then

he had no business pausing here at all. But he felt that

without a drink he might fall swooning to the floor.

    Geoffrey Alliburton did something then he had never done

before in his whole life; something he never did again. He

lifted the decanter directly to his mouth, and drank from the
neck.

Then he stepped back, and whispered: "We shall see about
this. We shall see about this, by heaven. And if I go on this
insane errand only to discover nothing at the end of it but
an old gravedigger's imagination after all, I will have good-
man Colter's earlobes on my watch chain, no matter how much
he loved Misery."

CHAPTER 3

He took the pony-trap, driving under an eerie, not-
quite-dark sky where a three-quarters moon ducked restlessly in and out between racing reefs of cloud. He had
paused to throw on the first thing in the downstairs hall closet
which came to hand--this turned out to be a dark-maroon smoking
jacket. The tails blew out behind him as he whipped Mary
on. The elderly mare did not like the speed upon which he
was insisting; Geoffrey did not like the deepening pain in
his shoulder and side...but the pain of neither could be
helped.

Scratchin' sounds, sair! It sounds as if she were still
alive down there and tryin' to work her way back up to the
land o' the livin'!

This by itself would not have put him in a state of near-
terror--but he remembered coming to Calthorpe Manor the day

after Misery's death. He and Ian had looked at each other,
and Ian had tried to smile, although his eyes were gemlike
with unshed tears.

"It would somehow be easier," Ian had said, "if she
looked...looked more dead. I know how that sounds--"

"Bosh," Geoffrey had said, trying to smile. "The
undertaker doubtless exercised all his wit and--"

"Undertaker!" Ian nearly screamed, and for the first
time Geoffrey had truly understood that his friend was tottering on the brink of madness. "Undertaker! Ghoul! I've
had no undertaker and I will have no undertaker to come in
and rouge my darling and paint her like a doll!"

"Ian! My dear fellow! Really, you mustn't--" Geoffrey
had made as if to clap Ian on the shoulder and somehow that
had turned into an embrace. The two men wept in each other's
arms like tired children, while in some other room Misery's
child, a boy now almost a day old and still unnamed, awoke and
began to cry. Mrs. Ramage, whose own kindly heart was broken,
began to sing it a cradle song in a voice cracked and full of
tears.

At the time, deeply afraid for Ian's sanity, he had
been less concerned with what Ian had said than how he had
said it--only now, as he whipped Mary ever faster toward
Little Dunthorpe in spite of his own deepening pain, did the
words come back, haunting in light of Colter's tale: If she
looked more dead. If she looked more dead, old chap.

Nor was that all. Late that afternoon, as the first of
the village people had begun wending their way up Calthorpe
Hill to pay their respects to the grieving lord, Shinebone had
returned. He had looked tired, not very well himself; nor
was this surprising in a man who claimed to have shaken hands
with Wellington--the Iron Duke himself--when he (Shinebone,
not Wellington) had been a boy. Geoffrey thought the
Wellington story was probably an exaggeration, but Old Shinny,
as he and Ian had called him as boys, had seen Geoffrey through
all his childhood illnesses, and Shinny had seemed a very
old man to him, even then. Always granting the eye of childhood, which tends to see anyone over the age of twenty-five
as elderly, he thought Shinny must be all of seventy-five now.

He was old...he'd had a hectic, terrible last twenty-four
hours...and might not an old, tired man have made a mistake?

A terrible, unspeakable mistake?

It was this thought more than any other which had sent
him out on this cold and windy night, under a moon which
stuttered uncertainly between the clouds.

Could he have made such a mistake? Part of him, a
craven, cowardly part which would rather risk losing Misery
forever tha   look upon the inevitable results of such a
mistake, denied it. But when Shinny came in...

Geoffrey had been sitting by Ian, who was remembering
in a broken, scarcely coherent way how he and Ian had rescued
Misery from the palace dungeons of the mad French viscount

Leroux, how they had escaped in a wagonload of hay, and how
Misery distracted one of the viscount's guards at a critical
moment by slipping one gorgeously unclad leg out of the hay
and waving it delicately. Geoffrey had been chiming in his
own memories of the adventure, wholly in the grip of his grief
by then, and he cursed that grief now, because to him (and
to Ian as well, he supposed), Shinny had barely been there.

Hadn't Shinny seemed strangely distant, strangely preoccupied? Was it only weariness, or had it been something
else...some suspicion...?

No, surely not, his mind protested uneasily. The pony-
trap was flying up Calthorpe Hill. The manor house itself
was dark, but--ah, good!--there was still a single light on
in Mrs. Ramage's cottage.

"Hup, Mary!" he cried, and cracked the whip, wincing.
"Not much further, girl, and you can rest a bit!"

Surely, surely not what you're thinking!!

But Shinny's examination of Geoffrey's broken ribs and
sprained shoulder had seemed purely perfunctory, and he had
spoken barely a word to Ian, in spite of the man's deep grief
and frequent incoherent cries. No--after a visit which now
seemed no longer than the most minimal sort of social con-
vention would demand, Shinny had asked quietly: "Is she--?"

"Yes, in the parlor," Ian had managed. "My poor darling
lies in the parlor. Kiss her for me, Shinny, a d tell her
I'll be with her soon!"

Ian then had burst into tears again, and after muttering some half-heard word of condolence, Shinny had passed
into the parlor. It now seemed to Geoffrey that the old saw-
bones had been in there a rather long time...or perhaps that
was only faulty recollection. But when he came out he had
looked almost cheerful, and there was nothing faulty about
this recollection, Geoffrey felt sure--that expression was
too out of place in that room of grief and tears, a room
where Mrs. Ramage had already hung the black funerary curtains.

Geoffrey had followed the old doctor out and spoke hesitantly to him in the kitchen. He hoped, he said, that the
doctor would prescribe a sleeping powder for Ian, who really
did seem quite ill.

Shinny had seemed completely distracted, however. "It's
not a bit like Miss Evelyn-Hyde," he said. "I have satisfied
myself of that."

And he had returned to his caleche without so much
as a response to Geoffrey's question. Geoffrey went back
inside, already forgetting the doctor's odd remark, already
chalking Shinny's equally odd behavior off to age, weariness,
and his own sort of grief. His thoughts had turned to Ian
again, and he determined that, with no sleeping powder forth-
coming, he would simply have to pour whiskey down Ian's
throat until the poor fellow passed out.

Forgetting...dismissing.

Until now.

It's not a bit like Miss Evelyn-Hyde. I have satisfied myself of that.

Of what?

Geoffrey did not know, but he intended to find out, no matter what the cost to his sanity might be--and he recognized that the cost might be high.

CHAPTER 4

Mrs. Ramage was still up when Geoffrey began to hammer on the cottage door, although it was already two hours past her normal bedtime. Since Misery had passed away, Mrs. Ramage found herself putting her bedtime further and further back. If she could not put an end to her restless tossing and turning, she could at least postpone the moment at which she began it.

Although she was the most levelheaded and practical of women, the sudden outburst of knocking startled a little scream from her, and she scalded herself with the hot milk she had been pouring from pot to cup. Lately she seemed always on edge, always on the verge of a scream. It was not grief, this feeling, although she was nearly overwhelmed with grief--this was a strange, thundery feeling that she couldn't ever remember having before. It sometimes seemed to her that thoughts better left unrecognized were

circli g around her, just beyond the grasp of her weary,
bitterly sad mind.

"Who knocks at ten?" she cried at the door. "Whoever
it is, I thank ye not for the burn I've given m'self!"

"It's Geoffrey, Mrs. Ramage! Geoffrey Alliburton!
Open the door, for God's sake!"

Mrs. Ramage's mouth dropped open and she was halfway
to the door before she remembered she was in her nightgown
and cap. She had never heard Geoffrey sound so, and would
not have believed it if someone had told her of it. If
there was a man in all England with a heart stouter than
that of her beloved My Lord, then it was Geoffrey--yet his
voice trembled like the voice of a woman on the verge of
hysterics.

"A minute, Mr. Geoffrey! I'm half-unclad!"

"Devil take it!" Geoffrey cried. "I don't care if
you're starkers, Mrs. Ramage! Open this door! Open it in
the name of Jesus!"

She stood only a second, then went to the door, unbarred
it, and threw it open. Geoffrey's look did more than stun
her, and again she heard the dim thunder of black thoughts
somewhere back in her head.

Geoffrey stood on the threshold of the housekeeper's
cottage in an odd slanting posture, as if his spine had been
warped out of shape by long years carrying a peddler's sack.
His right hand was pressed between his left arm and left side.

His hair was in a tangle. His dark-brown eyes burned out of
his white face. His dress was remarkable for one as careful
--dandified, some would have said--about his clothing as
Geoffrey Alliburton usually was. He wore an old smoking
jacket with the belt askew, an open-throated white shirt, and
a pair of rough serge pants that would have looked more at
home upon the legs of a itinerant gardener than upon those
of the richest man in Little Dunthorpe. On his feet were a
pair of threadbare slippers.

　　Mrs. Ramage, hardly dressed for a court ball herself in
her long white nightgown and muskrat's-nightcap with the un-
tied curling ribbons hanging around her face like the fringe
on a lampshade, stared at him with mounting concern. He had
re-injured the ribs he had broken riding after the doctor
three nights ago, that was obvious, but it wasn't just pain
that made his eyes blaze from his whitened face like that.
It was terror, barely held in check.

　　"Mr. Geoffrey! What--"

　　"No questions!" he said hoarsely. "Not yet--not until
you answer one question of my own."

　　"What question?" She was badly frightened now, her left
hand clenched into a tight fist just above her munificent
bosom.

　　"Does the name Miss Evelyn-Hyde mean anything to you?"

　　And suddenly she knew the reason for that terrible
thundery feeling that had been inside her ever since

Saturday night. Some part of her mind must already have
had this gruesome thought and suppressed it, for she
needed no explanation at all. Only the name of the unfortunate Miss Charlotte Evelyn-Hyde, late of Storping-
on-Firkill, the village just to the west of Little Dunthorpe,
was sufficient to bring a scream tearing from her.

"Oh, my saints! Oh, my dear Jesus! Has she been
buried alive? Has she been buried alive? Has my darling
Misery been buried alive?"

And now, before Geoffrey could even begin to answer,
it was tough old Mrs. Ramage's turn to do something she
had never done before that night and would never do again:
she fainted dead away.

CHAPTER 5

Geoffrey had no time to look for smelling salts. He
doubted if such a tough old soldier as Mrs. Ramage kept
them around anyway. But beneath her sink he found a rag
which smelled faintly of ammonia. He did not just pass this
beneath her nose but pressed it briefly against her lower
face. The possibility Colter had raised, however faint, was
too hideous to merit much in the way of consideration.

She jerked, cried out, and opened her eyes. For a
moment she looked at him with dazed, uncomprehending bewilderment. Then she sat up.

"No," she said. "No, Mr. Geoffrey, say ye don't mean it,
say it isn't true--"

"I don't know if it's true or not," he said. "But we
must satisfy ourselves immediately. Immediately, Mrs. Ramage.
I can't do all the digging myself, if there's digging that
must be done..." She was staring at him with horrified eyes,
her hands pressed so tightly over her mouth that the nails
were white. "Can you help me, if help is needed? There's
really no one else."

"My Lord," she said numbly. "My Lord Mr. Ian--"

"--must know nothing of this until we know more!" he
said. "If God is good, he need never know at all." He
would not voice to her the unspoken hope at the back of his
mind, a hope which seemed to him almost as monstrous as his
fears. If God was very good, he would find out about this
night's work...when his wife and only love was restored to
him, her return from the dead almost as miraculous as that of
Lazarus.

"Oh, this is terrible...terrible!" she said in a faint,
fluttery voice. Holding onto the table, she managed to
pull herself to her feet. She stood, swaying, little strag-
gles of hair hanging around her face among the muskrat-
tails of her cap.

"Are you well enough?" he asked, more kindly. "If not,
then I must try to carry on as best I can by myself."

She drew a deep, shuddering breath and let it out. The

side-to-side sway stopped. She turned and walked toward the
pantry. "There's a pair of spades in the shed out back," she
said. "A pick as well, I think. Throw them in your trap.
There's half a bottle of gin out here in the pantry. Been
here untouched since Bill died five years ago, on Lammas-
night. I'll have a bit and then join you, Mr. Geoffrey."

"You're a brave woman, Mrs. Ramage. Be quick."

"Aye, never fear me," she said, and grasped the bottle
of gin with a hand that trembled only slightly. There was
no dust on the bottle--not even the pantry was safe from the
relentless dust-clout of Mrs. Ramage--but the label reading
CLOUGH & POOR BOOZIERS was yellow. "Be quick yourself."

She had always hated spirits and her stomach wanted to
sick the gin, with its nasty junipery smell and oily taste,
back up. She made it stay down. Tonight she would need it.

CHAPTER 6

Under clouds that still raced east to west, blacker
shapes against a black sky, and a moon that was now settling
toward the horizon, the pony-trap sped toward the churchyard.
It was now Mrs. Ramage who drove, cracking the whip over the
bewildered Mary, who would have told them, if horses could
talk, that this was all wrong--she was supposed to be dozing
in her warm stall come this time of night. The spades and
the pick chattered coldly one against the other, and Mrs.

Ramage thought they would have given anyone who had seen them
a proper fright--they must look like a pair of Mr. Dickens's
resurrection men... or perhaps one resurrection man sitting in
a pony-trap driven by a ghost. For she was all in white--
had not even paused long enough to gather up her robe. Her
nightgown fluttered around her stout, vein-puffed ankles, and
the tails of her cap streamed wildly out behind her.

     Here was the church. She turned Mary up the lane
which ran beside it, shivering at the ghostly sound of the
wind playing along the eaves. She had a moment to wonder
why such a holy place as a church should seem so frightening
after dark, and then realized it was not the church...it
was the errand.

     Her first thought upon coming out of her faint was
that My Lord must help them--hadn't he been there in all
things, through thick and thin, never wavering? A moment
later she had realized how mad the idea was. This was not
a matter of My Lord's courage, but of his very sanity.

     She hadn't needed Mr. Geoffrey to tell her so; the
memory of Miss Evelyn-Hyde had done that.

     She realized that neither Mr. Geoffrey nor My Lord had
been in Little Dunthorpe when it had happened. This had
been almost half a year ago, in the spring. Misery had entered the rosy summer of her pregnancy, morning sickness
behind her, the final rising of her belly and its attendant
discomfort still ahead, and she had cheerfully sent the two
men off for a week of grouse-shooting and card-playing and

footballing and heaven alone knew what other masculine foolishness at Oak Hall in Doncaster. My Lord had been a bit
doubtful, but Misery assured him she would be fine, and
nearly pushed him out the door. That Misery would be fine
Mrs. Ramage had no doubt. But whenever My Lord and Mr.
Geoffrey left for Doncaster, she wondered if one of them--or
perhaps both--might not return on the back of a cart, toes up.

　　　Oak Hall was the inheritance of Albert Fossington, a
schoolmate of Geoffrey's and Ian's. Mrs. Ramage quite right-
ly believed that Bertie Fossington was mad. Some three years
ago he had eaten his favorite polo pony after it had broken
two legs and needed to be destroyed. It was a gesture of
affection, he said. "Learned it from the fuzzy-wuzzies in
Capetown," he said. "Griquas. Wonderful chaps. Put sticks
and things in their smoochers, what? Some of 'em look like
they could carry all twelve volumes of the Royal Navigation
Charts on their lower lips, ha-ha! Taught me that each man
must eat the thing he loves. Rather poetic in a grisly sort
of way, what?"

　　　In spite of such bizarre behavior, Mr. Geoffrey and My
Lord retained a great affection for Bertie (I wonder if
that means they'll have to eat him when he's dead? Mrs.
Ramage had once wondered after a visit from Bertie during
which he had tried to play croquet with one of the housecats,
quite shattering its poor little head), and they had spent
nearly ten days at Oak Hall this past spring.

　　　Not more than a day or two after they left, Miss Char-

lotte Evelyn-Hyde of Storping-on-Firkill had been found dead
on the back lawn of her home, Cove o' Birches. There had been
a freshly picked bunch of flowers near one outstretched hand.
The village doctor was a man named Billford--a capable man by
all accounts. Nevertheless, he had called old Dr. Shinebone
in to consult. Billford had diagnosed the fatal malady as a
heart attack, although the girl was very young--only eighteen
--and had seemed in the pink of health. Billford was puzzled.

Something seemed not at all right. Old Shinny had been
clearly puzzled as well, but in the end he had concurred with
the diagnosis. So did most of the village, for that matter--
the girl's heart had not been properly made, that was all,
such things were rare but everyone could recall such a sad
case at one time or another. It was probably this universal
concurrence that had saved Billford's practice--if not his
head--following the ghastly denouement. Although everyone
had agreed that the girl's death was puzzling, it had crossed
no one's mind that she might not be dead at all.

Four days following the interment, an elderly woman
named Mrs. Soames--Mrs. Ramage knew her slightly--had observed something white lying on the ground of the Congregation-
al church's cemetery as she entered it to put flowers on the
grave of her husband, who had died the previous winter. It
was much too big to be a flower petal, and she thought it
might be a dead bird of some sort. As she approached she became more and more sure that the white object was not just

lyi g on the ground, but protruding from it. She came two or
three hesitant steps closer yet, and observed a hand reaching
from the earth of a fresh grave, the fingers frozen in a
hideous gesture of supplication. Blood-streaked bones protruded from the ends of all the digits save the thumb.

Mrs. Soames ran shrieking from the cemetery, ran all
the way into Storping's high street--a run of nearly a mile
and a quarter--and reported her news to the barber, who was
also the local constable. Then she had collapsed in a dead
faint. She took to her bed later that afternoon and did not
arise from it for nearly a month. Nor did anyone in the village blame her in the least.

The body of the unfortunate Miss Evelyn-Hyde had been
exhumed, of course, and as Geoffrey Alliburton drew Mary to
a halt in front of the gate leading into Little Dunthorpe's
C of E churchyard, Mrs. Ramage found herself wishing fervently that she had not listened to the tales of the exhumation.
They had been dreadful.

Dr. Billford, shaken to within an inch of sanity himself, diagnosed catalepsy. The poor woman had apparently
fallen into some sort of deathlike trance, much like the
sort those Indian fakirs could voluntarily induce in themselves before allowing themselves to be buried alive or to
have needles passed through their flesh. She had remained in
this trance for perhaps forty-eight hours, perhaps sixty.
Long enough, at any rate, to have awakened not to find her-

self on her back lawn where she had been picki g flowers, but
buried alive in her own coffin.

She had fought grimly for her life, that girl, and Mrs.
Ramage found now, following Geoffrey through the gates and
into a thin mist that turned the leaning grave markers into
islands, that what should have redeemed with nobility only
made it seem all the more horrid.

The girl had been engaged to be married. In her left
hand-- n ot the one frozen above the soil like the hand of a
drowned woman--had been her diamond engagement ring. With it
she had slit the satin lining of her coffin and over God knew
how many hours she had used it to claw away at the coffin's
wooden lid. In the end, air running out, she had apparently
used the ring with her left hand to cut and excavate and her
right hand to dig. It had not been quite enough. Her complexion had been a deep purple from which her blood-rimmed
eyes stared in a bulging expression of terminal horror.

The clock in the church tower began to chime the hour
of twelve--the hour when, her mother had told her, the door
between life and death sways open a bit and the dead may
pass both ways--and it was all Mrs. Ramage could do to keep
herself from shrieking and fleeing in a panic which would
not abate but grow stronger with each step; if she began
running, she knew, she would simply run until she fell down
insensible.

Stupid, fearful woman! she berated herself, and then
amended that to: Stupid, fearful, selfish woman! It's My

Lord ye want to be thinkin' of now, and not yer own fears!
My Lord...and if there is even one chance that My Lady--

Ah, but no--it was madness to even think of such a
thing. It had been too long, too long, too long.

Geoffrey had led her to Misery's tombstone, and the
two of them stood looking down at it, as if mesmerized.
LADY CALTHORPE, the stone read. Other than the dates of
her birth and death, the only inscription was: LOVED BY
MANY.

She looked at Geoffrey and said, like one awakening from
a deep daze: "Ye've not brought the tools."

"N o--not yet," he responded, and threw himself full-
length on the ground and placed his ear against the earth,
which had already begun to show the first tender shoots of
new grass between the rather carelessly replaced sods.

For a moment the only expression she saw there by the
lamp she carried was the one Geoffrey had worn since she had
first opened her door to him--a look of agonized dread. Then
a new expression began to surface. This new expression was
one of utter horror mingled with an almost demented hope.

He looked up at Mrs. Ramage, eyes staring, mouth working.
"I believe she lives," he whispered strengthlessly. "Oh, Mrs.
Ramage--"

Suddenly he turned over onto his belly and screamed at
the ground--under other circumstances it would have been
comic. "Misery! MISERY! WE'RE HERE! WE KNOW! HOLD ON!
HOLD ON, MY DARLING!"

He was on his feet a moment later, sprinting back toward the pony-trap, where the digging tools were, his slippered feet sending the placid groundmist into excited little roils.

Mrs. Ramage's knees unlocked and she buckled forward, near to swooning again. Of its own accord, seemingly, her head slipped to one side so her right ear was pressed against the ground--she had seen children in similar postures by the railway line, listening for trains.

And she heard it--low, painful scraping sounds in the earth--not the sounds of a burrowing animal, these; these were the sounds of fingers scraping helplessly on wood.

She drew in breath in one great convulsive gulp, re-starting her own heart, it seemed. She shrieked: "WE'RE COMING, MY LADY! PRAISE GOD AND PLEAD SWEET JESUS WE BE IN TIME--WE'RE COMING!"

She began to pull half-healed turves out of the ground with her trembling fingers, and although Geoffrey returned in almost no time, she had by then already clawed a hole some eight inches deep.

7

He was already nine pages into Chapter 7—Geoffrey and Mrs. Ramage had managed to get Misery out of her grave in the barest nick of time only to realize that the woman had no idea at all who they were, or who she herself was—when Annie came into the room. This time Paul heard her. He stopped typing, sorry to be out of the dream.

She held the first six chapters at the side of her skirt. It had taken her less than twenty minutes to read his first stab at it; it had been an hour since she had taken this sheaf of twenty-one pages. He looked at her steadily, observing with faint interest that Annie Wilkes was a bit pale.

"Well?" he asked. "Is it fair?"

"Yes," she said absently, as if this was a foregone conclusion— and Paul supposed it was. "It's fair. And it's *good*. Exciting. But it's gruesome, too! It's not like *any* of the other *Misery* books. That poor woman who scraped the ends of her fingers off—" She shook her head and repeated: "It's not like any of the other *Misery* books."

The man who wrote these pages was in a rather gruesome frame of mind, my dear, Paul thought.

"Shall I go on?" he asked.

"I'll kill you if you don't!" she responded, smiling a little. Paul didn't smile back. This comment, which would once have struck him as in a league with such banalities as *You look so good I could just eat you up* now seemed not banal at all.

Yet something in her attitude as she stood in the doorway fascinated him. It was as if she was a little frightened to come any closer—as if she thought something in him might burn her. It wasn't the subject of premature burial that had done it, and he was wise enough to know it. No—it was the difference between his first try and this one. That first one had had all the life of an eighth-grader's "How I Spent My Summer Vacation" theme. This one was different. The furnace was on. Oh, not that he had written particularly well— the story was hot, but the characters as stereotyped and predictable as ever—but this time he had been able to at least generate some power; this time there was heat baking out from between the lines.

Amused, he thought: *She felt the heat. I think she's afraid to get too close in case I might burn her.*

"Well," he said mildly, "you won't have to kill me, Annie. I *want* to go on. So why don't I get at it?"

"All right," she said. She brought the pages to him, put them on the board, and then stepped back quickly.

"Would you like to read it as I go along?" he asked.

Annie smiled. "Yes! It would be almost like the chapter-plays, when I was a kid!"

"Well, I can't promise a cliff-hanger at the end of *every* chapter,"
he said. "It just doesn't work that way."

"It will for me," she said fervently. "I'd want to know what was
going to happen in Chapter 18 even if 17 ended with Misery and
Ian and Geoffrey sitting in armchairs on the porch, reading newspapers. I'm already wild to know what's going to happen next—
don't tell me!" she added sharply, as if Paul had offered to do this.

"Well, I generally don't show my work until it's all done," he
said, and then smiled at her. "But since this is a special situation,
I'll be happy to let you read it chapter by chapter." *And so began
the thousand and one nights of Paul Sheldon,* he thought. "But I
wonder if you'd do something for me?"

"What?"

"Fill in these damned n's," he said.

She smiled at him radiantly. "It would be an honor. I'll leave you
alone now."

She went back to the door, hesitated there, and turned back.
Then, with a deep and almost painful timidity, she offered the only
editorial suggestion she ever made to him. "Maybe it was a bee."

He had already dropped his gaze to the sheet of paper in the
typewriter; he was looking for the hole. He wanted to get Misery
back to Mrs. Ramage's cottage before he knocked off, and he looked
back up at Annie with carefully disguised impatience. "I beg pardon?"

"A bee," she said, and he saw a blush creeping up her neck and
over her cheeks. Soon even her ears were glowing. "One person
in every dozen is allergic to bee-venom. I saw lots of cases of it
before . . . before I retired from service as an R.N. The allergy can
show in lots of different ways. Sometimes a sting can cause a coma-
tose condition which is . . . is similar to what people used to
call . . . uh . . . catalepsy."

Now she was so red she was almost purple.

Paul held the idea up briefly in his mind and then tossed it on
the scrap-heap. A bee could have been the cause of Miss Evelyn-
Hyde's unfortunate live burial; it even made sense, since it had
happened in mid-spring; in the garden, to boot. But he had already
decided that credibility depended on the two live burials' being
related somehow, and Misery had succumbed in her bedroom. The
fact that late fall was hardly bee-season was not really the problem.
The problem was the rarity of the cataleptic reaction. He thought

Constant Reader would not swallow two unrelated women in neighboring townships being buried alive six months apart as a result of bee-stings.

Yet he could not tell Annie that, and not just because it might rile her up. He could not tell her because it would hurt her badly, and in spite of all the pain she had afforded him, he found he could not hurt her in that way. He had been hurt that way himself.

He fell back on that most common writers'-workshop euphemism: "It's got possibilities, all right. I'll drop it into the hopper, Annie, but I've already got some ideas in mind. It may not fit."

"Oh, I know that—you're the writer, not me. Just forget I said anything. I'm sorry."

"Don't be s—"

But she was gone, her heavy tread almost running down the hallway to the parlor. He was looking at an empty space. His eyes dropped—then widened.

On either side of the doorway, about eight inches up from the floor, was a black mark—they had been left, he understood at once, by the hubs of the wheelchair when he forced it through. So far she hadn't noticed them. It had been almost a week, and her failure to notice was a small miracle. But soon—tomorrow, perhaps even this afternoon—she would be in to vacuum, and then she would.

She would.

Paul managed very little during the rest of the day.

The hole in the paper had disappeared.

8

The following morning Paul was sitting up in bed, propped on a pile of pillows, drinking a cup of coffee, and eyeing those marks on the sides of the door with the guilty eye of a murderer who has just seen some bloody item of clothing of which he somehow neglected to dispose. Suddenly Annie came rushing into the room, her eyes wide and bulging. She held a dustcloth in one hand. In the other, incredibly, she held a pair of handcuffs.

"What—"

It was all he had time for. She seized him with panicky strength and pulled him into an upright sitting position. Pain—the worst in days—bellowed through his legs, and he screamed. The coffee cup flew out of his hand and shattered on the floor. *Things keep breaking in here,* he thought, and then: *She saw the marks. Of course. Probably a long time ago.* That was the only way he could account for this bizarre behavior—she had seen the marks after all, and this was the beginning of some new and spectacular punishment.

"Shut up, stupid," she hissed, and then his hands were pinned behind him, and just as he heard the click of the handcuffs, he also heard a car turning into the driveway.

He opened his mouth, meaning to speak or perhaps scream again, and she stuffed the rag into it before he could do either. There was some ghastly dead taste on the rag. Pledge, he supposed, or Endust, or something like that.

"Make no sound," she said, leaning over him with one hand on either side of his head, strands of her hair tickling his cheeks and forehead. "I warn you, Paul. If whoever that is hears something— or even if *I* hear something and *think* he might have heard something—I will kill him, or them, then you, then myself."

She stood up. Her eyes were bulging. There was sweat on her face and dried egg-yolk on her lips.

"Remember, Paul."

He was nodding but she didn't see. She was already running out.

An old but well-preserved Chevy Bel Air had pulled up behind Annie's Cherokee. Paul heard a door open somewhere off the parlor and then bang shut. It gave off the oddly interrogative squeak that told him it was the closet where she kept her outdoors stuff.

The man getting out of the car was as old and well preserved as the car itself—a Colorado Type if ever Paul had seen one. He looked sixty-five but might be eighty; he might be the senior partner of a law firm or the semi-retired patriarch of a construction company, but was more likely a rancher or a realtor. He would be a Republican of the sort who would no more put a bumper sticker on his car than he would put a pair of pointy-toed Italian shoes on his feet; he must also be some sort of town official, and here on town business, because it was only on town business that a man like this and a reclusive woman like Annie Wilkes would have occasion to meet.

Paul watched her hasten down the walk to the driveway, intent not on meeting but intercepting him. Here was something much like his earlier fantasy come true. Not a cop but someone IN AU-

THORITY. AUTHORITY had arrived at Annie's, and its arrival here could do nothing but shorten his own life.

Why not invite him in, Annie? he thought, trying not to choke on the dusty rag. *Why not invite him in and show him your African bird?*

Oh, no. She would no more invite Mr. Rocky Mountain Businessman in than she would drive Paul to Stapleton International and put a first-class ticket back to New York in his hand.

She was talking even before she reached him, the breath pluming out of her mouth in shapes like cartoon balloons with no words written inside them. He held out a hand dressed in a narrowly elegant black leather glove. She looked at it briefly, contemptuously, then began to shake a finger in his face, more of those empty white balloons puffing from her mouth. She finished struggling into her coat and stopped shaking her finger long enough to rake the zipper up.

He reached into the pocket of his topcoat and brought out a sheet of paper. He held it out to her almost apologetically. Although Paul had no way of knowing exactly what it was, he was sure that Annie had an adjective for it. *Cockadoodie,* maybe.

She led him along the driveway, still talking. They passed beyond his sightline. He could see their shadows lying like construction-paper cutouts on the snow, but that was all. She had done it on purpose, he realized dully. If he, Paul, couldn't see them, then there was no chance that Mr. Rancho Grande might look in through the guest-room window and see *him.*

The shadows remained on the melting snowpack of Annie's driveway for about five minutes. Once Paul actually heard Annie's voice, raised in an angry, hectoring shout. Those were a long five minutes for Paul. His shoulders ached. He found he couldn't move to ease the ache. After cuffing his hands together, she had somehow bound them to the bedstead.

But the dustcloth in his mouth was the worst. The stink of the furniture polish was making his head ache, and he was growing steadily more nauseated. He concentrated grimly on controlling it; he had no interest in choking to death, his windpipe full of vomit, while Annie argued with an elderly town official who got his hair trimmed once a week at the local tonsorial emporium and probably wore rubbers over his black oxfords all winter long.

Cold sick-sweat had broken on his forehead by the time they

reappeared. Now Annie was holding the paper. She followed Mr. Rancho Grande, shaking her finger at his back, those empty cartoon balloons issuing from her mouth. Mr. Rancho Grande would not look around at her. His face was carefully blank. Only his lips, pressed together so tightly that they almost disappeared, gave away some inward emotion. Anger? Perhaps. Distaste? Yes. That was probably closer.

You think she's crazy. You and all your poker cronies—who probably control this whole minor-league ballpark of a town—probably played a hand of Lowball or something to see who got this shit detail. No one likes to bring bad news to crazy people. But oh, Mr. Rancho Grande! If you knew just how crazy she really is, I don't think you'd turn your back on her like that!

He got into the Bel Air. He closed the door. Now she stood beside the car, shaking her finger at his closed window, and again Paul could dimly hear her voice: "—think you are so-so-so *smaa-aart!*"

The Bel Air began to back slowly down the driveway. Mr. Rancho Grande was ostentatiously not looking at Annie, whose teeth were bared.

Louder still: *"You think you are such a great big wheel!"*

Suddenly she kicked the front bumper of Mr. Rancho Grande's car, kicked it hard enough to knock packed chunks of snow out of the wheel-wells. The old guy had been looking over his right shoulder, guiding the car down the driveway. Now he looked back at her, startled out of the careful neutrality he had maintained all through his visit.

"Well I'll tell you something, you dirty bird! *LITTLE DOGS GO TO THE BATHROOM ALL OVER BIG WHEELS! What do you think of that? Hah?"*

Whatever he thought of it, Mr. Rancho Grande was not going to give Annie the satisfaction of seeing it—that neutral expression dropped over his face again like the visor on a suit of armor. He backed out of Paul's sight.

She stood there for a moment, hands fisted on hips, then stalked back toward the house. He heard the kitchen door open and explode shut.

Well, he's gone, Paul thought. *Mr. Rancho Grande is gone but I'm here. Oh yes, I'm here.*

9

But this time she didn't take her anger out on him.

She came into his room, her coat still on but now unzipped. She began to pace rapidly back and forth, not even looking his way. The piece of paper was still in her hand, and every now and then she would shake it in front of her own nose as if in self-chastisement.

"Ten-percent tax increase, he says! In arrears, he says! Liens! Lawyers! Quarterly payment, he says! Overdue! *Cockadoodie! Kaka! Kaka-poopie-DOOPIE!*"

He grunted into the rag, but she didn't look around. She was in a room by herself. She walked back and forth faster, cutting the air with her solid body. He kept thinking she would tear the paper to shreds, but it seemed she did not quite dare do this.

"Five hundred and six dollars!" she cried, this time brandishing the paper in front of his nose. She absently tore the rag that was choking him out of his mouth and threw it on the floor. He hung his head over to one side, dry-heaving. His arms felt as if they were slowly detaching themselves from their sockets. "Five hundred and six dollars *and seventeen cents!* They *know* I don't want anyone out here! I told them, didn't I? And look! *Look!*"

He dry-heaved again, making a desperate burping sound.

"If you vomit I guess you'll just have to lie in it. Looks like I've got other fish to fry. He said something about a lien on my house. What's that?"

"Handcuffs . . ." he croaked.

"Yes, yes," she said impatiently. "Sometimes you're such a *baby.*" She pulled the key from her skirt pocket and pushed him even farther to the left, so that his nose pressed the sheets. He screamed, but she ignored him. There was a click, a rattle, and then his hands were free. He sat up, gasping, then slid slowly down against his pillows, mindful to push his legs straight ahead as he did. There were pale furrows in his thin wrists. As he watched they began to fill in red.

Annie stuffed the cuffs absently into her skirt pocket, as if police restraints were found in most decent houses, like Kleenex or coat-hangers.

"What's a lien?" she asked again. "Does that mean they own my house? Is that what it means?"

"No," he said. "It means that you . . . ." He cleared his throat and got another after-taste of that fumey dust-rag. His chest hitched as he dry-heaved again. She took no notice of that; simply stood impatiently staring at him until he could talk. After awhile he could. "Just means you can't sell it."

"Just? *Just?* You got a funny idea of *just*, Mr. Paul Sheldon. But I suppose the troubles of a poor widow like me don't seem very important to a rich Mister Smart Guy like you."

"On the contrary. I think of your troubles as *my* troubles, Annie. I just meant that a lien isn't much compared to what they *could* do if you got seriously in arrears. *Are* you?"

"Arrears. That means in the bucket, doesn't it?"

"In the bucket, in the hole, behind. Yes."

"I'm no shanty-Irish moocher!" He saw the thin sheen of her teeth as her upper lip lifted. "I pay my bills. I just . . . this time I just . . ."

You forgot, didn't you? You forgot, just the way you keep forgetting to change February on that damned calendar. Forgetting to make the quarterly property-tax payment is a hell of a lot more serious than forgetting to change the calendar page, and you're upset because this is the first time you forgot something that big. Fact is, you're getting worse, Annie, aren't you? A little worse every day. Psychotics can cope in the world—after a fashion—and sometimes, as I think you well know, they get away with some very nasty shit. But there's a borderline between the lands of manageable and unmanageable psychosis. You're getting closer to that line every day . . . and part of you knows it.

"I just hadn't got around to it yet," Annie said sullenly. "Having you here has kept me busier than a one-armed paperhanger."

An idea occurred to him—a really fine one. The potential for brownie-points in this idea seemed almost unlimited. "I know," he said with quiet sincerity. "I owe you my life and I haven't been anything but a pain in the tail to you. I've got about four hundred bucks in my wallet. I want you to pay your arrears with it."

"Oh, Paul—" She was looking at him, both confused and pleased. "I couldn't take *your* money—"

"It's not mine," he said. He grinned at her, his number-one *Who loves ya, baby?* grin. And inside he thought: *What I want, Annie, is for you to do one of your forgetting acts when I've got access to one of your knives and I'm sure I can move well enough to use it. You'll be frying in hell ten seconds before you know you're dead.* "It's yours. Call it a down-payment, if you want." He paused, then took a calculated risk: "If you don't think I know I'd be dead if it wasn't for you, you're crazy."

"Paul . . . I don't know. . . ."

"I'm serious." He allowed his smile to melt into an expression of winning (or so he hoped—*please, God, let it be winning*) sincerity. "You did more than save *my* life, you know. You saved two lives— because without you, Misery would still be lying in her grave."

Now she was looking at him shiningly, the paper in her hand forgotten.

"And you showed me the error of my ways, got me back on track again. I owe you a lot more than four hundred bucks just for that. And if you don't take that money, you're going to make me feel bad."

"Well, I . . . all right. I . . . thank you."

"I should be thanking *you*. May I see that paper?"

She gave it to him with no protest at all. It was an overdue tax notice. The lien was little more than a formality. He scanned it quickly, then handed it back.

"Have you got money in the bank?"

Her eyes shifted away from his. "I've got a little put aside, but not in the bank. I don't believe in banks."

"This says they can't *execute* the lien on you unless the bill remains unpaid by March 25th. What's today?"

She frowned at the calendar. "Goodness! That's wrong."

She untacked it, and the boy on his sled disappeared—Paul watched this happen with an absurd pang of regret. March showed a white-water stream rushing pell-mell between snowy banks.

She peered myopically at the calendar for a moment and then said: "*Today* is March 25th."

Christ, so late, so late, he thought.

"Sure—that's why he came out." *He wasn't telling you they had slapped a lien on your house, Annie—he was telling you they would have to if you didn't cough up by the time the town offices closed tonight. Guy was actually trying to do you a favor.* "But if you pay this five hundred and six dollars before—"

"And seventeen cents," she put in fiercely. "Don't forget the cockadoodie seventeen cents."

"All right, and seventeen cents. If you pay it before they close the town offices this afternoon, no lien. If people in town really feel about you the way you say they do, Annie—"

"They hate me! They are all against me, Paul!"

"—then your taxes are one of the ways they'll try to pry you out. Hollering 'lien' at someone who has missed one quarterly property-tax payment is pretty weird. It smells. Well—it stinks. If you missed a couple of quarterly payments, they might try to take your home—sell it at auction. It's a crazy idea, but I guess they'd technically be within their rights."

She laughed, a harsh, barking sound. "Let them try! I'd guthole a few of them! I'll tell you that much. Yes, sir! Yessiree *Bob!*"

"In the end they'd guthole *you*," he said quietly. "But that isn't the point."

"Then what *is?*"

"Annie, there are probably people in Sidewinder who are two and three *years* behind on their taxes. No one is taking *their* homes or auctioning *their* furnishings down at the town hall. The worst that happens to people like that most of the time is that they lose their town water. The Roydmans, now." He looked at her shrewdly. "You think *they* pay their taxes on time?"

"*That* white trash?" she nearly shrieked. *"Hah!"*

"I think they are on the prod for you, Annie." He did in fact believe this.

"I'll never go! I'll stay up here just to spite them! I'll stay up here and spit in their eye!"

"Can you come up with a hundred and six bucks to go with the four hundred in my wallet?"

"Yes." She was beginning to look cautiously relieved.

"Good enough," he said. "Then I suggest you pay their crappy tax-bill today." *And while you're gone, I'll see what I can do about those damned marks on the door. And when that's done, I believe I'll see if I can do anything about getting the fuck out of here, Annie. I'm a little tired of your hospitality.*

He managed to smile.

"I think there must be at least seventeen cents there in the night-table," he said.

10

Annie Wilkes had her own interior set of rules; in her way she was strangely prim. She had made him drink water from a floor-bucket;

had withheld his medication until he was in agony; had made him burn the only copy of his new novel; had handcuffed him and stuck a rag reeking of furniture polish in his mouth; but she would not take the money from his wallet. She brought it to him, the old scuffed Lord Buxton he'd had since college, and put it in his hands.

All the ID had vanished. At *that* she had not scrupled. He did not ask her about it. It seemed wiser not to.

The ID was gone but the money was still there, the bills—mostly fifties—crisp and fresh. With a clarity that was both surprising and somehow ominous he saw himself pulling the Camaro up to the drive-in window of the Boulder Bank the day before he had finished *Fast Cars* and dropping his check for four hundred and fifty dollars, made out to cash and endorsed on the back, into the tray (perhaps even then the guys in the sweatshops had been talking vacation?— he thought it likely). The man who had done that had been free and healthy and feeling good, and had been without the wit to appreciate any of those fine things. The man who had done that had eyed the drive-up teller with a lively, interested eye—tall, blonde, wearing a purple dress that had cupped her curves with a lover's touch. And she had eyed him back. . . . What would she think, he wondered, of that man as he looked now, forty pounds lighter and ten years older, his legs a pair of crooked useless horrors?

"Paul?"

He looked up at her, holding the money in one hand. There was four hundred and twenty, in all.

"Yes?"

She was looking at him with that disconcerting expression of maternal love and tenderness—disconcerting because of the total solid blackness underlying it.

"Are you crying, Paul?"

He brushed his cheek with his free hand and, yes, there was moisture there. He smiled and handed her the money. "A little. I was thinking how good you've been to me. Oh, I suppose a lot of people wouldn't understand . . . but I think I know."

Her own eyes glistened as she leaned forward and gently touched his lips. He smelled something on her breath, something from the dark and sour chambers inside her, something that smelled like dead fish. It was a thousand times worse than the taste/smell of the dust-rag. It brought back the memory of her sour breath

(*!breathe goddammit BREATHE!*)

blowing down his throat like a dirty wind from hell. His stomach clenched, but he smiled at her.

"I love you, dear," she said.

"Would you put me in my chair before you go? I want to write."

"Of course." She hugged him. "Of course, my dear."

11

Her tenderness did not extend to leaving the bedroom door unlocked, but this presented no problem. He was not half-mad with pain and withdrawal symptoms this time. He had collected four of her bobby-pins as assiduously as a squirrel collects nuts for the winter, and had secreted them under his mattress along with the pills.

When he was sure she was really gone and not hanging around to see if he was going to "get up to didoes" (another Wilkesism for his growing lexicon), he rolled the wheelchair over to the bed and got the pins, along with the pitcher of water and the box of Kleenex from the night-table. Rolling the wheelchair with the Royal perched on the board in front of him was not very difficult—his arms had gotten a lot stronger. Annie Wilkes might be surprised to know just *how* strong they were now—and he sincerely hoped that someday soon she would be.

The Royal typewriter made a shitty writing machine, but as an exercise tool it was great. He had begun lifting it and setting it down whenever he was penned in the chair behind it and she was out of the room. Five lifts of six inches or so had been the best he could manage at first. Now he could do eighteen or twenty without a pause. Not bad when you considered the bastard weighed at least fifty pounds.

He worked on the lock with one of the bobby-pins, holding two spares in his mouth like a seamstress hemming a dress. He thought that the piece of bobby-pin still somewhere inside the lock might screw him up, but it didn't. He caught the rocker almost at once and pushed it up, drawing the lock's tongue along with it. He had just a moment to wonder if she might not have put a bolt on the outside of the door as well—he had tried very hard to seem weaker and sicker than he now really felt, but the suspicions of the true paranoiac spread wide and ran deep. Then the door was open.

He felt the same nervous guilt, the urge to do this *fast*. Ears attuned for the sound of Old Bessie returning—although she had only been gone for forty-five minutes—he pulled a bunch of the Kleenex, dipped the wad in the pitcher, and bent awkwardly over to one side with the soppy mass in his hand. Gritting his teeth and ignoring the pain, he began to rub at the mark on the right-hand side of the door.

To his intense relief, it began to fade almost at once. The hubs of the wheelchair had not actually scored through the paint, as he had feared, but only scuffed it.

He reversed away from the door, turned the chair, and backed up so he could work on the other mark. When he had done all he could, he reversed again and looked at the door, trying to see it through Annie's exquisitely suspicious eyes. The marks were there—but faint, almost unnoticeable. He thought he would be okay.

He *hoped* he would be okay.

"Tornado cellars," he said, licked his lips, and laughed dryly. "What the fuck, friends and neighbors."

He rolled back to the door and looked out at the corridor—but now that the marks were gone he felt no urge to go farther or dare more today. Another day, yes. He would know that day when it came around.

What he wanted to do now was to write.

He closed the door, and the click of the lock seemed very loud. *Africa.*

That bird came from Africa.

But you mustn't cry for that bird, Paulie, because after awhile it forgot about how the veldt smelled at noonday, and the sounds of the wildebeests at the waterhole, and the high acidic smell of the ieka-ieka *trees in the great clearing north of the Big Road. After awhile it forgot the cerise color of the sun dying behind Kilimanjaro. After awhile it only knew the muddy, smogged-out sunsets of Boston, that was all it remembered and all it* wanted *to remember. After awhile it didn't want to go back anymore, and if someone* took *it back and set it free it would only crouch in one place, afraid and hurting and homesick in two unknown and terribly ineluctable directions, until something came along and killed it.*

"Oh, Africa, oh, shit," he said in a trembling voice.

Crying a little, he rolled the wheelchair over to his wastebasket and buried the wet wads of Kleenex under the wastepaper. He repositioned the wheelchair by the window and rolled a piece of paper into the Royal.

And by the way, Paulie, is the bumper of your car sticking out of the snow yet? Is it sticking out, twinkling cheerily in the sun, just waiting for someone to come along and see it while you sit here wasting what may be your last chance?

He looked doubtfully at the blank sheet of paper in the typewriter.

I won't be able to write now anyway. That spoiled it.

But nothing had ever spoiled it, somehow. It *could* be spoiled, he knew that, but in spite of the reputed fragility of the creative act, it had always been the single toughest thing, the most abiding thing, in his life—nothing had ever been able to pollute that crazy well of dreams: no drink, no drug, no pain. He fled to that well now, like a thirsty animal finding a waterhole at dusk, and he drank from it; which is to say he found the hole in the paper and fell thankfully through it. By the time Annie got back home at quarter of six, he had done almost five pages.

12

During the next three weeks, Paul Sheldon felt surrounded by a queer electric peacefulness. His mouth was always dry. Sounds seemed too loud. There were days when he felt he could bend spoons simply by looking at them. Other days he felt like weeping hysterically.

Outside this, separate of the atmosphere and apart from the deep, maddening itch of his healing legs, its own serene thing, the work continued. The stack of pages to the right of the Royal grew steadily taller. Before this strange experience, he had considered four pages a day to be his optimum output (on *Fast Cars* it had usually been three—and only two on many days—before the final finishing sprint). But during this electric three-week period, which came to an end with the rainstorm of April 15th, Paul averaged *twelve pages a day*— seven in the morning, five more in an evening session. If anyone in his previous life (for so he had come to think of it, without even realizing it) had suggested he could work at such a pace, Paul would have laughed. When the rain began to fall, he had two hundred and sixty-seven pages of *Misery's Return*—first-draft stuff, sure, but he had scanned through it and thought it amazingly clean for a first.

Part of the reason was that he was living an amazingly straight life. No long, muddled nights spent bar-hopping, followed by long, muddled days spent drinking coffee and orange juice and gobbling vitamin-B tablets (days when if his glance so much as happened upon his typewriter, he would turn away, shuddering). No more waking up next to a big blonde or redhead he had picked up somewhere the night before—a lass who usually looked like a queen at midnight and a goblin at ten the next morning. No more cigarettes. He had once asked for them in a timid and tentative voice, and she had given him a look of such utter darkness that he had told her at once to forget it. He was Mr. Clean. No bad habits (except for his codeine jones, of course, still haven't done anything about that, have we, Paul?), no distractions. *Here I am,* he thought once, *the world's only monastic druggie.* Up at seven. Down two Novril with juice. At eight o'clock breakfast came, served at *monsieur's* bedside. A single egg, poached or scrambled, three days a week. High-fiber cereal the other four days. Then into the wheelchair. Over to the window. Find the hole in the paper. Fall into the nineteenth century, when men were men and women wore bustles. Lunch. Afternoon nap. Up again, sometimes to edit, sometimes just to read. She had everything Somerset Maugham had ever written (once Paul found himself wondering dourly if she had John Fowles's first novel on her shelves and decided it might be better not to ask), and Paul began to work his way through the twenty-odd volumes that comprised Maugham's *oeuvre,* fascinated by the man's canny grasp of story values. Over the years Paul had grown more and more resigned to the fact that he could not read stories as he had when he was a kid; by becoming a writer of them himself, he had condemned himself to a life of dissection. But Maugham first seduced him and then made him a child again, and that was wonderful. At five o'clock she would serve him a light supper, and at seven she would roll in the black-and-white television and they would watch *M*A*S*H* and *WKRP in Cincinnati.* When these were over, Paul would write. When he was done, he would roll the wheelchair slowly (he could have gone much faster, but it was just as well that Annie should not know that) over to the bed. She would hear, come in, and help

him back into bed. More medication. Boom. Out like a light. And
the next day would be just the same. And the next. And the next.

Being such a straight arrow was part of the reason for this amazing
fecundity, but Annie herself was a bigger one. After all, it was her
single hesitant suggestion about the bee-sting which had shaped the
book and given it its urgency when Paul had firmly believed he
could never feel urgent about Misery again.

He'd been sure of one thing from the start: there really *was* no
Misery's Return. His attention had been focused only on finding a
way to get the bitch out of her grave without cheating before Annie
decided to inspire him by giving him an enema with a handful of
Ginsu knives. Minor matters such as what the fucking book was
supposed to be *about* would have to wait.

During the two days following Annie's trip to town to pay her
tax-bill, Paul tried to forget his failure to take advantage of what
could have been a golden opportunity to escape and concentrated
on getting Misery back to Mrs. Ramage's cottage instead. Taking
her to Geoffrey's home was no good. The servants—most notably
Geoffrey's gossipy butler, Tyler—would see and talk. Also, he needed
to establish the total amnesia which had been caused by the shock
of being buried alive. Amnesia? Shit, the chick could barely talk.
Sort of a relief, given Misery's usual burblings.

So—what next? The bitch was out of her grave, now where was
the fucking *story?* Should Geoffrey and Mrs. Ramage tell Ian that
Misery was still alive? Paul didn't think so but he wasn't sure—*not
being sure of things,* he knew, was a charmless corner of purgatory
reserved for writers who were driving fast with no idea at all where
they were going.

Not Ian, he thought, looking out at the barn. *Not Ian, not yet.
The doctor first. That old asshole with all the n's in his name. Shinebone.*

The thought of the doctor brought Annie's comment about the
bee-stings to mind, and not for the first time. It kept recurring at
odd moments. *One person in every dozen . . .*

But it just wouldn't play. Two unrelated women in neighboring
townships, both allergic to stings in the same rare way?

Three days following the Great Annie Wilkes Tax Bail-out, Paul
had been drowsing his way into his afternoon nap when the guys
in the sweatshop weighed in, and weighed in heavy. This time it
wasn't a flare; this time it was an H-bomb explosion.

He sat bolt upright in bed, ignoring the flare of pain which shot
up his legs.

"Annie!" he bawled. *"Annie, come in here!"*

He heard her thump down the stairs two at a time and then run down the hallway. Her eyes were wide and scared when she came in.

"Paul! What's wrong? Are you cramping? Are you—"

"No," he said, but of course he was; his *mind* was cramping. "No. Annie, I'm sorry if I scared you, but you gotta help me into the chair. Mighty fuck! I got it!" The dreaded effword was out before he could help it, but this time it didn't seem to matter—she was looking at him respectfully, and with not a little awe. Here was the secular version of the Pentecostal fire, burning before her very eyes.

"Of course, Paul."

She got him into the chair as quickly as she could. She began to roll him toward the window and Paul shook his head impatiently. "This won't take long," he said, "but it's very important."

"Is it about the book?"

"It *is* the book. Be quiet. Don't talk to me."

Ignoring the typewriter—he never used the typewriter to make notes—he seized one of the ballpoints and quickly covered a single sheet of paper with a scrawl that probably no one but himself could have read.

They WERE related. It was bees and it affected them both the same way because they WERE related. Misery's an orph. And guess what? The Evelyn-Hyde babe was MISERY'S SISTER! Or maybe half-sister. That would probably work better. Who gets the first hint? Shinny? No. Shinny's a ninny. Mrs. R. She can go to see Charl. E-H's mommy and

And now he was struck by an idea of such intense loveliness—in terms of the plot at least—that he looked up, mouth open, eyes wide.

"Paul?" Annie asked anxiously.

"She *knew*," Paul whispered. "Of *course* she did. At least strongly suspected. But—"

He bent to his notes again.

she—Mrs. R.—realizes at once that Mrs. E-H has got to know M. is related to her daught. Same hair or something. Remember E-H's mom is starting to look like a maj. character. You'll

need to work her up. Mrs. R. starts to realize Mrs. E-H MAY
EVEN HAVE KNOWN MISERY WAS BURIED ALIVE!!
SHIT ON A SHINGLE! LOVE IT! Suppose the ole lady
guessed Misery was a leftover of her fuck-'em-and-leave-'em
days and

He put the pen down, looked at the paper, then slowly picked
the pen up again and scrawled a few more lines.

Three necessary points.

1. How does Mrs. E-H react to Mrs. R's suspicions? She should
be either murderous or puke-up scared. I prefer scared but
think A.W. would like murderous, so OK murd.

2. How does Ian get into this?

3. Misery's amnesia?

Oh, and here's one to grow on. Does Misery find out her mom
lived with the possibility that not just one but *two* of her
daughters had been buried alive rather than speak up?

Why not?

"You could help me back into bed now if you wanted," Paul
said. "If I sounded mad, I'm sorry. I was just excited."
"That's all right, Paul." She still sounded awed.
Since then the work had driven on famously. Annie was right;
the story was turning out to be a good deal more gruesome than
the other *Misery* books—the first chapter had not been a fluke but
a harbinger. But it was also more richly plotted than any *Misery*
novel since the first, and the characters were more lively. The latter
three *Misery* novels had been little more than straightforward adventure tales with a fair amount of piquantly described sex thrown
in to please the ladies. This book, he began to understand, was a
gothic novel, and thus was more dependent on plot than on situation. The challenges were constant. It was not just a question of
Can You? to begin the book—for the first time in years, it was Can
You? almost every day . . . and he was finding he *could*.
Then the rain came and things changed.

13

From the eighth of April until the fourteenth they enjoyed an unbroken run of fine weather. The sun beamed down from a cloud-less sky and temperatures sometimes rose into the mid-sixties. Brown patches began to appear in the field behind Annie's neat red barn. Paul hid behind his work and tried not to think about his car, the discovery of which was already overdue. His work did not suffer, but his mood did; he felt more and more that he was living in a cloud chamber, breathing an atmosphere thick with uncoalesced electricity. Whenever the Camaro stole into his mind, he imme-diately called the Brain Police and had the thought led away in handcuffs and leg-irons. Trouble was, the nasty thing had a way of escaping and coming back time after time, in one form or another.

One night he dreamed that Mr. Rancho Grande returned to Annie's place. He got out of his well-kept Chevrolet Bel Air, hold-ing part of the Camaro's bumper in one hand and its steering wheel in the other. *Do these belong to you?* he asked Annie in this dream.

Paul had awakened in a less-than-cheery frame of mind.

Annie, on the other hand, had never been in better spirits than she was during that sunny early-spring week. She cleaned; she cooked ambitious meals (although everything she cooked came out tasting strangely industrial, as if years of eating in hospital cafeterias had somehow corrupted any culinary talent she might once have had); each afternoon she bundled Paul up in a huge blue blanket, jammed a green hunting cap on his head, and rolled him out onto the back porch.

On those occasions he would take Maugham along, but rarely read him—being outside again was too great an experience to allow much concentration on other things. Mostly he just sat, smeiling sweet cool air instead of the bedroom's stale indoor smell, sly with sickroom undertones, listened to the drip of the icicles, and watched the cloud-shadows roll slowly and steadily across the melting field. That was somehow best of all.

Annie sang in her on-pitch but queerly tuneless voice. She giggled like a child at the jokes on *M*A*S*H* and *WKRP,* laughing especially hard at the jokes which were mildly off-color (which, in the case of *WKRP,* was most of them). She filled in n's tirelessly as Paul finished Chapters 9 and 10.

The morning of the fifteenth dawned windy and dull with clouds, and Annie changed. Perhaps, Paul thought, it was the falling barometer. It was as good an explanation as any.

She did not show up with his medication until nine o'clock, and by then he needed it quite badly—so badly that he had been thinking of going to his stash. There was no breakfast. Just the pills. When she came in she was still in her pink quilted housecoat. He noted with deepening misgivings that there were red marks like weals on her cheeks and arms. He also saw gooey splatters of food on the housecoat, and she had only managed to get on one of her slippers. *Thud-slush,* went Annie's feet as she approached him. *Thud-slush, thud-slush, thud-slush.* Her hair hung around her face. Her eyes were dull.

"Here." She threw the pills at him. Her hands were also covered with mixed streaks of goo. Red stuff, brown stuff, sticky white stuff. Paul had no idea what it was. He wasn't sure he wanted to know. The pills hit his chest and bounced into his lap. She turned to go. *Thud-slush, thud-slush, thud-slush.*

"Annie?"

She stopped, not turning around. She looked bigger that way, with her shoulders rounding the pink housecoat, her hair like some battered helmet. She looked like a Piltdown woman staring out of her cave.

"Annie, are you all right?"

"No," she said indifferently, and turned around. She looked at him with that same dullard's expression as she pinched her lower lip between the thumb and first finger of her right hand. She pulled it out and then twisted it, pinching inward at the same time. Blood first welled between lip and gum, then gushed down her chin. She turned and left without speaking a word, before his stunned mind could persuade itself that he had really seen her do that. She closed the door . . . and locked it. He heard her *thud-slushing* her way down the hall to the parlor. He heard the creak of her favorite chair as she sat down. Nothing else. No TV. No singing. No *click-clink* of silver or crockery. No, she was just sitting there. Just sitting there being not all right.

Then there *was* a sound. It was not repeated, but it was utterly distinctive. It was a slap. A damned hard one. And since he was in here on one side of a locked door and she was out there on the other side of it, you didn't have to be Sherlock Holmes to figure out that she'd slapped herself. Good and hard, from the sound. He saw her pulling her lip out, digging her short nails into its sensitive pink meat.

He suddenly remembered a note on mental illness he had taken for the first *Misery* book, where much of the action had been set in London's Bedlam Hospital (Misery had been railroaded there by the madly jealous villainess). *When a manic-depressive personality begins to slide deeply into a depressive period,* he had written, *one symptom he or she may exhibit is acts of self-punishment: slapping, punching, pinching, burning one's self w/ cigarette butts, etc.*

He was suddenly very scared.

14

Paul remembered an essay by Edmund Wilson where Wilson had said, in typically grudging Wilson manner, that Wordsworth's criterion for the writing of good poetry—strong emotion recalled in a time of tranquillity—would do well enough for most dramatic fiction as well. It was probably true. Paul had known writers who found it impossible to write after so much as a minor marital spat, and he himself usually found it impossible to write when upset. But there were times when a kind of reverse effect obtained—these were times when he had gone to the work not just because the work ought to be done but because it was a way to escape whatever was upsetting him. These were usually occasions when rectifying the source of the upset was beyond him.

This was one of those occasions. When she still hadn't returned to put him in his chair by eleven that morning, he determined to get into it himself. Getting the typewriter off the mantel would be beyond him, but he could write longhand. He was sure he could hoist himself into the chair, knew it was probably a bad idea to let Annie *know* he could, but he needed his *other* fix, goddammit, and he could not write lying here in bed.

He worked himself over to the edge of the bed, made sure the wheelchair brake was on, then grasped its arms and pulled himself slowly into the seat. Pulling his legs up onto the supports one at a time was the only part that hurt. He rolled himself over to the window and picked up his manuscript.

The key rattled in the lock. Annie was looking in at him, her eyes burned black holes in her face. Her right cheek was swelling up, and it looked like she was going to have a hell of a shiner in the morning. There was red stuff around her mouth and on her chin. For a moment Paul thought it was more blood from her torn lip and then he saw the seeds in it. It was raspberry jam or raspberry filling, not blood. She looked at him. Paul looked back. Neither said anything for a time. Outside, the first drops of rain splatted against the window.

"If you can get into that chair all by yourself, Paul," she said at last, "then I think you can fill in your own fucking n's."

She then closed the door and locked it again. Paul sat looking at it for a long time, almost as if there were something to see. He was too flabbergasted to do anything else.

15

He didn't see her again until late afternoon. After her visit, work was impossible. He made a couple of futile tries, wadded up the paper, and gave up. It was a bust. He rolled himself back across the room. In the process of getting out of the chair and into bed, one of his hands slipped and he came within an ace of falling. He brought his left leg down, and although it took his weight and saved him the fall, the pain was excruciating—it felt as if a dozen bolts had suddenly been driven into the bone. He screamed, scrabbled for the headboard, and pulled himself safely over onto the bed, his throbbing left leg trailing behind the rest of him.

That will bring her, he thought incoherently. *She'll want to see if Sheldon really turned into Luciano Pavarotti, or if it just sounds that way.*

But she didn't come and there was no way he could bear the rotted ache in his left leg. He rolled clumsily onto his stomach, burrowed one arm deep under the mattress, and brought out one of the Novril sample cards. He dry-swallowed two, then drifted for awhile.

When he came back he thought at first he must still be dreaming. It was just too surreal, like the night when she had rolled the barbecue pot in here. Annie was sitting on the side of his bed. She had set a water glass filled with Novril capsules on his bed-table. In her other hand she had a Victor rat-trap. There was a rat in it, too—a large one with mottled gray-brown fur. The trap had broken the rat's back. Its rear feet hung over the sides of the trap's board, twitching randomly. There were beads of blood in its whiskers.

This was no dream. Just another day lost in the funhouse with Annie.

Her breath smelled like a corpse decomposing in rotted food.

"Annie?" He straightened up, eyes moving between her and the rat. Outside it was dusk—a strange blue dusk filled with rain. It sheeted against the window. Strong gusts of wind shook the house, making it creak.

Whatever had been wrong with her this morning was worse tonight. *Much* worse. He realized he was seeing her with all her masks put aside—this was the real Annie, the inside Annie. The flesh of her face, which had previously seemed so fearsomely solid, now hung like lifeless dough. Her eyes were blanks. She had dressed, but her skirt was on inside out. There were more weals on her flesh, more food splattered on her clothes. When she moved, they exhaled too many different aromas for Paul to count. Nearly one whole arm of her cardigan sweater was soaked with a half-dried substance that smelled like gravy.

She held up the trap. "They come into the cellar when it rains." The pinned rat squeaked feebly, and snapped at the air. Its black eyes, infinitely more lively than those of its captor, rolled. "I put down traps. I have to. I smear the trip-plates with bacon grease. I always catch eight or nine. Sometimes I find others—"

She blanked then. Blanked for nearly three minutes, holding the rat in the air, a perfect case of waxy catatonia. Paul stared at her, stared at the rat as it squeaked and struggled, and realized that he had actually believed that things could get no worse. Untrue. Un-fucking-true.

At last, as he had begun to think she had just sailed off into oblivion forever with no fuss or fanfare, she lowered the trap and went on as if she had never stopped speaking.

"—drowned in the corners. Poor things."

She looked down at the rat and a tear fell onto its matted fur.

"Poor poor things."

She closed one of her strong hands around the rat and pulled back the spring with the other. It lashed in her hand, head twisting

as it tried to bite her. Its squeals were thin and terrible. Paul pressed
the heel of a palm against his wincing mouth.

"How its heart beats! How it struggles to get away! As we do,
Paul. As we do. We think we know so much, but we really don't
know any more than a rat in a trap—a rat with a broken back that
thinks it still wants to live."

The hand holding the rat became a fist. Her eyes never lost that
blank, distant cast. Paul wanted to look away and could not. Tendons
began to stand out on her inner arm. Blood ran from the rat's mouth
in an abrupt thin stream. Paul heard its bones break, and then the
thick pads of her fingers punched into its body, disappearing up to
the first knuckle. Blood pattered on the floor. The creature's dulling
eyes bulged.

She tossed the body into the corner and wiped her hand indifferently on the sheet, leaving long red smears.

"Now it's at peace." She shrugged, then laughed. "I'll get my
gun, Paul, shall I? Maybe the next world is better. For rats and
people both—not that there's much difference between the two."

"Not until I finish," he said, trying to enunciate each word carefully. This was difficult, because he felt as if someone had shot his
mouth full of Novocain. He had seen her low before, but he'd seen
nothing like this; he wondered if she'd ever *had* a low as low as this
before. This was how depressives got just before shooting all the
members of their families, themselves last; it was the psychotic
despair of the woman who dresses her children in their best, takes
them out for ice cream, walks them down to the nearest bridge,
lifts one into the crook of each arm, and jumps over the side.
Depressives kill themselves. Psychotics, rocked in the poison cra-
dles of their own egos, want to do everyone handy a favor and take
them along.

I'm closer to death than I've ever been in my life, he thought, *because
she means it. The bitch means it.*

"Misery?" she asked, almost as if she had never heard the word
before—but there had been a momentary fugitive sparkle in her
eyes, hadn't there? He thought so.

"Misery, yes." He thought desperately about how he should go
on. Every possible approach seemed mined. "I agree that the world
is a pretty crappy place most of the time," he said, and then added
inanely: "Especially when it rains."

Oh, you idiot, stop babbling!

"I mean, I've been in a lot of pain these last few weeks, and—"

"Pain?" she looked at him with sallow, sunken contempt. "You don't know what pain is. You don't have the slightest *idea*, Paul."

"No . . . I suppose not. Not compared to you."

"That's right."

"But—I want to finish this book. I want to see how it all turns out." He paused. "And I'd like you to stick around and see, too. A person might as well not write a book at all, if there's no one around to read it. Do you get me?"

He lay there looking at that terrible stone face, heart thumping. "Annie? Do you get me?"

"Yes . . ." She sighed. "I *do* want to know how it comes out. That's the *only* thing left in the world that I still want, I suppose." Slowly, apparently unaware of what she was doing, she began to suck the rat's blood from her fingers. Paul jammed his teeth together and grimly told himself he would *not* vomit, would *not*, would *not*. "It's like waiting for the end of one of those chapter-plays."

She looked around suddenly, the blood on her mouth like lipstick.

"Let me offer again, Paul. I can get my gun. I can end all of this for both of us. You are not a stupid man. You know I can never let you leave here. You've known that for some time, haven't you?"

Don't let your eyes waver. If she sees your eyes waver, she'll kill you right now.

"Yes. But it always ends, doesn't it, Annie? In the end we all swing."

A ghost of a smile at the corners of her mouth; she touched his face briefly, with some affection.

"I suppose you think of escape. So does a rat in a trap, I'm sure, in its way. But you're not going to, Paul. You might if this was one of your stories, but it's not. I can't let you leave here . . . but I could go with you."

And suddenly, for just a moment, he thought of saying: *All right, Annie—go ahead. Let's just call it off.* Then his need and will to live— and there was still quite a lot of each in him—rose up and clamored the momentary weakness away. Weakness was what it was. Weakness and cowardice. Fortunately or unfortunately, he did not have the crutch of mental illness to fall back on.

"Thank you," he said, "but I want to finish what I've started."

She sighed and stood up. "All right. I suppose I must have known you would, because I see I brought you some pills, although I don't remember doing it." She laughed—a small crazy titter which seemed to come from that slack face as if by ventriloquism. "I'll have to go away for awhile. If I don't, what you or I want won't matter. Because I do things. I have a place I go when I feel like this. A place in the hills. Did you ever read the Uncle Remus stories, Paul?"

He nodded.

"Do you remember Brer Rabbit telling Brer Fox about his Laughing Place?"

"Yes."

"That's what I call my place upcountry. My Laughing Place. Remember how I said I was coming back from Sidewinder when I found you?"

He nodded.

"Well, that was a fib. I fibbed because I didn't know you well then. I was really coming back from my Laughing Place. It has a sign over the door that says that. ANNIE'S LAUGHING PLACE, it says. Sometimes I *do* laugh when I go there.

"But mostly I just scream."

"How long will you be gone, Annie?"

She was drifting dreamily toward the door now. "I can't tell. I've brought you pills. You'll be all right. Take two every six hours. Or six every four hours. Or all of them at once."

But what will I eat? he wanted to ask her, and didn't. He didn't want her attention to return to him—not at all. He wanted her gone. Being here with her was like being with the Angel of Death.

He lay stiffly in his bed for a long time, listening to her movements, first upstairs, then on the stairs, then in the kitchen, fully expecting her to change her mind and come back with the gun after all. He did not even relax when he heard the side door slam and lock, followed by splashing steps outside. The gun could just as easily be in the Cherokee.

Old Bessie's motor whirred and caught. Annie gunned it fiercely. A fan of headlights came on, illuminating a shining silver curtain of rain. The lights began to retreat down the driveway. They swung around, dimming, and then Annie was gone. This time she was not heading downhill, toward Sidewinder, but up into the high country.

"Going to her Laughing Place," Paul croaked, and began to laugh himself. She had hers; he was already in his. The wild gales of mirth ended when he looked at the mangled body of the rat in the corner.

A thought struck him.

"Who *said* she didn't leave me anything to eat?" he asked the room, and laughed even harder. In the empty house Paul Sheldon's Laughing Place sounded like the padded cell of a madman.

16

Two hours later, Paul jimmied the bedroom's lock again and for the second time forced the wheelchair through the doorway that was almost too small. For the last time, he hoped. He had a pair of blankets in his lap. All the pills he had cached under the mattress were wrapped in a Kleenex tucked into his underwear. He meant to get out if he could, rain or no rain; this was his chance and this time he meant to take it. Sidewinder was downhill and the road would be slippery in the rain and it was darker than a mineshaft; he meant to try it all the same. He hadn't lived the life of a hero or a saint, but he did not intend to die like an exotic bird in a zoo.

He vaguely remembered an evening he'd spent drinking Scotch with a gloomy playwright named Bernstein at the Lion's Head, down in the Village (and if he lived to see the Village again he would get down on whatever remained of his knees and kiss the grimy sidewalk of Christopher Street). At some point the conversation had turned to the Jews living in Germany during the uneasy four or five years before the *Wehrmacht* rolled into Poland and the festivities began in earnest. Paul remembered telling Bernstein, who had lost an aunt and a grandfather in the Holocaust, that he didn't understand why the Jews in Germany—hell, all over Europe but *especially* in Germany—hadn't gotten out while there was still time. They were not, by and large, stupid people, and many had had first-hand experience of such persecution. Surely they had seen what was coming. So why had they stayed?

Bernstein's answer had struck him as frivolous and cruel and incomprehensible: *Most of them had pianos. We Jews are very partial to the piano. When you own a piano, it's harder to think about moving.*

Now he understood. Yes. At first it was his broken legs and crushed pelvis. Then, God help him, the book had taken off. In a crazy way he was even having fun with it. It would be easy—too easy—to blame everything on his broken bones, or the dope, when in fact so much of it had been the *book*. That and the droning passage of days with their simple convalescent pattern. Those things—but mostly the stupid goddam *book*—had been his piano. What would she do if he was gone when she came back from her Laughing Place? Burn the manuscript?

"I don't give a fuck," he said, and this was almost the truth. If he lived, he could write another book—re-create this one, even, if he wanted to. But a dead man couldn't write a book any more than he could buy a new piano.

He went into the parlor. It had been tidy before, but now there were dirty dishes stacked on every available surface; it looked to Paul as if every one in the house must be here. Annie apparently not only pinched and slapped herself when she was feeling depressed. It looked like she really chowed down as well, and never mind cleaning up after. He half-remembered the stinking wind that had blown down his throat during his time in the cloud and felt his stomach clench. Most of the remains were of sweet things. Ice-cream had dried or was drying in many of the bowls and soup-dishes. There were crumbs of cake and smears of pie on the plates. A mound of lime Jell-O covered with a crack-glaze of dried whipped cream stood on top of the TV next to a two-liter plastic bottle of Pepsi and a gravy-boat. The Pepsi bottle looked almost as big as the nosecone of a Titan-II rocket. Its surface was dull and smeary, almost opaque. He guessed she had drunk directly from it, and that her fingers had been covered with gravy or ice-cream when she did it. He had not heard the clink of silverware and that was not surprising because there was none here. Dishes and bowls and plates, but no cutlery. He saw drying drips and splashes—again, mostly of ice-cream—on the rug and couch.

That was what I saw on her housecoat. The stuff she was eating. And what was on her breath. His image of Annie as Piltdown woman recurred. He saw her sitting in here and scooping ice-cream into her mouth, or maybe handfuls of half-congealed chicken gravy with a Pepsi chaser, simply eating and drinking in a deep depressed daze.

The penguin sitting on his block of ice was still on the knick-knack table, but she had thrown many of the other ceramic pieces into the corner, where their littered remains were scattered—sharp little hooks and shards.

He kept seeing her fingers as they sank into the rat's body. The red smears of her fingers on the sheet. He kept seeing her licking the blood from her fingers, doing it as absently as she must have eaten the ice-cream and Jell-O and soft black jellyroll cake. These images were terrible, but they were a wonderful incentive to hurry.

The spray of dried flowers on the coffee-table had overturned; beneath the table, barely visible, lay a dish of crusted custard pudding and a large book. MEMORY LANE, it said. *Trips down Memory Lane when you're feeling depressed are never a very good idea, Annie—but I suppose you know that by this point in your life.*

He rolled across the room. Straight ahead was the kitchen. On the right a wide, short hallway went down to Annie's front door. Beside this hallway a flight of stairs went up to the second floor. Giving the stairs only a brief glance (there were drips of ice-cream on some of the carpeted stair levels and glazey smears of it on the banister), Paul rolled down to the door. He thought that if there was going to be a way out for him, tied to this chair as he was, it would be by way of the kitchen door—the one Annie used when she went out to feed the animals, the one she galloped from when Mr. Rancho Grande showed up—but he ought to check this one. He might get a surprise.

He didn't.

The porch stairs were every bit as steep as he had feared, but even if there had been a wheelchair ramp (a possibility he never would have accepted in a spirited game of Can You?, even if a friend had suggested it), he couldn't have used it. There were three locks on the door. The police-bar he could have coped with. The other two were Kreigs, the best locks in the whole world, according to his ex-cop friend Tom Twyford. And where were the keys? Umm . . . let me see. On their way to Annie's Laughing Place, maybe? *Yessiree Bob! Give that man a cigar and a blowtorch to light it with!*

He reversed down the hall, fighting panic, reminding himself he hadn't expected much from the front door anyway. He pivoted the chair once he was in the parlor and rolled into the kitchen. This was an old-fashioned room with bright linoleum on the floor and a pressed-tin ceiling. The refrigerator was old but quiet. There were three or four magnets stuck to its door—not surprisingly, they all looked like candy: a piece of bubble-gum, a Hershey Bar, a Tootsie Roll. One of the cabinet doors was open and he could see shelves neatly covered with oilcloth. There were big windows over the sink and they would let in a lot of light even on cloudy days. It should have been a cheery kitchen but wasn't. The open garbage can overflowed onto the floor and emitted the warm reek of spoiling food, but that wasn't the only thing wrong, or the worst smell. There was another that seemed to exist mostly in his mind, but which was no less real for that. It was *parfum de Wilkes;* a psychic odor of obsession.

There were three doors in the room, two to the left and one straight ahead, between the refrigerator and the pantry alcove.

He went to those on the left first. One was the kitchen closet— he knew that even before he saw the coats, hats, scarves, and boots. The brief, yapping squeak of the hinges was enough to tell him. The other was the one Annie used to go out. And here was another police-bar and two more Kreigs. Roydmans, stay out. Paul, stay in.

He imagined her laughing.

"You fucking *bitch!*" He struck his fist against the side of the door. It hurt, and he pressed the side of his hand against his mouth. He hated the sting of tears, the momentary doubling of his vision when he blinked, but there was no way he could stop it. The panic was yammering more loudly now, asking what was he going to do, what was he going to *do,* for Christ's sake, this might be his last chance—

What I'm going to do first is a thorough job of checking this situation out, he told himself grimly. *If you can stay cool for just awhile longer, that is. Think you can do that, chickenshit?*

He wiped his eyes—crying was not going to get him out of this— and looked out through the window which made up the top half of the door. It wasn't really just one window but sixteen small panes. He could break the glass in each, but he would have to bust the lathes, too, and that might take hours without a saw—they looked strong. And what then? A kamikaze dive out onto the back porch? A great idea. Maybe he could break his back, and that would take his mind off his legs for awhile. And it wouldn't take long lying out there in the pelting rain before he died of exposure. That would take care of the whole rotten business.

No way. No fucking way. Maybe I'm going to punch out, but I swear to God I'm not going to do it until I get a chance to show my number-one fan just how much I've enjoyed getting to know her. And that isn't just a promise—that's a sacred vow.

The idea of paying Annie back did more to still his panic than any amount of self-scolding had done. A little calmer, he flicked the switch beside the locked door. It turned on an outside light, which came in handy—the last of the daylight had drained away

during the time since he had left his room. Annie's driveway was
flooded, and her yard was a quagmire of mud, standing water, and
gobbets of melting snow. By positioning his wheelchair all the way
to the left of the door, he could for the first time see the road which
ran by her place, although it was really no big deal—two-lane black-
top between decaying snowbanks, shiny as sealskin and awash with
rainwater and snowmelt.

*Maybe she locked the doors to keep the Roydmans out, but she sure
didn't need to lock them to keep me in. If I got out there in this wheelchair,
I'd be bogged to the hubcaps in five seconds. You're not going anywhere,
Paul. Not tonight and probably not for weeks—they'll be a month into
the baseball season before the ground firms up enough for you to get out
to the road in this wheelchair. Unless you want to crash through a
window and crawl.*

No—he didn't want to do that. It was too easy to imagine how
his shattered bones would feel after ten or fifteen minutes of wriggling through cold puddles and melting snow like a dying tadpole.
And even supposing he could make it out to the road, what were
his chances of flagging down a car? The only two he'd ever heard
out here, other than Old Bessie, had been El Rancho Grande's Bel
Air and the car which had scared the life out of him passing the
house on the first occasion he had escaped his "guest-room."

He turned off the outside light and rolled across to the other
door, the one between the refrigerator and the pantry. There were
three locks on this one as well, and *it* didn't even open on the
outside—or at least not directly. There was another light-switch
beside this door. Paul flicked it and saw a neat shed addition which
ran the length of the house on its windward side. At one end was
a woodpile and a chopping block with an axe buried in it. At the
other was a work-table and tools hung on pegs. To its left there
was another door. The bulb out there wasn't terribly bright, but it
was bright enough for him to see another police bolt and another
two Kreig locks on that door as well.

The Roydmans . . . everybody . . . all out to get me . . .

"I don't know about *them*," he said to the empty kitchen, "but *I*
sure am."

Giving up on the doors, he rolled into the pantry. Before he
looked at the food stored on the shelves, he looked at the matches.
There were two cartons of paper book matches and at least two
dozen boxes of Diamond Blue Tips, neatly stacked up.

For a moment he considered simply lighting the place on fire, began to reject the idea as the most ridiculous yet, and then saw something which made him reconsider it briefly. In here was yet another door, and this one had no locks on it.

He opened it and saw a set of steep, rickety stairs pitching and yawing their way into the cellar. An almost vicious smell of dampness and rotting vegetables rose from the dark. He heard low squeaking sounds and thought of her saying: *They come into the cellar when it rains. I put down traps. I have to.*

He slammed the door shut in a hurry. A drop of sweat trickled down from his temple and ran, stinging, into the corner of his right eye. He knuckled it away. Knowing that door must lead to the cellar and seeing that there were no locks on it had made the idea of torching the place seem momentarily more rational—he could maybe shelter there. But the stairs were too steep, the possibility of being burned alive if Annie's flaming house collapsed into the cellar-hole before the Sidewinder fire engines could get here was too real, and the rats down there . . . the sound of the rats was somehow the worst.

How its heart beats! How it struggles to get away! As we do, Paul. As we do.

"Africa," Paul said, and didn't hear himself say it. He began to look at the cans and bags of food in the pantry, trying to assess what he could take with the least chance of raising her suspicions next time she came out here. Part of him understood exactly what this assessment meant: he had given up the idea of escape.

Only for the time being, his troubled mind protested.

No, a deeper voice responded implacably. *Forever, Paul. Forever.*

"I will never give up," he whispered. "Do you hear me? *Never.*"

Oh no? the voice of the cynic whispered sardonically. *Well . . . we'll see, won't we?*

Yes. They would see.

17

Annie's larder looked more like a survivalist's bomb shelter than a pantry. He guessed that some of this hoarding was a simple nod to the realities of her situation: she was a woman alone living in the high country, where a person must reasonably expect to spend a certain period—maybe only a day, but sometimes as long as a week or even two—cut off from the rest of the world. Probably even those cockadoodie Roydmans had a pantry that would make a home-owner from another part of the country raise his or her brows . . . but he doubted if the cockadoodie Roydmans or anyone else up here had anything which came close to what he was now looking at. This was no pantry; this was a goddam supermarket. He supposed there was a certain symbolism in Annie's pantry—the ranks of goods had something to say about the murkiness of the borderline between the Sovereign State of Reality and the People's Republic of Para-noia. In his current situation, however, such niceties hardly seemed worth examination. Fuck the symbolism. Go for the food.

Yes, but be careful. It wasn't just a matter of what she might miss. He must take no more than he could reasonably hope to hide if she came back suddenly . . . and how else did he *think* she would come? Her phone was dead and he somehow doubted if Annie would send him a telegram or Flowers by Wire. But in the end what she might miss in here or find in his room hardly mattered. After all, he had to eat. He was hooked on that, too.

Sardines. There were lots of sardines in those flat rectangular cans with the key under the paper. Good. He would have some of those. Tins of deviled ham. No keys, but he could open a couple of cans in her kitchen, and eat those first. Bury the empties deep in her own overflowing garbage. There was an open package of Sun-Maid raisins containing smaller boxes, which the ad-copy on the torn cellophane wrapper called "mini-snacks." Paul added four of the mini-snacks to the growing stash in his lap, plus single-serving boxes of Corn Flakes and Wheaties. He noted there were no single-serving boxes of pre-sweetened cereals. If there had been, Annie had chowed them down on her last binge.

On a higher shelf was a pile of Slim Jims, as neatly stacked as the kindling in Annie's shed. He took four, trying not to disturb the pyramidal structure of the pile, and ate one of them greedily, relishing the salty taste and the grease. He tucked the wrapping into his underwear for later disposal.

His legs were beginning to hurt. He decided that if he wasn't going to escape or burn the house down, he ought to go on back to his room. An anticlimax, but things could be worse. He could take a couple of pills and then write until he got drowsy. Then he could go to sleep. He doubted if she would be back tonight; far from abating, the storm was gaining strength. The idea of writing quietly and then sleeping with the knowledge that he was perfectly alone, that Annie was not going to burst in with some wild idea or even wilder demand, held great appeal, anticlimax or not.

He reversed out of the pantry, pausing to turn off the light, reminding himself that he must

(rinse)

put everything back in order as he made his retreat. If he ran out of food before she came back, he could always return for more

(like a hungry rat, right, Paulie?)

but he must not forget how careful he must be. It would not do to forget the simple fact that he was risking his life every time he left his room. Forgetting that would not do at all.

18

As he was rolling across the parlor, the scrapbook under the coffee table caught his eye again. MEMORY LANE. It was as big as a folio Shakespeare play and as thick as a family Bible.

Curious, he picked it up and opened it.

On the first page was a single column of newsprint, headed WILKES-BERRYMAN NUPTIALS. There was a picture of a pale gent with a narrow face and a woman with dark eyes and a pursy mouth. Paul glanced from the newspaper photo to the portrait over the mantel. No question. The woman identified in the clipping as Crysilda Berryman (*Now there's a name worthy of a* Misery *novel,* he thought) was Annie's mother. Neatly written in black ink below the clipping was: *Bakersfield Journal, May 30th, 1938.*

Page two was a birth announcement: Paul Emery Wilkes, born in Bakersfield Receiving Hospital, May 12th, 1939. Father, Carl Wilkes; mother, Crysilda Wilkes. The name of Annie's older brother gave him a start. He must have been the one with whom she had gone to the movies and seen the chapter-plays. Her brother had been Paul, too.

Page three announced the birth of Anne Marie Wilkes, d.o.b. April 1st, 1943. Which made Annie just past her forty-fourth birth-day. The fact that she had been born on April Fools' Day did not escape Paul.

Outside, the wind gusted. Rain tore against the house.

Fascinated, his pain temporarily forgotten, Paul turned the page.

The next clipping was from page one of the Bakersfield *Journal*. The photo showed a fireman on a ladder, silhouetted against a background of flames billowing from the windows of a frame building.

FIVE DIE IN APARTMENT HOUSE FIRE

Five persons, four of them members of the same family, died in the early hours of Wednesday morning, victims of a smoky three-alarm fire in a Bakersfield apartment house on Watch Hill Avenue. Three of the dead were children—Paul Krenmitz, 8, Frederick Krenmitz, 6, and Alison Krenmitz, 3. The fourth was their father, Adrian Krenmitz, 41. Mr. Krenmitz rescued the surviving Krenmitz child, Laurene Krenmitz, who is eighteen months old. According to Mrs. Jessica Krenmitz, her husband put the youngest of their four children in her arms and told her, "I'll be back with the others in a minute or two. Pray for us." "I never saw him again," she said.

The fifth victim, Irving Thalman, 58, was a bachelor who lived on the top floor of the building. The third-floor apartment was vacant at the time of the fire. The Carl Wilkes family, at first listed as missing, left the building Tuesday night because of a water leak in the kitchen.

"I weep for Mrs. Krenmitz and her loss," Crysilda Wilkes told a *Journal* reporter, "but I thank God for sparing my husband and my own two children."

Centralia Fire Chief Michael O'Whunn said that the fire began in the apartment building's basement. When asked about the possibility of arson, he said: "It's more likely that a wino crept into the basement, had a few drinks, and accidentally started the fire with a cigarette. He probably ran instead of trying to put the fire out, and five people died. I hope we catch up with the bum." When asked about leads, O'Whunn said, "The police have several, and they are following them up hard and fast, I can tell you."

Same neat black ink below the clipping. *October 28th, 1954.*

Paul looked up. He was totally still, but a pulse beat rapidly in his throat. His bowels felt loose and hot.

Little brats.
Three of the dead were children.
Mrs. Krenmitz's four brats downstairs.
Oh no, oh Christ, no.
I used to hate those little brats.
She was just a kid! Not even in the house!
She was eleven. Old enough and bright enough, maybe, to spill some kerosene around a cheap liquor bottle, then light a candle, and put the candle in the middle of the kerosene. Maybe she didn't even think it would work. Maybe she thought the kerosene would evaporate before the candle burned all the way down. Maybe she thought they'd get out alive . . . only wanted to scare them into moving. But she did it, Paul, she fucking did it, and you know it.

Yes, he supposed he did. And who would suspect her?

He turned the page.

Here was yet another Bakersfield *Journal* clipping, this one dated July 19th, 1957. It featured a picture of Carl Wilkes, looking slightly older. One thing was clear: it was as old as he was ever going to get. The clipping was his obituary.

BAKERSFIELD ACCOUNTANT DIES IN FREAK FALL

Carl Wilkes, a lifelong Bakersfield resident, died shortly after being admitted to Hernandez General Hospital last night. He apparently stumbled over a pile of loose clothing, which had been left on the stairs earlier, while on his way down to answer the phone. Dr. Frank Canley, the admitting physician, said that Wilkes died of multiple skull fractures and a broken neck. He was 44.

Wilkes is survived by his wife, Crysilda, a son, Paul, 18, and a daughter, Anne, 14.

When Paul turned to the next page, he thought for a moment that Annie had pasted in two copies of her father's obituary out of sentiment or by accident (he thought this latter the more likely possibility of the two). But this was a different accident, and the reason for the similarity was simplicity itself: neither had really been an accident at all.

He felt stark and simple terror steal into him.

The neat handwriting below this clipping read *Los Angeles Call, January 29th, 1962.*

USC STUDENT DIES IN FREAK FALL

Andrea Saint James, a USC nursing student, was pronounced dead on arrival at Mercy Hospital in North Los Angeles last night, the apparent victim of a bizarre accident.

Miss Saint James shared an off-campus apartment on Delorme Street with a sister nursing student, Anne Wilkes, of Bakersfield. Shortly before eleven P.M., Miss Wilkes heard a brief scream followed by "terrible thudding sounds." Miss Wilkes, who had been studying, rushed onto the third-floor landing and saw Miss Saint James lying on the landing below, "sprawled in a very unnatural position."

Miss Wilkes said that, in her effort to render aid, she almost fell herself. "We had a cat named Peter Gunn," she said, "only we hadn't seen him for days and thought the pound must have gotten him because we kept forgetting to get him a tag. He was lying dead on the stairs. It was the cat she tripped over. I covered Andrea with my sweater and then called the hospital. I knew she was dead, but I didn't know who else to call."

Miss Saint James, a native of Los Angeles, was 21.

"Jesus."

Paul whispered it over and over. His hand was shaking badly as he turned the page. Here was a *Call* clipping which said that the stray cat the student nurses adopted had been poisoned.

Peter Gunn. Cute name for a cat, Paul thought.

The landlord had rats in his basement. Tenant complaints had resulted in a warning from building inspectors the year before. The landlord had caused a ruckus at a subsequent City Council meeting which had been lively enough to get coverage in the papers. Annie would have known. Faced with a stiff fine by councilmen who didn't like being called names, the landlord had sown the cellar with poisoned bait. Cat eats poison. Cat languishes in cellar for two days. Cat then crawls as close to his mistresses as possible before expiring—and killing one of said mistresses.

An irony worthy of Paul Harvey, Paul Sheldon thought, and laughed wildly. *I bet it made his daily newscast, too.*

Neat. Very neat.

Except we know that Annie picked up some of the poisoned bait in the cellar and hand-fed it to the cat, and if old Peter Gunn didn't want to eat it, she probably rammed it down his gullet with a stick. When he was dead she put him on the stairs and hoped it would work. Maybe she had a pretty good idea her roommate would come home tiddly. I wouldn't be a bit surprised. A dead cat, a heap of clothes. Same M.O., as Tom Twyford would say. But why, *Annie? These clippings tell me everything but that.* WHY?

In an act of self-preservation, part of his imagination had, over the last few weeks, actually *become* Annie, and it was now this Annie-part that spoke up in its dry and uncontradictable voice. And while what it said was perfectly mad, it also made perfect sense.

I killed her because she played her radio late at night.

I killed her because of the dumb name she gave the cat.

I killed her because I got tired of seeing her soul-kissing her boyfriend on the couch, him with his hand shoved so far up her skirt he looked like he was prospecting for gold.

I killed her because I caught her cheating.

I killed her because she caught *me* cheating.

The specifics don't matter, do they? I killed her because she was a cockadoodie brat, and that was reason enough.

"And maybe because she was a Missus Smart Guy," Paul whispered. He threw back his head and donkeyed another shrill and frightened laugh. So this was Memory Lane, was it? Oh, what a variety of strange and poisonous flowers grew beside Annie's version of that quaint old path!

No one ever put those two freak falls together? First her father, then her roommate? Are you seriously telling me that?

Yes, he was seriously telling himself that. The accidents had happened almost five years apart, in two different towns. They had been reported by different papers in a populous state where people were probably always falling downstairs and breaking their necks.

And she was very, very clever.

Almost as clever as Satan himself, it seemed. Only now she was starting to lose it. It would be precious little consolation to him, however, if Annie were to be finally brought to bay for the murder of Paul Sheldon.

He turned the page and discovered another clipping from the Bakersfield *Journal*—the last, as it turned out. The headline read MISS WILKES IS NURSING SCHOOL GRADUATE. Home-town girl makes good. May 17th, 1966. The photo was of a younger, startlingly pretty Annie Wilkes, wearing a nurse's uniform and cap, smiling into the camera. It was a graduation photograph, of course. She had graduated with honors. *Only had to kill one roommate to do it, too,* Paul thought, and donkeyed his shrill, frightened laugh. The wind gusted around the side of the house as if in answer. Mom's picture chattered briefly on the wall.

The next cutting was from the Manchester, New Hampshire, *Union-Leader.* March 2nd, 1969. It was a simple obituary which seemed to have no connection with Annie Wilkes at all. Ernest Gonyar, age seventy-nine, had died in Saint Joseph's Hospital. No exact cause of death given. "After a long illness," the obit said. Survived by his wife, twelve children, and what looked like about four hundred grandchildren and great-grandchildren. There was nothing like the rhythm method for producing all descendants great and small, Paul thought, and donkeyed again.

She killed him. That's what happened to good old Ernie. Why else is his obituary here? This is Annie's Book of the Dead, isn't it?

Why, for God's sake? WHY?

With Annie Wilkes that is a question which has no sane answer. As you well know.

Another page, another *Union-Leader* obit. March 19th, 1969. The lady was identified as Hester "Queenie" Beaulifant, eighty-four. In the picture she looked like something whose bones might have been exhumed from the La Brea Tar Pits. The same thing that had gotten Ernie had gotten "Queenie"—seemed like that long-illness shit was going around. Like Ernie, she had expired at Saint Joe's. Viewings at 2:00 and 6:00 P.M. on March 20th at Foster's Funeral Home. Interment at Mary Cyr Cemetery on March 21st at 4:00 P.M.

Ought to've had a special rendition of "Annie, Won't You Come by Here," sung by the Mormon Tabersnackle Choir, Paul thought, and did the Donkey some more.

There were three more *Union-Leader* obits on the following pages. Two old men who had died of that perennial favorite, Long Illness. The third was a woman of forty-six named Paulette Simeaux. Paulette had died of that common runner-up, Short Illness. Although the picture accompanying the obit was even grainier and fuzzier than usual, Paul saw that Paulette Simeaux made "Queenie" Beaulifant look like Thumbelina. He thought her illness might have been short indeed—a thunderclap coronary, say, followed by a trip to Saint Joe's, followed by . . . followed by what? Exactly what?

He really didn't want to think about the specifics . . . but all three
obits identified Saint Joseph's as the place of expiration.

And if we looked at the nurses' register for March 1969, would we
find the name WILKES? *Friends, does a bear go cockadoodie in the woods?*

This book, dear God, this book was so *big*.

No more, please. I don't want to look at any more. I've got the idea.
I'm going to put this book down exactly where I found it. Then I am
going into my room. I guess I don't want to write after all; I think I'll
just take an extra pill and go to bed. Call it nightmare insurance. But
no farther down Annie's Memory Lane, if you please. Please, *if you*
please.

But his hands seemed to have a mind and a will of their own;
they kept on turning the pages, faster and faster.

Two more brief death notices in the *Union-Leader,* one in late
September of 1969, one in early October.

March 19th, 1970. This one was from the Harrisburg, Pennsylvania, *Herald.* A back page. NEW HOSPITAL STAFF ANNOUNCED.
There was a photo of a balding, bespectacled man who looked to
Paul like the type of fellow who might eat boogers in secret. The
article noted that in addition to the new publicity director (the
balding, bespectacled fellow), twenty others had joined the staff of
Riverview Hospital: two doctors, eight R.N.'s, assorted kitchen
staff, orderlies, and a janitor.

Annie was one of the R.N.'s.

On the next page, Paul thought, *I am going to see a brief death notice*
for an elderly man or woman who expired at Riverview Hospital in
Harrisburg, Pennsylvania.

Correct. An old duffer who had died of that all-time favorite,
Long Illness.

Followed by an elderly man who had died of that perennial
bridesmaid, Short Illness.

Followed by a child of three who had fallen down a well, sustained
grievous head injuries, and been brought to Riverview in a coma.

Numbly, Paul continued to turn the pages while the wind and
rain drove against the house. The pattern was inescapable. She got
a job, killed some people, and moved on.

Suddenly an image came, one from a dream his conscious mind
had already forgotten, which thus gained the delphic resonance of
déjà vu. He saw Annie Wilkes in a long aproned dress, her hair
covered with a mobcap, an Annie who looked like a nurse in Lon-

don's Bedlam Hospital. She held a basket over one arm. She dipped into it. Brought out sand and flung it into the upturned faces she passed. This was not the soothing sand of sleep but poisoned sand. It was killing them. When it struck them their faces went white and the lines on the machines monitoring their precarious lives went flat.

Maybe she killed the Krenmitz kids because they were brats . . . and her roommate . . . maybe even her own father. But these others?

But he knew. The Annie in him knew. Old and sick. All of them had been old and sick except Mrs. Simeaux, and she must have been nothing but a vegetable when she came in. Mrs. Simeaux and the kid who had fallen down the well. Annie had killed them because—

"Because they were rats in a trap," he whispered.

Poor things. Poor poor things.

Sure. That was it. In Annie's view all the people in the world were divided into three groups: brats, poor poor things . . . and Annie.

She had moved steadily westward. Harrisburg to Pittsburgh to Duluth to Fargo. Then, in 1978, to Denver. In each case the pattern was the same: a "welcome aboard" article in which Annie's name was mentioned among others (she had missed the Manchester "welcome aboard" probably because, Paul guessed, she hadn't known that local newspapers printed such things), then two or three unremarkable deaths. Following these, the cycle would start again.

Until Denver, that was.

At first, it seemed the same. There was the NEW ARRIVALS article, this time clipped from the in-house newspaper of Denver's Receiving Hospital, with Annie's name mentioned. The in-house paper was identified, in Annie's neat hand, as *The Gurney.* "Great name for a hospital paper," Paul told the empty room. "Surprised no one thought of calling it *The Stool Sample*." He donkeyed more terrified laughter, all unaware. Turned the page, and here was the first obit, cut from the Rocky Mountain *News.* Laura D. Rothberg. Long illness. September 21st, 1978. Denver Receiving Hospital.

Then the pattern broke wide open.

The next page announced a wedding instead of a funeral. The photo showed Annie, not in her uniform but in a white dress frothing with lace. Beside her, holding her hands in his, was a man named Ralph Dugan. Dugan was a physical therapist. DUGAN-WILKES NUPTIALS, the clipping was headed. Rocky Mountain *News,* January

2nd, 1979. Dugan was quite unremarkable save for one thing: he looked like Annie's father. Paul thought if you shaved off Dugan's singles-bar moustache—which she had probably gotten him to do as soon as the honeymoon was over—the resemblance would be just short of uncanny.

Paul thumbed the thickness of the remaining pages in Annie's book and thought Ralph Dugan should have checked his horoscope—whoops, make that *horrorscope*—the day he proposed to Annie.

I think the chances are very good that somewhere up ahead in these unturned pages I am going to find a brief article about you. Some people have appointments in Samarra; I think you may well have had one with a pile of laundry or a dead cat on a flight of stairs. A dead cat with a cute name.

But he was wrong. The next clipping was a NEW ARRIVALS from the Nederland newspaper. Nederland was a small town just west of Boulder. Not all that far from here, Paul judged. For a moment he couldn't find Annie in the short, name-filled clipping, and then realized he was looking for the wrong name. She was here, but had become part of a socio-sexual corporation called "Mr. and Mrs. Ralph Dugan."

Paul's head snapped up. Was that a car coming? No . . . just the wind. Surely the wind. He looked back down at Annie's book.

Ralph Dugan had gone back to helping the lame, the halt, and the blind at Arapahoe County Hospital; presumably Annie went back to that time-honored nurse's job of giving aid and comfort to the grievously wounded.

Now the killing starts, he thought. *The only real question is about Ralph: does he come at the beginning, in the middle, or at the end?*

But he was wrong again. Instead of an obit, the next clipping showed a Xerox of a realtor's one-sheet. In the upper left corner of the ad was a photo of a house. Paul recognized it only by the attached barn—he had, after all, never seen the house itself from the outside.

Beneath, in Annie's neat firm hand: *Earnest money paid March 3rd, 1979. Papers passed March 18th, 1979.*

Retirement home? Paul doubted it. Summer place? No; they couldn't afford the luxury. So . . . ?

Well, maybe it was just a fantasy, but try this. Maybe she really loves old Ralph Dugan. Maybe a year has passed and she still can't smell cockadoodie on him. *Something* has sure changed; there have been no obituaries since—

He flicked back to see.

Since Laura Rothberg in September 1978. She stopped killing around the same time she met Ralph. But that was then and this is now; now the pressure is starting to build up again. The depressive interludes are coming back. She looks at the old people . . . the terminally ill . . . and she thinks about what poor poor things they are, and maybe she thinks, *It's this environment that's depressing me. The miles of tiled corridor and the smells and the squeak of crepe-soled shoes and the sounds of people in pain. If I could get out of this place I'd be all right.*

So Ralph and Annie had apparently gone back to the land.

He turned the page and blinked.

Slashed into the bottom of the page was AUG 43rd 1880 FUCK YOU!

The paper, thick as it was, had torn in several places under the fury of the hand which had driven the pen.

It was the DIVORCES GRANTED column from the Nederland paper, but he had to turn it over to make sure that Annie and Ralph were a part of it. She had pasted it in upside down.

Yes, here they were. Ralph and Anne Dugan. Grounds: mental cruelty.

"Divorced after a short illness," Paul muttered, and again looked up, thinking he heard an approaching car. The wind, only the wind . . . still, he'd better get back to the safety of his room. It wasn't just the worsening pain in his legs; he was edging toward a state of terminal freak-out.

But he bent over the book again. In a weird way it was just too good to put down. It was like a novel so disgusting you just have to finish it.

Annie's marriage had been dissolved in a much more legal fashion than Paul had anticipated. It seemed fair to say that the divorce really *had* been after a short illness—a year and a half of wedded bliss wasn't all that much.

They had bought a house in March, and that was not a step you took if you felt that your marriage was falling apart. What happened? Paul didn't know. He could have made up a story, but a story was all it would have been. Then, reading the clipping again, he noticed something suggestive: *Angela Ford from John Ford. Kirsten Frawley*

from Stanley Frawley. Danna McLaren from Lee McLaren. And . . .
Ralph Dugan from Anne Dugan.
There's this American custom, right? No one talks about it much,
but it's there. Men propose in the moonlight; women file in court. That's
not always how it works, but usually that's it. So what tale does this
grammatical structure have to tell? Angela's saying "Slip out the back,
Jack!" Kirsten is saying "Make a new plan, Stan!" Danna is saying
"Drop off the key, Lee!" And what was Ralph, the only man who's listed
first in this column, saying? I think maybe he was saying "Let me the
hell out of here!"

"Maybe he saw the dead cat on the stairs," Paul said.

Next page. Another NEW ARRIVALS article. This one was from
the Boulder, Colorado, *Camera*. There was a photograph of a dozen
new staff members standing on the lawn of the Boulder Hospital.
Annie was in the second row, her face a blank white circle under
her cap with its black stripe. Another opening of another show.
The date underneath was March 9th, 1981. She had re-taken her
maiden name.

Boulder. That was where Annie really *had* gone crazy.

He turned the pages faster and faster, his horror mounting, and
the two thoughts which kept repeating were *Why in God's name
didn't they tip faster?* and *How in God's name did she slip through
their fingers?*

May 10th, 1981—long illness. May 14th, 1981—long illness.
May 23rd—long illness. June 9th—short illness. June 15th—short.
June 16th—long.

Short. Long. Long. Short. Long. Long. Short.

The pages stuttered through his fingers. He could smell the faint
odor of dried paper-paste.

"Christ, how many did she kill?"

If it was right to equate each obituary pasted in this book with
a murder, then her score was more than thirty people by the end
of 1981 . . . all without a single murmur from the authorities. Of
course most of the victims were old, the rest badly hurt, but
still . . . you would think . . .

In 1982 Annie had finally stumbled. The clipping from the January 14th *Camera* showed her blank, stonelike face rendered in
newsprint dots below a headline which read: NEW HEAD MATER-
NITY WARD NURSE NAMED.

On January 29th the nursery deaths had begun.

Annie had chronicled the whole story in her meticulous way. Paul had no trouble following it. *If the people after your hide had found this book, Annie, you would have been in jail—or some asylum— until the end of time.*

The first two infant deaths had not aroused suspicion—a story on one had mentioned severe birth defects. But babies, defective or not, weren't the same as old folks dying of renal failure or car-crash victims brought in still somehow alive in spite of heads which were only half there or steering-wheel-sized holes in their guts. And then she had begun killing the healthy along with the damaged. He supposed that, in her deepening psychotic spiral, she had begun to see all of them as poor poor things.

By mid-March of 1982 there had been five nursery deaths in the Boulder Hospital. A full-scale investigation was launched. On March 24th the *Camera* named the probable culprit as "tainted formula." A "reliable hospital source" was cited, and Paul wondered if perhaps the source had not been Annie Wilkes herself.

Another baby had died in April. Two in May.

Then, from the front page of the June 1st Denver *Post:*

HEAD MATERNITY NURSE QUESTIONED ON INFANT DEATHS
No Charges Made "As Yet," Sheriff's Office Spokeswoman Says
By Michael Leith

Anne Wilkes, the thirty-nine-year-old head nurse of the maternity ward at Boulder Hospital, is being questioned today about the deaths of eight infants—deaths which have taken place over a span of some months. All of the deaths took place following Miss Wilkes's appointment.

When asked if Miss Wilkes was under arrest, Sheriff's Office spokeswoman Tamara Kinsolving said she was not. When asked if Miss Wilkes had come in of her own free will to give information in the case, Ms. Kinsolving replied: "I would have to say that was not the case. Things are a bit more serious than that." Asked if Wilkes had been charged with any crime, Ms. Kinsolving replied: "No. Not as yet."

The rest of the article was a rehash of Annie's career. It was obvious that she had moved around a lot, but there was no hint that people in *all* of Annie's hospitals, not just the one in Boulder, had a way of croaking when she was around.

He looked at the accompanying photograph, fascinated.

Annie in custody. Dear God, Annie in custody; the idol not fallen but teetering . . . teetering . . .

She was mounting a set of stone steps in the company of a husky policewoman, her face dull, devoid of expression. She was wearing her nurse's uniform and white shoes.

Next page: WILKES RELEASED, MUM ON INTERROGATION.

She'd gotten away with it. Somehow, she'd gotten away with it. It was time for her to fade out and show up someplace else—Idaho, Utah, California, maybe. Instead, she went back to work. And instead of a NEW ARRIVALS column from somewhere farther west there was a huge headline from the Rocky Mountain *News* front page of July 2nd, 1982:

The Horror Continues:
THREE MORE INFANT DEATHS IN BOULDER HOSPITAL

Two days later the authorities arrested a Puerto Rican orderly, only to release him nine hours later. Then, on July 19th, both the Denver *Post* and the Rocky Mountain *News* announced Annie's arrest. There had been a short preliminary hearing in early August. On September 9th she went on trial for the murder of Girl Christopher, a female child one day of age. Behind Girl Christopher were seven other counts of first-degree murder. The article noted that some of Annie's alleged victims had even lived long enough to be given real names.

Interspersed among the accounts of the trial were Letters to the Editor printed in the Denver and Boulder newspapers. Paul understood that Annie had been driven to cull only the most hostile ones—those which reinforced her jaundiced view of mankind as *Homo brattus*—but they were vituperative by any standards. There seemed to be a consensus: hanging was too good for Annie Wilkes. One correspondent dubbed her the Dragon Lady, and the name stuck for the duration of the trial. Most seemed to feel that the Dragon Lady should be jabbed to death with hot forks, and most indicated they would be very willing to serve as a jabber.

Beside one such letter Annie had written in a shaky and somehow pathetic script entirely unlike her usual firm hand: *Sticks stones will break my bones words will never hurt me.*

It was apparent that Annie's biggest mistake had been not stopping when people finally realized *something* was going on. It was bad, but, unfortunately, not quite bad enough. The idol only tottered. The prosecution's case was entirely circumstantial, and in places thin enough to read a newspaper through. The district attorney had a hand-mark on Girl Christopher's face and throat which corresponded to the size of Annie's hand, complete with the mark of the amethyst ring she wore on the fourth finger of her right hand. The D.A. also had a pattern of observed entries and exits to the nursery which roughly corresponded to the infant deaths. But Annie was the head maternity nurse, after all, so she was *always* going in and out. Defense was able to show dozens of other occasions when Annie had entered the ward and *nothing* untoward had happened. Paul thought this was akin to proving that meteors never struck the earth by showing five days when not a single one had hit Farmer John's north field, but he could understand the weight the argument would have carried with the jury just the same.

The prosecution wove its net as well as it could, but the handprint with the mark of the ring was really the most damning bit of evidence it could come up with. The fact that the State of Colorado had elected to bring Annie to trial at all, given such a slight chance of conviction on the evidence, left Paul with one assumption and one certainty. The assumption was that Annie had said things during her original interrogation which were extremely suggestive, perhaps even damning; her attorney had managed to keep the transcript of that interrogation out of the trial record. The certainty was that Annie's decision to testify in her own behalf at the preliminary hearing had been extremely unwise. *That* testimony her attorney hadn't been able to keep out of the trial (although he had nearly ruptured himself trying), and while Annie had never confessed to anything in so many words during the three days in August she had spent "up there on the stand in Denver," he thought that she had really confessed to everything.

Excerpts from the clippings pasted in her book contained some real gems:

Did they make me feel sad? Of course they made me feel sad, considering the world we live in.

I have nothing to be ashamed of. I am never ashamed. What I do, that's final, I never look back on that type of thing.

Did I attend the funerals of any of them? Of course not. I find funerals very grim and depressing. Also, I don't believe babies are ensouled.

No, I never cried.

Was I sorry? I guess that's a philosophical question, isn't it?

Of *course* I understand the question. I understand *all* your questions. I know you're all out to get me.

If she had insisted on testifying in her own behalf at her trial, Paul thought, *her lawyer probably would have shot her to shut her up.*

The case went to the jury on December 13th, 1982. And here was a startling picture from the Rocky Mountain *News,* a photo of Annie sitting calmly in her holding cell and reading *Misery's Quest.* IN MISERY? the caption below asked. NOT THE DRAGON LADY. *Annie reads calmly as she waits for the verdict.*

And then, on December 16th, banner headlines: DRAGON LADY INNOCENT. In the body of the story a juror who asked not to be identified was quoted. "I had very grave doubts as to her innocence, yes. Unfortunately, I had very reasonable doubts as to her guilt. I hope she will be tried again on one of the other counts. Perhaps the prosecution could make a stronger case on one of those."

They all knew she did it but nobody could prove it. So she slipped through their fingers.

The case wound down over the next three or four pages. The D.A. said Annie surely *would* be tried on one of the other counts. Three weeks later, he said he never said that. In early February of 1983, the district attorney's office issued a statement saying that while the cases of infanticide at the Boulder Hospital were still very much alive, the case against Anne Wilkes was closed.

Slipped through their fingers.

Her husband never testified for either side. Why was that, I wonder?

There were more pages in the book, but he could tell by the snug way most lay against each other that he was almost done with Annie's history up to now. Thank God.

The next page was from the Sidewinder *Gazette,* November 19th, 1984. Hikers had found the mutilated and partly dismembered remains of a young man in the eastern section of Grider Wildlife Preserve. The following week's paper identified him as Andrew

Pomeroy, age twenty-three, of Cold Stream Harbor, New York. Pomeroy had left New York for L.A. in September of the previous year, hitchhiking. His parents had last heard from him on October 15th. He had called them collect from Julesburg. The body had been found in a dry stream-bed. Police theorized that Pomeroy might actually have been killed near Highway 9 and washed into the Wildlife Preserve during the spring run-off. The coroner's report said the wounds had been inflicted with an axe.

Paul wondered, not quite idly, how far Grider Wildlife Preserve was from here.

He turned the page and looked at the last clipping—at least so far—and suddenly his breath was gone. It was as if, after wading grimly through the almost unbearable necrology in the foregoing pages, he had come face to face with his *own* obituary. It wasn't quite, but . . .

"But close enough for government work," he said in a low, hoarse voice.

It was from *Newsweek*. The "Transitions" column. Listed below the divorce of a TV actress and above the death of a Midwestern steel potentate was this item:

REPORTED MISSING: *Paul Sheldon,* 42, novelist best known for his series of romances about sexy, bubbleheaded, unsinkable Misery Chastain; by his agent, Bryce Bell. "I think he's fine," Bell said, "but I wish he'd get in touch and ease my mind. And his ex-wives wish he'd get in touch and ease their bank accounts." Sheldon was last seen seven weeks ago in Boulder, Colorado, where he had gone to finish a new novel.

The clipping was two weeks old.

Reported missing, that's all. Just reported missing. I'm not dead, it's not like being dead.

But it *was* like being dead, and suddenly he needed his medication because it wasn't just his legs that hurt. *Everything* hurt. He put the book carefully back in its place and began rolling the wheelchair toward the guest room.

Outside, the wind gusted more strongly than it had yet done, slapping cold rain against the house, and Paul shrank away from it, moaning and afraid, trying desperately hard to hold himself together and not burst into tears.

19

An hour later, full of dope and drifting off to sleep, the sound of the howling wind now soothing rather than frightening, he thought: *I'm not going to escape. No way. What is it Thomas Hardy says in* Jude the Obscure? *"Someone could have come along and eased the boy's terror, but nobody did . . . because nobody does." Right. Correct. Your ship is not going to come in because there are no boats for nobody. The Lone Ranger is busy making breakfast-cereal commercials and Superman's making movies in Tinsel Town. You're on your own, Paulie. Dead flat on your own. But maybe that's okay. Because maybe you know what the answer is, after all, don't you?*

Yes, of course he did.

If he meant to get out of this, he would have to kill her.

Yes. That's the answer—the only one there is, I think. So it's that same old game again, isn't it? Paulie . . . Can You?

He answered with no hesitation at all. *Yes, I can.*

His eyes drifted closed. He slept.

20

The storm continued through the next day. The following night the clouds unravelled and blew away. At the same time the temperature plummeted from sixty degrees down to twenty-five. All the world outside froze solid. Sitting by the bedroom window and looking out at the ice-glittery morning world on that second full day alone, Paul could hear Misery the pig squealing in the barn and one of the cows bellowing.

He often heard the animals; they were as much a part of the general background as the chiming parlor-clock—but he had never heard the pig squeal so. He thought he had heard the cow bellow like that once before, but it had been an evil sound dimly heard in an evil dream, because then he had been full of his own pain. It had been when Annie had gone away that first time, leaving him with no pills. He had been raised in suburban Boston and had lived most of his life in New York City, but he thought he knew what those pained cow-bellows meant. One of the cows needed to be

milked. The other apparently didn't, possibly because Annie's er-
ratic milking habits had already dried her up.

And the pig?

Hungry. That was all. And that was enough.

They weren't going to get any relief today. He doubted if Annie
would be able to make it back even if she had wanted to. This part
of the world had turned into one big skating rink. He was a little
surprised at the depth of sympathy he felt for the animals and the
depth of his anger at Annie for how she had, in her unadmitting
and arrogant egoism, left them to suffer in their pens.

*If your animals could talk, Annie, they would tell you who the REAL
dirty birdie around here is.*

He himself was quite comfortable as those days passed. He ate
from cans, drank water from the new pitcher, took his medication
regularly, napped each afternoon. The tale of Misery and her amnesia and her previously unsuspected (and spectacularly rotten)
blood kin marched steadily along toward Africa, which was to be
the setting of the novel's second half. The irony was that the woman
had coerced him into writing what was easily the best of the Misery
novels. Ian and Geoffrey were off in Southampton outfitting a
schooner called the *Lorelei* for the run. It was on the Dark Continent
that Misery, who kept slipping into cataleptic trances at the most
inconvenient moments (and, of course, if she were to be stung by
another bee—ever, in her entire life—she would die almost in-
stantly), would either be killed or cured. For a hundred and fifty
miles inland from Lawstown, a tiny British-Dutch settlement on the
northernmost tip of the Barbary Coast's dangerous crescent, lived
the Bourkas, Africa's most dangerous natives. The Bourkas were
sometimes known as the Bee-People. Few of the whites who dared
to venture into Bourka country had ever returned, but those who
did had brought back fabulous tales of a woman's face jutting from
the side of a tall, crumbling mesa, a merciless face with a gaping
mouth and a huge ruby set in her stone forehead. There was another
story—only a rumor, surely, but strangely persistent—that within
the caves which honeycombed the stone behind the idol's jewelled
forehead there lived a hive of giant albino bees, swarming protec-
tively around their queen, a jellylike monstrosity of infinite poison . . . and infinite magic.

During the days he diverted himself with this pleasant foolishness. In the evenings he sat quietly, listening to the pig squeal and
thinking about how he would kill the Dragon Lady.

Playing Can You? in real life was quite different from playing it in a cross-legged circle as a kid or doing it in front of a typewriter as a grown-up, he discovered. When it was just a game (and even if they gave you money for it, a game was still all it was), you could think up some pretty wild things and make them seem believable— the connection between Misery Chastain and Miss Charlotte Evelyn-Hyde, for instance (they had turned out to be half-sisters; Misery would later discover her father down there in Africa hanging out with the Bourka Bee-People). In real life, however, the arcane had a way of losing its power.

Not that Paul didn't try. There were all those drugs in the down-stairs bathroom—surely there was some way he could use them to put her out of the way, wasn't there? Or to at least render her helpless long enough so he could do it? Take the Novril. Enough of that shit and he wouldn't even *have* to put her out of the way. She would float off on her own.

That's a very good idea, Paul. I tell you what to do. You just get a whole bunch of those capsules and stick them all through a pint of her ice cream. She'll just think they're pistachio nuts and gobble them right down.

No, of course *that* wouldn't work. Nor could he pull a cutie like opening the capsules and mixing the powder into some pre-softened ice cream. Novril in the raw was fabulously bitter. He had tasted it and knew. It was a taste she would recognize at once in the midst of the expected sweetness . . . *and then woe is you, Paulie. Woe to the max.*

In a story it would have been a pretty good idea. In real life, however, it simply did not make it. He wasn't sure he would have taken the chance even if the white powder inside the capsules had been almost or completely tasteless. It wasn't safe enough, it wasn't sure enough. This was no game; it was his life.

Other ideas passed through his mind and were rejected even more quickly. One was suspending something (the typewriter came immediately to mind) over the door so she would be killed or knocked unconscious when she came in. Another was running a tripwire across the stairway. But the problem in both cases was the same as the old Novril-in-the-ice-cream trick: neither was sure enough. He found himself literally unable to think of what might happen to him if he tried to assassinate her and failed.

As dark came down on that second night, Misery's squealing

went on as monotonously as ever—the pig sounded like an un-latched door with rusty hinges squealing in the wind—but Bossie No. 1 abruptly fell silent. Paul wondered uneasily if perhaps the poor animal's udder had burst, resulting in death by exsanguination. For a moment his imagination

so vivid!

tried to present him with a picture of the cow lying dead in a puddle of mixed milk and blood, and he quickly willed it away. He told himself not to be such a numbnuts—cows didn't die that way. But the voice doing the telling lacked conviction. He had no idea if they did or not. And, besides, it wasn't the *cow* that was his problem, was it?

All your fancy ideas come down to one thing—you want to kill her by remote control, you don't want her blood on your hands. You're like a man who loves nothing better than a thick steak but wouldn't last an hour in a slaughterhouse. But listen, Paulie, and get it straight: you must face reality at this point in your life if at no other. Nothing fancy. No curlicues. Right?

Right.

He rolled back into the kitchen and opened drawers until he found the knives. He selected the longest butcher-knife and went back to his room, pausing to rub away the hub-marks on the sides of the doorway. The signs of his passage were nevertheless becoming clearer.

Doesn't matter. If she misses them one more time, she misses them for good.

He put the knife on the night-table, hoisted himself into bed, then slid it under the mattress. When Annie came back he was going to ask her for a nice cold glass of water, and when she leaned over to give it to him he was going to plunge the knife into her throat.

Nothing fancy.

Paul closed his eyes and dropped off to sleep, and when the Cherokee came whispering back into the driveway that morning at four o'clock with both its engine and its lights shut off, he did not stir. Until he felt the sting of the hypo sliding into his arm and woke to see her face leaning over his, he hadn't the slightest idea she was back.

21

At first he thought he was dreaming about his own book, that the dark was the dream-dark of the caves behind the huge stone head of the Bourka Bee-Goddess and the sting was that of a bee—

"Paul?"

He muttered something that meant nothing—something that meant only *get out of here, dreamvoice, get gone.*

"Paul."

That was no dreamvoice; it was Annie's voice.

He forced his eyes open. Yes, it was her, and for a moment his panic grew even stronger. Then it simply seeped away, like fluid running down a partly clogged drain.

What the hell—?

He was totally disoriented. She was standing there in the shadows as if she had never been away, wearing one of her woolly skirts and frumpy sweaters; he saw the needle in her hand and understood it hadn't been a sting but an injection. What the fuck—either way it was the same thing. He had been gotten by the goddess. But what had she—?

That bright panic tried to come again, and once again it hit a dead circuit. All he could feel was a kind of academic surprise. That, and some intellectual curiosity about where she had come from, and why now. He tried to lift his hands and they came up a little . . . but *only* a little. It felt as if there were invisible weights dangling from them. They dropped back onto the sheet with little dull thumps.

Doesn't matter what she shot me up with. It's like what you write on the last page of a book. It's THE END.

The thought brought no fear. Instead he felt a kind of calm euphoria.

At least she's tried to make it kind . . . to make it . . .

"Ah, *there* you are!" Annie said, and added with lumbering coquettishness: "I *see* you, Paul . . . those blue eyes. Did I ever tell you what lovely blue eyes you have? But I suppose other women have—women who were much prettier than I am, and much bolder about their affections, as well."

Came back. Came creeping in the night and killed me, hypo or bee-sting, no difference, and so much for the knife under the bed. All I am now is the latest number in Annie's considerable body-count. And then, as the numbing euphoria of the injection began to spread, he thought almost with humor: *Some lousy Scheherazade I turned out to be.*

He thought that in a moment sleep would return—a more final sleep—but it did not. He saw her slip the hypo into the pocket of her skirt and then she sat down on the bed . . . not where she usually sat, however; she sat on its foot and for a moment he saw only her solid, impervious back as she bent over, as if to check on something. He heard a wooden *thunk,* a metallic *clunk,* and then a shaking sound he had heard someplace before. After a moment he placed it. *Take the matches, Paul.*

Diamond Blue Tips. He didn't know what else she might have there at the foot of the bed, but one of them was a box of Diamond Blue Tip matches.

Annie turned to him and smiled again. Whatever else might have happened, her apocalyptic depression had passed. She brushed an errant lock of hair back behind her ear with a girlish gesture. It went oddly with the lock's dull dirty half-shine.

Dull dirty half-shine oh boy you gotta remember that one that one ain't half-bad oh boy I am stoned now, all the past was prologue to this shit hey baby this here is the mainline oh fuck I'm fucked but this is crystal top-end shit this is going out on a mile-high wave in a fucking Rolls this is—

"What do you want first, Paul?" she asked. "The good news or the bad news?"

"Good news first." He managed a big foolish grin. "Guess the bad news is that this is THE END, huh? Guess you didn't like the book so great, huh? Too bad . . . I tried. It was even working. I was just starting to . . . you know . . . starting to drive on it."

She looked at him reproachfully. "I *love* the book, Paul. I told you that, and I never lie. I love it so much I don't want to read any more until the very end. I'm sorry to have to make you fill in the n's yourself, but . . . it's like peeking."

His big foolish grin stretched even wider; he thought soon it would meet in the back, tie a lover's knot there, and most of his poor old bean would just topple off. Maybe it would land in the bedpan beside the bed. In some deep, dim part of his mind where the dope hadn't yet reached, alarm bells were going off. She loved the book, which meant she didn't mean to kill him. Whatever was going on, she didn't mean to kill him. And unless his assessment of Annie Wilkes was totally off the beam, that meant she had something even worse in store.

Now the light in the room did not look dull; it looked marvellously pure, marvellously full of its own gray and eldritch charm; he could imagine cranes half-glimpsed in gunmetal mist standing in one-legged silence beside upland lakes in that light, could imagine the mica flecks in rocks jutting from spring grasses in upland meadows shining with the shaggy glow of glazed window-glass in that light, could imagine elves shucking their busy selves off to work in lines under the dew-soaked leaves of early ivy in that light. . . .

Oh BOY are you stoned, Paul thought, and giggled faintly.

Annie smiled in return. "The *good* news," she said, "is that your car is gone. I've been very worried about your car, Paul. I knew it would take a storm like this to get rid of it, and maybe even that wouldn't do the trick. The spring run-off got rid of that Pomeroy dirty bird, but a car is ever so much heavier than a man, isn't it? Even a man as full of cockadoodie as he was. But the storm and the run-off combined was enough to do the trick. Your car is gone. That's the *good* news."

"What . . ." More faint alarm bells. Pomeroy . . . he knew that name, but couldn't think exactly *how* he knew it. Then it came to him. Pomeroy. The late great Andrew Pomeroy, twenty-three, of Cold Stream Harbor, New York. Found in the Grider Wildlife Preserve, wherever *that* was.

"Now Paul," she said, in the prim voice he knew so well. "No need to be coy. I know you know who Andy Pomeroy was, because I know you've read my book. I suppose that I sort of hoped you would read it, you know; otherwise, why would I have left it out? But I made sure, you know—I make sure of everything. And sure enough, the threads were broken."

"The threads," he said faintly.

"Oh yes. I read once about a way you're supposed to find out for sure if someone has been snooping around in your drawers. You tape a very fine thread across each one, and if you come back and find one broken, why you know, don't you? You know someone's been snooping. You see how easy it is?"

"Yes, Annie." He was listening, but what he really wanted to do was trip out on the marvellous quality of the light.

Again she bent over to check whatever it was she had at the foot of the bed; again he heard a faint dull *clunk/clank,* wood thumping against some metallic object, and then she turned back, brushing absently at her hair again.

"I did that with my book—only I didn't really use threads, you know; I used hairs from my own head. I put them across the thickness of the book in three different places and when I came in this morning—very early, creeping like a little mousie so I wouldn't wake you up—all three threads were broken, so I *knew* you had been looking at my book." She paused, and smiled. It was, for Annie, a very winning smile, yet it had an unpleasant quality he could not quite put his finger on. "Not that I was surprised. I knew you had been out of the room. *That's* the bad news. I've known for a long, *long* time, Paul."

He should feel angry and dismayed, he supposed. She had known, known almost from the start, it seemed . . . but he could only feel that dreamy, floating euphoria, and what she was saying did not seem nearly as important as the glorious quality of the strengthening light as the day hovered on the edge of becoming.

"But," she said with the air of one returning to business, "we were talking about your car. I have studded tires, Paul, and at my place in the hills I keep a set of 10X tire chains. Early yesterday afternoon I felt ever so much better—I spent most of my time up there on my knees, deep in prayer, and the answer came, as it often does, and it was quite simple, as it often is. What you take to the Lord in prayer, Paul, He giveth back a thousandfold. So I put the chains on and I crept back down here. It was not easy, and I knew I might well have an accident in spite of the studs and the chains. I also knew that there is rarely such a thing as a 'minor accident' on those twisty upcountry roads. But I felt easy in my mind, because I felt safe in the will of the Lord."

"That's very uplifting, Annie," Paul croaked.

She gave him a look which was momentarily startled and narrowly suspicious . . . and then she relaxed and smiled. "I've got a present for you, Paul," she said softly, and before he could ask her what it was—he wasn't sure he wanted any sort of present from Annie—she went on: "The roads *were* terribly icy. I almost went off twice. . . . The second time, Old Bessie slid all the way around in a circle and kept right on going downhill while she did it!" Annie laughed cheerily. "Then I got stuck in a snowbank—this was around midnight—but a sanding-crew from the Eustice Public Works Department came along and helped me out."

"Bully for the Eustice Public Works Department," Paul said, but what came out was badly slurred—*Burry furdah Estice Pulleygurks Deparrent.*

"The two miles in from the county highway, that was the last hard patch. The county highway is Route 9, you know. The road you were on when you had your wreck. They had sanded that one to a fare-thee-well. I stopped where you went off and looked for your car. And I knew what I would have to do if I saw it. Because there would be questions, and I'd be just about the first one they'd ask those questions *to,* for reasons I think you know."

I'm way ahead of you, Annie, he thought. *I examined this whole scenario three weeks ago.*

"One of the reasons I brought you back was because it seemed like more than a coincidence . . . it seemed more like the hand of Providence."

"What seemed like the hand of Providence, Annie?" he managed.

"Your car was wrecked in almost exactly the same spot where I got rid of that Pomeroy creep. The one who said he was an artist." She flapped a hand in contempt, shifted her feet, and there was that wooden clunking sound as one of them brushed some of whatever it was she had down there on the floor.

"I picked him up on my way back from Estes Park. I was there at a ceramics show. I like little ceramic figurines."

"I noticed," Paul said. His voice seemed to come from light-years away. *Captain Kirk! There's a voice coming in over the sub-etheric,* he thought, and chuckled dimly. That deep part of him—the part the dope couldn't reach—tried to warn him to shut his mouth, just shut it, but what was the sense? She knew. *Of course she knows—the Bourka Bee-Goddess knows everything.* "I particularly liked the penguin on the block of ice."

"Thank you, Paul . . . he is cute, isn't he?

"Pomeroy was hitchhiking. He had a pack on his back. He said he was an artist, although I found out later he was nothing but a hippie dope-fiend dirty bird who had been washing dishes in an Estes Park restaurant for the last couple of months. When I told him I had a place in Sidewinder, he said that was a real coincidence. He said *he* was going to Sidewinder. He said he'd gotten an assignment from a magazine in New York. He was going to go up to the old hotel and sketch the ruins. His pictures were going to be with an article they were doing. It was a famous old hotel called the Overlook. It burned down ten years ago. The caretaker burned it down. He was crazy. Everybody in town said so. But never mind; he's dead.

"I let Pomeroy stay here with me.

"We were lovers."

She looked at him with her black eyes burning in her solid yet doughy white face and Paul thought: *If Andrew Pomeroy could get it up for you, Annie, he must have been as crazy as the caretaker that burned down the hotel.*

"Then I found out that he didn't really have an assignment to draw pictures of the hotel at all. He was just doing them on his own, hoping to sell them. He wasn't even sure the magazine was doing an article on the Overlook. I found *that* out pretty quick! After I did, I sneaked a look at his sketchpad. I felt I had a perfect right to do that. After all, he was eating my food and sleeping in my bed. There were only eight or nine pictures in the whole book and they were *terrible*."

Her face wrinkled, and for a moment she looked as she had when she had imitated the sound the pig made.

"*I* could have made better pictures! He came in while I was looking and he got mad. He said I was snooping. I said I didn't call looking at things in my own house snooping. I said if he was an artist, I was Madame Curie. He started to laugh. He laughed at me. So I . . . I . . ."

"You killed him," Paul said. His voice sounded dim and ancient.

She smiled uneasily at the wall. "Well, I guess it was something like that. I don't remember very well. Just when he was dead. I remember that. I remember giving him a bath."

He stared at her and felt a sick, soupy horror. The image came to him—Pomeroy's naked body floating in the downstairs tub like a piece of raw dough, head reclining aslant against the porcelain, open eyes staring up at the ceiling. . . .

"I *had* to," she said, lips drawing back a bit from her teeth. "You probably don't know what the police can do with just one piece of thread, or dirt under someone's fingernails or even dust in a corpse's hair! You don't know but I worked in hospitals all my life and I *do* know! I *do* know! I know about *for-EN-sics!*"

She was working herself into one of her patented Annie Wilkes frenzies and he knew he should try and say something which would at least temporarily defuse her, but his mouth seemed numb and useless.

"They're out to get me, all of them! Do you think they would have listened if I tried to tell them how it was? Do you? Do you? Oh no! They'd probably say something crazy like I made a pass at him and he laughed at me and so I killed him! They'd probably say something like that!"

And you know what, Annie? You know what? I think that just might be a little closer to the truth.

"The dirty birdies around here would say *anything* to get me in trouble or smear my name."

She paused, not quite panting but breathing hard, looking at him hard, as if inviting him to just dare and tell her different. *Just you dare!*

Then she seemed to get herself under some kind of control and she went on in a calmer voice.

"I washed . . . well . . . what was left of him . . . and his clothes. I knew what to do. It was snowing outside, the first real snow of the year, and they said we'd have a foot by the next morning. I put his clothes in a plastic bag and wrapped the body in sheets and took everything out to that dry wash on Route 9 after dark. I walked about a mile farther down from where your car ended up. I walked until I was in the woods and just dumped everything. You probably think I hid him, but I didn't. I knew the snow would cover him up, and I thought the spring melt would carry him away if I left him in the stream-bed. And that was what happened, except I had no idea he would go so *far*. Why, they found his body a whole year after . . . after he died, and almost twenty-seven miles away. Actually, it would have been better if he hadn't gone as far as he did, because there are always hikers and bird-watchers in the Grider Preserve. The woods around here are much less travelled."

She smiled.

"And that's where your car is now, Paul—somewhere between Route 9 and the Grider Wildlife Preserve, somewhere in the woods. It's far enough in so you can't see it from the road. I've got a spotlight on the side of Old Bessie, and it's plenty powerful, but the wash is empty all the way into the woods. I guess I'll go in on foot and check when the water goes down a little, but I'm almost positive it's safe. Some hunter will find it in two years or five years or seven years, all rusty and with chipmunks nesting in the seats, and by then you will have finished my book and will be back in New York or Los Angeles or wherever it is you decide to go, and I'll be living my quiet life out here. Maybe we will correspond sometimes."

She smiled mistily—the smile of a woman who sees a lovely castle in the sky—and then the smile disappeared and she was all business again.

"So I came back here and on the way I did some hard thinking. I had to, because your car being gone meant that you could really stay, you could really finish my book. I wasn't always sure you'd be able to, you know, although I never said because I didn't want to upset you. Partly I didn't want to upset you because I knew you wouldn't write as well if I did, but that sounds ever so much colder than I really felt, my dear. You see, I began by loving only the part of you that makes such wonderful stories, because that's the only part I had—the rest of you I didn't know anything about, and I thought that part might really be quite unpleasant. I'm not a dummy, you know. I've read about some so-called 'famous authors,' and I know that often they *are* quite unpleasant. Why, F. Scott Fitzgerald and Ernest Hemingway and that redneck fellow from Mississippi—Faulkner or whatever it was—those fellows may have won National Pulitzer Book Awards and things, but they were nothing but cockadoodie drunken bums just the same. Other ones, too—when they weren't writing wonderful stories they were drinking and whoring and shooting dope and heaven knows what else.

"But you're not like that, and after awhile I came to know the rest of Paul Sheldon, and I hope you don't mind me saying it, but I have come to love the rest of him, too."

"Thank you, Annie," he said from atop his golden glistening wave, and he thought: *But you may have read me wrong, you know—I mean, the situations that lead men into temptation have been severely curtailed up here. It's sort of hard to go bar-hopping when you've got a couple of broken legs, Annie. As for shooting dope, I've got the Bourka Bee-Goddess to do that for me.*

"But would you *want* to stay?" she resumed. "That was the question I had to ask myself, and as much as I may have wanted to pull the wool over my eyes, I knew the answer to *that*—I knew even before I saw the marks on the door over there."

She pointed and Paul thought: *I'll bet she did know almost from the very first. Wool-pulling? Not you, Annie. Never you. But I was doing enough of that for both of us.*

"Do you remember the first time I went away? After we had that silly fight over the paper?"

"Yes, Annie."

"That was when you went out the first time, wasn't it?"

"Yes." There was no point in denying it.

"Of course. You wanted your pills. I should have known you'd do anything to get your pills, but when I get mad, I get . . . you know." She giggled a little nervously. Paul did not join her, or even smile. The memory of that pain-wracked, endless interlude with the phantom voice of the sportscaster doing the play-by-play was still too strong.

Yes, I know how you get, he thought. *You get oogy.*

"At first I wasn't completely sure. Oh, I saw that some of the figures on the little table in the parlor had been moved around, but I thought I might have done that myself—I have times when I'm really quite forgetful. It crossed my mind that you'd been out of your room, but then I thought, *No, that's impossible. He's so badly hurt, and besides, I locked the door.* I even checked to make sure the key was still in my skirt pocket, and it was. Then I remembered you *were* in your chair. So maybe . . .

"One of the things you learn when you've been an R.N. for ten years is that it's always wise to check your maybes. So I took a look at the things I keep in the downstairs bathroom—they're mostly samples I brought home off and on while I was working; you should *see* all the stuff that just goes rolling around in hospitals, Paul! And so every now and then I helped myself to a few . . . well . . . a few *extras* . . . and I wasn't the only one. But I knew enough not to take any of the morphine-based drugs. They lock those up. They count. They keep records. And if they get an idea that a nurse is, you know, chipping—that's what they call it—they watch that nurse until they're sure. Then, *bang!*" Annie chopped her hand down hard. "Out they go, and most of them never put on the white cap again.

"I was smarter than that.

"Looking at those cartons was the same as looking at the figures on the little parlor table. I thought the stuff in them had been sort of stirred around, and I was pretty sure that one of the cartons that was on the bottom before was on top of some of the other cartons now, but I couldn't be *sure.* And I *could* have done it myself when I was . . . well . . . when I was preoccupied.

"Then, two days later, after I had just about decided to let it go, I came in to give you your afternoon medication. You were still having your nap. I tried to turn the doorknob, but for a few seconds it wouldn't turn—it was like the door was locked. Then it *did* turn, and I heard something rattle inside the lock. Then you started to stir around so I just gave you your pills like always. Like I didn't suspect. I'm very good at that, Paul. Then I helped you into your chair so you could write. And when I helped you into it that afternoon, I felt like Saint Paul on the road to Damascus. My eyes were opened. I saw how much of your color had come back. I saw that you were moving your legs. They were giving you pain, and you could only move them a little, but you *were* moving them. And your arms were getting stronger again, as well.

"I saw you were almost *healthy* again.

"That was when I started to realize I could have a problem with you even if no one from the outside suspected a thing. I looked at you and saw that I might not be the only one good at keeping secrets.

"That night I changed your medication for something a little stronger, and when I was sure you weren't going to wake up even if someone exploded a grenade under your bed, I got my little tool-kit from the cellar shelf and I took the keyplate off that door. And look what *I* found!"

She took something small and dark from one of the flap pockets of her mannish shirt. She put it in his numb hand. He brought it up close to his face and stared at it owlishly. It was a bent and twisted chunk of bobby-pin.

Paul began to giggle. He couldn't help it.

"What's so funny, Paul?"

"The day you went to pay your taxes. I needed to open the door again. The wheelchair—it was almost too big—it left black marks. I wanted to wipe them off if I could."

"So I wouldn't see them."

"Yes. But you already had, hadn't you?"

"After I found one of my bobby-pins in the lock?" She smiled herself. "You bet your rooty-patooties I had."

Paul nodded and laughed even harder. He was laughing so hard tears were squirting from his eyes. All his work . . . all his worry . . . all for nothing. It seemed deliciously funny.

He said, "I was worried that piece of bobby-pin might mess me up . . . but it didn't. I never even heard it rattling around. And there was a good reason for that, wasn't there? It never rattled because you took it out. What a fooler you are, Annie."

"Yes," she said, and smiled thinly. "What a fooler I am."

She moved her feet. That muffled wooden thump from the foot of the bed came again.

22

"How many times were you out in all?"

The knife. Oh Christ, the knife.

"Twice. No—wait. I went out again yesterday afternoon around five o'clock. To fill up my water pitcher." This was true; he *had* filled the pitcher. But he had omitted the real reason for his third trip. The real reason was under his mattress. The Princess and the Pea. Paulie and the Pig-Sticker. "Three times, counting the trip for the water."

"Tell the truth, Paul."

"Just three times, I swear. And never to get away. For Christ's sake I'm writing a book here, in case you didn't notice."

"Don't use the Saviour's name in vain, Paul."

"You quit using mine that way and maybe I will. The first time I was in so much pain that it felt like someone had put me into hell from the knees on down. And someone did. *You* did, Annie."

"Shut up, Paul!"

"The second time I just wanted to get something to eat, and make sure I had some extra supplies in here in case you were gone a long time," he went on, ignoring her. "Then I got thirsty. That's all there is. No big conspiracy."

"You didn't try the telephone either time, I suppose, or look at the locks—because you are just *such* a good little boy."

"Sure I tried the phone. Sure I looked at the locks . . . not that I would have gotten very far in the mudbath out there even if your doors had been wide open." The dope was coming in heavier and heavier waves, and now he just wished she would shut up and go away. She had already doped him enough to tell the truth—he was afraid he would have to pay the consequences in time. But first he wanted to sleep.

"How many times did you go out?"

"I told you—"

"How many times?" Her voice was rising. *"Tell the truth!"*

"I *am!* Three times!"

"*How many times, God damn it?*"

In spite of the cruiser-load of dope she'd shot into him, Paul began to be frightened.

At least if she does something to me it can't hurt too much . . . and she wants me to finish the book . . . she said so. . . .

"You're treating me like a fool." He noticed how shiny her skin was, like some sort of polymer plastic stretched tightly over stone. There seemed to be no pores at all in that face.

"Annie, I swear—"

"Oh, liars can swear! Liars *love* to swear! Well, go ahead and treat me like a fool, if that's what you want. That's fine. Goody-goody for you. Treat a woman who isn't a fool as if she were, and that woman always comes out ahead. Let me tell you, Paul—I've stretched thread and strands of hair from my own head all *over* this house and have found many of them snapped later on. Snapped or entirely gone . . . just disappeared . . . poof! Not just on my scrapbook but in this hallway and across my dresser drawers upstairs . . . in the shed . . . *all over.*"

Annie, how could I possibly get out in the shed with all those locks on the kitchen door? he wanted to ask, but she gave him no time, only plunged on.

"Now you go right ahead and keep telling me it was only *three times,* Mister Smart Guy, and I'll tell *you* who the fool is."

He stared at her, groggy but appalled. He didn't know how to answer her. It was so paranoid . . . so crazy. . . .

My God, he thought, suddenly forgetting the shed, *upstairs? Did she say UPSTAIRS?*

"Annie, how in God's name could I get upstairs?"

"Oh, *RIGHT!*" she cried, her voice cracking. "Oh, *SURE!* I came in here a few days ago and you'd managed to get into your wheel-chair *all by yourself!* If you could do that, you could get upstairs! *You could crawl!*"

"Yes, on my broken legs and my shattered knee," he said.

Again that black look of *crevasse;* the batty darkness under the meadow. Annie Wilkes was gone. The Bourka Bee-Goddess was here.

"You don't want to be smart to me, Paul," she whispered.

"Well, Annie, one of us has to at least try, and you're not doing a very good job. If you'd just try to see how cr—"

"How many times?"

"Three."

"The first time to get medication."

"Yes. Novril capsules."

"And the second time to get food."

"That's right."

"The third time it was to fill up the pitcher."

"Yes. Annie, I'm so dizzy—"

"You filled it in the bathroom up the hall."

"Yes—"

"Once for medication, once for food, and once for water."

"Yes, I told you!" He tried to yell, but what came out was a strengthless croak.

She reached into her skirt pocket again and brought out the butcher knife. Its keen blade glimmered in the brightening morning light. She suddenly twisted to the left and threw the knife. She threw it with the deadly, half-casual grace of a carnival performer. It stuck, quivering, in the plaster below the picture of the Arc de Triomphe.

"I investigated under your mattress a little before I gave you your pre-op shot. I expected to find capsules; the knife was a complete surprise. I almost cut myself. But *you* didn't put it there, did you?"

He didn't reply. His mind was spinning and diving like an out-of-control amusement-park ride. Pre-op shot? Was that what she had said? *Pre-op?* He was suddenly, utterly sure that she meant to pull the knife from the wall and castrate him with it.

"No, *you* didn't put it there. *You* went out once for medication, once for food, and once for water. This knife must have . . . why, it must have *floated* in here and slid under there all by itself. Yes, that's what must have happened!" Annie shrieked derisive laughter.

PRE-OP??? Dear God, is that what she said?

"Damn you!" she cried. "God *damn* you! *How many times?*"

"All right! All right! I got the knife when I went after the water! I confess! If you think that means I was out any number of times, go on and fill in the blank! If you want it to be five times, it was five. If you want it to be twenty, or fifty, or a hundred, that's what it was. I'll admit it. However many times you think, Annie, that's how many times I was out."

For a moment, in his anger and dopey befuddlement, he had lost sight of the hazy, frightening concept inherent in that phrase *pre-op shot*. He wanted to tell her so much, wanted to tell her even though he knew that a ravening paranoid like Annie would reject what was so obvious. It had been damp; Scotch tape did not like the damp; in many cases her Ludlumesque little traps had undoubtedly just peeled off and floated away on some random draft. And the rats. With a lot of water in the cellar and the mistress of the manor gone, he had heard them in the walls. Of course. They had the run of the house—and they would be attracted by all the oogy stuff Annie had left around. The rats were probably the gremlins who had broken most of Annie's threads. But she would only push such ideas away. In her mind, he was almost ready to run the New York Marathon.

"Annie . . . Annie, what did you mean when you said you gave me a pre-op shot?"

But Annie was still fixated on the other matter. "I say it was seven," she said softly. "At least seven. Was it seven?"

"If you want it to be seven, it was seven. What did you mean when you said—"

"I can see you mean to be stubborn," she said. "I guess fellows like you must get so used to lying for a living that you just can't stop doing it in real life. But that's all right, Paul. Because the *principle* doesn't change if you were out seven times, or seventy, or seventy times seven. The *principle* doesn't change, and neither does the *response*."

He was floating, floating, floating away. He closed his eyes and heard her speak as if from a long distance away . . . like a supernatural voice from a cloud. *Goddess,* he thought.

"Have you ever read about the early days at the Kimberly diamond mines, Paul?"

"I wrote the book on that one," he said for no reason at all, and laughed.

(pre-op? pre-op shot?)

"Sometimes, the native workers stole diamonds. They wrapped them in leaves and poked them up their rectums. If they got away from the Big Hole without being discovered, they would run. And do you know what the British did to them if they got caught before they could get over Oranjerivier and into Boer country?"

"Killed them, I suppose," he said, eyes still closed.

"Oh, no! That would have been like junking an expensive car

just because of a broken spring. If they caught them they made sure that they could go on working . . . but they *also* made sure they would never run again. The operation was called *hobbling,* Paul, and that is what I'm going to do to you. For my own safety . . . and yours as well. Believe me, you need to be protected from yourself. Just remember, a little pain and it will be over. Try to hold that thought."

Terror sharp as a gust of wind filled with razor-blades blew through the dope and Paul's eyes flew open. She had risen and now drew the bedclothes down, exposing his twisted legs and bare feet.

"No," he said. "No . . . Annie . . . whatever it is you've got on your mind, we can talk about it, can't we? . . . please . . ."

She bent over. When she straightened up she was holding the axe from the shed in one hand and a propane torch in the other. The blade of the axe gleamed. Written on the side of the propane torch was the word *Bernz-O-matiC.* She bent down again and this time came up with a dark bottle and the box of matches. There was a label on the dark bottle. Written on the label was the word *Betadine.*

He never forgot these things, these words, these names.

"Annie, no!" he screamed. *"Annie, I'll stay right here! I won't even get out of bed! Please! Oh God please don't cut me!"*

"It'll be all right," she said, and her face now had that slack, unplugged look—that look of perplexed vacuity—and before his mind was completely consumed in a forest fire of panic he understood that when this was over, she would have only the vaguest memories of what she had done, as she had only the vaguest memories of killing the children and the old people and the terminal patients and Andrew Pomeroy. After all, this was the woman who, although she'd gotten her cap in 1966, had told him only minutes ago that she had been a nurse for ten years.

She killed Pomeroy with that same axe. I know she did.

He continued to shriek and plead, but his words had become inarticulate babble. He tried to turn over, turn away from her, and his legs cried out. He tried to draw them up, make them less vulnerable, less of a target, and his knee screamed.

"Only a minute more, Paul," she said, and uncapped the Betadine. She poured a brownish-red muck over his left ankle. "Only a minute more and it's over." She tipped the blade of the axe flat, the tendons standing out in her strong right wrist, and he could see the wink of the amethyst ring she still wore on the pinkie finger of that hand. She poured Betadine on the blade. He could smell it, a doctor's-office smell. That smell meant you were going to get a shot.

"Just a little pain, Paul. It won't be bad." She turned the axe over and splashed the other side of the blade. He could see random flowers of rust blooming on this side before the goop covered it.

"Annie Annie oh Annie please please no please don't Annie I swear to you I'll be good I swear to God I'll be good please give me a chance to be good OH ANNIE PLEASE LET ME BE GOOD—"

"Just a little pain. Then this nasty business will be behind us for good, Paul."

She tossed the open bottle of Betadine over her shoulder, her face blank and empty and yet so inarguably solid; she slid her right hand down the handle of the axe almost to the steel head. She gripped the handle farther up in her left hand and spread her legs like a logger.

"ANNIE OH PLEASE PLEASE DON'T HURT ME!"

Her eyes were mild and drifting. "Don't worry," she said. "I'm a trained nurse."

The axe came whistling down and buried itself in Paul Sheldon's left leg just above the ankle. Pain exploded up his body in a gigantic bolt. Dark-red blood splattered across her face like Indian war-paint. It splattered the wall. He heard the blade squeal against bone as she wrenched it free. He looked unbelievingly down at himself. The sheet was turning red. He saw his toes wriggling. Then he saw her raising the dripping axe again. Her hair had fallen free of its pins and hung around her blank face.

He tried to pull back in spite of the pain in his leg and knee and realized that his leg was moving but his foot wasn't. All he was doing was widening the axe-slash, making it open like a mouth. He had time enough to realize his foot was now only held on his leg by the meat of his calf before the blade came down again, directly into the gash, shearing through the rest of his leg and burying itself deep in the mattress. Springs boinked and squoinked.

Annie pulled the axe free and tossed it aside. She looked absently at the jetting stump for a moment and then picked up the box of matches. She lit one. Then she picked up the propane torch with the word *Bernz-O-matiC* on the side and twisted the valve on the side. The torch hissed. Blood poured from the place where he no longer was. Annie held the match delicately under the nozzle of the *Bernz-O-matiC*. There was a *floof!* sound. A long yellow flame appeared. Annie adjusted it to a hard blue line of fire.

"Can't suture," she said. "No time. Tourniquet's no good. No central pressure point. Got to
(rinse)
cauterize."

She bent. Paul screamed as fire splashed over the raw and bleeding stump. Smoke drifted up. It smelled sweet. He and his first wife had honeymooned on Maui. There had been a luau. This smell reminded him of the smell of the pig when they brought it out of the pit where it had cooked all day. The pig had been on a stick, sagging, black, falling apart.

The pain was screaming. *He* was screaming.

"Almost over," she said, and turned the valve, and now the ground sheet caught fire around the stump that was no longer bleeding, the stump that was as black as the pig's hide had been when they had brought it out of the luau pit—Eileen had turned away but Paul had watched, fascinated, as they pulled off the pig's crackling skin as easily as you might skim off a sweater after a football game.

"Almost over—"

She turned the torch off. His leg lay in a line of flames with his severed foot wavering beyond it. She bent and now came up with his old friend the yellow floor-bucket. She dumped it over the flames.

He was screaming, screaming. The pain! The goddess! The pain! O Africa!

She stood looking at him, at the darkening, bloody sheet, with vague consternation—her face was the face of a woman who hears on her radio that an earthquake has killed ten thousand people in Pakistan or Turkey.

"You'll be all right, Paul," she said, but her voice was suddenly frightened. Her eyes began to dart aimlessly around as they had when it seemed that the fire of his burning book might get out of control. They suddenly fixed on something, almost with relief. "I'll just get rid of the trash."

She picked up his foot. Its toes were still spasming. She carried it across the room. By the time she got to the door they had stopped moving. He could see a scar on the instep and remembered how he had gotten that, how he had stepped on a piece of bottle when he was just a kid. Had that been at Revere Beach? Yes, he thought it had been. He remembered he had cried and his father had told him it was just a little cut. His father had told him to stop acting like someone had cut his goddam foot off. Annie paused at the door and looked back at Paul, who shrieked and writhed in the charred and blood-soaked bed, his face a deathly fading white.

"Now you're hobbled," she said, "and don't you blame me. It's your own fault."

She went out.

So did Paul.

23

The cloud was back. Paul dived for it, not caring if the cloud meant death instead of unconsciousness this time. He almost hoped it did. Just . . . no pain, please. No memories, no pain, no horror, no Annie Wilkes.

He dived for the cloud, dived *into* the cloud, dimly hearing the sounds of his own shrieks and smelling his own cooked meat.

As his thoughts faded, he thought: *Goddess! Kill you! Goddess! Kill you! Goddess!*

Then there was nothing but nothing.

PAUL

It's no good. I've been trying to sleep for the last half-hour, and I can't. Writing here is a sort of drug. It's the only thing I look forward to. This afternoon I read what I wrote. . . . And it seemed vivid. I know it seems vivid because my imagination fills in all the bits another person wouldn't understand. I mean, it's vanity. But it seems a sort of magic. . . . And I just can't live in this present. I would go mad if I did.

—John Fowles
The Collector

1

CHAPTER 32

"Oh blessed Jesus," Ia moa ed, a d made a co vul-
sive moveme t forward. Geoffrey grasped his frie d's arm.
The steady beat of the drums pulsed i his head like some-
thi g heard i a killi g delirium. Bees dro ed arou d
them, but o e paused; they simply flew past a d i to the
cleari g as if draw by a mag et--which, Geoffrey hough
sickly, hey

2

Paul picked up the typewriter and shook it. After a time, a small
piece of steel fell out onto the board across the arms of the wheelchair. He picked it up and looked at it.

It was the letter t. The typewriter had just thrown its t.

He thought: *I am going to complain to the management. I am going
to not just* ask *for a new typewriter but fucking* demand *one. She's got
the money—I know she does. Maybe it's squirrelled away in fruit-jars
under the barn or maybe it's stuffed in the walls at her Laughing Place,
but she's got the dough, and t, my God, the second-most-common letter
in the English language—!*

Of course he would ask Annie for nothing, much less demand.
Once there had been a man who would at least have *asked*. A man
who had been in a great deal more pain, a man who had had nothing
to hold onto, not even this shitty book. That man would have *asked*.

Hurt or not, that man had had the guts to at least *try* to stand up
to Annie Wilkes.

He had been that man, and he supposed he ought to be ashamed,
but *that* man had had two big advantages over this one: *that* man
had had two feet . . . and two thumbs.

Paul sat reflectively for a moment, reread the last line (mentally
filling in the omissions), and then simply went back to work.

Better that way.

Better not to ask.

Better not to provoke.

Outside his window, bees buzzed.

It was the first day of summer.

3

had been.

    "Let me go!" Ian snarled, and turned on Geoffrey,

his right hand curling into a fist. His eyes bulged madly

from his livid face, and he seemed totally unaware of who

was holding him back from his darling. Geoffrey realized

with cold certainty that what they had seen when Hezekiah

pulled the protective screen of bushes aside had come very

close to driving Ian mad. He still tottered on the brink,

and the slightest push would send him over. If that happened,

he would take Misery with him.

    "Ian --"

    "Let me go, I say!" Ian pulled backward with

furious strength, and Hezekiah moaned fearfully. "No boss,

make dem bees crazy, dem sting Mis'wess--"

    Ian seemed not to hear. Eyes wild and blank,

he lashed out at Geoffrey, striking his old friend high on

the cheekbone. Black stars rocketed through Geoffrey's head.

In spite of them, he saw Hezekiah beginning to swing the potentially deadly <u>gosha</u>--a sand-filled bag the Bourkas favored for close work--in time to hiss: "No! Let me handle this!"

Reluctantly, Hezekiah allowed the <u>gosha</u> to subside to the end of its leather string like a slowing pendulum.

Then Geoffrey's head was rocked back by a fresh blow. This one mashed his lips back against his teeth, and he felt the warm salt-sweet taste of blood begin to seep into his mouth. There was a rough purring sound as Ian's dress shirt, now sun-faded and already torn in a dozen places, began to come apart in Geoffrey's grasp. In another moment he would be free. Geoffrey realized with dazed wonder that it was the same shirt Ian had worn to the Baron and Baroness's dinner party three nights ago...of course it was. There had been no opportunity to change since then, not for Ian, not for any of them. Only three nights ago... but the shirt looked as if Ian had been wearing it for at least three years, and Geoffrey felt as if at least three hundred had passed since the party. <u>Only three nights ago,</u> he thought again with stupid wonder, and then Ian was raining blows into his face.

"<u>Let me go, damn you!</u>" Ian drove his bloody fist into Geoffrey's face again and again--his friend for whom, in his right mind, he would have died.

"Do you want to demonstrate your love for her by

killing her?" Geoffrey asked quietly. "If you want to
do that, then by all means, old boy, knock me senseless."

Ian's fist hesitated. Something at least approxi-
mating sense came back into his terrified, maddened gaze.

"I must go to her," he murmured like a man in a
dream. "I'm sorry I hit you, Geoffrey--truly sorry, my
dear old man, and I'm sure you know it--but I must... You
see her..." He looked again, as if to confirm the dread-
fulness of the sight, and again made as if to rush to where
Misery had been tied to a post in a jungle clearing, her arms
over her head. Glimmering on her wrists and fastening her
to the lowest branch of the eucalyptus, which was the only
tree in the clearing, was something the Bourkas had apparently
taken a fancy to before sending Baron Heidzig into the mouth
of the idol and to his undoubtedly terrible death: the Baron's
blued steel handcuffs.

This time it was Hezekiah who grabbed Ian, but
the bushes rustled again and Geoffrey looked into the
clearing, his breath momentarily catching in his throat,
as a bit of fabric may catch on a thorn--he felt like a
man who must walk up a rocky hill with a load of decayed
and dangerously volatile explosives in his arms. One
sting, he thought. Just one and it's all over for her.

"No, boss, mussun'," Hezekiah was saying with
a kind of terrified patience. "It like d'utha boss
be sayin'...if you go out dere, de bees wake up from

dey dream. And if de bees wake, it doan matter for her
if she be dine of one sting or one-de-one t'ousan' sting.
If de bees wake up from dey dream we all die, but she die
firs' and de mos' 'orrible."

Little by little Ian relaxed between the two
men, one of them black, the other white. His head
turned toward the clearing with dreadful reluctance, as
if he did not wish to look and yet could not forbear to.

"Then what are we to do? What are we to do for
my poor darling?"

I don't know came to Geoffrey's lips, and in his
own state of terrible distress, he was barely able to bite
them back. Not for the first time it occurred to him that
Ian's possession of the woman Geoffrey loved just as dearly
(if secretly) allowed Ian to indulge in an odd sort of
selfishness and an almost womanly hysteria that Geoffrey
himself must forgo; after all, to the rest of the world he
was only Misery's friend.

Yes, just her friend, he thought with half-
hysterical irony, and then his own eyes were drawn back
to the clearing. To his friend.

Misery wore not a stitch of clothing, yet Geoffrey
thought that even the most prudish church-thrice-a-week
village biddy could not have faulted her for indecency.
The hypothetical old prude might have run screaming from
the sight of Misery, but her screams would have been caused

by terror and revulsion rather than outraged propriety.
Misery wore not a stitch of clothing, but she was far from
naked.

　　　　She was dressed in bees. From the tips of her
toes to the crown of her chestnut hair, she was dressed
in bees. She seemed almost to be wearing some strange nun's
habit--strange because it moved and undulated across the
swells of her breasts and hips even though there was not even
a ghost of a breeze. Likewise, her face seemed encased in a
wimple of almost Mohammedan modesty--only her blue eyes
peered out of the mask of bees which crawled sluggishly over
her face, hiding mouth and nose and chin and brows. More
bees, giant Africa browns, the most poisonous and bad-tempered
bees in all the world, crawled back and forth over the Baron's
steel bracelets before joining the living gloves on Misery's
hands.

　　　　As Geoffrey watched, more and more bees flew into
the clearing from all points of the compass--yet it was clear
to him, even in his current distraction, that most of them
were coming from the west, where the great dark stone face of
the goddess loomed.

　　　　The drums pulsed their steady rhythm, in its
way as much a soporific as the sleepy drone of the bees.
But Geoffrey knew how deceptive that sleepiness was; he
had seen what happened to he Baroness, and only thanked
God that Ian had been spared that...and the sound of that

M   I   S   E   R   Y   217

sleepy hum suddenly rising to a furious buzz-saw squeal...
a sound which had at first muffled and then drowned the
woman's agonized dying screams. She had been a vain and
foolish creature, dangerous as well--she had almost gotten
them killed when she had freed Stringfellow's bushmaster--
but silly or not, foolish or not, dangerous or not, no
man or woman deserved to die like that.

In his mind Geoffrey echoed Ian's question:
What are we to do? What are we to do for our poor darling?

Hezekiah said: "Nothing can do now, boss--but
she in no danger. As long as de drums dey beat, de bees
will sleep. And Mis'wess, she is goan sleep, too."

Now the bees covered her in a thick and moving
blanket; her eyes, open but unseei g, seemed to be receding
into a living cave of crawling, stumbling, droning bees.

"And if the drums stop?" Geoffrey asked in a low,
almost strengthless voice, and just then , the drums did.

For a mom   h   hr   of h m

4

Paul looked unbelievingly at the last line, then picked the Royal
up—he had gone on lifting it like some weird barbell when she
was out of the room, God knew why—and shook it again. The keys
clittered, and then another chunk of metal fell out on the board
which served as his desk.

Outside he could hear the roaring sound of Annie's bright-blue riding lawnmower—she was around front, giving the grass a good trim so those cockadoodie Roydmans wouldn't have anything to talk about in town.

He set the typewriter down, then rocked it up so he could fish out this new surprise. He looked at it in the strong late-afternoon sunlight slanting in through the window. His expression of disbelief never altered.

Printed in raised and slightly ink-stained metal on the head of the key was:

E

e

Just to add to the fun, the old Royal had now thrown the most frequently used letter in the English language.

Paul looked at the calendar. The picture was of a flowered meadow and the month said May, but Paul kept his own dates now on a piece of scrap paper, and according to his home-made calendar it was June 21.

Roll out those lazy hazy crazy days of summer, he thought sourly, and threw the key-hammer in the general direction of the waste-basket.

Well, what do I do now? he thought, but of course he knew what came next. Longhand. That was what came next.

But not now. Although he had been tearing along like a house afire a few seconds ago, anxious to get Ian, Geoffrey, and the ever-amusing Hezekiah caught in the Bourkas' ambush so that the entire party could be transported to the caves behind the face of the idol for the rousing finale, he was suddenly tired. The hole in the paper had closed with an adamant bang.

Tomorrow.

He would go to longhand tomorrow.

Fuck longhand. Complain to the management, Paul.

But he would do no such thing. Annie had gotten too weird.

He listened to the monotonous snarl of the riding lawnmower, saw her shadow, and, as so often happened when he thought of how weird Annie was getting, his mind recalled the image of the axe rising, then falling; the image of her horrid impassive deadly face splattered with his blood. It was clear. Every word she had spoken, every word he had screamed, the squeal of the axe pulling away from the severed bone, the blood on the wall. All crystal-clear. And, as he *also* so often did, he tried to block this memory and found himself a second too late.

Because the crucial plot-twist of *Fast Cars* concerned Tony Bonasaro's near-fatal crack-up in his last desperate effort to escape the police (and this led to the epilogue, which consisted of the bruising interrogation conducted by the late Lieutenant Gray's partner in Tony's hospital room), Paul had interviewed a number of crash victims. He had heard the same thing time and time again. It came in different wrappers, but it always boiled down to the same thing: *I remember getting into the car, and I remember waking up here. Everything else is a blank.*

Why couldn't that have happened to *him?*

Because writers remember everything, Paul. Especially the hurts. Strip a writer to the buff, point to the scars, and he'll tell you the story of each small one. From the big ones you get novels, not amnesia. A little talent is a nice thing to have if you want to be a writer, but the only real requirement is that ability to remember the story of every scar.

Art consists of the persistence of memory.

Who had said that? Thomas Szasz? William Faulkner? Cyndi Lauper?

But that last name brought its own association, a painful and unhappy one under these circumstances: a memory of Cyndi Lauper hiccuping her way cheerfully through "Girls Just Want to Have Fun" that was so clear it was almost auditory: *Oh daddy dear, you're still number one / But girls, they wanna have fuh-un / Oh when the workin day is done / Girls just wanna have fun.*

Suddenly he wanted a hit of rock and roll worse than he had ever wanted a cigarette. It didn't have to be Cyndi Lauper. Anyone would do. Jesus Christ, Ted Nugent would be just fine.

The axe coming down.

The whisper of the axe.

Don't think about it.

But that was stupid. He kept telling himself not to think about it, knowing all the while that it was there, like a bone in his throat. Was he going to let it stay there, or was he going to be a man and sick the fucking thing up?

Another memory came then; it seemed like this was an All Request Oldies day for Paul Sheldon. This one was of Oliver Reed as the mad but silkily persuasive scientist in David Cronenberg's movie, *The Brood.* Reed urging his patients at The Institute of Psychoplasmatics (a name Paul had found deliciously funny) to "go through it! Go all the way through it!"

Well . . . maybe sometimes that wasn't such bad advice.

I went through it once. That was enough.

Bullshit was what *that* was. If going through things once was enough, he would have been a fucking vacuum-cleaner salesman, like his father.

Go through it, then. Go all the way through it, Paul. Start with Misery.

No.

Yes.

Fuck you.

Paul leaned back, put his hand over his eyes, and, like it or not, he began to go through it.

All the way through it.

5

He hadn't died, hadn't slept, but for awhile after Annie hobbled him the pain went away. He had only drifted, feeling untethered from his body, a balloon of pure thought rising away from its string.

Oh shit, why was he bothering? She had done it, and all the time between then and now had been pain and boredom and occasional bouts of work on his stupidly melodramatic book to escape the former two. The whole thing was meaningless.

Oh, but it's not—there is a theme here, Paul. It's the thread that runs through everything. The thread that runs so true. Can't you see it?

Misery, of course. That was the thread that ran through everything, but, true thread or false, it was so goddam silly.

As a common noun it meant pain, usually lengthy and often pointless; as a proper one it meant a character and a plot, the latter most assuredly lengthy and pointless, but one which would nonetheless end very soon. Misery ran through the last four (or maybe it was five) months of his life, all right, plenty of Misery, Misery day in and Misery day out, but surely that was too simple, surely—

Oh no, Paul. Nothing is simple about Misery. Except that you owe

*her your life, such as that may be . . . because you turned out to be
Scheherazade after all, didn't you?*

Again he tried to turn aside from these thoughts, but found
himself unable. The persistence of memory and all that. Hacks just
want to have fun. Then an unexpected idea came, a new one which
opened a whole new avenue of thought.

*What you keep overlooking, because it's so obvious, is that you were—
are—also Scheherazade to yourself.*

He blinked, lowering his hand and staring stupidly out into the
summer he had never expected he would see. Annie's shadow passed
and then disappeared again.

Was that true?

Scheherazade to myself? he thought again. If so, then he was faced
with an idiocy that was utterly colossal: he owed his survival to the
fact that he wanted to finish the piece of shit Annie had coerced
him into writing. He should have died . . . but couldn't. Not until
he knew how it all came out.

Oh you're fucking crazy.

You sure?

No. He was no longer sure. Not about anything.

With one exception: his whole life had hinged and continued to
hinge on Misery.

He let his mind drift.

The cloud, he thought. *Begin with the cloud.*

6

This time the cloud had been darker, denser, somehow smoother.
There was a sensation not of floating but of sliding. Sometimes
thoughts came, and sometimes there was pain, and sometimes, dimly,
he heard Annie's voice, sounding the way it had when the burning
manuscript in the barbecue had threatened to get out of control:
"Drink this, Paul . . . you've *got* to!"

Sliding?

No.

That was not quite the right verb. The right verb was *sinking.*
He remembered a telephone call which had come at three in the
morning—this was when he was in college. Sleepy fourth-floor

dorm proctor hammering on his door, telling him to come on and answer the fucking phone. His mother. *Come home as quick as you can, Paulie. Your father has had a bad stroke. He's sinking.* And he *had* come as fast as he could, pushing his old Ford wagon to seventy in spite of the front-end shimmy that developed at speeds over fifty, but in the end it had all been for nothing. When he got there, his father was no longer sinking but sunk.

How close had he himself come to sinking on the night of the axe? He didn't know, but the fact that he had felt almost no pain during the week following the amputation was a pretty clear indicator of just how close, perhaps. That, and the panic in her voice.

He had lain in a semi-coma, barely breathing because of the respiratory-depressant side-effects of the medication, the glucose drips back in his arms again. And what brought him out of it was the beat of drums and the drone of bees.

Bourka drums.

Bourka bees.

Bourka *dreams.*

Color bleeding slowly and relentlessly into a land and a tribe that never were beyond the margins of the paper on which he wrote.

A dream of the goddess, the *face* of the goddess, looming black over the jungle green, brooding and eroded. Dark goddess, dark continent, a stone head full of bees. Overlying even all this was a picture, which grew clearer and clearer (as if a giant slide had been projected against the cloud in which he lay) as time passed. It was a picture of a clearing in which one old eucalyptus tree stood. Hanging from the lowest branch of this tree was an old-fashioned pair of blued steel handcuffs. Bees were crawling over them. The cuffs were empty. They were empty because Misery had—

—escaped? She had, hadn't she? Wasn't that how the story was supposed to go?

It *had* been—but now he wasn't so sure. *Was* that what those empty handcuffs meant? Or had she been taken away? Taken into the idol? Taken to the queen bee, the Big Babe of the Bourkas?

You were also Scheherazade to yourself.

Who are you telling this story for, *Paul? Who are you telling it* to? *To Annie?*

Of course not. He did not look through that hole in the paper to see Annie, or please Annie . . . he looked through it to get *away* from Annie.

The pain had started. And the itch. The cloud began to lighten again, and rift apart. He began to glimpse the room, which was bad, and Annie, which was even worse. Still, he had decided to live. Some part of him that was as addicted to the chapter-plays as Annie had been as a child had decided he could not die until he saw how it all came out.

Had she escaped, with the help of Ian and Geoffrey?

Or had she been taken into the head of the goddess?

It was ridiculous, but these stupid questions actually seemed to need answering.

7

She didn't want to let him go back to work—not at first. He could see in her skittery eyes how frightened she had been and still was. How close he had come. She was taking extravagant care of him, changing the bandages on his weeping stump every eight hours (and at first, she had informed him with the air of one who knows she will never get a medal for what she has done—although she deserves one—she had done it every four hours), giving him sponge baths and alcohol rubs—as if to deny what she had done. Work, she said, would hurt him. *It would put you back, Paul. I wouldn't say it if it weren't so—believe me. At least you know what's ahead—I'm dying to find out what happens next.* It turned out she had read everything he had written—all his pre-surgery work, you might say—while he lingered near death . . . better than three hundred manuscript pages. He hadn't filled in the n's in the last forty or so; Annie had done that. She showed him these with an uneasily defiant sort of pride. Her n's were textbook neat, a striking comparison with his own, which had degenerated into a humpbacked scrawl.

Although Annie never said so, he believed she had filled in the n's either as another evidence of her solicitude—*How can you say I was cruel to you, Paul, when you see all the n's I have filled in?*—or as an act of atonement, or possibly even as a quasi-superstitious rite: enough bandage-changes, enough sponge baths, enough n's filled in, and Paul would live. *Bourka bee-woman work pow'ful mojo-magic, Bwana, fill in all dese hoodaddy n's an' all be well again.*

That was how she had begun . . . but then *the gotta* set in. Paul knew all the symptoms. When she said she was dying to find out what happened next, she wasn't kidding.

Because you went on living *to find out what happened next, isn't that what you're really saying?*

Crazy as it was—shameful, even, in its absurdity—he thought it was.

The gotta.

It was something he had been irritated to find he could generate in the *Misery* books almost at will but in his mainstream fiction erratically or not at all. You didn't know exactly where to find *the gotta,* but you always knew when you did. It made the needle of some internal Geiger counter swing all the way over to the end of the dial. Even sitting in front of the typewriter slightly hung-over, drinking cups of black coffee and crunching a Rolaid or two every couple of hours (knowing he should give up the fucking cigarettes, at least in the morning, but unable to bring himself to the sticking point), months from finishing and light-years from publication, you knew *the gotta* when you got it. Having it always made him feel slightly ashamed—manipulative. But it also made him feel vindicated in his labor. Christ, days went by and the hole in the paper was small, the light was dim, the overheard conversations witless. You pushed on because that was all you could do. Confucius say if man want to grow one row of corn, first must shovel one ton of shit. And then one day the hole widened to VistaVision width and the light shone through like a sunray in a Cecil B. De Mille epic and you knew you had *the gotta,* alive and kicking.

The gotta, as in: "I think I'll stay up another fifteen-twenty minutes, honey, I gotta see how this chapter comes out." Even though the guy who says it spent the day at work thinking about getting laid and knows the odds are good his wife is going to be asleep when he finally gets up to the bedroom.

The gotta, as in: "I know I should be starting supper now—he'll be mad if it's TV dinners again—but I gotta see how this ends."

I gotta know will she live.

I gotta know will he catch the shitheel who killed his father.

I gotta know if she finds out her best friend's screwing her husband.

The gotta. Nasty as a hand-job in a sleazy bar, fine as a fuck from the world's most talented call-girl. Oh boy it was bad and oh boy it was good and oh boy in the end it didn't matter how rude it was or how crude it was because in the end it was just like the Jacksons said on that record—don't stop til you get enough.

8

You were also Scheherazade to yourself.

That was not an idea he was able to articulate or even understand, not then; he had been in too much pain. But he had known just the same, hadn't he?

Not you. The guys in the sweatshop. They *knew.*

Yes. That had the ring of the right.

The sound of the riding mower swelled louder. Annie came into view for a moment. She looked at him, saw him looking back, and raised a hand to him. He raised one of his own—the one with the thumb still on it—in return. She passed from sight again. Good deal.

He was finally able to convince her that returning to work would put him forward, not back. . . . He was haunted by the specificity of those images which had lured him out of the cloud, and *haunted* was exactly the right word: until they were written down they were shades which would remain unlaid.

And while she hadn't believed him—not then—she had allowed him to go back to work just the same. Not because he had convinced her but because of *the gotta.*

At first he had been able to work only in painfully short bursts—fifteen minutes, maybe half an hour if the story really demanded it of him. Even short bursts were agony. A shift in position caused the stump to come brightly alive, the way a smouldering brand will burst into flame when fanned by a breeze. It hurt furiously while he wrote, but that was not the worst—the worst was the hour or two afterward, when the healing stump would madden him with a droney itch, like swarming, sleepy bees.

He had been right, not her. He never became really well—probably could not do so in such a situation—but his health did improve and some of his strength came back. He was aware that the horizons of his interest had shrunk, but he accepted this as the price of survival. It was a genuine wonder he had survived at all.

Sitting here in front of this typewriter with its increasingly bad teeth, looking back over a period which had consisted of work rather than events, Paul nodded. Yes, he supposed he had been his own Scheherazade, just as he was his own dream-woman when he grabbed hold of himself and jacked off to the feverish beat of his fantasies. He didn't need a psychiatrist to point out that writing had its autoerotic side—you beat a typewriter instead of your meat, but both acts depended largely on quick wits, fast hands, and a heartfelt commitment to the art of the farfetched.

But hadn't there also been some sort of fuck, even if of the driest variety? Because once he started again . . . well, she wouldn't interrupt him while he was working, but she would take each day's output as soon as he was done, ostensibly to fill in the missing letters, but actually—he knew this by now, just as sexually acute men know which dates will put out at the end of the evening and which ones will not—to get her fix. To get her *gotta*.

The chapter-plays. Yes. Back to that. Only for the last few months she's been going every day instead of just on Saturday afternoons, and the Paul who takes her is her pet writer instead of her older brother.

His stints at the typewriter grew gradually longer as the pain slowly receded and some of his endurance returned . . . but ultimately he wasn't able to write fast enough to satisfy her demands.

The gotta which had kept them both alive—and it had, for without it she surely would have murdered both him and herself long since— was also what had caused the loss of his thumb. It was horrible, but also sort of funny. *Have a little irony, Paul—it's good for your blood.*

And think how much worse it could have been.

It could have been his penis, for instance.

"And I only have one of those," he said, and began to laugh wildly in the empty room in front of the hateful Royal with its gaptoothed grin. He laughed until his gut and stump both ached. Laughed until his *mind* ached. At some point the laughter turned to horrible dry sobs that awoke pain even in what remained of his left thumb, and when that happened he was finally able to stop. He wondered in a dull sort of way how close he was to going insane.

Not that it really mattered, he supposed.

9

One day not long before the thumbectomy—perhaps even less than a week—Annie had come in with two giant dishes of vanilla ice cream, a can of Hershey's chocolate syrup, a pressure can of Reddi-Wip, and a jar in which maraschino cherries red as heart's blood floated like biology specimens.

"I thought I'd make us sundaes, Paul," Annie said. Her tone was spuriously jolly. Paul didn't like it. Not her tone of voice, nor the uneasy look in her eyes. *I'm being a naughty girl,* that look said. It made him wary, put his wind up. It was too easy for him to imagine her looking exactly the same way when she put a heap of clothes on one set of stairs, a dead cat on another.

"Why, thank you, Annie," he said, and watched as she poured the syrup and puffed two cumulus clouds of whipped cream out of the pressure can. She performed these chores with the practiced, heavy hand of the long-time sugar junkie.

"No need for thanks. You deserve it. You've been working so hard."

She gave him his sundae. The sweetness became cloying after the third bite, but he kept on. It was wiser. One of the key rules to survival here on the scenic Western Slope was, to wit, *When Annie's treatin, you best be eatin.* There was silence for awhile, and then Annie put her spoon down, wiped a mixture of chocolate syrup and melting ice cream off her chin with the back of her hand, and said pleasantly: "Tell me the rest."

Paul put his own spoon down. "I beg your pardon?"

"Tell me the rest of the story. I can't wait. I just can't."

And hadn't he known this was coming? Yes. If someone had delivered all twenty reels of the new Rocket Man chapter-play to Annie's house, would she have waited, parceling out only one a week, or even one a day?

He looked at the half-demolished avalanche of her sundae, one cherry almost buried in whipped cream, another floating in chocolate syrup. He remembered the way the living room had looked, with sugar-glazed dishes everywhere.

No. Annie was not the waiting type. Annie would have watched all twenty episodes in one night, even if they gave her eyestrain and a splitting headache.

Because Annie loved sweet things.

"I can't do that," he said.

Her face had darkened at once, but hadn't there been a shadowy relief there, as well? "Oh? Why not?"

Because you wouldn't respect me in the morning, he thought of saying, and clamped down on that. Clamped down hard.

"Because I'm a rotten story-teller," he answered instead.

She slurped up the remainder of her sundae in five huge spoonfuls that would have left Paul's throat gray with frostbite. Then she set her dish down and looked at him angrily, not as if he were the great Paul Sheldon but as if he were someone who had presumed to *criticize* the great Paul Sheldon.

"If you're such a rotten story-teller, how come you have bestsellers and millions of people love the books you write?"

"I didn't say I was a rotten story-*writer*. I actually happen to think I'm pretty good at *that*. But as a story-*teller,* I'm the pits."

"You're just making up a big cockadoodie excuse." Her face was darkening. Her hands were clenched into shiny fists on the heavy material of her skirt. Hurricane Annie was back in the room. Everything that went around came around. Except things no longer *had* been quite the same, had they? He was as scared of her as ever, but her hold over him had nonetheless diminished. His life no longer seemed like such a big deal, *gotta* or no *gotta*. He was only afraid she would hurt him.

"It's *not* an excuse," he had replied. "The two things are like apples and oranges, Annie. People who *tell* stories usually can't *write* stories. If you really think people who can write stories can talk worth a damn, you never watched some poor slob of a novelist fumbling his way through an interview on the *Today* show."

"Well, I don't want to wait," she sulked. "I made you that nice sundae and the least you could do is tell me a *few* things. It doesn't have to exactly be the whole story, I guess, but . . . did the Baron kill Calthorpe?" her eyes sparkled. "That's one thing I *really* want to know. And what did he do with the body if he did? Is it all cut up in that trunk his wife won't let out of her sight? That's what *I* think."

Paul shook his head—not to indicate she had it wrong but to indicate he would not tell.

She became even blacker. Yet her voice was soft. "You're making me very angry—you know that, don't you, Paul?"

"Of course I know it. But I can't help it."

"I could *make* you. I could *make* you help it. I could make you *tell*." But she looked frustrated, as if knowing that she could not. She could make him say some things, but she could not make him tell.

"Annie, do you remember telling me what a little kid says to his mother when she catches him playing with the cleaning fluid under the sink and makes him stop? *Mommy, you're mean!* Isn't that what you're saying now? *Paul, you're mean?*"

"If you make me much madder, I don't promise to be responsible," she said, but he sensed the crisis was already past—she was strangely vulnerable to these concepts of discipline and behavior.

"Well, I'll have to chance that," he said, "because I'm just like that mother—I'm not saying no to be mean, or to spite you—I'm saying no because I really want you to like the story . . . and if I give you what you want, you won't like it, and you won't want it anymore." *And then what will happen to me, Annie?* he thought but did not say.

"At least tell me if that nigger Hezekiah really *does* know where Misery's father is! At least tell me that!"

"Do you want the novel, or do you want me to fill out a questionnaire?"

"Don't you take that sarcastic tone to me!"

"Then don't you pretend you don't understand what I'm saying!" he shouted back. She recoiled from him in surprise and unease, the last of that blackness going out of her face, and all that was left was that weird little-girl look, that I've-been-naughty look. "You want to cut open the golden goose! That's what it comes down to! But when the farmer in the story finally did that, all he had was a dead goose and a bunch of worthless guts!"

"All right," she said. "All right, Paul. Are you going to finish your sundae?"

"I can't eat any more," he said.

"I see. I've upset you. I'm sorry. I expect that you're right. I was wrong to ask." She was perfectly calm again. He had half-expected another period of deep depression or rage to follow, but none had. They had simply gone back to the old routine, Paul writing, Annie reading each day's output, and enough time had passed between the argument and the thumbectomy that Paul had missed the connection. Until now.

I bitched about the typewriter, he thought, looking at it now and listening to the drone of the mower. It sounded fainter now, and he was marginally aware that wasn't because Annie was moving away but because *he* was. He was drowsing off. He did that a lot now, simply drowsed off like some old fart in a nursing home.

Not a lot; I only bitched about it that once. But once was enough, wasn't it? More than enough. That was—what?—a week after she brought those oogy sundaes? Just about that. Just one week and one bitch. About how the clunk of that dead key was driving me crazy. I didn't even suggest she get another used typewriter from Nancy Whoremonger or whoever that woman was, one with all its keys intact. I just said those clunks are driving me crazy, and then, in almost no time at all, presto chango, when it comes to Paul's left thumb, now you see it and now you don't. Except she didn't really do it because I bitched about the typewriter, did she? She did it because I told her no and she had to accept that. It was an act of rage. The rage was the result of realization. What realization? Why, that she didn't hold all the cards after all—that I had a certain passive hold over her. The power of the gotta. I turned out to be a pretty passable Scheherazade after all.

It was crazy. It was funny. It was also real. Millions might scoff, but only because they failed to realize how pervasive the influence of art—even of such a degenerate sort as popular fiction—could become. Housewives arranged their schedules around the afternoon soaps. If they went back into the workplace, they made buying a VCR a top priority so they could watch those same soap operas at night. When Arthur Conan Doyle killed Sherlock Holmes at Reichenbach Falls, all of Victorian England rose as one and demanded him back. The tone of their protests had been Annie's exactly— not bereavement but outrage. Doyle was berated by his own mother when he wrote and told her of his intention to do away with Holmes. Her indignant reply had come by return mail: "Kill that nice Mr. Holmes? Foolishness! *Don't you dare!*"

Or there was the case of his friend Gary Ruddman, who worked for the Boulder Public Library. When Paul had dropped over to see him one day, he had found Gary's shades drawn and a black crepe fluff on the door. Concerned, Paul had knocked hard until Gary answered. *Go away,* Gary had told him. *I'm feeling depressed today. Someone died. Someone important to me.* When Paul asked who, Gary had responded tiredly: *Van der Valk.* Paul had heard him walk away from the door, and although he knocked again, Gary had not

come back. Van der Valk, it turned out, was a fictional detective
created—and then uncreated—by a writer named Nicolas Freeling.

Paul had been convinced Gary's reaction had been more than
false; he thought it had been pretentiously arty. In short, a pose.
He continued to feel this way until 1983, when he read *The World
According to Garp.* He made the mistake of reading the scene where
Garp's younger son dies, impaled on a gearshift lever, shortly before
bed. It was hours before he slept. The scene would not leave his
mind. The thought that grieving for a fictional character was absurd
did more than cross his mind during his tossings and turnings. For
grieving was exactly what he was doing, of course. The realization
had not helped, however, and this had caused him to wonder if
perhaps Gary Ruddman hadn't been a lot more serious about Van
der Valk than Paul had given him credit for at the time. And this
had caused another memory to resurface: finishing William Gold-
ing's *Lord of the Flies* at the age of twelve on a hot summer day,
going to the refrigerator for a cold glass of lemonade . . . and then
suddenly changing direction and speeding up from an amble to an
all-out bolt which had ended in the bathroom. There he had leaned
over the toilet and vomited.

Paul suddenly remembered other examples of this odd mania:
the way people had mobbed the Baltimore docks each month when
the packet bearing the new installment of Mr. Dickens's *Little Dorrit*
or *Oliver Twist* was due (some had drowned, but this did not dis-
courage the others); the old woman of a hundred and five who had
declared she would live until Mr. Galsworthy finished *The Forsyte
Saga*—and who had died less than an hour after having the final
page of the final volume read to her; the young mountainclimber
hospitalized with a supposedly fatal case of hypothermia whose
friends had read *The Lord of the Rings* to him nonstop, around the
clock, until he came out of his coma; hundreds of other such in-
cidents.

Every "best-selling" writer of fiction would, he supposed, have
his own personal example or examples of radical reader involvement
with the make-believe worlds the writer creates . . . *examples of the
Scheherazade complex,* Paul thought now, half-dreaming as the sound
of Annie's mower ebbed and flowed at some great echoing distance.
He remembered getting two letters suggesting Misery theme parks,
on the order of Disney World or Great Adventure. One of these
letters had included a crude blueprint. But the blue-ribbon winner

(at least until Annie Wilkes had entered his life) had been Mrs. Roman D. Sandpiper III, of Ink Beach, Florida. Mrs. Roman D. Sandpiper, whose given name was Virginia, had turned an upstairs room of her home into Misery's Parlor. She included Polaroids of Misery's Spinning Wheel, Misery's Escritoire (complete with a half-completed bread-and-butter note to Mr. Faverey, saying she would be in attendance at the School Hall Recitation on 20th Nov. *inst.*— done in what Paul thought was an eerily apt hand for his heroine, not a round and flowing ladies' script but a half-feminine copperplate), Misery's Couch, Misery's Sampler (*Let Love Instruct You; Do Not Presume to Instruct Love*), etc., etc. The furnishings, Mrs. Roman D. ("Virginia") Sandpiper's letter said, were all genuine, not reproductions, and while Paul could not tell for sure, he guessed that it was the truth. If so, this expensive bit of make-believe must have cost Mrs. Roman D. ("Virginia") Sandpiper thousands of dollars. Mrs. Roman D. ("Virginia") Sandpiper hastened to assure him that she was not using his character to make money, nor did she have any plans in that direction—heaven forbid!—but she *did* want him to see the pictures, and to tell her what she had wrong (which, she was sure, must be a great deal). Mrs. Roman D. ("Virginia") Sandpiper also hoped for his opinion. Looking at these pictures had given him a feeling which was strange yet eerily intangible—it had been like looking at photographs of his own imagination, and he knew that from that moment on, whenever he tried to imagine Misery's little combination parlor and study, Mrs. Roman D. ("Virginia") Sandpiper's Polaroids would leap immediately into his mind, obscuring imagination with their cheery but one-dimensional concreteness. Tell *her* what was wrong? That was madness. From now on *he* would be the one to wonder about that. He had written back, a brief note of congratulations and admiration—a note which hinted not at all at certain questions concerning Mrs. Roman D. ("Virginia") Sandpiper which had crossed his mind: how tightly wrapped was she? for instance—and had received another letter in return, with a fresh slew of Polaroids. Mrs. Roman D. ("Virginia") Sandpiper's first communication had consisted of a two-page handwritten letter and seven Polaroids. This second consisted of a ten-page handwritten letter and *forty* Polaroids. The letter was an exhaustive (and ultimately exhausting) manual of where Mrs. Roman D. ("Virginia") Sandpiper had found each piece, how much she had paid, and the restoration processes involved. Mrs. Roman D. ("Virginia")

Sandpiper told him that she had found a man named McKibbon who owned an old squirrel-rifle, and had gotten him to put the bullet-hole in the wall by the chair—while she could not swear to the historical accuracy of the gun, Mrs. Roman D. ("Virginia") Sandpiper admitted, she knew the caliber was right. The pictures were mostly close detail shots. But for the handwritten captions on the backs, they could have been photos in one of those WHAT IS THIS PICTURE? features in puzzle magazines, where maxi-photography makes the straight-arm of a paper-clip look like a pylon and the pop-top of a beer-can like a Picasso sculpture. Paul had not answered this letter, but that had not deterred Mrs. Roman D. ("Virginia") Sandpiper, who had sent five more (the first four with additional Polaroids) before finally lapsing into puzzled, slightly hurt silence.

The last letter had been simply, stiffly signed Mrs. Roman D. Sandpiper. The invitation (however parenthetically made) to call her "Virginia" had been withdrawn.

This woman's feelings, obsessed though they might have been, had never evolved into Annie's paranoid fixation, but Paul understood now that the wellspring had been the same. The Scheherazade complex. The deep and elemental drawing power of *the gotta*.

His floating deepened. He slept.

10

He dozed off these days as old men doze off, abruptly and sometimes at inappropriate times, and he slept as old men sleep—which is to say, only separated from the waking world by the thinnest of skins. He didn't stop hearing the riding mower, but its sound became deeper, rougher, choppier: the sound of the electric knife.

He had picked the wrong day to start complaining about the Royal and its missing n. And, of course, there was never a *right* day to say no to Annie Wilkes. Punishment might be deferred . . . but never escaped.

Well, if it bothers you so much, I'll just have to give you something to take your mind off that old n. He heard her rummaging around in the kitchen, throwing things, cursing in her strange Annie Wilkes language. Ten minutes later she came in with the syringe, the Betadine, and the electric knife. Paul began to scream at once. He was, in a way, like Pavlov's dogs. When Pavlov rang a bell, the dogs salivated. When Annie came into the guest bedroom with a hypo, a bottle of Betadine, and a sharp cutting object, Paul began to scream. She had plugged the knife into the outlet by his wheelchair and there had been more pleading and more screaming and more promises that he would be good. When he tried to thrash away from the hypo she told him to sit still and be good or what was going to happen would happen without the benefit of even light anesthesia. When he continued to pull away from the needle, mewling and pleading, Annie suggested that if that was really the way he felt, maybe she just ought to use the knife on his throat and be done with it.

Then he had been still and let her give him the injection and this time the Betadine had gone over his left thumb as well as the blade of the knife (when she turned it on and the blade began to saw rapidly back and forth in the air the Betadine flew in a spray of maroon droplets she seemed not to notice) and in the end of course there had been much redder droplets spraying into the air as well. Because when Annie decided on a course of action, she carried it through. Annie was not swayed by pleas. Annie was not swayed by screams. Annie had the courage of her convictions.

As the humming, vibrating blade sank into the soft web of flesh between the soon-to-be-defunct thumb and his first finger, she assured him again in her this-hurts-Mother-more-than-it-hurts-Paulie voice that she loved him.

Then, that night . . .

You're not dreaming, Paul. You're thinking about things you don't dare think about when you're awake. So wake up. For God's sake, WAKE UP!

He couldn't wake up.

She had cut his thumb off in the morning and that night she swept gaily into the room where he sat in a stupid daze of drugs and pain with his wrapped left hand held against his chest and she had a cake and she was bellowing "Happy Birthday to You" in her on-key but tuneless voice although it was not his birthday and there were candles all over the cake and sitting in the exact center pushed into the frosting like an extra big candle had been his thumb his gray dead thumb the nail slightly ragged because he sometimes chewed it when he was stuck for a word and she told him *If you*

*promise to be good Paul you can have a piece of birthday cake but you
won't have to eat any of the special candle* so he promised to be good
because he didn't want to be forced to eat any of the special candle
but also because mostly because surely because Annie was great
Annie was good let us thank her for our food including that we
don't have to eat girls just wanna have fun but something wicked
this way comes please don't make me eat my thumb Annie the mom
Annie the goddess when Annie's around you better stay honest she
knows when you've been sleeping she knows when you're awake
she knows if you've been bad or good so be good for goddess' sake
you better not cry you better not pout but most of all you better
not scream don't scream don't scream don't scream don't

He hadn't.

And now, as he awoke, he did so with a jerk that hurt him all
over, hardly aware that his lips were pressed tightly together to
keep the scream inside, although the thumbectomy had happened
over a month ago.

He was so preoccupied with not screaming that for a moment
he didn't even see what was coming into the driveway, and when
he *did* see it, he believed at first that it must be a mirage.

It was a Colorado State Police car.

11

Following the amputation of his thumb there had been a dim period
when Paul's greatest single accomplishment, other than working on
the novel, had been to keep track of the days. He had become
pathological about it, sometimes spending as long as five minutes
lost in a daze, counting back, making sure he hadn't somehow
forgotten one.

I'm getting as bad as she is, he thought once.

His mind had returned wearily: *So what?*

He had done pretty well with the book following the loss of his
foot—during what Annie so mincingly called his "convalescent period." No—*pretty well* was false modesty if ever there was such a
thing. He had done *amazingly* well for a man who had once found
it impossible to write if he was out of cigarettes or if he had a
backache or a headache a degree or two above a low drone. It would

be nice to believe he had performed heroically, but he supposed it was only that escape thing again, because the pain had been really dreadful. When the healing process finally did begin, he thought the "phantom itch" of the foot which was no longer there was even worse than the pain. It was the arch of the missing foot which bothered him the most. He awoke time after time in the middle of the night using the big toe of his right foot to scratch thin air four inches below the place where, on that side, his body now ended.

But he had gone on working just the same.

It wasn't until after the thumbectomy, and that bizarre birthday cake like a left-over prop from *Whatever Happened to Baby Jane,* that the balls of crumpled-up paper had begun to proliferate in the wastebasket again. Lose a foot, almost die, go on working. Lose a thumb and run into some kind of weird trouble. Wasn't it supposed to be the other way around?

Well, there was the fever—he had spent a week in bed with that. But it was pretty minor-league stuff; the highest his temperature had ever gone was 100.7, and that wasn't exactly the stuff of which high melodrama was made. The fever had probably been caused more by his general run-down condition than any specific infection, and an oogy old fever was no problem for Annie; among her other souvenirs, Annie had Keflex and Ampicillin up the old kazoo. She dosed him and he got better . . . as better as it was possible to get under such bizarre circumstances, at any rate. But something was wrong. He seemed to have lost some vital ingredient, and the mix had become a lot less potent as a result. He tried to blame it on the missing n, but he'd had that to contend with before, and, really, what was a missing n compared to a missing foot and now, as an extra added attraction, a missing thumb?

Whatever the reason, something had disturbed the dream, some-thing was whittling away the circumference of that hole in the paper through which he saw. Once—he would have sworn it was so!—that hole had been as big as the bore of the Lincoln Tunnel. Now it was no more than the size of a knothole through which a sidewalk superintendent might stoop to snoop on an interesting piece of building construction. You had to peer and crane to see anything at all, and more often than not the really important things happened outside your field of vision . . . not surprising, considering the field of vision was so small.

In practical terms, what had happened following the thumbec-tomy and ensuing bout of fever was obvious. The language of the book had grown florid and overblown again—it was not self-parody yet, not quite, but it was floating steadily in that direction and he seemed helpless to stop it. Continuity lapses had begun to proliferate with the stealth of rats breeding in cellar corners: for a space of thirty pages, the Baron had become the Viscount from *Misery's Quest*. He'd had to go back and tear that all out.

It doesn't matter, Paul, he told himself again and again in those last few days before the Royal coughed up first its t and then its e, *the damned thing is almost done.* So it was. Working on it was torture, and finishing it was going to mean the end of his life. That the latter had begun to look slightly more attractive than the former said all that probably needed to be said about the worsening state of his body, mind, and spirit. And the book moved on in spite of everything, seemingly independent of them. The continuity drops were annoying but minor. He was having more problems with the actual make-believe than he ever had before—the game of Can You? had become a labored exercise rather than simple good fun. Yet the book had continued to roll in spite of all the terrible things Annie had subjected him to, and he could bitch about how something— his guts, maybe—had run out of him along with the half-pint or so of blood he'd lost when she took his thumb, but it was still a goddam good yarn, the best *Misery* novel by far. The plot was melodramatic but well constructed, in its own modest way quite amusing. If it were ever to be published in something other than the severely limited (first printing: one copy) Annie Wilkes Edition, he guessed it might sell like a mad bastard. Yeah, he supposed he would get through it, if the goddam typewriter held together.

You were supposed to be so tough, he had thought once, after one of his compulsive lifting exercises. His thin arms were trembling, the stump of his thumb aching feverishly, his forehead covered with a thin oil of sweat. *You were the tough young gunsel looking to make a rep off the tired old turd of a sheriff, right? Only you've already thrown one key and I see the way some of the others—the t, the e, and the g, for instance, are starting to look funny . . . sometimes leaning one way, sometimes leaning the other, sometimes riding a little high on the line, sometimes dipping a little low. I think maybe the tired old turd is going to win this one, my friend. I think maybe the tired old turd is going to beat you to death . . . and it could be that the bitch knew it. Could be that's why she took my left thumb. Like the old saying goes, she may be crazy but she sure ain't dumb.*

He had looked at the typewriter with tired intensity.

Go on. Go on and break. I'll finish anyway. If she wants to get me a replacement, I'll thank her kindly, but if she doesn't, I'll finish on my goddam legal pads.

The one thing I won't do is scream.

I won't scream.

I.

I won't.

12

I won't scream!

He sat at the window, totally awake now, totally aware that the police car he was seeing in Annie's driveway was as real as his left foot had once been.

Scream! Goddammit, scream!

He *wanted* to, but the dictum was too strong—just too strong. He couldn't even open his mouth. He tried and saw the brownish droplets of Betadine flying from the blade of the electric knife. He tried and heard the squeal of axe against bone, the soft *flump* as the match in her hand lit the Bernz-O-matiC.

He tried to open his mouth and couldn't.

Tried to raise his hands. Couldn't.

A horrible moaning sound passed between his closed lips and his hands made light, haphazard drumming sounds on either side of the Royal, but that was all he could do, all the control of his destiny he could seem to take. Nothing which had gone before— except perhaps for the moment when he had realized that, although his left leg was moving, his left foot was staying put—was as terrible as the hell of this immobility. In real time it did not last long; perhaps five seconds and surely no longer than ten. But inside Paul Sheldon's head it seemed to go on for years.

There, within plain sight, was salvation: all he had to do was break the window and the dog-lock the bitch had put on his tongue and scream *Help me, help me, save me from Annie! Save me from the goddess!*

At the same time another voice was screaming: *I'll be good, Annie! I won't scream! I'll be good, I'll be good for goddess' sake! I promise not to scream, just don't chop off any more of me!* Had he known, before this had he really *known* how badly she had cowed him, or how much of his essential self—the liver and lights of his spirit—she had scraped away? He knew how constantly he had been terrorized, but did he know how much of his own subjective reality, once so strong he had taken it for granted, had been erased?

He knew one thing with some certainty—a lot more was wrong with him than paralysis of the tongue, just as a lot more was wrong with what he had been writing than the missing key or the fever or continuity lapses or even a loss of guts. The truth of everything was so simple in its horridness; so dreadfully simple. He was dying by inches, but dying that way wasn't as bad as he'd already feared. But he was also *fading,* and that was an awful thing because it was moronic.

Don't scream! the panicky voice screamed just the same as the cop opened the door of his cruiser and stepped out, adjusting his Smokey Bear hat as he did so. He was young, no more than twenty-two or -three, wearing sunglasses as black and liquid-looking as dollops of crude oil. He paused to adjust the creases of his khaki uniform pants and thirty yards away a man with blue eyes bulging from his white and whiskery old-man's face sat staring at him from behind a window, moaning through closed lips, hands rattling uselessly on a board laid across the arms of a wheelchair.

don't scream

(yes scream)

scream and it will be over scream and it can end

(never never going to end not until I'm dead that kid's no match for the goddess)

Paul oh Christ are you dead already? *Scream,* you chickenshit motherfucker! *SCREAM YOUR FUCKING HEAD OFF!!!*

His lips pulled apart with a minute tearing sound. He hitched air into his lungs and closed his eyes. He had no idea what was going to come out or if anything really was—until it came.

"AFRICA!" Paul screamed. Now his trembling hands flew up like startled birds and clapped against the sides of his head, as if to hold in his exploding brains. *"Africa! Africa! Help me! Help me! Africa!"*

13

His eyes snapped open. The cop was looking toward the house. Paul could not see the Smokey's eyes because of the sunglasses, but the tilt of his head expressed moderate puzzlement. He took a step closer, then stopped.

Paul looked down at the board. To the left of the typewriter was a heavy ceramic ashtray. Once upon a time it would have been filled with crushed butts; now it held nothing more hazardous to his health than paper-clips and a typewriter eraser. He seized it and threw it at the window. Glass shattered outward. To Paul it was the most liberating sound he had ever heard. *The walls came tumbling down,* he thought giddily, and screamed: *"Over here! Help me! Watch out for the woman! She's crazy!"*

The state cop stared at him. His mouth dropped open. He reached into his breast pocket and brought out something that could only be a picture. He consulted it and then advanced to the edge of the driveway. There he spoke the only four words Paul ever heard him say, the last four words *anyone* ever heard him say. Following them he would make a number of inarticulate sounds but no real words.

"Oh, shit!" the cop exclaimed. "It's you!"

Paul's attention had been so fiercely focused on the trooper that he did not see Annie until it was too late. When he did see her, he was struck by a real superstitious horror. Annie had *become* a goddess, a thing that was half woman and half Lawnboy, a weird female centaur. Her baseball cap had fallen off. Her face was twisted in a frozen snarl. In one hand she held a wooden cross. It had marked the grave of the Bossie—Paul didn't remember if it was No. 1 or No. 2—which had finally stopped bawling.

That Bossie had indeed died, and when spring had softened the ground enough, Paul had watched from his window, sometimes dumbstruck with awe and sometimes overcome with shrieking attacks of the giggles, as she first dug the grave (it had taken her most of the day) and then dragged Bossie (who had also softened considerably) out from behind the barn. She had used a chain attached to the Cherokee's trailer-hitch to do this. She had looped the other end of the chain around Bossie's middle. Paul made a mental bet with himself that Bossie would tear in half before Annie got her to the grave, but that one he lost. Annie tumbled Bossie in, then stolidly begun refilling the hole, a job she hadn't finished until long after dark.

Paul had watched her plant the cross and then read the Bible over the grave by the light of a new-risen spring moon.

Now she was holding the cross like a spear, the dirt-darkened point of its vertical post pointed squarely at the trooper's back.

"Behind you! Look out!" Paul shrieked, knowing he was too late but shouting anyway.

With a thin warbling cry, Annie plunged Bossie's cross into the trooper's back.

"AG!" the cop said, and walked slowly onto the lawn, his pierced back arched and his gut sticking out. His face was the face of a man either trying to pass a kidney stone or having a terrible gas attack. The cross began to droop toward the ground as the trooper approached the window in which Paul sat, his gray invalid's face framed by jags of broken glass. The cop reached slowly over his shoulders with both hands. He looked to Paul like a man trying very hard to scratch that one itch you can never quite reach.

Annie had dismounted the Lawnboy and had been standing frozen, her tented fingers pressed against the peaks of her breasts. Now she lunged forward and snatched the cross out of the trooper's back.

He turned toward her, groping for his service pistol, and Annie drove the cross point-first into his belly.

"OG!" the cop said this time, and dropped to his knees, clutching his stomach. As he bent over Paul could see the slit in his brown uniform shirt where the first blow had gone home.

Annie pulled the cross free again—its sharpened point had broken off, leaving a jagged, splintery stump—and drove it into his back between the shoulderblades. She looked like a woman trying to kill a vampire. The first two blows had perhaps not gone deep enough to do much damage, but this time the cross's support post went at least three inches into the kneeling trooper's back, driving him flat.

"THERE!" Annie cried, wrenching Bossie's memorial marker out of his back. *"HOW DO YOU LIKE THAT, YOU OLD DIRTY BIRD?"*

"Annie, stop it!" Paul shouted.

She looked up at him, her dark eyes momentarily as shiny as coins, her hair fungus-frowzy around her face, the corners of her mouth drawn up in the jolly grin of a lunatic who has, at least for the moment, cast aside all restraints. Then she looked back down at the state trooper.

"THERE!" she cried, and drove the cross into his back again. And his buttocks. And the upper thigh of one leg. And his neck. And his crotch. She stabbed him with it half a dozen times, screaming

"THERE!" every time she brought it down again. Then the cross's upright split.

"There," she said, almost conversationally, and walked away in the direction from which she had come running. Just before she passed from Paul's view she tossed the bloody cross aside as if it no longer interested her.

14

Paul put his hands on the wheels of the chair, not at all sure where he intended to go or what, if anything, he meant to do when he got there—to the kitchen for a knife, perhaps? Not to try to kill her with, oh no; she would take one look at the knife in his hand and step back into the shed for her .30.30. Not to kill her but to defend himself from her revenge by cutting his wrists open. He didn't know if that had been his intention or not, but it surely did seem like a hell of a good idea, because if there had ever been a time to *exeunt* stage left, this was it. He was tired of losing pieces of himself to her fury.

Then he saw something which froze him in place.

The cop.

The cop was still alive.

He raised his head. His sunglasses had fallen off. Now Paul could see his eyes. Now he could see how young the cop was, how young and hurt and scared. Blood ran down his face in streams. He managed to get to his hands and knees, fell forward, and then got painfully back up again. He began to crawl toward his cruiser.

He worked his way halfway down the mild slope of grass between the house and the driveway, then overbalanced and fell on his back. For a moment he lay there with his legs drawn up, looking as helpless as a turtle on its shell. Then he slowly rolled over on his side and began the terrible job of getting to his knees again. His uniform shirt and pants were darkening with blood—small patches were slowly spreading, meeting other patches, growing bigger still.

The Smokey reached the driveway.

Suddenly the noise of the riding lawnmower was louder.

"Look out!" Paul screamed. *"Look out, she's coming!"*

The cop turned his head. Groggy alarm surfaced on his face, and he grappled for his gun once more. He got it out—something big and black with a long barrel and brown woodgrips—and then Annie reappeared, sitting tall in the saddle and driving the Lawnboy as fast as it would go.

"*SHOOT HER!*" Paul screamed, and instead of shooting Annie Wilkes with his big old Dirty
(birdie)
Harry gun, he first fumbled, then dropped it.

He stretched out his hand for it. Annie swerved and ran over both his reaching hand and his forearm. Blood squirted from the Lawnboy's grass-exhaust in an amazing jet. The kid in the trooper uniform screamed. There was a sharp clang as the mower's whirling blade struck the pistol. Then Annie was swerving up the side lawn, using it to turn, and her gaze fell on Paul for one second and Paul felt sure he knew what that momentary gaze meant. First the Smokey, then him.

The kid was lying on his side again. When he saw the mower bearing down on him he rolled over on his back and dug frantically at the driveway dirt with his heels, trying to push himself under the cruiser where she couldn't get him.

He didn't even come close. Annie throttled the riding lawn-mower up to a scream and drove it over his head.

Paul caught a last glimpse of horrified brown eyes, saw tatters of brown khaki uniform shirt hanging from an arm raised in a feeble effort at protection, and when the eyes were gone, Paul turned away.

The Lawnboy's engine suddenly lugged down and there was a series of fast, strangely liquid thudding sounds.

Paul vomited beside the chair with his eyes closed.

15

He only opened them when he heard the rattle of her key in the kitchen door. His own door was open; he watched her approach down the hall in her old brown cowboy boots and her blue-jeans with the keyring dangling from one of the belt-loops and her man's tee-shirt now spotted with blood. He cringed away from her. He wanted to say: *If you cut anything else off me, Annie, I'm going to die.*

It won't take the shock of another amputation, either. I'll die on purpose.
But no words came out—only terrified chuffing noises that disgusted him.

She gave him no time to speak anyway.

"I'll deal with you later," she said, and pulled his door closed.
One of her keys rattled in the lock—a new Kreig that would have
defeated even Tom Twyford himself, Paul thought—and then she
was striding down the hall again, the thud of her bootheels mercifully diminishing.

He turned his head and looked dully out the window. He could
see only part of the trooper's body. His head was still under the
mower, which was, in turn, canted at a drunken angle against the
cruiser. The riding mower was a small tractor-like vehicle meant
for keeping larger-than-average lawns neat and clipped. It had not
been designed to keep its balance as it passed over jutting rocks,
fallen logs, or the heads of state troopers. If the cruiser hadn't been
parked exactly where it was, and if the trooper hadn't gotten exactly
as close to it as he had before Annie struck him, the mower would
almost surely have tipped over, spilling her off. This might have
caused her no harm at all, but it might have hurt her quite badly.

She has the luck of the devil himself, Paul thought drearily, and
watched as she put the mower in neutral and then pushed it off the
trooper with one hard shove. The side of the mower squalled along
the side of the cruiser and took off some paint.

Now that he was dead, Paul could look at him. The cop looked
like a big doll that has been badly treated by a gang of nasty children.
Paul felt a terrible aching sympathy for this unnamed young man,
but there was another emotion mixed with that. He examined it
and was not much surprised to find it was envy. The trooper would
never go home to his wife and kids, if he had had them, but on the
other hand, he had escaped Annie Wilkes.

She grabbed a bloody hand and dragged him up the driveway
and through the barn doors, which stood ajar on their tracks. When
she came out, she pushed them along their tracks as far as they
would go. Then she walked back down to the cruiser. She was
moving with a calm that was almost serenity. She started the cruiser
and drove it into the barn. When she came out again she closed
the doors almost completely, leaving a gap just wide enough for
her to slip in and out.

She walked halfway down the driveway and looked around,

hands on her hips. Again Paul saw that remarkable expression of
serenity.

The bottom of the mower was smeared with blood, particularly
around the grass-exhaust, which was still dripping. Little scraps of
khaki uniform lay in the driveway or fluttered in the freshly cut
grass of the side lawn. There were daubs and splashes of blood
everywhere. The trooper's gun, with a long slash of bright metal
now scarring its barrel, lay in the dust. A square of stiff white paper
had caught on the spines of a small cactus Annie had set out in
May. Bossie's splintered cross lay in the driveway like a comment
on the whole filthy mess.

She moved out of his field of vision, heading toward the kitchen
again. When she came in he heard her singing. *"She'll be driving six
white horses when she COMES . . . she'll be driving six white horses when
she COMES! She'll be driving six white HORSES, driving six white
HORSES . . . she'll be driving six white HORSES when she COMES!"*

When he saw her again, she had a big green garbage bag in her
hands and three or four more sticking out of the back pockets of
her jeans. Big sweatstains darkened her tee-shirt around her armpits
and neck. When she turned, he saw a sweatstain that looked vaguely
tree-like rising up her back.

That's a lot of bags for a few scraps of cloth, Paul thought, but he
knew that she would have plenty to put in them before she was
done.

She picked up the shreds of uniform and then the cross. She
broke it into two pieces, and dropped it into the plastic bag. Incredibly, she genuflected after doing this. She picked up the gun,
rolled the cylinder, dumped the slugs, put them in one hip pocket,
snapped the cylinder back in with a practiced flick of her wrist, and
then stuck the gun in the waistband of her jeans. She plucked the
piece of paper off the saguaro and looked at it thoughtfully. She
stuck it into the other hip pocket. She went to the barn, tossed the
garbage bags inside the doors, then came back to the house.

She walked up the side lawn to the cellar bulkhead which was
almost directly below Paul's window. Something else caught her
eye. It was his ashtray. She picked it up and handed it politely to
him through the broken window.

"Here, Paul."

Numbly, he took it.

"I'll get the paper-clips later," she said, as if this were a question which must already have occurred to him. For one moment he thought of bringing the heavy ceramic ashtray down on her head as she bent over, cleaving her skull with it, letting out the disease that passed for her brains.

Then he thought of what would happen to him—what *could* happen to him—if he only hurt her, and put the ashtray where it had been with his shaking thumbless hand.

She looked up at him. "I didn't kill him, you know."

"Annie—"

"*You* killed him. If you had kept your mouth shut, I would have sent him on his way. He'd be alive now and there would be none of this oogy mess to clean up."

"Yes," Paul said. "Down the road he would have gone, and what about me, Annie?"

She was pulling her hose out of the bulkhead and looping it over her arm. "I don't know what you mean."

"Yes you do." In the depth of his shock he had achieved his own serenity. "He had my picture. It's in your pocket right now, isn't it?"

"Ask me no questions and I will tell you no lies." There was a faucet bib on the side of the house to the left of his window. She began to screw the end of the hose onto it.

"A state cop with my picture means someone found my car. We both knew someone would. I'm only surprised it took so long. In a novel a car might be able to float right out of the story—I guess I could make people believe it if I had to—but in real life, no way. But we went on fooling ourselves just the same, didn't we, Annie? You because of the book, me because of my life, miserable as it has become to me."

"I don't know what you're talking about." She turned on the faucet. "All I know is you killed that poor kid when you threw the ashtray through the window. You're getting what might happen to *you* mixed up with what already happened to *him*." She grinned at him. There was craziness in that grin, but he saw something else in it as well, something that really frightened him. He saw conscious evil in it—a demon capering behind her eyes.

"You bitch," he said.

"*Crazy* bitch, isn't that right?" she asked, still smiling.

"Oh yeah—you're crazy," he said.

"Well, we'll have to talk about that, won't we? When I have more time. We'll have to talk about that a *lot*. But right now I'm very busy, as I think you can see."

She unreeled the hose and turned it on. She spent nearly half an hour hosing blood off the mower and driveway and the side lawn, while interlinked rainbows glimmered in the spray.

Then she twisted the nozzle off and walked back along the hose's length, looping it over her arm. There was still plenty of light but her shadow trailed long behind her. It was now six o'clock.

She unscrewed the hose, opened the bulkhead, and dropped the green plastic snake inside. She closed the bulkhead, shot the bolt, and stood back, surveying the puddly driveway and the grass, which looked as though a heavy dew had fallen upon it.

Annie walked back to the mower, got on, started it up, and drove it around back. Paul smiled a little. She had the luck of the devil, and when she was pressed she had almost the cleverness of the devil—but *almost* was the key word. She had slipped in Boulder and wriggled away mostly due to luck. Now she had slipped again. He had seen it. She had washed the blood off the mower but forgotten the blade underneath—the whole blade housing, for that matter. She might remember later, but Paul didn't think so. Things had a way of dropping out of Annie's mind once the immediate moment was past. It occurred to him that the mind and the mower had a lot in common—what you could see looked all right. But if you turned the thing over to take a look at the works, you saw a blood-slimed killing machine with a very sharp blade.

She returned to the kitchen door and let herself into the house again. She went upstairs and he heard her rummaging there for awhile. Then she came down again, more slowly, dragging something that sounded soft and heavy. After a moment's consideration, Paul rolled the wheelchair across to his door and leaned his ear against the wood.

Dim, diminishing footfalls—slightly hollow. And still that soft flumping sound of something being dragged. Immediately his mind lit up with panicky floodlights and his skin flushed with his terror. *Shed! She's gone to the shed to get the axe! It's the axe again!*

But this was only a momentary atavism, and he pushed it roughly away. She hadn't gone into the shed; she was going down cellar. Dragging something down cellar.

He heard her come up again and he rolled back to the window. As her bootheels approached his door, as the key slid into the lock again, he thought: *She's come to kill me.* And the only emotion this thought engendered was tired relief.

16

The door opened and Annie stood there, looking at him contemplatively. She had changed into a fresh white tee-shirt and a pair of chinos. A small khaki bag, too big to be a purse and not quite big enough to be a knapsack, was slung over one shoulder.

As she came in, he was surprised to find himself able to say it, and say it with a certain amount of dignity: "Go ahead and kill me, Annie, if that's what you mean to do, but at least have the decency to make it quick. Don't cut anything more off me."

"I'm not going to kill you, Paul." She paused. "At least, not if I have just a little luck. I *should* kill you—I know that—but I'm crazy, right? And crazy people often don't look after their best interests, do they?"

She went behind him and propelled him across the room, out the door, and down the hall. He could hear her bag slapping solidly against her side, and it occurred to him that he had never seen her carrying a bag like that before. If she went to town in a dress, she carried a big, clunky purse—the sort of purse maiden aunts tote to church jumble sales. If she went in pants, she went with a wallet stuck in her hip pocket, like a man.

The sunlight slanting into the kitchen was strong bright gold. Shadows from the legs of the kitchen table lay across the linoleum in horizontal stripes like the shadows of prison bars. It was quarter past six according to the clock over the range, and while there was no reason to believe she was any less sloppy about her clocks than her calendars (the one out here had actually made it to May), that seemed about right. He could hear the first evening crickets tuning up in Annie's field. He thought, *I heard that same sound as a small, unhurt boy,* and for a moment he nearly wept.

She pushed him into the pantry, where the door to the basement stood open. Yellow light staggered up the stairs and fell dead on the pantry floor. The smell of the late-winter rainstorm which had flooded it still lingered.

Spiders down there, he thought. *Mice down there. Rats down there.*

"Uh-uh," he told her. "Count me out."

She looked at him with a level sort of impatience, and he realized that since killing the cop, she had seemed almost sane. Her face was the purposeful if slightly harried face of a woman making ready for a big dinner party.

"You're going down there," she said. "The only question is whether you're going down piggy-back or bum over teakettle. I'll give you five seconds to decide."

"Piggy-back," he said at once.

"Very wise." She turned around so he could put his arms around her neck. "Don't do anything stupid like trying to choke me, Paul. I took a karate class in Harrisburg. I was good at it. I'll flip you. The floor is dirt but very hard. You'll break your back."

She hoisted him easily. His legs, now unsplinted but as crooked and ugly as something glimpsed through a rip in the canvas of a freak-show tent, hung down. The left, with the salt-dome where the knee had been, was fully four inches shorter than the right. He had tried standing on the right leg and had found he could, for short times, but doing so produced a low, primal agony that lasted for hours. The dope couldn't touch that pain, which was like a deep physical sobbing.

She carried him down and into a thickening smell of old stone and wood and flood and rotting vegetables. There were three naked light-bulbs. Old spiderwebs hung in rotting hammocks between bare beams. The walls were rock, carelessly chinked—they looked like a child's drawing of rock walls. It was cool, but not a pleasant cool.

He had never been as close to her as he was then, as she carried him piggy-back down the steep stairs. He would only be as close once again. It was not a pleasant experience. He could smell the sweat of her recent exertions, and while he actually liked the smell of fresh perspiration—he associated it with work, hard effort, things he respected—this smell was secretive and nasty, like old sheets thick with dried come. And below the smell of sweat was a smell of very old dirt. Annie, he guessed, had gotten as casually catch-as-catch-can about showering as she had about changing her calendars. He could see dark-brown wax plugging one ear and wondered with faint disgust how the hell she could hear anything.

Here, by one of the rock walls, was the source of that flumping, dragging sound: a mattress. Beside it she had placed a collapsed TV tray. There were a few cans and bottles on it. She approached the mattress, turned around, and squatted.

"Get off, Paul."

He released his hold cautiously and allowed himself to fall back on the mattress. He looked up at her warily as she stood and reached into the little khaki bag.

"No," he said immediately when he saw the tired yellow cellar-light gleam on the hypodermic needle. "No. No."

17

"Oh boy," she said. "You must think Annie's in a real poopie-doopie mood today. I wish you'd *relax,* Paul." She put the hypo on the TV tray. "That's scopolamine, which is a morphine-based drug. You're lucky I have any morphine at all. I told you how closely they watch it in the hospital pharmacies. I'm leaving it because it's damp down here and your legs may ache quite badly before I get back.

"Just a minute." She gave him a wink which had strangely un-settling undertones—a wink one conspirator might give another. "You throw one cockadoodie ashtray and I'm as busy as a one-armed paperhanger. I'll be right back."

She went upstairs and came back shortly with the cushions from the sofa in the parlor and the blankets from his bed. She arranged the cushions behind him so he could sit up without too much discomfort—but he could feel the sullen chill of the rocks even through the cushions, waiting to steal out and freeze him.

There were three bottles of Pepsi on the collapsed TV tray. She opened two of them, using the opener on her keyring, and handed him one. She upended her own and drank half of it without stop-ping; then she stifled a burp, ladylike, against her hand.

"We have to talk," she said. "Or, rather, I have to talk and you have to listen."

"Annie, when I said you were crazy—"

"Hush! Not a word about that. Maybe we'll talk about that later. Not that I would ever try to change your mind about anything you chose to think—a Mister Smart Guy like you who thinks for a living. All I ever did was pull you out of your wrecked car before you could freeze to death and splint your poor broken legs and give you medicine to ease your pain and take care of you and talk you out of a bad book you'd written and into the best one you *ever* wrote. And if that's crazy, take me to the loonybin."

Oh, Annie, if only someone would, he thought, and before he could stop himself he had snapped: "You also cut off my fucking foot!"

Her hand flickered out whip-quick and rocked his head over to one side with a thin spatting sound.

"Don't you use that effword around me," Annie said. "I was raised better even if you weren't. You're lucky I didn't cut off your man-gland. I thought of it, you know."

He looked at her. His stomach felt like the inside of an ice-maker. "I know you did, Annie," he said softly. Her eyes widened, and for just a moment she looked both startled and guilty—Naughty Annie instead of Nasty Annie.

"Listen to me. Listen closely, Paul. We're going to be all right if it gets dark before anyone comes to check on that fellow. It'll be full dark in an hour and a half. If someone comes sooner—"

She reached into the khaki bag again and brought out the trooper's .44. The cellar lights shone on the zigzagging lightning-bolt the Lawnboy's blade had chopped into the gun's barrel.

"If someone comes sooner there's this," she said. "For whoever comes, and then you, and then me."

18

Once it was dark, she said, she was going to drive the police cruiser up to her Laughing Place. There was a lean-to beside the cabin where she could park it safely out of sight. She thought the only danger of being noticed would come on Route 9, but even there the risk would be small—she only had to drive four miles of it. Once she was off 9, the way into the hills was by little-travelled meadow-line roads, many fallen into casual disuse as grazing cattle this high up became a rarity. A few of these roads, she said, were still gated off—she and Ralph had obtained keys to them when they bought the property. They didn't have to ask; the owners of the land between the road and the cabin gave them the keys. This was called *neighboring,* she told Paul, managing to invest a pleasant word with unsuspected depths of nuance: suspicion, contempt, bitter amusement.

"I would take you with me just to keep an eye on you, now that you've shown how untrustworthy you can be, but it wouldn't work. I could get you up there in the back of the police-car, but getting you back down would be impossible. I'm going to have to ride Ralph's trail-bike. I'll probably fall off and break my cockadoodie *neck!*"

She laughed merrily to show what a joke on her *that* would be, but Paul did not join her.

"If that *did* happen, Annie, what would happen to *me?*"

"You'll be fine, Paul," she said serenely. "Gosh, you're such a worry-wart!" She walked over to one of the cellar windows and stood there a moment, looking out, measuring the fall of the day. Paul watched her moodily. If she fell off her husband's bike or drove off one of those unpaved ridge-roads, he did not actually believe he would be fine. What he actually believed was that he would die a dog's death down here, and when it was finally over he would make a meal for the rats which were even now undoubtedly watching these two unwelcome bipeds who had intruded upon their domain. There was a Kreig lock on the pantry door now, and a bolt on the bulkhead almost as thick as his wrist. The cellar windows, as if reflecting Annie's paranoia (and there was nothing strange about that, he thought; didn't all houses come, after awhile, to reflect the personalities of their inhabitants?), were not much more than dirty gun-slits, about twenty inches long by fourteen wide. He didn't think he could have wriggled through one of those even on his fittest day, which this wasn't. He might be able to break one and yell for help if someone showed up here before he starved to death, but that wasn't much comfort.

The first twinges of pain slipped down his legs like poisoned water. And the want. His body yelling for Novril. It was *the gotta,* wasn't it? Sure it was.

Annie came back and took the third bottle of Pepsi. "I'll bring down another couple of these before I go," she said. "Right now I need the sugar. You don't mind, do you?"

"Absolutely not. My Pepsi is your Pepsi."

She twisted the cap off the bottle and drank deeply. Paul thought: *Chug-a-lug, chug-a-lug, make ya want to holler hi-de-ho.* Who was that? Roger Miller, right? Funny, the stuff your mind coughed up. Hilarious.

"I'm going to put him in his car and drive it up to my Laughing Place. I'm going to take all his things. I'll put the car in the shed up there and bury him and his . . . you know, his *scraps* . . . in the woods up there."

He said nothing. He kept thinking about Bossie, bawling and bawling and bawling until she couldn't bawl anymore because she was dead, and another of those great axioms of Life on the Western Slope was just this: *Dead cows don't bawl.*

"I have a driveway chain. I'm going to use it. If the police come, it may raise suspicion, but I'd rather have them suspicious than have them drive up to the house and hear you making a big cockadoodie fuss. I thought of gagging you, but gags are dangerous, especially if you're taking drugs that affect respiration. Or you might vomit. Or your sinuses might close up because it's so damp down here. If your sinuses closed up tight and you couldn't breathe through your mouth . . ."

She looked away, unplugged, as silent as one of the stones in the cellar wall, as empty as the first bottle of Pepsi she had drunk. *Make ya want to holler hi-de-ho.* And had Annie hollered hi-de-ho today? Bet your ass. O brethren, Annie had yelled hi-de-ho until the whole yard was oogy. He laughed. She made no sign she had heard him.

Then, slowly, she began to come back.

She looked around at him, blinking.

"I'm going to stick a note through one of the links in the fence," she said slowly, re-gathering her thoughts. "There's a town about thirty-five miles from here. It's called Steamboat Heaven, isn't that a funny name for a town? They're having what they call The World's Biggest Flea Market this week. They have it every summer. There's always lots of people there who sell ceramics. I'll write in my note that I'm there, in Steamboat Heaven, looking at ceramics. I'll say I'm staying overnight. And if anyone asks me later where I stayed, so they can check the register, I'll say there were no good ceramics so I started back. Only I got tired. That's what I'll say. I'll say I pulled over to take a nap because I was afraid I might fall asleep behind the wheel. I'll say I only meant to take a short nap but I was so tired from working around the place that I slept all night."

Paul was dismayed by the depth of this slyness. He suddenly realized that Annie was doing exactly what he could not: she was playing Can You? in real life. *Maybe,* he thought, *that's why she doesn't write books. She doesn't have to.*

"I'll get back just as soon as I can, because policemen *will* come here," she said. The prospect did not seem to disturb Annie's weird serenity in the least, although Paul could not believe that, in some part of her mind, she did not realize how close to the end of the game they had now come. "I don't think they'll come tonight— except maybe to cruise by—but they *will* come. As soon as they know for sure he's really missing. They'll go all along his route, looking for him and trying to find out where he stopped, you know, showing up. Don't you think so, Paul?"

"Yes."

"I *should* be back before they come. If I start out on the bike at first light, I might even be able to make it back before noon. I should be able to beat them. Because if he started from Sidewinder, he would have stopped at lots of places before he got here.

"By the time they come, you should be back in your own room, snug as a bug in a rug. I'm not going to tie you up, or gag you, or anything like that, Paul. You can even peek when I go out to talk to them. Because it will be two next time, I think. At least two, don't you think so?"

Paul did.

She nodded, satisfied. "But I can handle two, if I have to." She patted the khaki purse. "I want you to remember that kid's gun while you're peeking, Paul. I want you to remember that it's going to be in here all the time I'm talking to those police when they come tomorrow or the next day. The bag won't be zipped. It's all right for *you* to see *them,* but if *they* see *you,* Paul—either by accident or because you try something tomorrow like you did today—if that happens, I'm going to take the gun out of the bag and start shooting. You're already responsible for that kid's death."

"Bullshit," Paul said, knowing she would hurt him for it but not caring.

She didn't, though. She only smiled her serene, maternal smile.

"Oh, you know," she said. "I don't kid myself that you *care,* I don't kid myself about that at all, but you *know.* I don't kid myself that you'd care about getting another *two* people killed, if it would help you . . . but it wouldn't, Paul. Because if I have to do two, I'll do four. Them . . . and us. And do you know what? I think you still care about your own skin."

"Not much," he said. "I'll tell you the truth, Annie—every day that passes, my skin feels more and more like something I want to get out of."

She laughed.

"Oh, I've heard *that* one before. But let them see you put one hand on their oogy old respirators! Then it's a different story! Yes! When they see *that,* they yell and cry and turn into a bunch of real *brats!*"

Not that you ever let that stop you, right, Annie?

"Anyway," she said, "I just wanted you to know how things are. If you really don't care, yell your head off when they come. It's entirely up to you."

Paul said nothing.

"When they come I'll stand right out there in the driveway and say yes, there was a state trooper that came by here. I'll say he came just when I was getting ready to leave for Steamboat Heaven to look at the ceramics. I'll say he showed me your picture. I'll say I hadn't seen you. Then one of them will ask me, 'This was last winter, Miss Wilkes, how could you be so positive?' And I'll say, 'If Elvis Presley was still alive and you saw him last winter, would *you* remember seeing him?' And he'll say yes, probably so, but what does that have to do with the price of coffee in Borneo, and I'll say Paul Sheldon is my favorite writer and I've seen his picture lots of times. I have to say that, Paul. Do you know why?"

He knew. Her slyness continued to astound him. He supposed it shouldn't, not anymore, but it did. He remembered the caption below the picture of Annie in her detainment cell, the picture taken in the *caesura* between the end of the trial and the return of the jury. He remembered it word for word. *IN MISERY? NOT THE DRAGON LADY. Annie reads calmly as she waits for the verdict.*

"So then," she continued, "I'll say the policeman wrote it all down in his book and thanked me. I'll say I asked him in for a cup of coffee even though I was in a hurry to be on my way and they'll ask me why. I'll say he probably knew about my trouble before, and I wanted to satisfy his mind that everything was on the up-and-up here. But he said no, he had to move along. So I asked if he'd like to take a cold Pepsi along with him because the day was so hot and he said yes, thanks, that was very kind."

She drained her second Pepsi and held the empty plastic bottle between her and him. Seen through the plastic her eye was huge and wavering, the eye of a Cyclops. The side of her head took on a ripply, hydrocephalic bulge.

"I'm going to stop and put this bottle in the ditch about two

miles up the road," she said. "But first I'll put his fingers on it, of
course."

She smiled at him—a dry, spitless smile.

"Fingerprints," she said. "They'll know he went past my house
then. Or they'll *think* they do, and that's just as good, isn't it, Paul?"

His dismay deepened.

"So they'll go up the road and they won't find him. He'll just be
gone. Like those swamis who toot their flutes until ropes come out
of baskets and they climb the ropes and disappear. Poof!"

"Poof," Paul said.

"It won't take them long to come back. I know that. After all,
if they can't find any trace of him except that one bottle after here,
they'll decide they better think some more about me. After all, I'm
crazy, aren't I? All the papers said so. Nutty as a fruitcake!

"But they'll believe me at first. I don't think they'll actually want
to come in and search the house—not at first. They'll look in other
places and try to think of other things before they come back. We'll
have some time. Maybe as much as a week."

She looked at him levelly.

"You're going to have to write faster, Paul," she said.

19

Dark fell and no police came. Annie did not spend the time before
it did with Paul, however; she wanted to re-glaze his bedroom
window, and pick up the paper-clips and broken glass scattered on
the lawn. When the police come tomorrow looking for their missing
lamb, she said, we don't want them to see anything out of the
ordinary, do we, Paul?

*Just let them look under the lawnmower, kiddo. Just let them look
under there and they'll see plenty out of the ordinary.*

But no matter how hard he tried to make his vivid imagination
work, he could not make it come up with a scenario which would
lead up to that.

"Do you wonder why I told you all of this, Paul?" she asked
before going upstairs to see what she could do with the window.
"Why I went into my plans for dealing with this in such great detail?"

"No," he said wanly.

"Partly because I wanted you to know exactly what the stakes

are, and exactly what you'll have to do to stay alive. I also wanted
you to know that I'd end it right now. Except for the book. I still
care about the book." She smiled. It was a smile which was both
radiant and strangely wistful. "It really *is* the best *Misery* story of
them all, and I do so much want to know how it all comes out."

"So do I, Annie," he said.

She looked at him, startled. "Why . . . you *know,* don't you?"

"When I start a book I always *think* I know how things will turn
out, but I never actually had one end *exactly* that way. It isn't even
that surprising, once you stop to think about it. Writing a book is
a little like firing an ICBM . . . only it travels over time instead of
space. The book-time the characters spend living in the story and
the real time the novelist spends writing it all down. Having a novel
end exactly the way you thought it would when you started out
would be like shooting a Titan missile halfway around the world
and having the payload drop through a basketball hoop. It looks
good on paper, and there are people who build those things who'd
tell you it was easy as pie—and even kept a straight face while they
said it—but the odds are always against."

"Yes," Annie said. "I see."

"I must have a pretty good navigation system built into the equipment, because I usually get close, and if you have enough high
explosive packed into the nosecone, close is good enough. Right
now I see *two* possible endings to the book. One is very sad. The
other, while not your standard Hollywood happy ending, at least
holds out some hope for the future."

Annie looked alarmed . . . and suddenly thunderous. "You're not
thinking of killing her *again,* are you, Paul?"

He smiled a little. "What would you do if I did, Annie? Kill me?
That doesn't scare me a bit. I may not know what's going to happen
to Misery, but I know what's going to happen to me . . . and you.
I'll write THE END, and you'll read, and then *you'll* write THE END,
won't you? The end of us. That's one I don't have to guess at. Truth
really isn't stranger than fiction, no matter what they say. Most
times you know *exactly* how things are going to turn out."

"But—"

"I think I know which ending it's going to be. I'm about eighty
percent sure. If it turns out that way, you'll like it. But even if it
turns out the way I think, neither of us will know the actual details
until I get them written down, will we?"

"No—I suppose not."

"Do you remember what the old Greyhound Bus ads used to say? 'Getting there is half the fun.' "

"Either way, it's almost over, isn't it?"

"Yes," Paul said. "Almost over."

20

Before she left she brought him another Pepsi, a box of Ritz crackers, sardines, cheese . . . and the bedpan.

"If you bring me my manuscript and one of those yellow legal pads, I'll work in longhand," he said. "It will pass the time."

She considered, then shook her head regretfully. "I wish you could, Paul. But that would mean leaving at least one light on, and I can't risk it."

He thought of being left alone down here in the cellar and felt panic flush his skin again, but just for a moment. Then it went cold. He felt tiny hard goosebumps rising on his skin. He thought of the rats hiding in their holes and runs in the rock walls. Thought of them coming out when the cellar went dark. Thought of them smelling his helplessness, perhaps.

"Don't leave me in the dark, Annie. Please don't do that."

"I have to. If someone noticed a light in my cellar, they might stop to investigate, driveway chain or no driveway chain, note or no note. If I gave you a flashlight, you might try to signal with it. If I gave you a candle, you might try to burn the house down with it. You see how well I know you?"

He hardly dared mention the times he had gotten out of his room, because it always made her furious; now his fear of being left alone down here in the dark drove him to it. "If I had wanted to burn the house down, Annie, I could have done it long before this."

"Things were different then," she said shortly. "I'm sorry you don't like being left in the dark. I'm sorry you have to be. But it's your own fault, so quit being a brat. I've got to go. If you feel like you need that injection, stick it in your leg."

She looked at him.

"Or stick it up your ass."

She started for the stairs.

"Cover the windows, then!" he yelled after her. "Use some pieces of sheet . . . or . . . or . . . paint them black . . . or . . . Christ, Annie, the rats! The *rats!*"

She was on the third stair. She paused, looking at him from those dusty-dime eyes. "I haven't time to do any of those things," she said, "and the rats won't bother you, anyway. They may even recognize you for one of their own, Paul. They may adopt you."

Annie laughed. She climbed the stairs, laughing harder and harder. There was a click as the lights went out and Annie went on laughing and he told himself he wouldn't scream, wouldn't beg; that he was past all that. But the damp wildness of the shadows and the boom of her laughter were too much and he shrieked for her not to do this to him, not to leave him, but she only went on laughing and there was a click as the door was shut and her laughter was muted but her laughter was still there, her laughter was on the other side of the door, where there was light, and then the lock clicked, and then another door closed and her laughter was even more muted (but still there), and another lock clicked and a bolt slammed, and her laughter was going away, her laughter was outside, and even after she had started the cruiser up, backed out, put the chain across the driveway, and driven away, he thought he could still hear her. He thought he could still hear her laughing and laughing and laughing.

21

The furnace was a dim bulk in the middle of the room. It looked like an octopus. He thought he would have been able to hear the chiming of the parlor clock if the night had been still, but a strong summer wind had blown up, as it so often did these nights, and there was only time, spreading out forever. He could hear crickets singing just outside the house when the wind dropped . . . and then, sometime later, he heard the stealthy noises he had been afraid of: the low, momentary scuff-and-scurry of the rats.

Only it wasn't rats he was afraid of, was it? No. It was the trooper. His so-fucking-vivid imagination rarely gave him the horrors, but when it did, God help him. God help him once it was warmed up. It was not only warmed up now, it was hot and running on full choke. That there was no sense at all in what he was thinking made not a whit of difference in the dark. In the dark, rationality seemed stupid and logic a dream. In the dark he thought with his skin. He kept seeing the trooper coming back to life—*some* sort of life—out in the barn, sitting up, the loose hay with which Annie had covered him falling to either side of him and into his lap, his face plowed into bloody senselessness by the mower's blade. Saw him crawling out of the barn and down the driveway to the bulkhead, the torn streamers of his uniform swinging and fluttering. Saw him melting magically through the bulkhead and reintegrating his corpse's body down here. Saw him crawling across the packed dirt floor, and the little noises Paul heard weren't rats but the sounds of his approach, and there was but a single thought in the cooling clay of the trooper's dead brain: *You killed me. You opened your mouth and killed me. You threw an ashtray and killed me. You cockadoodie son of a bitch, you murdered my life.*

Once Paul felt the trooper's dead fingers slip, tickling, down his cheek, and he screamed loudly, jerking his legs and making them bellow. He brushed frantically at his face and knocked away not fingers but a large spider.

The movement ended the uneasy truce with the pain in his legs and the drug-need in his nerves, but it also diffused his terror a little. His night vision was coming on strong now, he could see better, and that was a help. Not that there was much to look at— the furnace, the remains of a coal-pile, a table with a bunch of shadowy cans and implements lying on it . . . and to his right, up a way from where he was propped . . . what was that shape? The one next to the shelves? He *knew* that shape. Something about it that made it a *bad* shape. It stood on three legs. Its top was rounded. It looked like one of Welles's death-machines in *The War of the Worlds,* only in miniature. Paul puzzled over this, dozed a little, woke, looked again, and thought: *Of course. I should have known from the first. It* is *a death-machine. And if anyone on Earth's a Martian, it's Annie-fucking-Wilkes. It's her barbecue pot. It's the crematorium where she made me burn* Fast Cars.

He shifted a little because his ass was going to sleep, and moaned. Pain in his legs—particularly in the bunched remains of his left knee—and pain in his pelvis as well. That probably meant he was in for a really bad night, because his pelvis had gotten pretty quiet over the last two months.

He felt for the hypo, picked it up, then put it back. A very light dose, she had said. Best to save it for later, then.

He heard a light shuffle-scuffle and looked quickly in the corner, expecting to see the trooper crawling toward him, one brown eye peering from the hash of his face. *If not for you I could be home watching TV now with my hand on my wife's leg.*

No cop. A dim shape which was maybe just imagination but was more likely a rat. Paul willed himself to relax. Oh what a long night this was going to be.

22

He dozed a little and woke up slumped far over to the left with his head hung down like a drunk in an alley. He straightened up and his legs cursed him roundly. He used the bedpan and it hurt to piss and he realized with some dismay that a urinary infection was probably setting in. He was so vulnerable now. So fucking vulnerable to *everything.* He put the urinal aside and picked up the hypo again.

A light dose of scopolamine, she said—well, maybe so. Or maybe she loaded it with a hot shot of something. The sort of stuff she used on folks like Ernie Gonyar and "Queenie" Beaulifant.

Then he smiled a little. Would that really be so bad? The answer was a resounding *HELL, NO!* It would be good. The pilings would disappear forever. No more low tide. Forever.

With that thought in mind he found the pulse in his left thigh, and though he had never injected himself in his life, he did it efficiently now, even eagerly.

23

He did not die and he did not sleep. The pain went away and he drifted, feeling almost untethered from his body, a balloon of thought drifting at the end of a long string.

You were also Scheherazade to yourself, he thought, and looked at the barbecue pot. He thought of Martian death-rays, burning London in fire.

He thought suddenly of a song, a disco tune, something by a group called the Trammps: *Burn, baby, burn, burn the mother down. . . .*

Something flickered.

Some idea.

Burn the mother down. . . .

Paul Sheldon slept.

24

When he woke up the cellar was filled with the ashy light of dawn. A very large rat sat on the tray Annie had left him, nibbling cheese with its tail neatly curled around its body.

Paul screamed, jerked, then screamed again as pain flowed up his legs. The rat fled.

She had left him some capsules. He knew that the Novril wouldn't take care of the pain, but it was better than nothing.

Besides, pain or no pain, it's time for the old morning fix, right, Paul?

He washed two of the caps down with Pepsi and then leaned back, feeling the dull throb in his kidneys. He was growing something down there, all right. Great.

Martians, he thought. Martian death-machines.

He looked toward the barbecue pot, expecting it to *look* like a barbecue pot in the morning light: a barbecue pot and nothing else. He was surprised to find it still looked to him like one of Welles's striding machines of destruction.

You had an idea—what was it?

The song came back, the one by the Trammps:

Burn, baby, burn, burn the mother down!

Yeah? And just what mother is that? She wouldn't even leave you a candle. You couldn't light a fart.

Up came a message from the boys in the sweatshop.

You don't need to burn anything now. Or here.

What the fuck are we talking about, guys? Could you let me in on—

Then it came, it came at once, the way all the really good ideas came, rounded and smooth and utterly persuasive in its baleful perfection.

Burn the mother down....

He looked at the barbecue pot, expecting the pain of what he had done—what she had *made* him do—to return. It did, but it was dull and faint; the pain in his kidneys was worse. What had she said yesterday? *All I ever did was ... talk you out of a bad book you'd written and into the best one you* ever *wrote....*

Maybe there was a queer sort of truth in that. Maybe he had wildly overestimated just how good *Fast Cars* had been.

That's just your mind trying to heal itself, part of him whispered. *If you ever get out of this, you'll work yourself around in much the same fashion to thinking you never needed your left foot anyway—hell, five less nails to clip. And they do wonders with prosthetics these days. No, Paul, one was a damned good book and the other was a damned good foot. Let's not kid ourselves.*

Yet a deeper part of him suspected that to think that way *was* kidding himself.

Not kidding yourself, Paul. Tell the goddam truth. Lying *to yourself. A guy who makes up stories, a guy like that is lying to everyone, so that guy can't* ever *lie to himself. It's funny, but it's also the truth. Once you start that shit, you might as well just cover up your typewriter and start studying for a broker's license or something, because you're down the toilet.*

So what was the truth? The *truth,* should you insist, was that the increasing dismissal of his work in the critical press as that of a "popular writer" (which was, as he understood it, one step—a small one—above that of a "hack") had hurt him quite badly. It didn't jibe with his self-image as a Serious Writer who was only churning out these shitty romances in order to subsidize his (flourish of trumpets, please!) REAL WORK! Had he hated Misery? Had he really? If so, why had it been so easy to slip back into her world? No, more than easy; blissful, like slipping into a warm bath with a good book by one hand and a cold beer by the other. Perhaps all he had hated was the fact that her face on the dust jackets had overshadowed his in his author photographs, not allowing the critics to see that they were dealing with a young Mailer or Cheever here— that they were dealing with a *heavyweight* here. As a result, hadn't his "serious fiction" become steadily more self-conscious, a sort of scream? *Look at me! Look how good this is! Hey, guys! This stuff has got a sliding perspective! This stuff has got stream-of-consciousness interludes! This is my REAL WORK, you assholes! Don't you DARE turn away from me! Don't you DARE, you cockadoodie brats! Don't you DARE turn away from my REAL WORK! Don't you DARE, or I'll—*

What? What would he do? Cut off their feet? Saw off their thumbs?

Paul was seized by a sudden fit of shivering. He had to urinate. He grabbed the bedpan and finally managed, although it hurt worse than before. He moaned while he was pissing, and continued moaning for a long while after it was done.

Finally, mercifully, the Novril began to kick in—a little—and he drowsed.

He looked at the barbecue pot with heavy-lidded eyes.

How would you feel if she made you burn Misery's Return? the interior voice whispered, and he jumped a little. Drifting away, he realized that it would hurt, yes, it would hurt terribly, it would make the pain he had felt when *Fast Cars* went up in smoke look like the pain of this kidney infection compared with what he had felt when she brought the axe down, cutting off his foot, exercising editorial authority over his body.

He also realized that wasn't the real question.

The real question was how it would make *Annie* feel.

There was a table near the barbecue pot. There were maybe half a dozen jars and cans on it.

One was a can of charcoal lighter fluid.

What if Annie *was the one screaming in pain? Are you curious about how that might sound? Are you curious at all? The proverb says revenge is a dish best eaten cold, but Ronson Fast-Lite had yet to be invented when they made that one up.*

Paul thought: *Burn the mother down,* and fell asleep. There was a little smile on his pale and fading face.

25

When Annie arrived back at quarter of three that afternoon, her normally frizzy hair flattened around her head in the shape of the helmet she had been wearing, she was in a silent mood that seemed to indicate tiredness and reflection rather than depression. When Paul asked her if everything had gone all right, she nodded.

"Yes, I think so. I had some trouble starting the bike, or I would have been back an hour ago. The plugs were dirty. How are your legs, Paul? Do you want another shot before I take you upstairs?"

After almost twenty hours in the dampness, his legs felt as if someone had studded them with rusty nails. He wanted a shot very badly, but not down here. That would not do at all.

"I think I'm all right."

She turned her back to him and squatted. "All right, grab on. But remember what I said about choke-holds and things like that. I'm very tired, and I don't think I'd react very well to funny jokes."

"I seem to be all out of jokes."

"Good."

She lifted him with a moist grunt, and Paul had to bite back a scream of agony. She walked across the floor toward the stairs, her head turned slightly, and he realized she was—or might be—looking at the can-littered table. Her glance was short, seemingly casual, but to Paul it seemed to go on for a very long time, and he was sure she would realize the can of lighter fluid was no longer there. It was stuffed down the back of his underpants instead. Long months after his earlier depredations, he had finally summoned up the courage to steal something else . . . and if her hands slipped up his legs as she climbed the stairs, she was going to grab more than a handful of his skinny ass.

Then she glanced away from the table with no change of expression, and his relief was so great that the thudding, shifting ascent up the stairs to the pantry was almost bearable. She kept up a very good poker face when she wanted to, but he thought—*hoped*—that he had fooled her.

That this time he had really fooled her.

26

"I guess I'd like that shot after all, Annie," he said when she had him back in bed.

She studied his white, sweat-beaded face for a moment, then nodded and left the room.

As soon as she was gone, he slid the flat can out of his underwear and under the mattress. He had not put anything under there since the knife, and he did not intend to leave the lighter fluid there long, but it would have to stay there for the rest of the day. Tonight he intended to put it in another, safer place.

She came back and gave him an injection. Then she put a steno pad and some freshly sharpened pencils on the windowsill and rolled his wheelchair over so it was by the bed.

"There," she said. "I'm going to get some sleep. If a car comes in, I'll hear it. If we're left alone, I'll probably sleep right through until tomorrow morning. If you want to get up and work in long-hand, here's your chair. Your manuscript is over there, on the floor. I frankly don't advise it until your legs start to warm up a little, though."

"I couldn't right now, but I guess I'll probably soldier along awhile tonight. I understand what you meant about time being short now."

"I'm glad you do, Paul. How long do you think you need?"

"Under ordinary circumstances, I'd say a month. The way I've been working just lately, two weeks. If I really go into overdrive, five days. Or maybe a week. It'll be ragged, but it'll be there."

She sighed and looked down at her hands with dull concentration. "I know it's going to be less than two weeks."

"I wish you'd promise me something."

She looked at him with no anger or suspicion, only faint curiosity. "What?"

"Not to read any more until I'm done . . . or until I have to . . . you know . . ."

"Stop?"

"Yes. Or until I have to stop. That way you'll get the conclusion without a lot of fragmentation. It'll have a lot more punch."

"It's going to be a good one, isn't it?"

"Yes." Paul smiled. "It's going to be very hot stuff."

27

That night, around eight o'clock, he hoisted himself carefully into the wheelchair. He listened and heard nothing at all from upstairs. He had been hearing the same nothing ever since the squeak of the bedsprings announced her lying down at four o'clock in the afternoon. She really *must* have been tired.

Paul got the lighter fluid and rolled across to the spot by the window where his informal little writer's camp was pitched: here was the typewriter with the three missing teeth in its unpleasant grin, here the wastebasket, here the pencils and pads and typing paper and piles of scrap-rewrite, some of which he would use and some of which would go into the wastebasket.

Or would have, before.

Here, all unseen, was the door to another world. Here too, he thought, was his own ghost in a series of overlays, like still pictures which, when riffled rapidly, give the illusion of movement.

He wove the chair between the piles of paper and the casually stacked pads with the ease of long practice, listened once more, then reached down and pulled out a nine-inch section of the base-board. He had discovered it was loose about a month ago, and he could see by the thin film of dust on it (*Next you'll be taping hairs across it yourself just to make sure,* he had thought) that Annie hadn't known this loose piece of board was here. Behind it was a narrow space empty save for dust and a plentiful scattering of mouse-turds.

He stowed the can of Fast-Lite in the space and pushed the board back into place. He had an anxious moment when he was afraid it would no longer fit flush against its mates (and God! her eyes were so *fucking* sharp!), and then it slipped neatly home.

Paul regarded this for a moment, then opened his pad, picked up a pencil, and found the hole in the paper.

He wrote undisturbed for the next four hours—until the points on all three of the pencils she had sharpened for him were written flat—and then he rolled himself back to the bed, got in, and went easily off to sleep.

28

CHAPTER 37

Geoffrey's arms were beginning to feel like white iron. He had been standing in the deep shadows outside the hut which belonged to M'Chibi "Beautiful

One" for the last five minutes, looking
rather like a too-slim version of the
circus strongman with the Baroness's
trunk poised over his head.

Just as he came to believe that
nothing Hezekiah could say would convince
M'Chibi to leave his hut, he heard sounds
of ~~rapid~~ movement. Geoffrey turned even
farther, the muscles in his arms now twitching
wildly. Chief M'Chibi "Beautiful One" was
the keeper of the Fire, and inside his hut
were better than a hundred torches, the
head of each coated with a thick, gummy
resin. This resin oozed from the low
trees of the area, and the Boukras called
it Fire-Oil or Fire-Blood-Oil. Like
most essentially ~~simple~~ languages, that
of the Boukras could at times be oddly
elusive. Whatever you called the stuff,
however, there were enough torches in there
to set this whole village afire — it would
burn like a Guy Fawkes dummy, Geoffrey
thought ... if, that was, M'Chibi could
be gotten out of the way.

Fear not to strike, Boss Ge'ff'y,
Hezekiah had said. M'Chibi, he come out

fire' one, 'cause he the fire-man.
Hezekiah, he be comin' out secon' one. So
you don't be waitin' to see my gold
toot' flash! You break that brat's
head, damn quick!

But when he actually did hear them
coming, Geoffrey felt a moment's doubt
in spite of the agony in his arms. Suppose
that, just this once, the ou~

29

His pencil paused in mid-word at the sound of an approaching
engine. He was surprised at how calm he felt—the strongest emotion in him right now was mild annoyance at being interrupted just
when it was starting to float like a butterfly and sting like a bee.
Annie's bootheels rattled staccato down the hallway.

"Get out of sight." Her face was tight and grim. The khaki bag,
unzipped, was over her shoulder. "Get out of s—"

She paused and saw that he had already rolled the wheelchair
back from the window. She looked to make sure that none of his
things were on the sill, then nodded.

"It's the State Police," she said. She looked tense but in control.
The shoulder-bag was within easy reach of her right hand. "Are
you going to be good, Paul?"

"Yes," he said.

Her eyes searched his face.

"I'm going to trust you," she said finally, and turned away, closing
the door but not bothering to lock it.

The car turned into the driveway, the smooth, sleepy beat of that
big 442 Plymouth engine almost like a trademark. He heard the
kitchen screen door bang shut and eased the wheelchair close enough
to the window so he could remain in an angle of shadow and still
peek out. The cruiser pulled up to where Annie stood, and the

engine died. The driver got out and stood almost exactly where the young trooper had been standing when he spoke his last four words . . . but there all resemblance ended. That trooper had been a weedy young man hardly out of his teens, a rookie cop pulling a shit detail, chasing the cold trail of some numbnuts writer who had wrecked up his car and then either staggered deeper into the woods to die or walked blithely away from the whole mess with his thumb cocked.

The cop currently unfolding himself from behind the cruiser's wheel was about forty, with shoulders seemingly as wide as a barn-beam. His face was a square of granite with a few narrow lines carved into it at the eyes and the corners of the mouth. Annie was a big woman, but this fellow made her look almost small.

There was another difference as well. The trooper Annie killed had been alone. Getting out of the shotgun seat of this cruiser was a small, slope-shouldered plainclothesman with lank blonde hair. *David and Goliath,* Paul thought. *Mutt and Jeff. Jesus.*

The plainclothesman did not so much walk around the cruiser as mince around it. His face looked old and tired, the face of a man who is half-asleep . . . except for his faded blue eyes. The eyes were wide-awake, everywhere at once. Paul thought he would be quick.

They bookended Annie and she was saying something to them, first looking up to speak to Goliath, then half-turning and looking down to reply to David. Paul wondered what would happen if he broke the window again and screamed for help again. He thought the odds were maybe eight in ten that they would take her. Oh, she was quick, but the big cop looked as if he might be quicker in spite of his size, and strong enough to uproot middling-sized trees with his bare hands. The plainclothesman's self-conscious walk might be as deliberately deceptive as his sleepy look. He thought they would take her . . . except what surprised them wouldn't surprise her, and that gave her an outside chance, anyway.

The plainclothesman's coat. It was buttoned in spite of the glaring heat. If she shot Goliath first, she might very well be able to put a slug in David's face before he could get that oogy goddam coat unbuttoned and his gun out. More than anything else, that buttoned coat suggested that Annie had been right: so far, this was just a routine check-back.

So far.

I didn't kill him, you know. You *killed him. If you had kept your mouth shut, I would have sent him on his way. He'd be alive now. . . .*

Did he believe that? No, of course not. But there was still that strong, hurtful moment of guilt—like a quick deep stab-wound. Was he going to keep his mouth shut because there were two chances in ten that she would off these two as well if he opened it?

The guilt stabbed quickly again and was gone. The answer to that was also no. It would be nice to credit himself with such selfless motives, but it wasn't the truth. The fact was simple: he wanted to take care of Annie Wilkes himself. *They could only put you in jail, bitch,* he thought. *I know how to hurt you.*

30

There was always the possibility, of course, that they would smell a rat. Rat-catching was, after all, their job, and they would know Annie's background. If that was the way things turned out, so be it . . . but he thought Annie might just be able to wriggle past the law this one last time.

Paul now knew as much of the story as he needed to know, he supposed. Annie had listened to the radio constantly since her long sleep, and the missing state cop, whose name was Duane Kushner, was big news. The fact that he had been searching for traces of a hotshot writer named Paul Sheldon was reported, but Kushner's disappearance had not been linked, even speculatively, with Paul's own. At least, not yet.

The spring runoff had sent his Camaro rolling and tumbling five miles down the wash. It might have lain undiscovered in the forest for another month or another year but for merest coincidence. A couple of National Guard chopper-jockeys sent out as part of a random drug-control sweep (looking for back-country pot-farmers, in other words) had seen a sunflash on what remained of the Camaro's windshield and set down in a nearby clearing for a closer look. The seriousness of the crash itself had been masked by the violent battering the Camaro had taken as it travelled to its final resting place. If the car had yielded traces of blood to forensic analysis (if, indeed, there had *been* a forensic analysis), the radio did not say so. Paul knew that even an exhaustive analysis would turn up precious few traces of blood—his car had spent most of the spring with snowmelt running through it at flood-speed.

And in Colorado, most of the attention and concern were focussed on Trooper Duane Kushner—as he supposed these two visitors proved. So far all speculation centered on three illegal substances: moonshine, marijuana, and cocaine. It seemed possible that Kushner might have stumbled across the growing, distilling, or stockpiling of one of these substances quite by accident during his search for signs of the tenderfoot writer. And as hope of finding Kushner alive began to fade, questions about why he had been out there alone in the first place began to grow louder—and while Paul doubted if the State of Colorado had money enough to finance a buddy system for its vehicle police, they were obviously combing the area for Kushner in pairs. Taking no chances.

Goliath now gestured toward the house. Annie shrugged and shook her head. David said something. After a moment she nodded and led them up the path to the kitchen door. Paul heard the screen's hinges squeak, and then they were in. The sound of so many footfalls out there was frightening, almost a profanation.

"What time was it when he came by?" Goliath asked—it *had* to be Goliath. He had a rumbling Midwestern voice, roughened by cigarettes.

Around four, Annie said. Give or take. She had just finished mowing the grass and she didn't wear a watch. It had been devilish hot; she remembered that well enough.

"How long did he stay, Mrs. Wilkes?" David asked.

"It's *Miss* Wilkes, if you don't mind."

"Excuse me."

Annie said she couldn't reckon on how long for sure, only it hadn't been long. Five minutes, maybe.

"He showed you a picture?"

Yes, Annie said, that was why he came. Paul marvelled at how composed she sounded, how pleasant.

"And had you seen the man in the picture?"

Annie said certainly, he was Paul Sheldon, she knew that right away. "I have all his books," she said. "I like them very much. That disappointed Officer Kushner. He said if that was the case, he guessed I probably knew what I was talking about. He looked very discouraged. He also looked very hot."

"Yeah, it was a hot day, all right," Goliath said, and Paul was alarmed by how much closer his voice was. In the parlor? Yes, almost certainly in the parlor. Big or not, the guy moved like a goddamned lynx. When Annie responded, her own voice was closer. The cops had moved into the parlor. She was following. She hadn't asked them, but they had gone in there anyway. Looking the place over.

Although her pet writer was now less than thirty-five feet away, Annie's voice remained composed. She had asked if he would like to come in for an iced coffee; he said he couldn't. So she had asked if he'd like to take along a cold bottle of—

"Please don't break that," Annie interrupted herself, her voice sharpening. "I like my things, and some of them are quite fragile."

"Sorry, ma'am." That had to be David, his voice low and whispery, both humble and a little startled. That tone coming from a cop would have been amusing under other circumstances, but these were not other circumstances and Paul was not amused. He sat stiffly, hearing the small sound of something being set carefully back down (the penguin on his block of ice, perhaps), his hands clasped tightly on the arms of the wheelchair. He imagined her fiddling with the shoulder-bag. He waited for one of the cops— Goliath, probably—to ask her just what the hell it was she had in there.

Then the shooting would start.

"What were you saying?" David asked.

"That I asked him if he'd like to take along a cold Pepsi from the fridge because it was such a hot day. I keep them right next to the freezer compartment, and that keeps them as cold as you can get them without freezing them. He said that would be very kind. He was a very polite boy. Why did they let such a young boy out alone, do you know?"

"Did he drink the soda here?" David asked, ignoring her question. His voice was closer still. He had crossed the parlor. Paul didn't have to close his eyes to imagine him standing there, looking down the short hall which passed the little downstairs bathroom and ended in the closed guest-room door. Paul sat tight and upright, a pulse beating rapidly in his scrawny throat.

"No," Annie said, as composed as ever. "He took it along. He said he had to keep rolling."

"What's down there?" Goliath asked. There was a double thud of booted heels, the sound slightly hollow, as he stepped off the parlor carpet and onto the bare boards of the hallway.

"A bath and a spare bedroom. I sometimes sleep there when it's very hot. Have a look, if you like, but I promise you I don't have your trooper tied to the bed."

"No, ma'am, I'm sure you don't," David said, and, amazingly, their footfalls and voices began to fade toward the kitchen again. "Did he seem excited about anything while he was here?"

"Not at all," Annie said. "Just hot and discouraged." Paul was beginning to breathe again.

"Preoccupied about anything?"

"No."

"Did he say where he was going next?"

Although the cops almost surely missed it, Paul's own practiced ear sensed the minutest of hesitations—there could be a trap here, a snare which might spring at once or after a short delay. No, she said at last, although he had headed west, so she assumed he must have gone toward Springer's Road and the few farms out that way.

"Thank you, ma'am, for your cooperation," David said. "We may have to check back with you."

"All right," Annie said. "Feel free. I don't see much company these days."

"Would you mind if we looked in your barn?" Goliath asked abruptly.

"Not at all. Just be sure to say howdy when you go in."

"Howdy to who, ma'am?" David asked.

"Why, to Misery," Annie said. "My pig."

31

She stood in the doorway looking at him fixedly—so fixedly that his face began to feel warm and he supposed he was blushing. The two cops had left fifteen minutes ago.

"You see something green?" he asked finally.

"Why didn't you holler?" Both cops had tipped their hats to her as they got in their cruiser, but neither had smiled, and there had been a look in their eyes Paul had been able to see even from the narrow angle afforded by the corner of his window. They knew who she was, all right. "I kept expecting you to holler. They would have fallen on me like an avalanche."

"Maybe. Maybe not."

"But why didn't you?"

"Annie, if you spend your whole life thinking the worst thing you can imagine is going to happen, you have to be wrong some of the time."

"Don't be smart with me!" He saw that beneath her assumed impassivity she was deeply confused. His silence did not fit well into her view of all existence as a sort of Big-Time Wrestling match: Honest Annie *vs.* that all-time, double-ugly tag-team of The Cockadoodie Brats.

"Who's being smart? I told you I was going to keep my mouth shut and I did. I want to finish my book in relative peace. And I want to finish it for you."

She looked at him uncertainly, wanting to believe, afraid to believe . . . and ultimately believing anyway. And she was right to believe, because he was telling the truth.

"Get busy, then," she said softly. "Get busy right away. You saw the way they looked at me."

32

For the next two days life went on just as it had before Duane Kushner; it was almost possible to believe Duane Kushner had never happened at all. Paul wrote almost constantly. He had given the typewriter up for the nonce. Annie put it on the mantel below the picture of the Arc de Triomphe without comment. He filled three legal pads in those two days. There was only one left. When he had filled that one, he would move on to the steno pads. She sharpened his half-dozen Berol Black Warrior pencils, he wrote them dull, and Annie sharpened them again. They shrank steadily as he sat in the sun by the window, bent over, sometimes scratching absently with the great toe of his right foot at the air where the sole of his left foot had been, looking through the hole in the paper. It had yawned wide open again, and the book rushed toward its climax the way the best ones did, as if on a rocket sled. He saw everything with perfect clarity—three groups all hellbent for Misery in the crenellated passages behind the idol's forehead, two wanting to kill her, the third—consisting of Ian, Geoffrey, and Hezekiah—trying to save her . . . while below, the village of the Bourkas burned and the survivors massed at the one point of egress—the idol's left ear—to massacre *anyone* who happened to stagger out alive.

This hypnotic state of absorption was rudely shaken but not broken when, on the third day after the visit of David and Goliath, a cream-colored Ford station wagon with *KTKA/Grand Junction* written on the side pulled into Annie's driveway. The back was full of video equipment.

"Oh God!" Paul said, frozen somewhere between humor, amazement, and horror. "What's *this* fuck-a-row?"

The wagon had barely stopped before one of the rear doors flew open and a guy dressed in combat-fatigue pants and a Deadhead tee-shirt leaped out. There was something big and black pistol-gripped in one hand and for one wild moment Paul thought it was a tear-gas gun. Then he raised it to his shoulder and swept it toward the house, and Paul saw it was a minicam. A pretty young woman was getting out of the front passenger seat, fluffing her blow-dried hair and pausing for one final appraising look at her makeup in the outside rear-view mirror before joining her camera-man.

The eye of the outside world, which had slipped away from the Dragon Lady these last few years, had now returned with a vengeance.

Paul rolled backward quickly, hoping he had been in time.

Well, if you want to know for sure, just check the six o'clock news, he thought, and then had to raise both hands to his mouth to plug up the giggles.

The screen door banged open and shut.

"Get the hell out of here!" Annie screamed. "Get the hell off my land!"

Dimly: "Ms. Wilkes, if we could have just a few—"

"You can have a couple of loads of double-ought buck up your cockadoodie *bumhole* if you don't get out of here!"

"Ms. Wilkes, I'm Glenna Roberts from KTKA—"

"I don't care if you're John Q. Jesus Johnnycake Christ from the planet Mars! Get off my land or you're DEAD!"

"But—"

KAPOW!

Oh Annie oh my Jesus Annie killed that stupid broad—

He rolled back and peeked through the window. He had no choice—he had to see. Relief gusted through him. Annie had fired into the air. That seemed to have done quite well. Glenna Roberts was diving head-first into the KTKA newsmobile. The camera-man swung his lens toward Annie; Annie swung her shotgun toward the camera-man; the camera-man, deciding he wanted to live to see the Grateful Dead again more than he wanted to roll tape on the Dragon Lady, immediately dropped into the back seat again. The wagon was reversing down the driveway before he got his door all the way closed.

Annie stood watching them go, the rifle held in one hand, and then she came slowly back into the house. He heard the clack as she put the rifle on the table. She came down to Paul's room. She looked worse than he had ever seen her, her face haggard and pale, her eyes darting constantly.

"They're back," she whispered.

"Take it easy."

"I knew all those brats would come back. And now they have."

"They're gone, Annie. You made them go."

"They *never* go. Someone told them that cop was at the Dragon Lady's house before he disappeared. So here they are."

"Annie—"

"You know what they want?" she demanded.

"Of course. I've dealt with the press. They want the same two things they always want—for you to fuck up while the tape's running and for someone else to buy the martinis when Happy Hour rolls around. But, Annie, you've got to settle d—"

"*This* is what they want," she said, and raised one hooked hand to her forehead. She pulled down suddenly, sharply, opening four bloody furrows. Blood ran into her eyebrows, down her cheeks, along either side of her nose.

"Annie! Stop it!"

"And this!" She slapped herself across the left cheek with her left hand, hard enough to leave an imprint. "And *this!*" The right cheek, even harder, hard enough to make droplets of blood fly from the fingernail gouges.

"*STOP it!*" he screamed.

"*It's what they want!*" she screamed back. She raised her hands to her forehead and pressed them against the wounds, blotting them. She held her bloody palms out toward him for a moment. Then she plodded out of the room.

After a long, long time, Paul began to write again. It went slowly at first—the image of Annie pulling those furrows into her skin kept intruding—and he thought it was going to be no good, he had just better pack it in for the day, when the story caught him and he fell through the hole in the paper again.

As always these days, he went with a sense of blessed relief.

33

More police came the next day: local yokels this time. With them was a skinny man carrying a case which could only contain a steno machine. Annie stood in the driveway with them, listening, her face expressionless. Then she led them into the kitchen.

Paul sat quietly, a steno pad of his own on his lap (he had finished the last legal pad the previous evening), and listened to Annie's voice as she made a statement which consisted of all the things she had told David and Goliath four days ago. This, Paul thought, was nothing more than blatant harassment. He was amused and appalled to find himself feeling a little sorry for Annie Wilkes.

The Sidewinder cop who asked most of the questions began by telling Annie she could have a lawyer present if she wanted. Annie declined and simply re-told her story. Paul could detect no deviations.

They were in the kitchen for half an hour. Near the end one of them asked how she had come by the ugly-looking scratches on her forehead.

"I did it in the night," she said. "I had a bad dream."

"What was that?" the cop asked.

"I dreamed that people remembered me after all this time and started coming out here again," Annie said.

When they were gone, Annie came to his room. Her face was doughy and distant and ill.

"This place is turning into Grand Central," Paul said.

She didn't smile. "How much longer?"

He hesitated, looked at the pile of typescript with the ragged stack of handwritten pages on top, then back at Annie. "Two days," he said. "Maybe three."

"The next time they come they'll have the search warrant," she said, and left before he could reply.

34

She came in that evening around quarter of twelve and said: "You should have been in bed an hour ago, Paul."

He looked up, startled out of the story's deep dream. Geoffrey—who had turned out to be very much the hero of this one—had just come face to face with the hideous queen bee, whom he would have to battle to the death for Misery's life.

"It doesn't matter," he said. "I'll turn in after awhile. Sometimes you get it down or it gets away." He shook his hand, which was sore and throbbing. A large hard growth, half callus and half blister, had risen on the inside of his index finger, where the pencil pressed most firmly. He had pills, and they would take away the pain, but they would also blur his thoughts.

"You think it's good, don't you?" she asked softly. "Really good. You're not doing it just for me anymore, are you?"

"Oh no," he said. For a moment he trembled on the edge of saying something more—of saying, *It was never for you, Annie, or all the other people out there who sign their letters "Your number-one fan." The minute you start to write all those people are at the other end of the galaxy, or something. It was never for my ex-wives, or my mother, or for my father. The reason authors almost always put a dedication on a book, Annie, is because their selfishness even horrifies themselves in the end.*

But it would be unwise to say such a thing to her.

He wrote until dawn was coming up in the east and then fell into bed and slept for four hours. His dreams were confused and unpleasant. In one of them Annie's father was climbing a long flight of stairs. He had a basket of what appeared to be newspaper clippings in his arms. Paul tried to cry out to him, to warn him, but every time he opened his mouth nothing came out but a neatly reasoned paragraph of narration—although this paragraph was different each time he tried to scream, it always opened the same way: "One day, about a week later . . ." And now came Annie Wilkes, screaming, rushing down the hall, hands outstretched to give her father the killing push . . . only her screams were becoming weird buzzing noises, and her body was rippling and humping and changing under her skirt and cardigan sweater, because Annie was changing into a bee.

35

No one official came by the following day, but lots of unofficial people showed up. Designated Gawkers. One of the cars was full of teen-agers. When they turned into the driveway to reverse direction, Annie rushed out and screamed at them to get off her land before she shot them for the dirty dogs they were.

"Fuck off, Dragon Lady!" one of them shouted.

"Where'd you bury him?" another yelled as the car backed out in a boil of dust.

A third threw a beer-bottle. As the car roared away, Paul could make out a bumper sticker pasted to the rear window. SUPPORT THE SIDEWINDER BLUE DEVILS, it read.

An hour later he saw Annie stalk grimly past his window, drawing on a pair of work-gloves as she headed for the barn. She came back some time later with the chain. She had taken the time to interlace its stout steel loops with barbed wire. When this prickly knitting was padlocked across the driveway, she reached into her breast pocket, and took out some red pieces of cloth. These she tied to several of the links to aid visibility.

"It won't keep the cops out," she said when she finally came in, "but it'll keep the rest of the brats away."

"Yes."

"Your hand . . . it looks swollen."

"Yes."

"I hate to be a cockadoodie pest, Paul, but . . ."

"Tomorrow," he said.

"Tomorrow? Really?" She brightened at once.

"Yes, I think so. Probably around six."

"Paul, that's wonderful! Shall I start reading now, or—"

"I'd prefer that you wait."

"Then I will." That tender, melting look had crept into her eyes again. He had come to hate her most of all when she looked that way. "I love you, Paul. You know that, don't you?"

"Yes," he said. "I know." And bent over his pad again.

36

That evening she brought him his Keflex pill—his urinary infection was improving, but very slowly—and a bucket of ice. She laid a neatly folded towel beside it and left without saying a word.

Paul put his pencil aside—he had to use the fingers of his left hand to unbend the fingers of his right—and slipped his hand into the ice. He left it there until it was almost completely numb. When he took it out, the swelling seemed to have gone down a little. He wrapped the towel around it and sat, looking out into the darkness, until it began to tingle. He put the towel aside, flexed the hand for awhile (the first few times made him grimace with pain, but then the hand began to limber up), and started to write again.

At dawn he rolled slowly over to his bed, lurched in, and was asleep at once. He dreamed he was lost in a snowstorm, only it wasn't snow; it was flying pages which filled the world, destroying direction, and each page was covered with typing, and all the n's and t's and e's were missing, and he understood that if he was still alive when the blizzard ended, he would have to fill them all in himself, by hand, deciphering words that were barely there.

37

He woke up around eleven, and almost as soon as Annie heard him stirring about, she came in with orange juice, his pills, and a bowl of hot chicken soup. She was glowing with excitement. "It's a very special day, Paul, isn't it?"

"Yes." He tried to pick up the spoon with his right hand and could not. It was puffy and red, so swollen the skin was shiny. When he tried to bend it into a fist, it felt as though long rods of metal had been pushed through it at random. The last few days, he thought, had been like some nightmare autographing session that just never ended.

"Oh, your poor *hand!*" she cried. "I'll get you another pill! I'll do it right now!"

"No. This is the push. I want my head clear for it."

"But you can't write with your hand like that!"

"No," he agreed. "My hand's shot. I'm going to finish this baby

the way I started—with that Royal. Eight or ten pages should see
it through. I guess I can fight my way through that many n's, t's,
and e's."

"I should have gotten you another machine," she said. She looked
honestly sorry; tears stood in her eyes. Paul thought that the occasional moments like this were the most ghastly of all, because in
them he saw the woman she might have been if her upbringing had
been right or the drugs squirted out by all the funny little glands
inside her had been less wrong. Or both. "I goofed. It's hard for
me to admit that, but it's true. It was because I didn't want to admit
that Dartmonger woman got the better of me. I'm sorry, Paul. Your
poor hand."

She raised it, gentle as Niobe at the pool, and kissed it.

"That's all right," he said. "We'll manage, Ducky Daddles and I.
I hate *him,* but I've got a feeling he hates *me* as well, so I guess
we're even."

"Who are you talking about?"

"The Royal. I've nicknamed it after a cartoon character."

"Oh . . ." She trailed away. Turned off. Came unplugged. He
waited patiently for her to return, eating his soup as he did so,
holding the spoon awkwardly between the first and second fingers
of his left hand.

At last she did come back and looked at him, smiling radiantly
like a woman just awakening and realizing it was going to be a
beautiful day. "Soup almost gone? I've got something very special,
if it is."

He showed her the bowl, empty except for a few noodles stuck
to the bottom. "See what a Do-Bee I am, Annie?" he said without
even a trace of a smile.

"You're the most goodest Do-Bee there ever was, Paul, and you
get a whole *row* of gold stars! In fact . . . wait! Wait till you see
this!"

She left, leaving Paul to look first at the calendar and then at the
Arc de Triomphe. He looked up at the ceiling and saw the interlinked W's waltzing drunkenly across the plaster. Last of all he
looked across at the typewriter and the vast, untidy pile of manuscript. *Goodbye to all that,* he thought randomly, and then Annie
was bustling back in with another tray.

On it were four dishes: wedges of lemon on one, grated egg on
a second, toast points on a third. In the middle was a larger plate,
and on this one was a vast

(oogy)

gooey pile of caviar.

"I don't know if you like this stuff or not," she said shyly. "I don't even know if *I* like it. I never had it."

Paul began to laugh. It hurt his middle and it hurt his legs and it even hurt his hand; soon he would probably hurt even more, because Annie was paranoid enough to think that if someone was laughing it must be at *her.* But still he couldn't stop. He laughed until he was choking and coughing, his cheeks red, tears spurting from the corners of his eyes. The woman had cut off his foot with an axe and his thumb with an electric knife, and here she was with a pile of caviar big enough to choke a warthog. And for a wonder, that black look of *crevasse* did not dawn on her face. She began to laugh with him, instead.

38

Caviar was supposed to be one of those things you either loved or hated, but Paul had never felt either way. If he was flying first class and a stewardess stuck a plate of it in front of him, he ate it and then forgot there was such a thing as caviar until the next time a stewardess stuck a plate of it in front of him. But now he ate it hungrily, with all the trimmings, as if discovering the great principle of food for the first time in his life.

Annie didn't care for it at all. She nibbled at the one dainty teaspoonful she'd put on a toast point, wrinkled her face in disgust, and put it aside. Paul, however, plowed ahead with undimmed enthusiasm. In a space of fifteen minutes he had eaten half of Mount Beluga. He belched, covered his mouth, and looked guiltily at Annie, who went off into another gay gust of laughter.

I think I am going to kill you, Annie, he thought, and smiled warmly at her. *I really do. I may go with you—probably will, in fact—but I am going to go with a by-God bellyful of caviar. Things could be worse.*

"That was great, but I can't eat any more," he said.

"You'd probably throw up if you did," she said. "That stuff is very rich." She smiled back. "There's another surprise. I have a bottle of champagne. For later . . . when you finish the book. It's called Dom Pérignon. It cost seventy-five dollars! For *one bottle!* But Chuckie Yoder down at the liquor store says it's the best there is."

"Chuckie Yoder is right," Paul said, thinking that it was partly Dom's fault that he'd gotten himself into this hell in the first place. He paused a moment and then said: "There's something else I'd like, as well. For when I finish."

"Oh? What's that?"

"You said once you had all of my things."

"I do."

"Well . . . there was a carton of cigarettes in my suitcase. I'd like to have a smoke when I finish."

Her smile had faded slowly. "You know those things are no good for you, Paul. They cause cancer."

"Annie, would you say that cancer is something I have to worry about just now?"

She didn't answer.

"I just want that one single cigarette. I've always leaned back and smoked one when I finished. It's the one that always tastes the best, believe me—even better than the one you have after a really fine meal. At least that's how it used to be. I suppose this time it'll make me feel dizzy and like puking, but I'd like that little link with the past. What do you say, Annie? Be a sport. *I* have been."

"All right . . . but before the champagne. I'm not drinking a seventy-five-dollar bottle of fizzy beer in the same room where you've been blowing that poison around."

"That's fine. If you bring it to me around noon, I'll put it on the windowsill where I can look at it once in awhile. I'll finish, and then I'll fill in the letters, and then I'll smoke it until I feel like I'm going to fall down unconscious, and then I'll butt it. Then I'll call you."

"All right," she said. "But I'm still not happy about it. Even if you don't get lung cancer from just one, I'm still not happy about it. And do you know why, Paul?"

"No."

"Because only Don't-Bees smoke," she said, and began to gather up the dishes.

39

"Mis†uh Boss Ia∩, is sh℮--?"

"Shhhhh!" Ia∩ hissed fierc℮ly, and Hez℮kiah sub-

sided. Geoffrey felt a pulse beating with wild rapidity
in his throat. From outside came the steady soft creak of
lines and rigging, the slow flap of the sails in the first
faint breezes of the freshening trade winds, the occasional
cry of a bird. Dimly, from the afterdeck, Geoffrey could
hear a gang of men singing a shanty in bellowing, off-key
voices. But in here all was silence as the three men,
two white and one black, waited to see if Misery would live
...or--

        Ian groaned hoarsely, and Hezekiah gripped his
arm. Geoffrey merely tightened his already hysterically
tight hold on himself. After all of this, could God really
be cruel enough to let her die? Once he would have denied
such a possibility confidently, and with humor rather than
indignation. The idea that God could be cruel would in
those days have struck him as absurd.

        But his ideas about God--like his ideas about so
many things, had changed. They had changed in Africa. In
Africa he had discovered that there was not just one God
but many, and some were more than cruel--they were insane,
and that changed all. Cruelty, after all, was under-
standable. With insanity, however, there was no arguing.

        If his Misery were truly dead, as he had come to
fear, he intended to go up on the foredeck and throw himself over the rail. He had always known and accepted the
fact that the gods were hard; he had no desire, however,
to live in a world where the gods were insane.

These wretched musings were interrupted by a harsh, half-superstitious gasp from Hezekiah.

"Mist' Boss Ian! Mist' Boss Geoffrey! Look! She eyes! Look she eyes!"

Misery's eyes, that gorgeously delicate shade of cornflower blue, had fluttered open. They passed from Ian to Geoffrey and then back to Ian again. For a moment Geoffrey saw only puzzlement in those eyes...and then recognition dawned in them, and he felt gladness roar through his soul.

"Where am I?" she asked, yawning and stretching. "Ian--Geoffrey--are we at sea? Why am I so hungry?"

Laughing, crying, Ian bent and hugged her, speaking her name over and over again.

Bewildered but pleased, she hugged him back--and because he knew she was all right, Geoffrey found he could abide their love, now and forever. He would live alone, could live alone, in perfect peace.

Perhaps the gods were not insane after all...at least, not all of them.

He touched Hezekiah on the shoulder. "I think we should leave them alone, old man, don' you?"

"I guess that be right, Mist' Boss Geoffrey," Hezekiah said. He grinned widely, flashing all seven of his gold teeth.

Geoffrey stole one last look at her, and for just

a moment those cornflower eyes flashed his way, warming him,
filling him. <u>Fulfilli g him.</u>

    <u>I love you, my darling,</u> he thought. <u>Do you hear
me?</u>

    Perhaps the answer which came back was only the
wistful call of his own mind, but he thought not--it was
too clear, too much her own voice.

    <u>I hear...and I love you, too.</u>

    Geoffrey closed the door and went up to the after-
deck. Instead of throwing himself over the rail, as he might
have done, he lit his pipe and smoked a bowl of tobacco slowly, watching the sun go down behind that distant, disappearing
cloud on the horizon--that cloud which was the coast of
Africa.

And then, because he could not stand to do otherwise, Paul
Sheldon rolled the last page out of the typewriter and scrawled the
most loved and hated phrase in the writer's vocabulary with a pen:

THE END

40

His swollen right hand had not wanted to fill in the missing letters,
but he had forced it through the work nonetheless. If he wasn't
able to work at least some of the stiffness out of it, he was not
going to be able to carry through with this.

When it was done, he put the pen aside. He regarded his work
for a moment. He felt as he always did when he finished a book—
queerly empty, let down, aware that for each little success he had
paid a toll of absurdity.

It was always the same, always the same—like toiling uphill through

jungle and breaking out to a clearing at the top after months of
hell only to discover nothing more rewarding than a view of a
freeway—with a few gas stations and bowling alleys thrown in for
good behavior, or something.

Still, it was good to be done—always good to be done. Good to
have produced, to have caused a thing to be. In a numb sort of way
he understood and appreciated the bravery of the act, of making
little lives that weren't, creating the appearance of motion and the
illusion of warmth. He understood—now, finally—that he was a
bit of a dullard at doing this trick, but it was the only one he knew,
and if he always ended up doing it ineptly, he at least never failed
to do it with love. He touched the pile of manuscript and smiled
a little bit.

His hand left the big pile of paper and stole to the single Marlboro
she had put on the windowsill for him. Beside it was a ceramic
ashtray with a paddlewheel excursion boat printed on the bottom
encircled by the words SOUVENIR OF HANNIBAL, MISSOURI—HOME
OF AMERICA'S STORY TELLER!

In the ashtray was a book of matches, but there was only one
match in it—all she had allowed him. One, however, should be
enough.

He could hear her moving around upstairs. That was good. He
would have plenty of time to make his few little preparations, plenty
of warning if she decided to come down before he was quite ready
for her.

Here comes the real *trick, Annie. Let's see if I can do it. Let's see—
can I?*

He bent over, ignoring the pain in his legs, and began to work
the loose section of baseboard out with his fingers.

41

He called for her five minutes later, and listened to her heavy,
somehow toneless tread on the stairs. He had expected to feel
terrified when things got to this point, and was relieved to find he
felt quite calm. The room was filled with the reek of lighter fluid.
It dripped steadily from one side of the board which lay across the
arms of the wheelchair.

"Paul, are you *really* done?" she called down the length of hallway.

Paul looked at the pile of paper sitting on the board beside the hateful Royal typewriter. Lighter fluid soaked the stack. "Well," he called back, "I did the best I could, Annie."

"Wow! Oh, great! Gee, I can hardly believe it! After all this time! Just a minute! I'll get the champagne!"

"Fine!"

He heard her cross the kitchen linoleum, knowing where each squeak was going to come the instant before it did come. *I am hearing all these sounds for the last time,* he thought, and that brought a sense of wonder, and wonder broke the calm open like an egg. The fear was inside . . . but there was something else in there as well. He supposed it was the receding coast of Africa.

The refrigerator door was opened, then banged shut. Here she came across the kitchen again; here she came.

He had not smoked the cigarette, of course; it still lay on the windowsill. It had been the match he wanted. That one single match.

What if it doesn't light when you strike it?

But it was far too late for such considerations.

He reached over to the ashtray and picked up the matchbook. He tore out the single match. She was coming down the hallway now. Paul struck the match and, sure enough, it didn't light.

Easy! Easy does it!

He struck it again. Nothing.

Easy . . . easy . . .

He scratched it along the rough dark-brown strip on the back of the book a third time and a pale-yellow flame bloomed at the end of the paper stick.

42

"I just hope this—"

She stopped, the next word pulled back inside her as she sucked in breath. Paul sat in his wheelchair behind a barricade of heaped paper and ancient Royal stenomongery. He had purposely turned the top sheet around so she could read this:

MISERY'S RETURN

By Paul Sheldon

Above this sopping pile of paper Paul's swollen right hand hovered, and held between the thumb and first finger was a single burning match.

She stood in the doorway, holding a bottle of champagne wrapped in a strip of towelling. Her mouth dropped open. She closed it with a snap.

"Paul?" Cautiously. "What are you doing?"

"It's done," he said. "And it's good, Annie. You were right. The best of the *Misery* books, and maybe the best thing I ever wrote, mongrel or not. Now I'm going to do a little trick with it. It's a good trick. I learned it from you."

"*Paul, no!*" she screamed. Her voice was full of agony and understanding. Her hands flew out, the bottle of champagne dropping from them unheeded. It hit the floor and exploded like a torpedo. Curds of foam flew everywhere. "*No! No! PLEASE DON'T—*"

"Too bad you'll never read it," Paul said, and smiled at her. It was his first real smile in months, radiant and genuine. "False modesty aside, I've got to say it was better than good. It was *great,* Annie."

The match was guttering, printing its small heat on the tips of his fingers. He dropped it. For one terrible moment he thought it had gone out, and then pale-blue fire uncoiled across the title page with an audible sound—*foomp!* It ran down the sides, tasted the fluid that had pooled along the outer edge of the paper-pile, and shot up yellow.

"*OH GOD NO!*" Annie shrieked. "*NOT MISERY! NOT MISERY! NOT HER! NO! NO!*"

Now her face had begun to shimmer on the far side of the flames. "Want to make a wish, Annie?" he shouted at her. "Want to make a *wish,* you fucking goblin?"

"*OH MY GOD OH PAUL WHAT ARE YOU DOOOOOING?*" She stumbled forward, arms outstretched. Now the pile of paper was not just burning; it was blazing. The gray side of the Royal had begun to turn black. Lighter fluid had pooled under it and now pale-blue tongues of flame shot up between the keys. Paul could feel his face baking, the skin tightening.

"*NOT MISERY!*" she wailed. "*YOU CAN'T BURN MISERY, YOU COCKADOODIE BRAT, YOU CAN'T BURN MISERY!*"

And then she did exactly what he had almost known she would do. She seized the burning pile of paper and wheeled about, meaning to run to the bathroom with it, perhaps, and douse it in the tub.

When she turned Paul seized the Royal, unmindful of the blisters its hot right side was printing on his already swollen right hand. He lifted it over his head. Little blue firedrops still fell from its undercarriage. He paid them no more mind than he paid the flare of pain in his back as he strained something there. His face was an insane grimace of effort and concentration. He brought his arms forward and down, letting the typewriter fly out of his hands. It struck her squarely in the center of her wide solid back.

"HOO-OWWG!" It was not a scream but a vast, startled grunt. Annie was driven forward onto the floor with the burning stack of paper under her.

Small bluish fires like spirit-lanterns dotted the surface of the board which had served as his desk. Gasping, each breath smooth hot iron in his throat, Paul knocked it aside. He pushed himself up and tottered erect on his right foot.

Annie was writhing and moaning. A lick of flame shot up through the gap between her left arm and the side of her body. She screamed. Paul could smell frying skin, burning fat.

She rolled over, struggling to her knees. Most of the paper was on the floor now, either still burning or hissing to ruin in puddles of champagne, but Annie still held some, and it was still burning. Her cardigan sweater was burning, too. He saw green hooks of glass in her forearms. A larger shard poked out of her right cheek like the blade of a tomahawk.

"I'm going to kill you, you lying cocksucker," she said, and staggered toward him. She knee-walked three "steps" toward him and then fell over the typewriter. She writhed and managed to turn over halfway. Then Paul fell on her. He felt the sharp angles of the typewriter beneath her even through her body. She screamed like a cat, writhed like a cat, and tried to claw out from under him like a cat.

The flames were going out around them but he could still feel savage heat coming off the twisting, heaving mound beneath him, and knew that at least some of her sweater and brassiere must be cooked onto her body. He felt no sympathy at all.

She tried to buck him off. He held on, and now he was lying squarely on top of her like a man who means to commit rape, his face almost on hers; his right hand groped, knowing exactly what it was looking for.

"Get off me!"

He found a handful of hot, charry paper.

"Get off me!"

He crumpled the paper, squeezing flames out between his fingers. He could smell her—cooked flesh, sweat, hate, madness.

"GET OFF ME!" she screamed, her mouth yawning wide, and he was suddenly looking into the dank red-lined pit of the goddess. *"GET OFF ME YOU COCKADOODIE BR—"*

He stuffed paper, white bond and black charred onionskin, into that gaping, screaming mouth. Saw the blazing eyes suddenly widen even more, now with surprise and horror and fresh pain.

"Here's your book, Annie," he panted, and his hand closed on more paper. This bunch was out, dripping wet, smelling sourly of spilt wine. She bucked and writhed under him. The salt-dome of his left knee whammed the floor and there was excruciating pain, but he stayed on top of her. *I'm gonna rape you, all right, Annie. I'm gonna rape you because all I can do is the worst I can do. So suck my book. Suck my book. Suck on it until you fucking CHOKE.* He crumpled the wet paper with a convulsive closing jerk of his fist and slammed it into her mouth, driving the half-charred first bunch farther down.

"Here it is, Annie, how do you like it? It's a genuine first, it's the Annie Wilkes Edition, how do you like it? Eat it, Annie, suck on it, go on and *eat it,* be a Do-Bee and eat your book *all up.*"

He slammed in a third wad, a fourth. The fifth was still burning; he put it out with the already blistered heel of his right hand as he stuffed it in.

Some weird muffled noise was coming out of her. She gave a tremendous jerk and this time Paul was thrown off. She struggled and flailed to her knees. Her hands clawed at her blackened throat, which had a hideously swelled look. Little was left of her sweater but the charred ring of the neck. The flesh of her belly and diaphragm bubbled with blisters. Champagne was dripping from the wad of paper which protruded from her mouth.

"Mumpf! Mark! Mark!" Annie croaked. She got to her feet somehow, still clawing at her throat. Paul pushed himself backward, legs sticking untidily out in front of him, watching her warily. *"Harkoo? Dorg? Mumpf!"*

She took one step toward him. Two. Then she tripped over the typewriter again. As she fell this time her head twisted at an angle and he saw her eyes looking at him with an expression that was questioning and somehow terrible: *What happened, Paul? I was bringing you champagne, wasn't I?*

The left side of her head connected with the edge of the man-

telpiece and she went down like a loose sack of bricks, striking the
floor in a vast tumble that shook the house.

43

Annie had fallen on the bulk of the burning paper; her body had
put it out. It was a smoking black lump in the middle of the floor.
The puddles of champagne had put out most of the individual pages.
But two or three had wafted against the wall to the left of the door
while still burning brightly, and the wallpaper was alight in
spots . . . but burning with no real enthusiasm.

Paul crawled over to his bed, pulling himself on his elbows, and
got hold of the coverlet. Then he worked his way over to the wall,
pushing the shards of broken bottle out of his way with the sides
of his hands as he went. He had strained his back. He had burned
his right hand badly. His head ached. His stomach roiled with the
sick-sweet smell of burned meat. But he was free. The goddess was
dead and he was free.

He got his right knee under him, reached up clumsily with the
coverlet (which was damp with champagne and striped with smeary
black swaths of ash), and began to beat at the flames. When he let
the coverlet fall into a smoking heap at the baseboard, there was
a big smoking bald spot in the middle of the wall, but the paper
was out. The bottom page of the calendar had curled up, but that
was all.

He began to crawl back toward the wheelchair. He was halfway
there when Annie opened her eyes.

44

Paul stared, unbelieving, as she got slowly to her knees. Paul himself
was propped on his hands, legs trailing out behind him. He looked
like a strange adult version of Popeye's nephew, Swee' Pea.

No . . . no, you're dead.

*You are in error, Paul. You can't kill the goddess. The goddess is
immortal. Now I must rinse.*

Her eyes were staring, horrible. A huge wound, pink-red, glared through her hair on the left side of her head. Blood sheeted down her face.

"Durd!" Annie cried through her throatful of paper. She began to crawl toward him, hands outstretched, flexing. *"Ooo durd!"*

Paul pulled himself around in a half-circle and began to crawl for the door. He could hear her behind him. And then, as he entered the zone of broken glass, he felt her hand close around his left ankle and squeeze his stump excruciatingly. He screamed.

"DIRT!" Annie cried triumphantly.

He looked over his shoulder. Her face was turning slowly purple, and seemed to be swelling. He realized she actually *was* turning into the Bourkas' idol.

He yanked with all his might and his leg slithered footlessly out of her grasp, leaving her with nothing but the circlet of leather with which she had capped the stump.

He crawled on, beginning to cry, sweat pouring down his cheeks. He pulled himself along on his elbows like a soldier advancing beneath heavy machine-gun fire. He heard the thud of first one knee from behind him, then the other, then the first again. She was still coming. She was as solid as he had always feared. He had burned her broken her back stuffed her tubes full of paper and still still still she was coming.

"BIRT!" Annie screamed now. *"DIRT . . . BIRT!"*

One of his elbows came down on a hook of glass and it jabbed up into his arm. He crawled forward anyway with it sticking out of him like a push-pin.

Her hand closed over his left calf.

"AW! GAW . . . OOO OW . . . AW!"

He turned back again and yes, her face had gone black, a dusky rotted-plum black from which her bleeding eyes bulged wildly. Her pulsing throat had swelled up like an inner-tube, and her mouth was writhing. She was, he realized, trying to grin.

The door was just in reach. Paul stretched out and laid hold of the jamb in a death-grip.

"GAW . . . OOO . . . OW!"

Her right hand on his right thigh.

Thud. One knee. *Thud.* The other.

Closer. Her shadow. Her shadow falling over him.

"No," he whimpered. He felt her tugging, pulling. He held onto the jamb grimly, eyes now squeezed shut.

"GAW . . . OOO . . . AW!"

Over him. Thunder. Goddess-thunder.

Now her hands scuttled up his back like spiders and settled upon his neck.

"GAW . . . OOO . . . DIRT . . . BIRT!"

His air was gone. He held the jamb. He held the jamb and felt her over him felt her hands sinking into his neck and he screamed *Die can't you die can't you ever die can't you—*

"GAW . . . G—"

The pressure slackened. For a moment he could breathe again. Then Annie collapsed on top of him, a mountain of slack flesh, and he couldn't breathe at all.

45

He worked his way out from under her like a man burrowing his way out of a snowslide. He did it with the last of his strength.

He crawled through the door, expecting her hand to settle around his ankle again at any moment, but that did not happen. Annie lay silent and face-down in blood and spilled champagne and fragments of green glass. Was she dead? She *must* be dead. Paul did not believe she was dead.

He slammed the door shut. The bolt she had put on looked like something halfway up a high cliff, but he clawed his way up to it, shot it, and then collapsed in a shuddery huddle at the door's foot.

He lay in a stupor for some unknown length of time. What roused him from it was a low, minute scratching sound. *The rats,* he thought. *It's the r—*

Then Annie's thick, blood-grimed fingers poked under the door and tugged mindlessly at his shirt.

He shrieked and jerked away from them, his left leg creaking with pain. He hammered at the fingers with his fist. Instead of pulling back, they jerked a little and lay still.

Let that be the end of her. Please God let that be the end of her.

In horrible pain now, Paul began to crawl slowly toward the bathroom. He got halfway there and looked back. Her fingers were still poking out from under the door. As bad as his pain was, he could not stand to look at that, or even think of that, and so he reversed direction, went back, and pushed them under. He had to nerve himself to do it; he was certain that the moment he touched them, they would clutch him.

He finally reached the bathroom, every part of him throbbing. He pulled himself inside and shut the door.

God, what if she's moved the dope?

But she hadn't. The untidy litter of boxes was still there, including the ones containing the sample packets of Novril. He took three dry, then crawled back to the door and lay down against it, blocking it with the weight of his body.

Paul slept.

46

When he woke up it was dark, and at first he didn't know where he was—how had his bedroom gotten so *small?* Then he remembered everything, and with his remembering a queer certainty came: she was not dead, even now not dead. She was standing right outside this door, she had the axe, and when he crawled out she would amputate his head. It would go rolling off down the hallway like a bowling ball while she laughed.

That is crazy, he told himself, and then he heard—or thought he did—a little rustling sound, the sound of a woman's starched skirt, perhaps, brushing lightly against the wall.

You just made it up. Your imagination . . . it's so vivid.

I didn't. I heard it.

He *hadn't*. He knew that. His hand reached for the doorknob, then fell uncertainly back. Yes, he knew he had heard nothing . . . but what if he *had?*

She could have gone out the window.

Paul, she's DEAD!

The return, implacable in its illogic: The goddess never dies.

He realized he was frantically biting his lips and made himself stop it. Was this what going crazy was like? Yes. He was close to that, and who had a better right? But if he gave in to it, if the cops finally returned tomorrow or the day after to find Annie dead in the guest-room and a blubbering ball of protoplasm in the downstairs bathroom, a blubbering ball of protoplasm who had once been a writer named Paul Sheldon, wouldn't that be Annie's victory?

*You bet. And now, Paulie, you're going to be a good little Do-Bee and
follow the scenario. Right?*

Okay.

His hand reached for the knob again . . . and faltered again. He
couldn't follow the original scenario. In it he had seen himself lighting the paper and her picking it up, and that had happened. Only
he was to have bashed her *brains* in with the fucking typewriter
instead of hitting her in the back with it. Then he had meant to
work his way out into the parlor and light the house on fire. The
scenario had called for him to effect his escape through one of the
parlor windows. He would take a hell of a thump, but he had already
seen how fastidious Annie was about locking her doors. Better
thumped than crisped, as he believed John the Baptist had once said.

In a book, all would have gone according to plan . . . but life was
so fucking untidy—what could you say for an existence where some
of the most crucial conversations of your life took place when you
needed to take a shit, or something? An existence where there
weren't even any *chapters?*

"Very untidy," Paul croaked. "Good thing there's guys like me,
just to keep things rinsed." He cackled.

The champagne bottle hadn't been in the scenario, but that was
minor compared with the woman's hideous vitality and his current
painful uncertainty.

And until he knew whether or not she was dead, he couldn't
burn the house down, making a beacon that would bring help on
the run. Not because Annie might still be alive; he could roast her
alive with no qualms at all.

It wasn't *Annie* that was holding him back; it was the manuscript. The *real* manuscript. What he had burned had been nothing
more than an illusion with a title page on top—blank pages interspersed with written rejects and culls. The *actual* manuscript of
Misery's Return had been safely deposited under the bed, and there
it still was.

*Unless she's still alive. If she's still alive, maybe she's in there read-
ing it.*

So what are you going to do?

Wait right in here, part of him advised. *Right in here, where it's
nice and safe.*

But another, braver, part of him urged him to go through with
the scenario—as much of it as he could, anyway. Get to the parlor,
break the window, get out of this awful house. Work his way to

the edge of the road and flag down a car. Under previous circumstances this might have meant waiting for days, but not anymore. Annie's house had become a drawing card.

Summoning all of his courage, he reached for the doorknob and turned it. The door swung slowly open on darkness, and yes, there was Annie, there was the goddess, standing there in the shadows, a white shape in a nurse's uniform—

He blinked his eyes tightly shut and then opened them. Shadows, yes. Annie, no. Except in the newspaper photographs, he had never seen her in her nurse's uniform. Only shadows. Shadows and
(so vivid)
imagination.

He crawled slowly into the hall and looked back down toward the guest-room. It was shut, blank, and he began to crawl toward the parlor.

It was a pit of shadows. Annie could be hidden in any of them; Annie could *be* any of them. And she could have the axe.

He crawled.

There was the overstuffed sofa, and Annie was behind it. There was the kitchen door, standing open, and Annie was behind *that*. The floorboards creaked in back of him . . . of course! Annie was *behind* him!

He turned, heart hammering, brains squeezing at his temples, and Annie was there, all right, the axe upraised, but only for a second. She blew apart into shadows. He crawled into the parlor and that was when he heard the drone of an approaching motor. A faint wash of headlights illuminated the window, brightened. He heard the tires skid in the dirt and understood they had seen the chain she had strung across the driveway.

A car door opened and shut.

"Shit! Look at this!"

He crawled faster, looked out, and saw a silhouette approaching the house. The shape of the silhouette's hat was unmistakable. It was a state cop.

Paul groped on the knick-knack table, knocking figurines over. Some fell to the floor and shattered. His hand closed around one, and that at least was like a book; it held the roundness novels delivered precisely because life so rarely did.

It was the penguin sitting on his block of ice.

NOW MY TALE IS TOLD! the legend on the block read, and Paul thought: *Yes! Thank God!*

Propped on his left arm, he made his right hand close around the penguin. Blisters broke open, dribbling pus. He drew his arm back and heaved the penguin through the parlor window, just as he had thrown an ashtray through the window of the guest bedroom not so long ago.

"Here!" Paul Sheldon cried deliriously. *"Here, in here, please, I'm in here!"*

47

There was yet another novelistic roundness in this denouement: they were the same two cops who had come the other day to question Annie about Kushner, David and Goliath. Only tonight David's sport-coat was not only unbuttoned, his gun was out. David turned out to be Wicks. Goliath was McKnight. They had come with a search warrant. When they finally broke into the house in answer to the frenzied screams coming from the parlor, they found a man who looked like a nightmare sprung to life.

"There was a book I read when I was in high school," Wicks told his wife early the next morning. *"Count of Monte Cristo,* I think, or maybe it was *The Prisoner of Zenda.* Anyway, there was a guy in that book who'd spent forty years in solitary confinement. He hadn't seen anybody in forty years. That's what *this* guy looked like." Wicks paused for a moment, wanting to better express how it had been, the conflicting emotions he had felt—horror and pity and sorrow and disgust—most of all wonder that a man who looked this bad should still be alive. He could not find the words. "When he saw us, he started to cry," he said, and finally added: "He kept calling me David. I don't know why."

"Maybe you look like somebody he knew," she said.

"Maybe so."

48

Paul's skin was gray, his body rack-thin. He huddled by the occasional table, shivering all over, staring at them with rolling eyes.

"Who—" McKnight began.

"Goddess," the scrawny man on the floor interrupted. He licked his lips. "You have to watch out for her. Bedroom. That's where she kept me. Pet writer. Bedroom. She's there."

"Anne Wilkes?" Wicks. "In that bedroom?" He nodded toward the hall.

"Yes. Yes. Locked in. But of course. There's a window."

"Who—" McKnight began a second time.

"Christ, can't you see?" Wicks asked. "It's the guy Kushner was looking for. The writer. I can't remember his name, but it's him."

"Thank God," the scrawny man said.

"What?" Wicks bent toward him, frowning.

"Thank God you can't remember my name."

"I'm not tracking you, buddy."

"It's all right. Never mind. Just . . . you have to be careful. I think she's dead. But be careful. If she's still alive . . . danger-ous . . . like a rattlesnake." With tremendous effort he moved his twisted left leg directly into the beam of McKnight's flashlight. "Cut off my foot. Axe."

They stared at the place where his foot wasn't for long long seconds and then McKnight whispered:

"Good Christ."

"Come on," Wicks said. He drew his gun and the two of them started slowly down the hall to Paul's closed bedroom door.

"Watch out for her!" Paul shrieked in his cracked and broken voice. *"Be careful!"*

They unlocked the door and went in. Paul pulled himself against the wall and leaned his head back, eyes closed. He was cold. He couldn't stop shivering. They would scream or she would scream. There might be a scuffle. There might be shots. He tried to prepare his mind for either. Time passed, and it seemed to be a very long time indeed.

At last he heard booted feet coming back down the hall. He opened his eyes. It was Wicks.

"She *was* dead," Paul said. "I knew it—the *real* part of my mind did—but I can still hardly be—"

Wicks said: "There's blood and broken glass and charred paper in there . . . but there's no one in that room at all."

Paul Sheldon looked at Wicks, and then he began to scream. He was still screaming when he fainted.

IV

GODDESS

"You will be visited by a tall, dark stranger," the gipsy woman told Misery, and Misery, startled, realized two things at once: this was no gipsy, and the two of them were no longer alone in the tent. She could smell Gwendolyn Chastain's perfume in the moment before the madwoman's hands closed around her throat.

"In fact," the gipsy who was not a gipsy observed, "I think she is here now."

Misery tried to scream, but could no longer even breathe.

—Misery's Child

"It always look dat way, Boss Ian," Hezekiah said. "No matter how you look at her, she seem like she be lookin' at you. I doan know if it be true, but the Bourkas, dey say even when you get behin' her, the goddess, she seem to be lookin' at you."

"But she is, after all, only a piece of stone," Ian remonstrated.

"Yes, Boss Ian," Hezekiah agreed. "Dat what give her her powah."

—Misery's Return

1

umber whunnnn
yerrrnnn umber whunnnn
fayunnnn
These sounds: even in the haze.

2

Now I must rinse she said, and this is how it rinses out:

3

Nine months after Wicks and McKnight carried him from Annie's
house on a makeshift litter, Paul Sheldon was dividing his time
between Doctors Hospital in Queens and a new apartment on the
East Side of Manhattan. His legs had been re-broken. His left was
still in a cast from the knee down. He would walk with a limp for
the rest of his life, the doctors told him, but he *would* walk, and
eventually he would walk without pain. His limp would have been
deeper and more pronounced if he had been walking on his own
foot instead of a custom-made prosthesis. In an ironic sort of way,
Annie had done him a favor.

He was drinking too much and not writing at all. His dreams
were bad.

When he got out of the elevator on the ninth floor one afternoon
in May, he was for a change thinking not of Annie but of the bulky
package tucked clumsily under his arm—it contained two bound
galleys of *Misery's Return.* His publishers had put the book on a

very fast track, and considering the world-wide headlines generated by the bizarre circumstances under which the novel had been written, that was hardly surprising. Hastings House had ordered an unprecedented first printing of a million copies. "And that's only the beginning," Charlie Merrill, his editor, had told him at lunch that day—the lunch from which Paul was now returning with his bound galleys. "This book is going to outsell everything in the world, my friend. We all just ought to be down on our knees thanking God that the story *in* the book is almost as good as the story *behind* the book."

Paul didn't know if that was true, and didn't really care anymore. He only wanted to get it behind him and find the *next* book . . . but as dry days became dry weeks became dry months, he had begun to wonder if there ever *would* be a next book.

Charlie was begging him for a nonfiction account of his ordeal. That book, he said, would outsell even *Misery's Return*. Would, in fact, outsell *Iacocca*. When Paul asked him, out of idle curiosity, what he thought the paperback rights for such a book might fetch, Charlie brushed his long hair away from his forehead, lit a Camel, and said: "I believe we could set a floor at ten million dollars and then conduct one *hell* of an auction." He did not bat an eye when he said it; after a moment or two Paul realized he either was serious or thought he was.

But there was no way he could write such a book, not yet, probably not ever. His job was writing novels. He *could* write the account Charlie wanted, but to do so would be tantamount to admitting to himself that he would never write another novel.

And the joke is, it would be a novel, he almost said to Charlie Merrill . . . and then held back at the last moment. The joke *was,* Charlie wouldn't care.

It would start out as fact, and then I'd begin to tart it up . . . just a little at first . . . then a little more . . . then a little more. Not to make myself look better (although I probably would) and not to make Annie look worse (she couldn't). Simply to create that roundness. I don't want to fictionalize myself. Writing may be masturbatory, but God forbid it should be an act of autocannibalism.

His apartment was 9-E, farthest from the elevator, and today the corridor looked two miles long. He began to stump his way grimly down to it, a t-shaped walking-stick in each hand. *Clack . . . clack . . . clack . . . clack.* God, he hated that sound.

His legs ached sickeningly and he yearned for Novril. Sometimes he thought it would be worth being back with Annie just to have the dope. The doctors had weaned him from it. The booze was his substitute, and when he got inside he was going to have a double bourbon.

Then he would look at the blank screen of his word processor for awhile. What fun. Paul Sheldon's fifteen-thousand-dollar paperweight.

Clack . . . clack . . . clack . . . clack.

Now to get the key out of his pocket without dropping either the manila envelope containing the bound galleys or the sticks. He propped the sticks against the wall. While he was doing that, the galleys dropped out from under his arm and fell to the rug. The envelope split open.

"Shit!" he growled, and then the sticks fell over with a clatter, adding to the fun.

Paul closed his eyes, swaying unsteadily on his twisted, aching legs, waiting to see if he was going to get mad or cry. He hoped he would get mad. He didn't want to cry out here in the hall, but he might. He had. His legs hurt all the time and he wanted his dope, not the heavy-duty aspirin they gave him at the hospital dispensary. He wanted his *good* dope, his Annie-dope. And oh he was so tired all the time. What he needed to prop him up were not those shitty sticks but his make-believe games and stories. They were the good dope, the never-fail fix, but they had all fled. It seemed playtime was finally over.

This is what it's like after the end, he thought, opening the door and tottering into the apartment. *This is why no one ever writes it. It's too fucking dreary. She should have died after I stuffed her head full of blank paper and busted pages, and I should have died then, too. At that moment if at no other we really were like characters in one of Annie's chapter-plays—no grays, only blacks and whites, good and bad. I was Geoffrey and she was the Bourka Bee-Goddess. This . . . well, I've heard of denouement, but this is ridiculous. Never mind the mess back there on the floor. Drinky-poo first, pick-uppy-poo second. First be a Don't-Be and then be a—*

He stopped. He had time to realize the apartment was too dark. And there was a smell. He knew that smell, a deadly mixture of dirt and face-powder.

Annie rose up from behind the sofa like a white ghost, dressed in a nurse's uniform and cap. The axe was in her hand and she was screaming: *Time to rinse, Paul! Time to rinse!*

He shrieked, tried to turn on his bad legs. She leaped the sofa with clumsy strength, looking like an albino frog. Her starched uniform rustled briskly. The first sweep of the axe did no more than knock the wind from him—this was really what he thought until he landed on the carpet smelling his own blood. He looked down and saw he was cut nearly in half.

"Rinse!" she shrieked, and there went his right hand.

"Rinse!" she shrieked again, and his left was gone; he crawled toward the open door on the jetting stumps of his wrists, and incredibly the galleys were still there, the bound galleys Charlie had given him at lunch in Mr. Lee's, sliding the manila envelope to him across gleaming white napery while Muzak drifted down from overhead speakers.

"Annie you can read it now!" he tried to scream, but only got out *Annie you* before his head flew off and rolled to the wall. His last dimming glimpse of the world was his own collapsing body and Annie's white shoes standing astride it:

Goddess, he thought, and died.

4

Scenario: An outline or synopsis. A plot outline.
—*Webster's New Collegiate*

Writer: One who writes, esp. as an occupation.
—*Webster's New Collegiate*

Make-believe: Pretense or pretend.
—*Webster's New Collegiate*

5

Paulie, Can You?

6

Yes; of course he could. "The *writer's scenario* was that Annie was still alive, although he understood this was only *make-believe*."

7

He really did go to lunch with Charlie Merrill. All the conversation was the same. Only when he let himself into his apartment he knew it was the cleaning woman who had pulled the drapes, and although he fell down and had to smother a scream of fright when Annie rose up like Cain from behind the sofa, it was just the cat, a cross-eyed Siamese named Dumpster he had gotten last month at the pound.

There was no Annie because Annie had not been a goddess at all, only a crazy lady who had hurt Paul for reasons of her own. Annie had managed to pull most of the paper out of her mouth and throat and had gotten out through Paul's window while Paul was sleeping the sleep of drugs. She had gotten to the barn and had collapsed there. She was dead when Wicks and McKnight found her, but not of strangulation. She had actually died of the fractured skull she had received when she struck the mantel, and she had struck the mantel because she had tripped. So in a way she had been killed by the very typewriter Paul had hated so much.

But she'd had plans for him, all right. Not even the axe would suffice this time.

They had found her outside of Misery the pig's stall, with one hand wrapped around the handle of her chainsaw.

That was all in the past, though. Annie Wilkes was in her grave. But, like Misery Chastain, she rested there uneasily. In his dreams and waking fantasies, he dug her up again and again. You couldn't kill the goddess. Temporarily dope her with bourbon, maybe, but that was all.

He went to the bar, looked at the bottle, then looked back at where his galleys and walking sticks lay. He gave the bottle a good-bye look and worked his way back to his stuff.

8

Rinse.

9

Half an hour later he was sitting in front of the blank screen,
thinking he had to be a glutton for punishment. He had taken the
aspirin instead of the drink, but that didn't change what was going
to happen now; he was going to sit here for fifteen minutes or
maybe half an hour, looking at nothing but a cursor flashing in
darkness; then he was going to turn the machine off and have that
drink.

Except . . .

Except he had seen something funny on the way home from
lunch with Charlie, and it had given him an idea. Not a big one.
Just a small one. After all, it had only been a small incident. Just a
kid pushing a shopping cart up 48th Street, that was all, but there
had been a cage in the cart, and in it had been a rather large furry
animal which Paul at first thought was a cat. A closer look had
shown him a wide white stripe up the cat's back.

"Sonny," he said, "is that a skunk?"

"Yeah," the kid said, and pushed the shopping cart along a little
faster. You didn't stop for long conversations with people in the
city, especially weird-looking guys with bags the size of Samsonite
two-suiters under their eyes who were lurching along on metal
walking-sticks. The kid turned the corner and was gone.

Paul went on, wanting to take a cab, but he was supposed to
walk at least a mile every day and this was his mile and it hurt like
hell and to take his mind off the mile he started wondering where
that kid had come from, where the shopping cart had come from,
and most of all where the skunk had come from.

He heard a noise behind him and turned from the blank screen
to see Annie coming out of the kitchen dressed in jeans and a red
flannel logger's shirt, the chainsaw in her hands.

He closed his eyes, opened them, saw the same old nothing, and was suddenly angry. He turned back to the word processor and wrote fast, almost bludgeoning the keys:

-1-

The kid heard a sound in the back of the building and although the thought of rats crossed his mind, he turned the corner anyway--it was too early to go home because school didn't let out for another hour and a half and he had gone truant at lunch.

What he saw crouched back against the wall in a dusty shaft of sunlight was not a rat but a great big black cat with the bushiest tail he had ever seen.

10

He stopped, heart suddenly pounding.

Paulie, Can You?

This was a question which he did not dare answer. He bent over the keyboard again, and after a moment began to hit the keys . . . but more gently now.

11

It _wasn't_ a cat. Eddie Desmond had lived in New York City all his life, but he had been to the Bronx Zoo, and Christ, there were picture-books, weren't there? He knew what that thing was, although he hadn't the slightest idea how such a thing could have gotten into this deserted East 105th Street tenement, but the long white stripe down its back was a dead give-away. It was a skunk.

Eddie started slowly toward it, feet gritting in the plaster dust

12

He could. He *could.*

So, in gratitude and in terror, he *did.* The hole opened and Paul stared through at what was there, unaware that his fingers were picking up speed, unaware that his aching legs were in the same city but fifty blocks away, unaware that he was weeping as he wrote.

Lovell, Maine: September 23rd, 1984 / Bangor, Maine: October 7th, 1986: *Now my tale is told.*